Book
3 of 7

K'Narf Etaguf

By:

Steven A. Vaughn

ISBN 978-0-9914575-8-8(Print)
ISBN 978-0-9653330-1-6(E-Book)
TXu 1-735-679(L. of C.)

Cover Design by M. Joyce

Dedicated

To my best friend and only son who both now sleep waiting for the final resurrection, and to my mother who has now joined them for gifting me with a love for words. Finally, and with a grateful heart, to my wife who patiently listened to each chapter being described and then diligently reviewed them after they had been written.

PROLOGUE

First and foremost, this is a work of fiction. The characters, even though some of them were drawn from the Bible, are still fictitious and none of them reflect negatively on anyone currently living in this century.

Second, the Bible, by its very nature becomes a primary source and, to a limited degree, a central theme when writing about prophetic events. However, I am not a preacher, nor a Sabbath or Sunday school teacher and have therefore deliberately avoided using this book as a pulpit.

Third, all biblical quotes were drawn from the King James Version.

Enjoy!

Table of Contents

Chapter One

"K'Narf, that's an unusual name Mr. Fugate. I don't think I've ever heard it before. What about a middle name?" the candy striper asked, as she typed the information for the birth certificate.

"No, no middle name, just K'Narf Fugate, exactly the way I've written it down." She obviously hadn't seen his son yet or she wouldn't have been so inquisitive.

Leaving the girl to her typing, Joe Fugate headed for his wife's room determined not to look at his son as he passed the nursery window. Suddenly feeling as if an invisible force had literally reached out and grabbed him he stopped, and with a feeling of lingering disbelief looked again at his son. He didn't totally fit his grandfather's description of his dead uncle, but the differences weren't worth arguing about. Heavy coarse black hair, low jutting forehead, thick eyebrows that almost touched, a bulbous nose with a small dark birthmark slightly off center, thick fleshy lips and a recessed chin that just barely qualified as such. Born nine days late, thirteen and a quarter pounds and twenty-three inches long. He had almost killed Robbie. Thank God that the birth of their first son, Joe Junior, had been normal.

Glancing at the only other baby in the nursery, a beautiful little oriental girl, he turned and headed for his wife's room.

Stepping just inside the door he found himself studying his wife as she slept quietly in her bed. Her beautiful dark hair wildly disarrayed against the white pillow framed the small delicate oval of her face. Her closed eyelids covered the dark brown pools that were her eyes. He often wondered why she had picked him for her husband, for pick him she had.

Robin Louise Steinbeck, she had been one of the prettiest girls in college and literally had to beat the fellows away from her dorm. Why she had singled him out in the cafeteria that afternoon and started up the relationship that had quickly led to marriage he'd never figure out. He wasn't bad looking, he just wasn't considered real good looking. Average height and weight, his only distinctive feature was his dark reddish hair and a smattering of freckles.

Selecting him like she had didn't make a lot of sense, and probably never would. What with the birth of this baby she might even leave him since it was obvious what side of the family he came from. If only he hadn't told her about the existence of his great uncle K'Narf, but then she'd have found out eventually. Even good old Doctor Easley couldn't conceal his revulsion when he delivered K'Narf, mask or no mask his eyes expressed his thoughts as if he had spoken them out loud.

"Joe, is that you?" Robbie asked groggily.

"Yes hon, I'm right here." Joe said, as he stepped over to the bed and took her hand.

"Oh Joe, I'm so sorry." Tears welled up as she pulled her hand away and rolled her face into the pillow.

"Sorry, what are you sorry for. He came from my side of the family, not yours."

"I know, but I gave him to you." She said as she half rolled out of the pillow.

"Hon, it's not your fault. I guess it's not my fault either, but it will be if we start blaming each other. The one who's at fault is God, and how do you go about blaming Him?"

"Just don't be mad at me please. I love you so much. I couldn't live without you. Hold me please." Robbie stammered, as she turned her tear-stained face to him and held out her arms.

Joe, taking her in his arms, gave her a gentle squeeze then told her what he had done. "Robbie, I named him after my Great Uncle K'Narf." Her fingers dug into his arm, but she didn't raise her head or utter a single sound in protest.

Chapter Two

"I don't care what your father says, we are not going to put him in an institution. The Steinbeck's take care of their own. Always have and always will." Robbie said, as she stomped her foot in frustrated anger.

"Well you're not a Steinbeck anymore, you're a Fugate, and there is no way we can continue to take care of him in this apartment, and don't start in on me about moving to the country. I'm city-bred and city-oriented and no little moron is going to force me to become a country hick." Joe yelled, his face now a livid red reminding her more and more of his narrow-minded father.

"Don't you call our son a moron!"

"Why not, that's what he is isn't he. Those school people that tested him said so didn't they?"

"No! Not exactly. They said he had a very unusual and puzzling handicap. Something they had never encountered before."

"Yeah! Real unusual, he's a complete idiot!"

"He is not! And how... how would you know. You wouldn't even go with me to talk to them." Robbie stammered in anger, as her eyes began to water. Making her as furious with herself as she was with him.

"Why should I go down there and let some stranger tell me what I already know. That my son is so stupid that he can't even remember his own name!" Anger making Joe's blood veins stand out against his temples.

"I refuse to listen to anymore of your vicious accusations about Bubba! It's his sixth birthday and he's going to have a party just like every other kid his age. Now please go get the ice cream before mom and dad get here." Robbie half-cried and half-sobbed, quickly turning away so he wouldn't see her tears.

"Some birthday party. Couldn't get anyone to come but your parents. Some birthday party." Joe repeated, as he headed for the door.

"Mom, why is dad mad at Bubba? He hasn't done anything wrong has he?" Asked the miniature version of Joe senior, popping out of his bedroom just as the door slammed on his father's retreating back.

"No Junior, Bubba hasn't done anything wrong. Your father is just... your father just doesn't understand him that's all. Where is Bubba anyway?"

"I told him to go stand in the closet when I heard you and dad fighting."

"We weren't fighting... exactly. We were just talking loud." Robbie said, as she wiped at her eyes with her apron.

"Yeah, I know, fighting." Junior said.

"You just go get Bubba out of the closet and make sure he's memorized his list and the pictures. We wouldn't want him to forget who Grandma and Grandpa are would we? Now go on, they'll be here any minute now."

It's impossible to argue with Joe Junior when he knows he's right she thought. But Joe is wrong, just plain wrong! Bubba is not a moron! He's abnormal yes, and he will probably need special care the rest of his life. But he is not a moron since he is trainable.

The retarded children specialist and the schools resident psychologist both tested Bubba and they even co-wrote a paper on him. They said he was unique in all the case histories they had studied. He was bright, well coordinated, highly active and healthy.

He could learn anything they wanted to take the time to teach him including in one long session the entire multiplication table up to a hundred. They said he was exceptionally fast at learning something new and faster at learning a previously taught lesson. But for all their knowledge they didn't know why everything they taught him faded from his memory within seventy-two hours unless it was re-stressed each and every day. She had their report ready to show her parents.

At least I have the satisfaction of knowing that they couldn't improve on my method of pictures and study lists to maintain in his memory those things essential to his daily routine she thought.

Now if she could only convince her father that Bubba could be trained to help him on the farm. He'd always wanted a son and now with the Lord's blessing he was going to have one. Bubba already towered over Junior, and he was showing no sign of slowing his growth rate. He needed to be on a farm where he could stretch and grow, not cooped up in a small apartment.

Joe was right about their inability to raise Bubba and care for him properly, and that he would have to go, but for all the wrong reasons. That's why she hadn't told him that the real reason for the birthday party was to convince her father and mother to take Bubba to live with them on the farm. If she could only get her mother on her side, then her father would be easy. He'd never been a match for both of them when they wanted the same thing.

"Junior, get the door. That should be Grandma and Grandpa." She yelled. Joe had better come home with that ice cream she thought.

Chapter Three

"Hi Gramps!" Junior half yelled as he bounded up onto the old wooden porch.

"Junior, how are ya? What are ya doing here? How's your father and that daughter of mine? Well, speak up. Don't just stand there, come on in." Wheezing out the last word Junior's grandfather pushed back the dilapidated screen door and half pulled his grandson into what had once been a spotless kitchen.

It was the exact opposite now. Dirty dishes in the sink, week old food stains on the table, and the inevitable coffee pot.

"Can I get you a cup of coffee?"

Junior started to say no but it was too late, Gramps was already pouring him some into an obviously dirty cup. He could only hope the coffee was strong enough to kill anything in it.

"Do you have any cream Gramps?"

"Think so, check the ice box there." Gramps said, with a nod of his head at the modern stainless steel double door freezer refrigerator mom and dad had bought for Grandma just before she died last year.

Junior regretted opening it immediately as the odor of spoiled and dried out leftovers assailed his already over-taxed senses. He quickly closed the door and decided he really liked his coffee black. Mom would have to know about this so she could arrange for another housekeeper. This would make the fourth one that had walked out on Gramps and Bubba.

"Where is Bubba, Gramps?"

"Up in his room I guess. He's usually there unless he's doing his chores. He doesn't come down much since your Grandma left us. Just sits up there staring out the window all the time."

"Have you varied his routine any lately?"

"Naw, your Grandma used ta teach him something new each week and type it into his memory lists, but I just don't have the time. Your Grandma, bless her soul, said I didn't have the patience. I get mad and start yelling and he drops his eyes and kinda bows

16

his head and that's the end of the lesson. So I just don't try anymore. He don't seem to mind anyway."

"Does he still have a picture of me in his memory package?"

"Yup, same one ya gave him two years ago on his birthday. Say, what day is this?" Gramps asked as he arched his right eyebrow.

"October the eleventh." Junior said breaking out in a grin.

"So that's what brought ya up here. It's his birthday again. Let's see, he's eighteen now isn't he."

"Yup." Junior said, mimicking his grandfather.

"Eighteen years, it's kinda hard to believe Bubba's that old." Gramps said, shaking his head from side to side.

"Remember when I turned sixteen and you let me drive Bubba into town for an ice cream cone and Herman and his gang made fun of him. I managed to belt Herman one good one before they all jumped me, then good old Bubba seen them hitting me so he started hitting them. He put that dumb Herman and three of his buddies in the hospital, and the cops told you not to allow Bubba into town again unless he was with you and they were to be notified first, remember?" Junior said, as the memory triggered a burst of laughter.

"Yup, after all the commotion settled down Sheriff Anderson told me it was the best thing that could have happened ta Herman and his bunch. Ya know Herman's shoulder never did heal right. He still has trouble with it."

"I know, Bubba really did a job on those guys. I didn't realize how strong he was until that fight. When you treat him as a five-year-old you tend to think of him the same way."

"Yup, know just what ya mean." Gramps said, nodding his head up and down this time.

"Gramps, if I was to try something special with Bubba, would you promise not to tell mom?"

"Depends on what ya mean by something special. I won't tolerate your hurting him none."

"Oh, I won't hurt him any. You ought to know that. I'm trying to help him. The chances are pretty slim that I'll do any good, it's just that mom is kinda paranoid about doing anything to Bubba."

"Yup, daughter or no daughter, she's just a bit tetched about that kid, always has been."

"That's why I want you to promise me that you won't tell mom that I tried to hypnotize Bubba." Junior said, as he eyed his grandfather very carefully for his reaction.

"Hypnotize him! What on earth for?" Gramps asked, as both eyebrows arched up.

"Well, I've been studying mind control through self-hypnotism in college and I've learned quite a bit about how the subconscious mind functions. That's where all your memories are stored." Junior said, still eyeing his grandfather very carefully.

"Yup, done a little reading about that myself, but what's that got ta do with Bubba?" Gramps asked, as he looked Junior straight in the eye.

"Well, the problem with Bubba seems to be a block that doesn't allow his conscious mind access to his subconscious mind." Junior said, as he looked down at his coffee cup, unable to maintain eye contact with his grandfather.

"Yup, understand that too, but I still don't see what hypnotism has to do with Bubba." Gramps said, as he leaned his chair back on two legs still holding onto his coffee cup. Something his wife had never allowed him to do.

"Well, if I can hypnotize him and take him down to his mind's Theta level and sort of reprogram him so that he will be able to recall at least some of the things he has been taught. Well, I thought it would at least be worth a try." Junior said, thinking that it had seemed like such a good idea at school.

"Yup, might just be worth a try, but what do ya know about this here hypnotism stuff?" Gramps asked, leaning forward and putting his elbows on the table. Something else his wife had never allowed him to do.

"We had to hypnotize each other as part of our class studies, and I've watched our instructor do it a lot of times. It's really not that hard." Junior said, excited again now that his grandfather was showing some interest in his idea.

"What do ya plan ta do to him after you get him all hypnotized? Ya do have ta do something other than just hypnotize him don't ya?"

"Yes, I spent several days working on the exact wording of what I will do and say. After I get him under as far as I possibly can I am going to turn on a tape recorder that I have pre-recorded. It will repeat over and over just one phrase. *Your conscious mind and your subconscious mind shall become as one. You shall have total memory recall.* At the end of forty-five minutes I'll shut it off and bring him out. I really think it's worth a try Gramps." Junior said, as he watched his grandfather's reaction.

"Yup, your mother would skin ya alive. As a matter of fact, she would skin both of us alive." Gramps said, as he swirled his coffee around in his cup, watching it as though it would provide an answer to his dilemma.

"Gramps, I really think it might help Bubba, but if it didn't and mom ever found out there'd be hell to pay." Junior said, watching his grandfather very closely now.

"I may be old, but I'm not senile, and I'm not about to give that mother of yours an excuse to light into me. Daughter or no daughter that woman has a vicious tongue. When do you want to try this here hypnotizing?" Gramps asked, as he watched the excitement light up the eyes of his grandson.

"Right now, if it's all right with you?" Junior said, as he got up from the table.

"Ya mean ta say ya got all that stuff with ya? Your awful blinkin' sure of yourself aren't ya. Well, get on with it before I change my mind. I'll stay down here and wait. Won't help none my watching and all." Gramps said nervously, now that he had committed himself.

"Okay, but first I'll go out to the van and get my stuff. Be right back." The screen door slammed behind him as he dashed to his van and grabbed the box with the recorder and his notebook. Slamming the screen door again on his return. "When I put him on the recorder I'll come back down and join you for another cup of whatever it is that's in that pot." Nervousness giving Junior's laugh a high-pitched quality.

"Now don't you get persnickety and insult my coffee." Gramps said, laughing as his grandson's excitement rubbed off on him.

Still grinning, Junior bounded up the stairs two at a time. Thirty-seven minutes later he came back down at a much slower pace. Dropping into a kitchen chair he reached for the steaming cup of coffee that his grandfather placed in front of him.

"Well, aren't ya going ta tell me what happened, or are ya just going ta sit there like a bump on a log." Gramps said, wheezing out the last word.

"I'm not real sure I know myself." Junior said, staring into his coffee cup.

19

"What do you mean by that? Look at me when I talk to you. If you've harmed that boy your mother will skin both of us. Tetched that woman is when it concerns Bubba." Gramps sputtered, as he scooted back his chair and stood up. Only five feet eight inches and one hundred and forty-five pounds, but he was still formidable when he got riled.

"No, I didn't hurt him. I'm just not sure what really happened. He had all the symptoms of already being in a trance, even though he spoke to me and recognized that I was his older brother. I told him what I was going to do and asked him to go along with my little game just like he used to when we were kids. Then I started in trying to hypnotize him and he immediately went under and from what little I know I think he went all the way down to the Delta level." Junior said, looking back down at his coffee.

"The what level?" Gramps asked, still standing and obviously upset.

"The Delta level. That's the level where you're totally unconscious. Anyway, I went ahead and turned on the tape recorder. It's been on twenty-three minutes, so I have to go back up at exactly ten-thirty-eight to turn it off, Okay?" Junior asked, as he hesitantly looked up at his grandfather.

"I'm starting ta wish ya hadn't talked me into this. If your mother ever finds out she won't let me have a moments peace the rest of my life." Gramps said, as he slowly settled back down in his chair.

"I'm not so sure that you shouldn't have talked me out of doing it too." Junior said, staring into his coffee cup again.

"Now ya decide that it's not such a good idea. I thought ya were so blinkin' sure of yourself. I think ya had better git up there right now and bring him out of that hypnotism stuff before something goes wrong. I mean it, git up there and shut that recorder thing off and wake Bubba up. Go on, git!" Gramps said, standing again and pointing at the stairs.

Taking the stairs two at a time again, Junior quickly disappeared into Bubba's room. Moments later he was yelling for his grandfather who also took the stairs two at a time.

"Gramps, help me get him back on the bed."

"What's he all curled up like that for?"

"He's in what's known as the fetal position and I can't get him to wake up. I think you'd better call the doctor." Junior said, his voice rising with a note of fear.

"I knew it, felt it in my bones. Your mother is going ta skin both of us... if we tell her." Gramps mumbled to himself as he hurried down the stairs.

Chapter Four

"Mr. Steinbeck, I'm sure glad to see you." The doctor said, as he ushered Gramps through the double doors of the hospital's emergency entrance. "You made excellent time. Did you finally trade in that old pick-up of yours?"

"Not a chance doc, that old truck's like a member of the family. Speaking of family, where's Bubba? You did say he was awake didn't you?" Gramps asked, as he hurried to keep up with the fast walking doctor.

"Yes, he's just around the corner in room thirteen." The doctor said, as they turned the corner. Opening the door the doctor stood back and let Gramps through first, and then with a slight shudder, he followed.

Gramps stopped just inside the door. Looking at his grandson the odd reality of the situation struck him. They had brought Bubba into this place exactly three weeks ago. He had been in a coma so deep, that even the doc with all of his science and medicines hadn't been able to bring him out of it. He and Junior had agreed to tell Bubba's mother that they had found him that way when Junior went up to wish him a happy birthday. The doctor and Robbie, not suspecting anything, had believed them.

Now this wild call from the doc in the middle of the night telling him to get down here right away, that Bubba was awake.

"What in blue blazes have you done to my grandson?" Gramps suddenly squalled. "My God, he's been beat to a pulp. Look at his face, and what the... what's he doing in a straight jacket?" Gramps stammered, not believing what his eyes were seeing.

"He's been unconscious for three weeks and...."

"That doesn't explain the blood on his face and a straight jacket!" Gramps almost screamed, as he turned on the doctor.

Taking a deep breath, the doctor exhaled slowly and said, "If you'll calm down, I'll try to explain."

"I'm as calm as I'm gonna git so start explaining. Gramps half-yelled, standing ramrod stiff and glaring at the doctor.

"Well, a little past midnight I was in the duty lounge resting when your Bubba woke up. He was apparently frightened by his strange surroundings and started bellowing at the top of his lungs. Nothing intelligible understand, just a wild, animalistic sound that woke up and petrified the entire east wing.

The first one to get to him was Karen Shuck, our head nurse. He had ripped out his I.V. tubes and his arm was bleeding. Karen immediately went for the arm to stop the bleeding. Bubba apparently thought she was going to harm him and struck out to protect himself."

"Is she hurt bad?" Gramps asked, his anger and his spine beginning to soften.

"Karen? Yes, he gave her a compound fracture of the right arm, but it's been set and I put a balloon splint on it so she's resting quietly now, along with Harry and little Sally."

"Harry and little Sally?"

"Yes, Bubba started swinging at everybody that came into the room after that. Fractured poor Harry's jaw I'm afraid. Little Sally's really the heroine since she was the one that crawled under the bed in order to get behind him. Then, when Johnny, Bill and I grabbed his arms she hit him in his right buttock with a syringe full of sedative. He immediately tossed Bill and me against the wall and tried to get at Sally. That's when Johnny, who's rather a large man himself, started hitting him. Johnny's rather sweet on Sally and I'm afraid he over reacted. I believe they're planning to be married soon." The doctor said, as his thoughts seemed to wander a little.

"Was she hurt bad, Sally I mean? Gramps asked, all traces of anger now gone.

"Sally? Oh no, I gave her a sedative and made her lie down. Very emotional that girl, don't really think she's cut out for this kind of work."

"Well, thank God for that. Did he hurt anybody else?" Gramps asked, looking back at his grandson who was hunkered down in the far corner.

"Oh, Johnny had a few slight bruises and one small laceration on his hand where Bubba bit him, but nothing serious. We backed off and simply waited for the sedative to take affect, and then put him in that straight jacket. Actually he looks pretty good considering what he did to half my staff. Not to mention the fact that it should be physically impossible to come out of a coma of twenty-one days and even get out of bed!" The doctor exclaimed, his face livid and his voice going up several decibels.

"Has he said anything, or asked for anyone?" Gramps asked, trying to change the subject.

"No, not a word since he stopped screaming, just sits there staring at us. I called you as soon as we had him sedated." The doctor said, his voice again carefully controlled.

"Do you mind if I try to talk to him?" Gramps asked, turning to look at Bubba again.

"No, that's why I called you in, just be careful. He's been watching the two of us since we came into the room, and he can still kick, bite, and butt, and it looks like the sedative is wearing off so be careful please, I'll stay here by the door." The doctor said, as he gave Gramps a nervous nudge toward the creature squatting in the far corner of the room. Not only did he not act human he really doesn't look all that human either the doctor thought to himself.

Gramps moved very slowly toward Bubba, noting as he got closer just how badly his grandson had been beaten. No sign that they had tried to treat him either. His left eye was almost swollen shut, and he had a nasty cut just below it. Most of the blood seemed to have come from that cut; at least he couldn't see any others. Then, as he hunkered down in front of Bubba he really noticed for the first time what the doc had mentioned a few moments before. Bubba was staring at him in a fashion that sent chills down his back and made him avert his own eyes, something he'd never done with Bubba before.

"Go home Grandpa, want go home." Bubba said, as big tears suddenly started rolling down his face.

Gramps, who had never felt very close to Bubba in the twelve years they had been together, was suddenly over whelmed by emotion at the sight of his grandson's tears, and by the fact that he had recognized and spoke to him.

"Bubba, you can talk, you remember me! I'm your old Gramps, talk to me, say something, anything! Gramps almost yelled, as he gave Bubba a big hug and then started tearing at the buckles of the straight jacket.

"Hey, don't take that off!" Yelled the doctor, as he backed out of the room locking the door behind him.

Cautiously opening the door to room thirteen, Doctor Robert E. Donavan didn't quite know what to expect. A motley crew of sleepy interns and two nurses backed him up, so in his mind he was ready for anything except what confronted him. There was Bubba sitting on a chair while Grandpa Steinbeck worked on his face with a washcloth from the sink. The straight jacket had been tossed on the bed.

"Oh, there you are doc. What do I have to do to get Bubba outta here? You got some papers for me to sign or something?" Gramps asked, as he tossed the bloody washcloth at the sink.

"No, no you just take him if you want. We'll mail you our bill." He added as an after thought. Turning around he shooed his troops back up the hall giving Steinbeck and his grandson plenty of room. He would really liked to have studied that boy, but not at the risks involved with an unstable personality, especially at my age, he thought.

Standing at the end of the corridor he watched as they emerged from their room and headed for the exit. He didn't miss the long baleful look that Bubba stopped and gave him, just before his grandfather pulled him out the door. He felt a twinge of guilt for not stitching up that cut but, then again, maybe a scar would improve his looks. It sure couldn't make him any uglier. One thing was obvious though, that boy wasn't the imbecile his medical record showed him to be. I'll bet my reputation on that, he thought, as he turned and walked toward the lounge and a much needed cup of coffee.

Chapter Five

Gramps called Junior as soon as he had got home with Bubba, leaving it up to him to call his mother.

When he hung up the phone Bubba was standing there like he had been listening and then said the one word, "hurt", and pointed at his head. Not knowing what else to do, Gramps offered him some aspirin. Bubba took about a half-a-dozen of them, swallowed them with a glass of water and then turned and went upstairs calling for his cat Thomas. The full-blooded Manx his mother had bought him several years ago.

Gramps stood there for a long time listening to the sounds of a methodical search going on upstairs. Then, feeling more than just a little disoriented, he went out to feed his chickens. They were the only animals his wife had allowed on the farm and which, by that time, were raising a ruckus. They knew it was way past their breakfast time. Afterwards, with a hat full of fresh warm eggs; he had headed back into the house to do the same for him and Bubba.

To his surprise he found Bubba sitting in what had been his wife's favorite chair holding her old and well-worn Bible in his hands. Thomas was snuggled up in his lap.

"You all right, Bubba?" He asked, looking carefully at his grandson.

"Grandma used to read this to me every evening before bed." Bubba said, holding up his Grandmother's Bible. "She always read two pages every day, that way she could read the whole Bible through in a year." He added.

"I know." Gramps said, sitting down in the chair Bubba used to set in when she read to him. "They didn't come any better'n her. You know this was her farm when she married me." He confessed, not knowing exactly why.

"No, that I didn't know." Bubba said, looking quizzically at his grandfather.

"She inherited it when her parents were killed in an auto accident. Her father bought the initial forty acres, but my Angie is the one that laid out the fields, orchards and green houses. She said that if the Lord had cursed a fig tree because it wouldn't produce fruit, then nothing was going to be planted on her farm that didn't give something back. That's why there's nothing growing on this farm that doesn't produce something, even if it's just a flower." Gramps said, smiling at the memory of his wife.

"How well I know." Bubba said, smiling along with his grandfather. "Twenty-one, one acre plots plus seven quarter acre greenhouses. Each year she retired three of the one acre plots and one greenhouse in honor of what God said in this book about resting the land." He added, holding up his grandmother's Bible.

"Yup, she made this farm the envy of all our neighbors. When the acres were resting she had us plant cover crops and plow them into the ground, replace the greenhouse cover, and put new compost in all the greenhouse beds. Always got the highest bids on our produce too." Gramps bragged. "Still do." He added, giving his grandson a long measuring look.

"You know I won't be staying." Bubba said, looking seriously at his grandfather.

"Kinda figured as much." Gramps said, nodding. "You know she ain't going ta like it." Both of them knew he was referring to Bubba's mother.

"I'll handle that when she gets here." Bubba said, then added. "Do you mind if I take this with me?"

Gramps looked at the Bible in Bubba's hand and nodded his head. "Your welcome to it. She would have liked that."

"I also took a few pictures out of her album upstairs. I didn't take a lot, just a picture of her and her parents when she was a young girl, one of the two of you right after you got married and one of mom before she married dad. I hope you don't mind." Bubba said, knowing by the look on his grandfather's face that he didn't.

"I'm right pleased you'd want'em. Now, how about I fix us some breakfast before they get here." Gramps said, getting up and heading for the kitchen without waiting for an answer. Looking back briefly at his grandson, he watched as he pulled what appeared to be the dictionary from the bookshelf.

"It's on the table!" Gramps yelled from the kitchen almost an hour later.

27

"Looks like a Sabbath meal." Bubba said, stepping into the kitchen and looking at the breakfast his grandfather had made.

"I know it's not Saturday, but somehow it jus' felt right. Sides, I always liked fried lamb chops with my eggs an' taters."

"Me too!" Bubba said, as he pulled out a chair and sat down. "How come Grandma was so set on what kind of meat we could and couldn't eat?" He asked, as he quickly bowed his head and said grace.

"Simple enough." Gramps said, as he pulled out his own chair and sat down. "She cooked mostly vegetarian dishes as you know. She wouldn't of let us have eggs, butter and cheese if I hadn't thrown a fit about it right after we got married. Meat on the other hand she didn't approve of at all; however, as she put it, since the Lord had eaten both whilst he was here on earth, she allowed that we could properly eat fish or lamb on the Sabbath."

"You almost sound like her when you say it like that." Bubba said, smiling at his grandfather. Seconds later he was finishing the last of his fried eggs. "Have a few things to do upstairs. Don't worry; I'll hear'em when they come up the drive. Oh, and by the way, my given name is K'Narf, not Bubba." He added, as he got up from the table.

Gramps watched as Bubba walked through the living room and headed for the stairs. Sitting there with his still half eaten breakfast, the strangeness of the conversation he had just had with his grandson struck him as surreal. It was almost like the mentally retarded boy who had lived with him for the last twelve years had never existed. Finally he got up and cleared the table and poured himself a fresh cup of coffee. He expected his grandson, Junior, to arrive any time now. His mother shouldn't be far behind if she'd left right after Junior phoned.

Having let his coffee grow cold, he dumped it out in the sink and was reaching for the coffee pot when he heard the sound of squealing brakes out on the highway, and then the roar of an accelerating engine. Letting the screen door slam behind him he ran to intercept the small red van speeding up the drive.

Slamming on the brakes and stopping short of where he usually parked kept Junior from running over his grandfather by inches only. "Gramps, what's wrong, where's Bubba, is he all right?" Junior asked, as he jumped from his van expecting the worst from the jumbled phone call he'd received early that morning.

"He may be all right, but I'm sure the blue blazes not!" Gramps wheezed, as he grabbed Junior for support.

Thinking he meant being out of breath from running, Junior started helping his grandfather back to the house. "Well, you know better than to run with your lungs the way they are. Now let's get you inside and sitting down." Junior said.

"It ain't my lungs that'er giving me fits, it's K'Narf!" Gramps wheezed, getting his breath back a little.

"Who's Keenarf?" Junior asked, as they reached the warped boards of the old porch.

"I am, and you pronounce my name KahNarf. Not KeeNarf." K'Narf said, as he opened the screen door for his older brother.

Looking up at the sound of K'Narf's voice, Junior's brain seemed to choke up and backfire. For the first time in his life he locked eyes with his brother. Gone was the simple-minded boy who always bowed his head and averted his eyes to avoid any form of confrontation. In his place stood a massive shouldered six foot four inch man glaring at him with ramrod intensity.

Junior hadn't seen his brother in anything except hobnail boots, bib overalls, flannel shirts and his hair shorn close to the skull by Gramps, since he'd been brought to the farm twelve years ago.

The hobnail boots were the same, but that was all. He now had on a pair of dark slacks and a white dress shirt that was at least one size to small forcing the top two buttons open. He had somehow trimmed his eyebrows and oiled and brushed his newly grown hair into questionable respectability. His left eye was swollen badly, but not totally shut, and he had a double band-aid stuck just below the same eye. He had shaved off what had once been an almost beard, nicking himself in several places. All in all, what with his bulging forehead and miniscule chin, and that awful nose decorated as it was with that small black birthmark, he still had to be the ugliest man Junior had ever seen in his short life. A conclusion Junior instinctively knew better than to voice out loud.

"Well, don't just stand there gawking, come on in. I believe we have a few scores to settle up." K'Narf said, as he stepped back into the kitchen.

That ominous sounding statement sent Junior on a fast tour of those memories that involved Bubba as he helped Gramps up the steps and into the kitchen. What he dredged up sent cold chills down his spine.

"Sit down, I'll get the coffee. If my memory serves me right you take both cream and sugar, right?" K'Narf asked, smiling ominously at his brother.

Junior sat down, numbly shook his head and barely managed a weak "Uh huh."

"Well, well." K'Narf said, sitting down himself after serving the coffee. "I don't know whether to shake your hand, or toss you through that window head first." He added, looking seriously into Junior's eyes.

"I don't understand. I'm the one who fixed your memory so... so why are you mad at me?" Junior stammered, holding tight to his coffee cup.

"That questionable assumption is all that's keeping you from a trip through the window at the moment. I say questionable because I believe I was starting to achieve the same results on my own. I don't honestly know if you saved me or almost killed me with that hypnotism stunt of yours. Either way, at the moment I'm giving you the benefit of the doubt, so relax." K'Narf said, as he removed the spoon from his coffee and took a sip.

"You look so different, and you talk educated." Junior said, trying to get his coffee cup up to his mouth without spilling any, finally giving up due to the shakes.

"That's more than I can say for you." K'Narf said, grinning. "Anyway, why shouldn't I? I can recall every conversation I've ever heard and every T.V. Program I was allowed to see; added to the fact that I memorized Gramps' dictionary this morning."

"You what!" Junior exclaimed, raising his head for the first time and looking at his brother straight on.

"You heard me, I memorized Gramps' dictionary this morning." K'Narf said again, obviously enjoying himself.

"The whole dictionary?" Junior asked, as he raised his coffee cup for a drink, not caring that he spilled some. "The whole thing!" He repeated, stammering slightly as he put his cup down.

"Sure, why should that surprise you? You're the one who fixed my memory, remember!" K'Narf said, trying hard not to laugh at the expression on his brother's face.

"So that's what you were doing." Gramps said, remembering when he had glanced into the living room and saw K'Narf turning pages so fast he thought he was looking for pictures.

"That's right grandfather. I also reviewed my memories of you and grandmother, and even though you didn't want to take me in, you still treated me fairly once you had. I want to thank you for that, and tell you what you already know. Your wife, my grandmother, was as close to a saint as it's humanly possible to be and I suffer her loss as grievously as do you. You both will have my eternal gratitude." K'Narf said, as tears started forming at the thought of his grandmother and the love she had given him.

"Thank ya son, ya don't know what your words mean to me." Gramps said, his own eyes beginning to show signs of wetness.

"Unfortunately I can't say the same for you." K'Narf said, as he pointed his finger at Junior, breaking the mood of common bond between himself and his grandfather. Then, hearing the sound of a car coming up the drive, he got up and went to the window.

Junior, knowing it was his mother, breathed the sigh of relief known only by the condemned man who receives a stay of execution at the last possible second.

K'Narf stood at the window and watched as his mother drove up and parked next to Junior's van, step gracefully out, and headed for the house at a fast, almost running walk. She had opted for a short hairstyle several years ago; however, she hadn't lost her figure, and in that form-fitting custom made suit she was still every inch a beautiful woman. Watching her he felt mixed emotions of love and almost hate. He knew she loved him but not enough to have kept him with her. His mind understood her problems with keeping him, but his heart wasn't in a logical mood. Determined not to start anything, he stood mute as she opened the door and stormed into the kitchen.

"All right, what have you two done to, uh, Bubba, is that, uh, are you all right?" She stammered, as she started to reach for him. The strange look in his eyes stopping her from actually touching him.

"Sit down mother, and I'll get you a cup of coffee. You still take it black I presume." K'Narf said, as he stepped over to the table and pulled the fourth chair out and held it for her. Then, to her surprise and delight, he assisted her by pushing it in after she'd sat down. Moving to the cupboard for a clean cup and filling it from the coffee pot on the stove, K'Narf, using his peripheral vision, could see her giving his brother and grandfather one of those palms-up shrugs that asked the question, what gives? "I hope your trip out here didn't impose to great an inconvenience on you mother." K'Narf added, as he sat down and reached for his own coffee.

"I'm afraid, I uh, I don't quite understand..."

"Bubba's got his memory back. I mean he can remember everything that ever happened to..."

"Including what my name is, and it's not Bubba! It's K'Narf, pronounced KahNarf, and if I have to tell you again I will toss you through that window!" K'Narf said, as he pointed at Junior with his coffee cup.

"You've got your memory back? I don't... Would someone please...."

"It's very simple mother. I remember everything that ever happened to me, everything I ever heard, everything I've ever seen, and I remember them in vivid detail right down to the sounds and smells. I can remember when Doctor Easley delivered me and his nurse said 'Oh my God!'" Then you started screaming, "No, no, it can't be. It can't be him!" Then they took me out of the delivery room and put me in the nursery. Later I learned that you were referring to my great, great uncle K'Narf. He was so ugly at birth that his father reversed the name he was going to give him so that he wouldn't unwittingly offend anyone with the name of Frank. Remember, dad named me for the same reason and you signed the birth certificate." K'Narf said, as he locked eyes with his mother.

"I don't, it's been so long, I...." Robbie stammered, as she lowered her eyes unable to look at her son.

"Now that K'Narf can remember things he can come back to school with me. Heck, with his memory and my tutoring I'll have him caught up to me in no time." Junior said.

"No, Bub, Uh, K'Narf is going back to New York with me and I'll see that he gets the proper training to bring him up to college entry level, and that's final." Robbie said, looking at Junior and her father in turn.

"No." K'Narf said quietly.

All three of them turned as one and looked at K'Narf. Each with their private memories of past associations with him, none of which included a time when he had said no to anything.

"Now Bub, uh, K'Narf, don't be difficult. As your mother I know what's best for you and you're coming to New York with me. I know of a very nice private school and I'm sure I can get you enrolled." Robbie said, as her normal assertive personality returned.

"No!" K'Narf said, slamming his fist down on the table hard enough to make all the coffee cups jump.

"Bubba...."

"Don't call me Bubba!" K'Narf said, as he glared at his mother. "I said no! I will not go to New York with you, and I will not go to college with you, nor will I stay on this farm any longer." He added, as he stared at each one of them in turn. "I have already made plans of my own."

"Which are?" Robbie asked icily.

"To go wherever the mood takes me, do whatever I feel like doing, and stay until I decide it's time to move on!" K'narf said, returning his mother's stare until she dropped her eyes.

"You can't do that. You can't just walk out on the only ones who love you. It wouldn't be fair to us." Robbie said, still unable to look her son in the eye.

"Love!" K'Narf exclaimed, raising his voice as he stood up from the table. "Love! Grandmother loved me. She proved it on a day-to-day basis by fixing my hurts and teaching me new things. She sat with me when I was sick and played with me when I was well. She cooked me special treats and hugged me and told me she loved me at least once a day. I know of love, but the woman who loved me died last year. Grandfather likes me, he took me in and always treated me kindly, but it was because he loved his wife not because he loved me." K'Narf said, as he paced around the kitchen stopping to stare at his mother, then added. "You couldn't wait to get rid of me because dad was ashamed to have me around. He threatened to put me in an institution so you conned your mother and father into taking me to live on the farm. I owe you for that, and for my birth, but the first six years of my life were totally devoid of love."

"No, I took care of you. I loved you. I really did. I...." Robbie stammered, searching for the right words.

"No, I have searched my memories of those years. Oh, you took care of me, dressed me and invented the memory list and picture system that enabled me to function on my own, and you violently defended me against any verbal assault that besmirched my unusual mental state, but not once in the six years did you ever hug me and say you loved me." K'narf said, looking at his mother's downcast face, knowing that he had hurt her deeply.

"As for Junior, you might say he liked me there toward the last. My ineptitude made him feel superior, but during my last year with you when you made him take me to the park every Sunday so I could get some sunshine and exercise, and you thought it was so sweet of him to do it and not complain. Well, for your information, he and his buddies built a makeshift ladder and each Sunday they put it up against a tree and made me climb up it and crawl out on a limb. Then they took the ladder away and left me sitting up there crying while they ran off and played. When it was time to go home they came and got me down." K'Narf said, his face simmering in anger at the memory.

Robbie and Gramps, their faces registering shock, both turned to look at Junior. Only his bloodshot ears were visible since both hands covered his face as he slowly slid down in his chair making a weird moaning sound.

K'Narf, his anger subsiding as he watched the reaction his words were having on his brother, started to smile, then burst out laughing. Gramps, seeing that Junior was seriously humiliated and ashamed joined in, and even Robbie found herself smiling mostly because by now they were all laughing including Junior. However, her eyes conveyed to Junior in unmistakable terms the world of trouble he was destined to inherit at a later date.

"I refuse to allow you to throw your life away gallivanting around the country, it's just not right." Robbie said, as the laughter died down.

"I'm afraid you don't have a voice in my decision since I am of age." K'Narf said, getting serious again. "However, you can prove this love you speak of by helping, rather than hindering me in my leaving." He said, looking first at his mother and then at Gramps and Junior.

"Ya name it son, and if it's in my powers, ya got it." Gramps said, looking more at his daughter than at K'Narf as he spoke.

"Yeah, me too." Junior said, as he joined ranks with his grandfather.

K'Narf looked at his mother's bowed head as the seconds ticked into minutes. Finally she raised her head and looked at him through her tears, nodding her head in agreement."

K'Narf, looking at his mother's tear stained face, realized that in this eleventh hour of their lives together, her love for him was truly genuine. As was his love for her he realized. Sitting back down at the table he reached over and lightly touched her hand. A touch that told her all was forgiven.

34

"What is it ya'd have me do for ya son?" Gramps asked, breaking the timeless moment between K'Narf and his mother.

"How long have I worked for you Gramps?" K'Narf asked.

"Why, just a shade over twelve years, but you know that as well as I do." Gramps said, looking puzzled.

"Would you say that on the average I was worth at least five thousand dollars a year in labor alone?" K'Narf asked, looking sharply at his grandfather.

The mention of money made Gramps eyes narrow as he looked at his grandson suspiciously and asked. "Maybe, why?"

You have three hundred and thirty seven thousand, ninety-seven dollars and eleven cents in your savings account, and sixty seven thousand, four hundred dollars and sixteen cents in the farm's business account. I want you to give me sixty thousand dollars. Five thousand dollars for each of the twelve years I worked for you, money that I feel I have earned as a stake on a new life. Grandmother would not disapprove." K'Narf said, knowing that it had been his grandmother that had made Gramps save against the time when they'd have to pay someone to take care of him.

Gramps, knowing the meaning of K'Narf's words surprised both Junior and his daughter by saying "Okay son, is there anything else I can do." Feeling as he said the words that a burden weighing twelve years had suddenly lifted from his shoulders.

"Yes, I need you to drive me to town. I need to get a drivers license. Then I want to put together a wardrobe that would include traveling as well as dress clothes. Junior, I'd like you to go along to help me pick out a reliable van. Something like the one you're driving if we can find a used one." K'Narf said, as his grandmother's words, waste not want not, echoed in his ears.

"What would you have me do?" Robbie asked, as she looked at her son in the light of his newly acquired manhood.

"I want you to drive back to New York and bring me back two things before I leave tomorrow morning. One is my original birth certificate, and the other is my father. I would very much like to say my goodbyes to him in person. Do you think you can do this for me?" K'Narf asked, looking at his mother as she seemed to square her shoulders and assert herself once again.

"Your father and I will be here no later than eight A.M. tomorrow morning with your original birth certificate. Also I would like to leave with you a blank check. When you find the vehicle you wish to buy, just fill in the required amount. Call it a going away present from your father and I." So saying, she signed and tore a blank check out of her checkbook. Handing it to him, she smiled saying, "Your father is in for a double shock."

"I really hate to break up this cozy little chit chat." Gramps said, "But it's almost ten o'clock, and if you're serious about leaving tomorrow, we'd better git."

Knowing the truth of Gramps' statement, K'Narf folded the check and put it in his shirt pocket. Standing up, he held the chair for his mother and without a word spoken walked her out to her car, opening and closing the door for her. She started it up, and then giving him one last glance, she backed out and headed for the main highway.

"Let's take my van Gramps, and I can give K'Narf a driving lesson on the way into town. That way he can see if he really wants to buy a van." Junior said, as he and Gramps caught up with K'Narf.

"Suits me, but let's git. I want to see Sheriff Anderson's face when K'Narf asks for a driver's license." Gramps said, his face lighting up with a slightly sadistic smile.

"Okay lets go." K'Narf said, turning around as his mother's car disappeared from sight. "Did I hear you say I could drive your van, brother?" He asked, as he reached out and deftly took the keys out of Junior's hand and climbed into the driver's seat.

Chapter Six

Having pictured himself awake at six A.M. before going to sleep, K'narf obediently opened his eyes at that exact hour. He and Junior had staggered in just five hours before, loaded down with his purchases and Gramps, who had fell asleep on the way back from town. Junior was now snoring on the couch, and Gramps was safely tucked away in his bed. Thomas, noticing he was awake, snuggled up against him demanding attention. "Hey boy, you like having your back scratched don't you. Well, I guess I'd better get up and get at it, and you'd better mark territory one last time. I won't let you do it in that new van of ours, and it could be a long time before we have a place to call our own. Now git, unless you want to take a shower." K'Narf said, as he tossed Thomas lightly to the floor followed quickly by his own size thirteen bare feet pounding down the path, worn in the old linoleum floor, that led to the bathroom and a hot shower and a shave with his new razor.

After a rigorous rub down with a stiff line dried towel, he started opening his many packages. Sorting out and putting on a new pair of shorts and a tee shirt, he then chose a pair of light blue denims and a matching pale blue long sleeve shirt. Blue socks, black leather loafers and a black leather belt completed the dressing process.

He admired himself in his dresser mirror by jumping up and down to see all of himself. Quickly deciding that folding back the sleeves of his shirt made him look more casual and relaxed. Satisfied, he picked up the black pants he had worn yesterday. Reaching into the pockets he transferred his new pocketknife, keys to his new van, comb, handkerchief, and his new wallet with its drivers license.

Sheriff Anderson had been real reluctant to give him a license, even after he quoted the entire drivers manual to him verbatim, until Gramps told him he wouldn't be able to leave town without one. Sheriff Anderson had personally delivered it to him laminated and all, an hour later at the barbershop.

The barber had shaped his hair the best he could, and plucked out the center of his eyebrows and trimmed them again so they looked even neater. He also cut the hair growing in his nose. Looking out from his eyes, he could see a marked improvement, even if no one else could.

Reaching for his shirt, he unpinned the fifty five thousand dollar bank draft sticking it in his new shirt pocket and re-pinning it. Then he took the thick wad of traveling money left over from his purchases and stuffed it into his left front pants pocket.

Looking around his old room for the last time, he reached over and took the small picture of the sailor guiding his ship on a stormy sea with Christ looking over his shoulder and pointing the way. His grandmother had given it to him his first day on the farm. Then, not knowing exactly why, he picked up his old memory list with its associated pictures and opening up his new metal trunk, he packed them both away. Then he started sorting out and packing the rest of his new clothes. A lot of the stuff he'd bought he'd left in the van the night before, such as his sleeping bag, cool box and a traveling litter box for Thomas.

Hauling out the trunk and stowing it in the van, he went back to the kitchen. Looking at his reflection in the window over the sink he pulled out his comb, and wetting it down he re-combed his hair. Realizing that he was ready to leave he looked at the clock. It was seven thirty-three. His mother had twenty-seven minutes to keep her promise. Junior was still snoring on the couch, and Gramps wouldn't wake up until past noon. He decided to make a pot of coffee, feed Thomas and maybe fry up a couple of eggs before they got here.

The eggs tasted good and K'Narf had just cleared the table and sat down to a second cup of coffee, when he heard a car turn off the main highway and start up the drive to the house. It was seven fifty six. His mother was very punctual K'Narf thought, as he listened to the car stop and doors slam shut. He stood up as he heard footsteps on the porch.

His mother stepped through first and he could see the surprise register on her face as she looked at him. Then, giving him a soft smile, she stepped aside thus allowing his father into the room.

K'Narf looked at his father for the first time in twelve years. His hair was still dark red, only now he had a mustache and a van-dike. He had on a dark pin striped business suit, white shirt and a

38

dark solid color tie. Looking every inch the successful businessman that he was. He suddenly realized that his father was studying him with a cold unnerving stare. Just then his mother spoke.

"I brought you your birth certificate as you requested." Robbie said, as she took a yellowed envelope out of her purse and handed it to him.

"Thank you Mother." K'Narf said, taking it. Opening it up he noticed that both his mother and father had good strong signatures. "You might be interested to know that my last name is no longer Fugate, it's now legally Etaguf." He added, casually mentioning what he thought would be a shock to his father.

"Why, why would you, how?" His mother stammered.

"Bill Michaels, a lawyer friend of Gramps drew up the papers, Judge Rhone signed them and they were duly recorded at the Court House." K'Narf said, watching his father for a reaction. "Had it done before I got my new drivers license." He added.

"But why?" Robbie asked again, surprise very evident on her face.

"Same reason great, great grandfather reversed the name of Frank and named his son K'Narf. I don't want anyone to worry that I might bring shame or disgrace on the name of Fugate, so I had it reversed too." K'Narf said, unable to see so much as a glimmer of emotion on his father's face.

"I, uh, did you have any trouble with my check?" Robbie asked, suddenly fearing her husband's reaction and trying to change the subject.

"Yes, a little. They wouldn't take a two party check for that amount over at Reese's Truck Palace, so Gramps paid cash and I filled your check out and signed it over to him. He's already deposited it in his account. He seemed to think you were good for it even if Reese's didn't." K'Narf said, looking sideways at his father who so far hadn't said a word or showed any visible emotion.

"And you didn't have any trouble getting your drivers license?" Robbie asked, still looking nervously at her husband.

"Not at all, Sheriff Anderson had no objection after Gramps assured him that I was going to be leaving." K'Narf said, grinning slightly at the memory. "And that I couldn't leave without it." He added, looking directly at his father and thinking he was going to have to speak first.

"They say seeing is believing. I see you and I hear you, but I still have trouble believing. I guess it's because in my mind you have been an object of pity for so long." Joe Sr. said, locking eyes with his son.

"Well, I'm no longer a case deserving of your pity, or anything else. I wanted to meet you face to face before I left mainly to impress that fact on you, and to thank you for naming me K'Narf after your great uncle. He sounds like a man that carried his name proudly." K'Narf said, glaring at his father.

"He did, right up to the moment his enemies drugged him and wrapped him in chains. Then, after he recovered his senses, they toasted him with a half empty whisky bottle and booted him into the Mississippi. That was the day before he would have turned twenty-one. See that your pride doesn't land you in a river." His father said, glaring back.

"I knew he had been murdered, but I'd never heard anyone speak of how." K'Narf said, his voice much softer than it had been.

"You seem to have inherited some of the abilities that made your great, great uncle special; see that you use them cautiously and sparingly. If perchance you find yourself in some difficulty along the way where my assistance may be beneficial, I offer you this letter of introduction. Also included is mine, and my lawyers, private business phone numbers in case of an emergency." Joe Sr. said, reaching into his inside coat pocket and pulling out a long white envelope with his firm's insignia on it and handing it to him. "And if you're ever in New York, feel free to drop in." He added, not realizing what those casual words would someday lead too.

"Auditor's Auditor." K'Narf said, reading his father's insignia. "What...."

"We are an auditing firm. If you ever find yourself in the position of wanting to buy a business, give us a call. We will tell you if their books accurately reflect their assets prior to your purchase." Joe Sr. said, stating what was obviously a well-rehearsed statement of fact.

"Mother." K'Narf said, not knowing what else to say to his father as he held out his hands to his mother.

"Take care of yourself, and be careful driving. Especially in heavy traffic, and I just love that blue color you picked out." Robbie said, taking her son's hands and giving them a squeeze. "It looks almost new." She added.

"It is. They didn't have any used ones so I bought the one off their show room floor." K'Narf said, looking at his father for a reaction.

"Enjoy it in good health." Joe Sr. said, holding out his hand in an obvious act of dismissal.

Shaking his father's hand, K'Narf felt very young and foolish, which wasn't exactly the feeling that he had imagined when he had planned this meeting. "Thank you father." He said, unable to think of anything else to say.

Then, scooping up Thomas who had been rubbing against his leg, he walked out of the kitchen letting the screen door slam behind him. Getting into the van, he realized he had forgotten Thomas' cat pole. Nothing on earth could force him to face his father again; especially if it was just to tell him he'd forgotten his cat's pole. Starting the van he backed out of the driveway, headed for the main highway and swung in the westbound lane with the rising sun at his back.

"Meowwrr!"

"You've ate, and you have fresh litter in your litter box. So just settle down and relax. You'd think he'd have gotten angry when I said I bought a new van! Now I wish I'd bought that tan one that was outfitted for camping, instead of this stripped down version!" K'Narf growled at Thomas, as he glanced behind him at the bare metal walls and plain blue carpeting. At least it had these nice captain's chairs. One for him and one for Thomas, he thought, as Thomas curled up in his seat and prepared to take a nap. Looking at the highway stretching out before him, K'Narf settled down to the job of driving. K'Narf, having had to stop for gas once already, noticed that his gauge was approaching empty again. His stomach was signaling the same condition, so it was no surprise when Thomas stretched and let out with an unmistakable meow that said, "feed me". Their mutual hunger was compounded by the sun, which had dropped low enough in the west to start blinding him to oncoming traffic. He filed a mental note to buy a pair of sun glasses the first chance he got; which may just be that truck stop coming up on the right, he thought, letting his foot ease off the gas peddle.

"Meeoowaarrr!"

"Okay Thomas! I'd tell you not to get your tail in a twist if you had one." K'Narf said, grinning at his own humor. "Besides, I'm the one who drove all day; all you did was curl up and go to

41

sleep, so don't yowl at me." He added, as he slowed and swung into the gravel off-ramp that angled toward the blinking "Gas" sign, and the motley collection of buildings surrounding it.

"Can I help you sir?" A young boy asked, running out from between two of the buildings.

"You sure can, how about washing off that windshield of mine." K'Narf said, as he headed inside to pay for his gas. Coming back out he noticed the boy was industrially scrubbing at the bugs that had spattered his windshield. Moments later, his gas tank full again, he gave the boy a five-dollar tip for doing such a good job. Then, getting back in his van he looked around and realized that there was a small grocery store, with an adjoining restaurant, attached to the gas station.

"We're in luck Thomas. We should be able to get everything we need right here." K'Narf said, as he started the van and pulled over and parked out of the main drive. You wait here, and don't let anyone mess with the van." He added, as he headed for the grocery store.

The store was old and poorly illuminated, but it seemed to be well stocked with a wide variety of goods. There was a heavyset woman perched on a stool behind a makeshift counter, and a young girl looking at a magazine over in the corner. Picking up a cardboard box from the pile stacked by the door, he began methodically filling it from the store's shelves. Bread, mayonnaise, mustard, pickles, potato chips, sliced cheese and a small package of kosher baloney, "Best I can do for right now." K'Narf mumbled to himself, thinking of his grandmother and her views on eating meat.

Continuing on with his shopping, he added cookies, napkins, paper plates, can-opener, bottled water, cat food, two heavy flat bottomed ceramic bowls so he could feed and water Thomas and two bags of ice for the cool box. Not exactly a gourmet's delight, he thought, but it would have to do. Moving toward the woman at the counter, he noticed a rack of sunglasses. Putting down his box, he selected a pair with heavy black frames that felt comfortable. Adding them to his box, he picked it up, stepped over and placed it on the counter in front of the woman.

Grunting, she heaved herself off her stool and started adding up his purchases on an old adding machine. K'Narf had already done this mentally and knew that the total should be seventy-nine dollars and thirty-seven cents with tax.

"Seventy-nine dollars and thirty-nine cents." She said, holding out her hand.

Seeing no advantage in arguing over two cents, K'Narf pulled out his money and peeled off four twenties. Then, getting his change he picked up his box and headed out the door.

"Harriet, did I see what I thought I did?" the young girl asked, as she dropped her magazine and walked over to the counter.

"Ya sure did. Tha' roll was big enough to choke a horse." Harriet said, grunting as she plopped herself back down on her stool.

Moving to the window the girl watched K'Narf open the back of a van and load his cool box with ice and food. Then he opened a can and fed a large grey and white cat that didn't seem to have any tail; closing up the van and headed for the restaurant. "He's going into Mike's." She said, glancing back at Harriet.

"Ya gon'na give it a try?" Harriet asked.

"Yeah, guess so, but if it weren't for all that money... geeze he's ugly." She said, as she opened the door and headed for Mike's place.

K'Narf, feeling the need for some hot food decided at the last minute to get something here and save the cold cuts for later. Stepping into the restaurant he walked over to a booth and slid in picking up the menu, noticing that he was the only customer made him wonder where all the truckers were.

Concentrating on the menu, he only half heard the front door open and close behind him. Having decided on a roast beef on rye bread and a Coke, he was startled when he looked up for a waitress and found the girl from the store standing at his table. She was clutching her coat at the throat and the middle like she was cold and was obviously waiting for him to notice her.

"Please mister, don't yell or Mike'll throw me out. All I want is something to eat. It's been two days since I had a good meal... please! Just a hamburger and maybe a glass of milk." She said, pleading with her eyes and gripping her coat tighter.

"Okay, sure, be my pleasure." K'narf said, as the girl quickly slid into the seat opposite him. Mike came out of his kitchen just then and walked over. K'Narf caught the look he gave the girl so he quickly said, "She's with me. I'll have your roast beef on rye and a Coke. Give her anything she wants."

"Ya mean it mister! Anything I want, gee thanks." She said, turning to Mike. "I'll have your open face steak sandwich with all the trimmings and a strawberry shake." She added, glaring at Mike in triumph as he turned and headed back to his kitchen.

"That's Mike, he owns this place. He doesn't like me hanging around, says I'm bad for business. Mostly he's mad 'cause I told him he was fat and to quit bothering me." She said, turning her full green eyed smile on K'narf.

K'Narf, not quite following her conversation just smiled back. "Is he a good cook?" He asked, unable to think of anything else to say.

"Mike? Yeah, he's one of the best. Don't judge him by this place. He could cook any place he wanted if he could leave his own cooking alone." She said, still smiling at K'Narf.

"What's your name?" K'Narf asked, thinking it was a proper question to ask.

"Terry Jean, after my mother. She had beautiful red hair and was a model. I have her hair, but I ain't never been no model." She said, finally letting go of her coat allowing it to fall open in front.

K'Narf, noticing immediately that her dress was cut exceedingly low, felt himself blushing and quickly turned his gaze to the kitchen door. She continued to talk, but he didn't really understand much of what she said, then finally the door opened and Mike came out with their food. Setting both the food and the bill down in front of them, he retreated back to his kitchen without saying a word.

"Ooh! That looks good." Terry Jean said, as she shrugged her shoulders forward and started pulling her arms out of her coat sleeves.

K'Narf, his eyes on Terry Jean, reached blindly for the salt, his second shock came when the saltshaker came to him. His hand had been inches away when it had literally jumped into his hand. Suddenly the room got very close as his breathing became rapid and his heart started pounding. Sliding out of the booth, he picked up his sandwich and wrapped it in his napkin, took a long swallow of Coke and set the glass back down on the table. Reaching into his pocket he pulled out his money and peeled off two twenties and tossed them on the table. "That will cover the ticket, you can keep the change. I, uh, I got'ta go." He stammered, as he almost ran from the room.

Jumping into the van, he quickly started it up and headed for the highway. Thomas, sensing his master's troubled mind, jumped in his lap and started purring. Later, turning on his headlights, K'Narf finally settled down enough to chew on his now cold sandwich. He didn't know which had terrified him more, the girl or the saltshaker. "Thomas, I may just have a few problems in this new life of mine that I haven't counted on." He said, as the nighttime highway unwound ahead of him.

Three days, and almost twenty-five hundred miles later, a very tired K'Narf pulled off the Interstate and drove slowly down a street named "Central". The name told him it would take him through the heart of Phoenix, the capital city of Arizona. One more town, one more detour, he thought as he looked at the lights ahead.

Then, approaching the center of town, he saw a small green sign titled "Library". He made a hard left into the libraries' parking lot, drove around until he found the entrance, parked the van and walked over. The dedication plaque stated 1951. Then, not wanting to go in he looked through the double glass doors. There was a guard checking parcels and bags, and beyond him he could see books; more books than he had ever imagined.

That settled it, all he needed now was living quarter's close by, but today was Friday and the Sabbath starts at sundown, he thought, "I need a motel where I can hole up and rest; a hot bath and a soft bed sounds awful good too." K'Narf mumbled to himself, as he turned and headed for the van.

Chapter Seven

The sign simply stated "Room" and was thumb tacked to the porch post. The house itself was old, but had been kept in good repair, at least from an outsider's view. K'Narf had slept nearly all day Saturday. The Lord said to rest on the Sabbath and he had taken Him literally. Then, having left the motel while it was still dark he had found an all night restaurant, and by buying two breakfast specials managed to pacify his stomach. Leaving the restaurant right after daybreak, he had spent the next hour combing the residential area around the library. He finally found exactly what he was looking for. It was within easy walking distance to the library, five blocks to be exact. Even though it was still rather early he pulled into the driveway and parked.

"Thomas, you stay here and be quiet. I want this room, and your yowling might cause a problem." K'Narf said, seeing a light go on in the house. Getting out of the van he quickly shut the door in Thomas' face and walked up to the door. Not seeing a doorbell he hit the door with three sharp raps.

He somehow expected the door to be opened by a little old lady, not by a large powerfully built, but obviously elderly black man. Never having had any associations with a member of the black race, K'Narf found himself staring. The man of the house, having never opened his door on anything quite like K'Narf, stared back.

Feeling slightly disoriented, K'Narf pointed at the small sign and half grunted. "Room, uh, your room. It's for rent?"

"Uh huh, yeah. It's just a room though, no, uh, house privileges." The black man stammered, still staring at K'Narf. "You can have a hot-plate though." He added, as an after thought.

"How much?" K'Narf asked, beginning to regain his composure.

The black man's eyes seemed to tighten as he looked past K'Narf at the new van sitting in the driveway. "Sixty dollars a

46

week, no women, no pets!" He said, spitting the words out as though expecting an argument.

"K'Narf pulled out his money and started to peel off three twenties, then stopped in mid action. "Oh, I'm sorry, I almost forgot my cat Thomas. I guess he could stay in the van at night though."

The black man, his eyes glued to K'Narf's money roll, seemed to come to life. "Cat! Oh, I guess a cat would be all right, but I'll need the first and last weeks rent in advance, and there's a twenty dollar cleaning deposit." He said, defensively.

"Okay." K'Narf said, as he counted out seven twenties into his new landlords hand. "By the way, my name's K'Narf Etaguf. What's yours?"

"Rudy, Rudy Marcus. Uh, come on in and I'll show you the room and give you your keys." Rudy said, as he folded the money and put it in his shirt pocket.

"Keys?"

"Yeah, one for the room, and one for the house in case I'm not home." Rudy said, glancing back quizzically at K'Narf as they climbed the stairs.

Following Rudy as he opened an ancient wood door, K'Narf stepped into a beautifully furnished room. It had a four-poster bed, dresser with a mirror, and a full sized chest-of-drawers all in dark cherry wood. There was a small corner desk with a lamp and chair, and a large over-stuffed chair with its back to the window. The floor was polished wood, with two Indian-looking throw rugs positioned in front of the bed and the reading chair.

Turning to Rudy he noticed the expectant look in his eyes. "It's beautiful, much more than I expected. I...."

"Everything, except the desk and chair, has been in my family for generations. Please bare that in mind during your stay here." Rudy said, obviously pleased, as he handed K'Narf the two keys that had been lying on the dresser. "You'll find the bathroom at the end of the hall." He added, as he turned and left the bedroom.

Following Rudy back downstairs, K'Narf noticed that the rest of the house echoed the neatness of the bedroom. There must be a woman around somewhere he thought, as he went out to the van to get his things and Thomas.

At ten o'clock sharp he was standing on the front steps of the library along with eleven others. Five minutes later he was wandering wide-eyed among stack, after stack, of books. Titles such as *Universe, Earth, and Atom: The Story of Physics*, *Evolution of the Solar System*, *Chemistry: A Study of Matter*, *The Textbook of Microbiology*, *Janes Weapon Systems*, and *Psychophysiological Aspects of Space Flight*, boggled his mind. He finally decided to start with something more basic, which was the Collier's Encyclopedia, after making himself a promise that he would not leave this library until he'd scanned and memorized every book that fired his imagination.

He was almost finished with PHYFE to RENI when the librarian, the same one who had asked him several times that day if he needed help finding something, informed him that it was eight-forty-five and they'd be closing at nine. Doing a fast mental calculation, K'Narf added up the total pages scanned, subtracted his own personal time used, divided the remainder by total pages, and concluded that he was scanning at the rated of one page every two-point-five seconds. At that rate he should be finished with Collier's by twelve-thirty tomorrow. Staggering out of the library, he headed for a restaurant he'd spotted a block over and up from the Library. His first day at school had drained all thought of exploring Phoenix from his mind.

Approaching Rudy's house, K'Narf could detect no sign of life. Assuming Rudy was asleep, he opened the front door and crept up to his room with all the stealth at his command. Just as he was about to open the door to his room, he heard what sounded like a moan coming from further down the hall. Walking catlike, he slipped down the dark hall to the bedroom at the far end. Putting his ear to the door he listened as muffled sounds of activity filtered through. Hearing Rudy cry out in anguish, he opened the door and stepped in and crouched in one smooth violent motion. Ready, so he thought, for whatever kind of trouble he might find in the room.

In the space of a heart beat K'Narf took in the room and the scene in front of him. To his left, pushed up against a wall, was a short little bald-headed fat man whose bright blue eyes were full of fear. Crouched in front of him, arms wide in a fighting stance was a dark skinned man with a weather beaten face, framed by long blackish gray hair brandishing a formidable knife in his right hand. Next to him was Rudy, also in a fighting stance with a stiletto like knife in his hand. Behind Rudy and to his right was another older man, he too had fear in his eyes, and judging by the glint of red on top of his head he used to have bright red hair. Finally, standing in front of him in a fighting crouch, was another black man. He was old like Rudy, but wiry and thin looking and he too had a stiletto looking knife in his hand. Seeing Rudy, K'Narf straightened up and started backing out of the room. "I, uh, I thought you were in some kind of trouble. I heard you moaning and then I heard them laughing." K'Narf said defensively, looking at Rudy as he nodded at his friends.

Suddenly Rudy burst out laughing "And you was gon'na save me was you! Well, get in here an close the door." Turning around Rudy looked at his friends, waving his knife casually at them as he folded it up. They picked up the signal, and the knives disappeared as quickly as they had appeared. "K'Narf, I'd like you to meet my friends, Jimmy, Mickey, Andrew and Turk. This is my new roomer Mister K'Narf Etaguf." Rudy said, as he pointed at each man in turn. "The reason I was moaning, was because these gentleman just relieved me of half the rent you gave me this morning." Rudy added, as he turned his attention to K'Narf.

"Half of it?" K'Narf asked questioningly.

This brought a roll of laughter from Rudy's friends, as Rudy bent over and straightened up an old grey blanket that had been spread out on the floor; a blanket with a printed U.S. Navy emblem still visible on it, and sat back down on the floor with his back to K'Narf. The others followed suit, leaving K'narf standing.

"I don't mind if you watch, as long as you keep quiet. Now who owned the bones when Mister Etaguf rescued me?" Rudy asked, grinning at his friends.

In the next half hour K'Narf learned not only the game of *Craps*, but also the highly colorful language that goes along with the game. Finally it was Rudy's turn with the dice, or bones as they were referred to, and K'Narf found himself mentally rooting for Rudy to win. Six straight wins later no one was laughing. Rudy had won back more than he'd lost in the first four wins, and now with what was left of his friends money in the pot, the silence could be cut with a knife.

Rudy, suddenly very conscious of K'Narf's standing silently behind him paused, then laid down the dice and stood up. "Excuse me bro's, I'll be right back." He said, as he grabbed K'Narf, and opening the door pushed him out into the hall. Shutting the door, he pushed K'narf further down the hall and then in a harsh whisper he asked "You doing anything to those bones boy, or is it just my imagination running amuck?"

"Well, yeah, I, uh, I think I am." K'Narf stammered.

"What do you mean, you think! Either you're controlling the bones or you're not!" Rudy said, fighting to keep his voice down.

"Well, I, uh, concentrate on the numbers you need on each dice, and when they stop rolling that's the numbers that shows up. I...."

"Sweet Jesus!" Rudy moaned, cutting K'Narf off in mid-sentence. "I don't know what kind of a gift the Good Lord has given you, but here's what you're gon'na do with it! When we go back in there you're gon'na make sure I lose. I'm gon'na keep losing until my friends are even again, then you're gon'na git. This is a friendly game and no one has ever got bad hurt, and I'm not gon'na change the rules tonight." Rudy said, as he half shoved K'narf toward the door. "Mister Etaguf, I appreciate what you tried to do." He added, squeezing K'Narf's arm just before he opened the door.

Twenty minutes later K'Narf quietly slipped out and headed for his bedroom. Opening his door he was met by a very agitated and hungry cat. "Thomas." K'Narf said thoughtfully. "I think I just found out why my great, great uncle K'Narf was murdered, and if I'm not real careful it could happen to me." He added, as he dug out a can of cat food and the can-opener.

Opening his door early the next morning, K'Narf almost stepped on a pair of dice and a knife. No note, they were just lying on the throw rug in front of his door. The knife was a work of art in itself. Thumbing back the catch, its one long single blade fell out, locking into placed when he relaxed his thumb. The blade was razor sharp, with the tip honed on both edges, its intended use was obvious even to him. The dice, like the knife, were also works of art; translucent white, they seemed to glow with a life of their own. K'Narf, knowing who the gifts were from felt a strong feeling of satisfaction. He had made his first friend.

By eight-forty-five that evening, when the librarian informed him that it was closing time, he had finished with *Collier's Encyclopedia, Van Nostrand's Scientific Encyclopedia*, which covered twenty-nine sciences starting with Aeronautics and ending with Zoology, and *Mathematics for Engineers and Scientist, Calculus and Analytic Geometry, Physics in Perspective, Electro-Magnetism, The Electro Magnetic Field*, plus *The Storage of Fruits and Vegetables*. He was also halfway through *The Natural Radiation Environment* and his head felt like it was radiating at a steady forty beats to the second itself.

At the restaurant that evening he practiced with his dice, being very careful not to expose his ability to manipulate them to the inquisitive stares of his waitress and several other customers.

Several days later, just as he was finishing *Basic Physiology and Anatomy*, he looked out the window and noticed that the light was getting dim. Checking his mental clock, he realized that not only was it Friday, but that he had barely twenty minutes before the sun would be setting. Replacing the book he had been reading back to its exact spot on the bookshelf, he headed for the door.

Walking up to the house, he saw Rudy sitting out on the front porch smoking a pipe. It reminded him of evenings on the farm before his grandfather had been forced to give up smoking. As K'Narf stepped up on the porch, Rudy grunted and nodded his head toward the other porch rocker in an obvious invitation to join him.

"Quitting the library a little early today, aren't you?" Rudy asked, in a soft drawl.

"It's Friday," K'Narf answered, surprised that Rudy knew where he spent his days as he sat down in the rocker and relaxed.

"Friday?" Rudy asked, using the word as a question.

"Yeah, Friday. Sabbath began just a few minutes ago." K'Narf answered, thinking everyone should know that as he looked over at Rudy.

"Sabbath, you mean like those Adventist people?" Rudy asked, thinking of the Seventh Day Adventist Church.

"Don't know about any Adventist people, it's just the Sabbath. Starts at sundown today and ends at sundown tomorrow, supposed to rest according to the Bible." K'Narf said, thinking it odd that Rudy didn't know this. "How did you know that I was at the Library?" He asked, more interested in how Rudy knew where he spent his days.

"Oh... curiosity mostly. Seen you going into the library the other morning and followed you." Rudy stated flatly. "I know you go to the library each day and do nothing but turn pages all day. I also know that the head librarian was considering calling the police and having you picked up. Lucky for you that I overheard them talking and managed to explained to them that you were a college student living at my place, and that you were writing a term paper on high speed reading. Not sure how much they believed, but it was enough to keep them from calling the law." He concluded, puffing hard on his pipe to bring it back to life, after what was for him a long speech.

"So that's why she didn't bother me with her silly, 'Can I help you find something?' question today." K'Narf said, still not totally sure why Rudy had taken the time to check up on him, but deciding not to push the issue.

"Could be, but if I was you I'd be very polite and civil to them librarians. They ain't all that convinced that you ain't a loony." Rudy said, grinning around his pipe stem.

"Guess I'd better, since I want to be there at least another month, and I'll want to come back from time to time." K'Narf said, with a brooding look on his face.

"Did you ever consider just getting a library card?" Rudy asked, looking purposefully at K'Narf. "You can use me for a reference if you want." He added, taking a last long drag on his pipe.

"Library Card!" K'Narf said, surprised at the thought. "Do you think they'd give me one?" He added, asking the question as though he really didn't believe they would.

"Don't see why not." Rudy said, getting up and stretching. "You ate yet?" He added, asking the question as he looked down at K'Narf.

"No, but...." K'Narf stammered, standing up himself.

"No buts about it then, come on in and I'll rustle us something up." Rudy said, stopping K'Narf's excuse in mid-sentence as he headed for the door.

Rudy, as it turned out was an excellent cook, and the conversation had been stimulating. He was a wealth of information about life in general and specifically about Arizona having been born and raised in the state.

K'Narf, with a growing interest in a place of his own where he could do some experimentation, had learned of a small mountainous community called New River located just north of Phoenix. Far enough out for the glimmerings of an idea that was just starting to germinate, and close enough to Phoenix to initiate and maintain the necessary contacts. His suddenly active imagination held sleep at bay until almost dawn, making him an hour late to the library.

Getting a library card turned out to be a very simple matter once he showed them his father's letter of introduction, *and* they made a copy for their records, *and* he paid them what they said was the customary fee, *and* he filled out all their forms. Anyway, after all their questions, he was the proud owner of a library card that allowed him to check out books. More important, he was no longer an object of suspicion to them.

He finished the *Natural Radiation Environment and Principles of Physical Geology, California Manufacturer's Register, Power Plant Engineers Guide, The Machine Shop Training Course Volume I & II, Water and Wastewater Engineering, Instrument Flying,* and was starting one titled *Plant Breeding* when the librarian came over.

"Mister Etaguf, we'll be closing in twenty minutes. Why don't you select some books to take with you tonight? We'll be closed tomorrow due to the holiday you know." She said, in her soft librarian voice.

"Thank you, I believe I will." K'Narf said, looking up and giving her his best smile.

Actually it wasn't a bad idea he thought, as he got up and started prowling among the stacks, picking up any book that grabbed his imagination. Finally, loaded down with nine volumes, he headed for the front desk. Jeannette, that was her name, didn't question his choices at all; she just checked them out to him. Her curiosity had obviously been satisfied years ago.

Four weeks, and hundreds of books later, he checked in the last three books he had out in his name. It had been a fast six and a half weeks, and he would never forget the feeling of satisfaction he had found here. Taking a last walk among the stacks of pure fascination called books, he promised himself that he would be back. There were still many of them he wanted to read, but right now his mind was crammed-full of ideas that he had to try. With mixed emotions he waved a casual goodbye to Jeannette and left; he didn't really feel like he was graduating, more like he was being let out for the summer.

Chapter Eight

"Morning Rudy." K'Narf called out from the top of the stairs.

"Morning yourself." Rudy hollered back, looking up at K'Narf. "Why ain't you at the library?"

"You might say I'm on summer break. Do you have anything special planned for today?" K'Narf asked, as he descended the stairs followed closely by Thomas.

"Nothing that couldn't be changed, why? You got something in mind?" Rudy asked, lowering his voice as K'Narf hit the bottom step.

"Yeah, I'd like to go look at that New River place you told me about."

"When you wan'na go?"

"Right after breakfast if it's all right with you." K'Narf said, sniffing at the aroma coming from the kitchen.

Rudy, grinning an ear-to-ear grin, his idea of happiness was to have someone to cook for, took K'Narf by the arm and led him into the kitchen. Just a shade over half an hour later they were backing out of the driveway.

"One thing I'll say for you Mister Etaguf, you shore can eat."

"The name is K'Narf, Rudy, and you might say I was starved for some good home cooking, and your cooking is exceptionally good. In fact, I'd say you were the best cook I've ever known." K'Narf said, mentally apologizing to his grandmother. "Where'd you learn to cook like that anyway?"

"Navy." Rudy said. "Spent thirty years cooking for the Navy!" He added, smiling at the memory. "Retired off'en the U.S.S. Providence."

"Thirty years, wow, no wonder you can cook. Now, where is this New River Place?" K'Narf asked, changing the subject as he headed the van toward Central avenue.

"Hang a right at Central, then a left at the light and swing north when you hit the canyon." Rudy said, as he settled into his seat.

"The canyon?"

"The Black Canyon Highway or Interstate seventeen if you prefer to call it that. Anyway, you just drive and I'll tell you when and which way to turn, okay?" Rudy asked, looking over at K'Narf for agreement just as Thomas jumped up into his lap. "New River's about twenty five miles to the North." He added, rubbing Thomas behind the ears.

Twenty-seven minutes later K'Narf swung onto the New River off ramp. Turning right, the first thing he saw was a service station and some small outbuildings. K'Narf continued on past the station, turned left onto the frontage road, then right onto New River Road.

Immediately to his left was a single building touting a Realty and a Tavern as tenants. Continuing on he crossed the New River Bridge, and in an undeclared, but mutually agreed upon silence, he drove down New River Road. Rudy had said "Mountainous Community," foothills would have been more appropriate. Meander Road, Coyote Pass, Country Road, Quail Run, Venado Drive, Circle Mountain Road then empty desert.

"So that was new River." K'Narf said, turning the van around.

"What were you expecting, a suburb of New York?" Rudy asked, grinning.

"No, don't know exactly what I was expecting, but nice homes and a beautiful church, intermingled with a random collection of slum-like shacks wasn't it." K'Narf said, as he turned north on Circle Mountain Road.

"If you don't like the place, why are we on this dirt road?" Rudy grunted, asking the question as the van hit a chuckhole.

"Didn't say I didn't like it, just surprised at the zoning a little; and the reason we're on this dirt road is because the terrain fits my requirements." K'narf said, looking more at the surrounding countryside than at the road. "Now, if I can just find the place I want." He added, suddenly hitting the brakes as he tried to avoid another large chuckhole.

"If you'd slow down a mite, you might see something." Rudy half-yelled, as the van barreled around a curve and hit a heavily wash-boarded section of road.

"I'm looking for a well-built house with a large double garage and no close neighbors." K'Narf said, raising his voice just enough to be heard over the noise caused by the dirt road, and at the same time slowing the van as they topped a small rise.

"Ya mean like that one over yonder." Rudy said, pointing toward a slump-block house with a double garage that had been built literally into a mountainside.

"That's exactly what I'm looking for." K'Narf said, as he swung the van into the long winding driveway leading to the house.

"Hey, where do you think you're going, there ain't no for sale sign on this place."

"Won't hurt none to ask." K'Narf said, as he pulled up and parked.

"I think someone put something funny in your pipe." Rudy said, as K'Narf opened his door and got out.

"Pipe? What pipe? I don't smoke a pipe." K'Narf said, giving Rudy a puzzled look.

"Forget it. I was just thinking out loud." Rudy said, giving K'Narf one of his ear-to-ear grins as he got out and joined him.

"I can hear music playing so somebody's home." K'Narf said, as he punched the doorbell and stood back.

Minutes later the door was opened by a tall thin elderly man, dressed in bright yellow golf knickers and a pale green sweater, drying his hands on a dishtowel. "May I help you?" He asked.

"Yes, I'd like to buy your house." K'Narf said, seeing Rudy shaking his head in disbelief out of the corner of his eye.

"Well, uh, I'd like nothing better than to sell it to you, but I doubt if you could afford it." He said, slightly taken aback.

"Why, how much are you asking?"

"It's not just how much I'm asking, it's the fact that you can't get financing up here, and I can't afford to carry the mortgage myself. I tried for six months to sell it after my wife died and I couldn't find anyone with cash." He said, tossing the towel on a chair beside the door.

"How much are you asking?" K'Narf asked again.

"Two-hundred and fifty-seven thousand." The thin man said, looking at K'Narf almost apologetically.

"Would you accept twenty-five thousand down and the remainder in sixty days?" K'Narf asked, seeing a look of surprise in the thin man's eyes.

"Well yes, but you haven't even seen the house yet." He said, shock replacing the look of surprise in his eyes.

"It's not necessary, I already know I want to buy it. If you can have someone draw up the necessary papers, I'll bring out a certified cashier's check tomorrow morning no later than eleven." K'Narf said, extending his hand in a manner that implied a deal had been made and agreed upon.

"Why yes, I'll have Ted draw them up tonight. Wouldn't you like to come in and at least look at the house first though? I built most of it myself you know." He asked hopefully, accepting K'Narf's hand as he spoke.

"Not right now, I have to get to the Bank before they close. My name is K'Narf Etaguf and this is my friend Rudy Marcus." K'Narf said bluntly.

"My name is Bill Kent." He said offering his hand to Rudy.

"Good, then we have a deal. I'll see you tomorrow." K'Narf said, as he abruptly turned and headed back to the van leaving Rudy shaking Bill's hand.

Jumping into the van, K'Narf started it up and waited as Rudy hurried over, opened his door and climbed in.

"Did anyone ever tell you that you're rude?" Rudy asked, as K'Narf headed the van out of the drive.

"Nope." K'Narf said matter-of-factly, dust boiling out from behind the van as he hit the gas.

"Well you are!" Rudy squalled, as the van slid sideways going around the same wash-boarded curve they had passed earlier. "And who in the world taught you to drive?"

"Taught myself." K'Narf yelled back as he hit the brakes, which was the wrong thing to do.

The van didn't tip over, but it did manage to tilt briefly up on two wheels, as it slid sideways off the road and stalled. Rudy, choking on the dust pouring in his window, said a few choice words from his days in the Navy as he slapped at the window's up button. "Why'd you hit the brakes? Any fool kid knows better than to hit the brakes in a slide! How long you been driving anyway?" He asked, as his tirade finally ran out of steam.

"Got my license the same week I showed up at your place." K'Narf said, looking sideways at the shocked look on Rudy's face.

"I'm driving." Rudy stated in a flat no-nonsense voice that reminded K'Narf of his grandfather.

K'Narf, not about to argue with that tone of voice, obligingly got out of the drivers chair and allowed Rudy to take his place at the wheel. Seating himself on the passenger's side, he watched as Rudy started up the van and eased it back onto the road.

Halfway back to Phoenix, Rudy finally broke the uneasy silence. "You got that kind of money?"

"The twenty five thousand? Yeah, I've got it." K'Narf answered.

"No, I mean the two hundred and fifty-seven thousand!" Rudy said, in an exasperated voice.

"No, but I know where I can get it." K'Narf said, avoiding Rudy's scrutinizing gaze.

"Don't tell me, let me guess. You're going to Las Vegas and win it at the crap tables." Rudy said, glancing at the astonished look on K'Narf's face.

"How'd you know that? I haven't told anyone, I've never said anything about...."

"Didn't take any brains to figure out why you were practicing every night with them dice I gave you." Rudy said, cutting K'Narf off in mid-sputter.

"Well, I need the money and I'm not about to go out and get a job even if I could find one." K'Narf said defensively, quickly getting his composure back.

"Are you going to ask me, or am I going to have to invite myself along?" Rudy asked, glancing over at K'Narf. "I have a strange feeling you're gon'na need me for something more than just driving this here van." He added, more to himself than to K'narf.

K'Narf mutely nodded his head up and down; a feeling of warmth flowing through him at Rudy's offer to go with him. "Okay, but remember, you're just along for the ride." K'Narf said, petting Thomas who had jumped in his lap; his mind swirling with plans as they silently followed the highway back down into the Valley of the Sun.

Thirty-two hours later, with the contract for the house in his pocket, they topped a rise, and he looked at the lights of the fabled Las Vegas for the first time. "Somebody forgot to turn the lights off." K'Narf said, thinking of his grandmother's oft repeated admonition about that very subject. "Haven't these people ever heard of the energy crisis?"

"Energy crisis, Vegas don't even know the meaning of the word crisis, much less an energy crises." Rudy said, giving K'Narf one of those special looks he reserved for what he privately thought of as "dumb" comments.

"Well, maybe when we get through with them, they won't be able to afford their electric bill." K'Narf said grinning.

"What do you mean we? I'm just along for the ride, remember!" Rudy said, giving K'Narf a hard look.

"No you ain't! You faded your bet back there in New River and the dice just came up snake-eyes." K'Narf said seriously, staring directly at Rudy who had his eyes riveted on the road ahead.

"What do you mean by that?" Rudy asked, deliberately refusing to look over at K'Narf.

"Meaning I've been listening to you all the way from Phoenix about Vegas gamblers, their spotters, mafia hit-men and the I.R.S. and their forms for excessive winnings. I agree with you, I can't just walk into Vegas, make a big win and leave; but I can walk into Vegas, make a lot of small wins and leave." K'Narf said, daring Rudy to contradict him.

"You'd still get caught by the cashiers at the windows. They're trained to watch for repeaters, you'd never get away with it." Rudy said, almost desperately.

"No, but with your help I can...."

"Man, there ain't any way I'm gon'na...." Rudy stuttered.

"Listen to me!" K'Narf said, raising his voice slightly as he interrupted Rudy in mid-sentence.

"Okay, okay, I'm listening." Rudy said, as he pulled up and stopped at a red light.

"First we separate, and go into each casino as if we were total strangers."

"Now that sounds like a good plan." Rudy said, chuckling as the light turned green.

"I said *as if.*" K'Narf grunted back, not seeing any humor in what he had said. "When we get inside, I'll go to the cashier's window and get a thousand dollars in chips. Then I'll go to the first crap table, and by very carefully controlling the dice, allow some other player to get real hot. Now, like any good gambler I'll ride his or her luck until I've won about three thousand dollars, then I'll chicken out. I'll continue to control the dice until my hot gambler either makes a big win, or a big loss if he or she rides it too long.

Either way, no one will notice me as I walk away with my winnings. Then I'll meet you in the rest room and slip you a thousand in chips."

"Why can't I just buy myself a thousand in chips when we come in and play along with you, we could still pretend we didn't know each other?" Rudy asked, his interest and natural gambling spirit coming alive.

"Because our biggest problem will be cashing in our chips, not winning them. Don't worry, before we leave Vegas you'll have hit every table and dealer in town. You'll also have cashed in thousands of dollars in chips, to every cashier, on every shift, in every casino. I'll be doing the same, so that's the reason I want us to pretend not to know each other. We can come and go in separate taxis, take our breaks in separate lounges, enjoy separate shows. We'll only come together at the crap tables when you're gambling; you'll stay away when I'm gambling. I'll give you the signal when it's okay to cash in, and at which window. We'll only meet at our room, which will not be in or near any of the casinos." K'narf said, laying everything out like a military strategy.

"It might just work, and as long as we don't cash in enough to get the attention of the I.R.S, there won't be any record of how much we've won." Rudy said, obviously excited.

"That's right, and by not hitting any one twice, we should be able to confuse even your illustrious spotters." K'Narf said, knowing Rudy was hooked.

"How much money you after?" Rudy asked, getting serious again.

"I want at least five hundred thousand, but I'd settle for four and a half in a pinch." K'Narf said yawning. It had been a long trip. "How about that place?" He asked, pointing at a motel sign with a flashing vacancy sign. "It's not to close to the main part of town, but it's close enough to the main strip to make catching a taxi easy."

Rudy obediently pulled into the Fox and Hound motel and parked. It was several hours later that he finally managed to go to sleep, and it wasn't just because K'Narf was snoring.

Two weeks later Rudy counted and bundled another ten thousand dollars, bringing their grand total to four hundred and thirty thousand dollars. They were starting to run out of sources; plenty of dealers but not enough cashiers. K'Narf had mentioned Reno this morning, and after tonight's schedule they would probably go there. K'Narf had located two new cashiers over at

M.G.M., one at Circus-Circus, and one that came on duty at three A.M. at Caesar's palace. That was their schedule for tonight, unless K'narf could come up with another new face in his travels. One thing he knew for sure, gambling was simply work when there was no gamble involved.

K'Narf watched as Rudy casually sauntered into Caesar's. The new cashier had just set-up at his window, and there was an unused dealer at table three. He had already hit that same table, two hours earlier for a little over fifteen hundred dollars. He had also cashed a fifty-dollar chip in on a very nice dinner at the casino's dining room, before turning in his chips.

He and Rudy, using individual casino chips, had managed to buy a lot of clothes and some nice art pieces in casino-operated shops. In fact, Rudy was wearing that new sport coat he'd bought here at Caesar's just two nights ago. He'd warned him before about letting them cool off before wearing them. The last thing they needed was to call attention to themselves, but Rudy was obstinate about what he called trivialities.

Giving Rudy the signal for crap table number three, K'Narf started wandering in that direction himself. He noticed the girl immediately. She was the same one that had watched him play earlier. She unnerved him because she kept looking directly at him. What with mirrors mounted on walls, columns, doors, and even ceilings in some of the casinos, he had quickly adjusted to the fact that he was extremely ugly, especially with that birthmark on his nose. He kept trying to imagine what he would look like without it and as soon as he could arrange it he was going to have it surgically removed; however he had become used to the fact that girls, pretty ones like this one in particular, always avoided looking at him.

Ignoring her, he concentrated on the crap game, picking a little old lady who had just received the dice as his shill. Four passes later Rudy had won seventeen hundred dollars and had casually moved on to the next table. He would lose a hundred there for the benefit of any hidden spotter, and then in mild disgust would head for the window and cash in his remaining chips.

His little old lady backed off her run of luck with over five thousand dollars, so he dropped his control and wandered toward the cashiers window; leaving the happy squeals of the big winner behind him.

The new cashier was still at his window, so he signaled Rudy by simply rubbing his chin with two fingers indicating window two. Turning around he noticed that the girl who had been watching him earlier was now talking to two large rough looking men, and she seemed to be indicating him as both men turned and looked directly at him.

Catching Rudy's eye he nodded toward a side door and headed that way. He'd wait for Rudy outside, since he didn't like the way that girl was acting and wanted to warn him.

Outside, he found himself in a parking lot, which at this hour was packed full. He started wandering around looking at license plates. It seemed that all fifty states were represented, from Alaska to Maine.

People were constantly coming and going, so he didn't pay any particular attention to the sound of footsteps coming up behind him, until both his arms were grabbed in vice-like grips. He was picked up bodily and turned round by his captors, the two large men that he'd seen talking to the girl, and held almost dangling as she walked toward him. A small crippled woman with long black hair was following her.

Suddenly he recognized the cripple; it was the shill he'd used three days ago in the Safari. He'd felt sorry for her, old and crippled up the way she was, and allowed her to win over seven thousand dollars. He remembered that the dice had been hard to control there toward the last roll; he had thought he was getting tired. He also remembered thinking that those large black oriental eyes didn't look old, even though they were set in a time worn face. Now here she was hobbling toward him and his captors with that young brown-eyed brunette that had been watching him all evening.

Just as the brunette started to speak, the man holding his right arm sagged forward dropping him as his vice-like grip released his arm. Without thinking, K'narf shoved the man's body into the girl knocking her down hard with the man's body landing on top of her. Then with his right arm free, he came around with a hard right to the stomach of the man on his left, who immediately let go of his arm and doubled over. K'Narf brought up his left to the man's face, and crossed with a hard right which tossed the man backward onto the hood of a parked car.

Rudy was standing there with a blackjack in his hand, which explained why the first man had folded. Then, an unholy screaming something landed on his back. It was clawing at his face and in a pure reflex action he grabbed it and threw it, realizing as he hand released that it was the crippled old oriental. She sailed over two cars and landed with a sickening thud.

He started to move toward where he had tossed the old woman, when Rudy grabbed his arm and started pulling him toward the main strip. Moments later they were in a taxi heading for the Fox and Hound.

An anxious thirty minutes later, they were loaded up and headed back toward Phoenix. Rudy hadn't said more than three words the whole time, and it was starting to get on his nerves the way Rudy kept glancing over at him.

"Okay, it was my fault. I didn't realize that old cripple was a spotter for the casino. I'm sorry. Now will you please say something? I don't even care if you yell at me." K'Narf said, looking at Rudy.

"I ain't gon'na say anything until you tell me where that mark on your nose went." Rudy said, staring straight ahead at the road.

"What mark? What are you talking about?" K'narf asked, confused.

"That black mark that used to be on your nose! That's what mark!"

K'Narf, grabbing the rear-view mirror, twisted it to look at his face. In the dim light from the dashboard, and an occasional passing car, he could tell that he was scratched up pretty good but that wasn't what riveted his attention. His birthmark, the black blotchy little birthmark he'd been born with was gone. It hadn't been scratched off either; there was only a mildly pink spot where it had been. He stared dumb-founded at his new face as Rudy steered the van down the road.

Chapter Nine

"Breakfast is ready!" Rudy yelled from the kitchen door.

"Okay, I'll be right there, K'Narf hollered back from his new garage-cum laboratory.

Rudy, turning back to the kitchen, walked over to the stove and picked up the platter of eggs, lamb chops and hash browns. Holding the platter in one hand, he opened the refrigerator and grabbed a half-gallon of soymilk and headed for the kitchen table, nudging the refrigerator door shut with his heel as he stepped away.

"Man that smells good Rudy." K'narf said, as he grabbed a chair and set down; impatiently waiting until Rudy sat down so he could say grace and eat before the eggs got cold.

"By the way, you got any more batteries for the glasses?" Rudy asked, as soon as K'Narf finished thanking the Lord; he was trying to get in his question before K'Narf started eating.

"You mean you already burned out the set I put in Tuesday?" K'Narf asked, noticing immediately the stubborn look that came across Rudy's face. "It's okay, I don't mind, I'm just surprised that the batteries burned out so fast. I'll put in a new set right after we finish breakfast." He said, shoveling in a heaping forkful of hash browns and eggs.

"They didn't burn up that fast, I just use them a lot." Rudy said defensively.

"I'd think you'd run out of things to look at." K'Narf said, trying to swallow and talk at the same time.

"I look at my garden every day, and I can tell if any of my plants are getting sick or anything just by looking at their auras. I can also tell what kind of mood the mail man's in, and if anyone is upset or angry when I'm out on a shopping run." Rudy answered, pausing to take a bite out of a lamb chop.

"I know about the plants, but how do you tell about people?" K'Narf asked, looking up from his food.

"Easy, if their aura shimmers an even white, they're in a good mood. If they have small reddish spikes in their auras, then they're upset. If their aura is all ragged with dark red spikes, then they're angry. And if they're looking specifically at me, then it's me they're angry with." Rudy said in his matter-of-fact tone of voice.

"Can you read me that way?" K'Narf asked, a fork full of food poised halfway between his plate and mouth.

"Nope, like I told you before. I don't know how you invented these Kirlian glasses, but they don't work on you. Other people's auras are only a soft glow around their heads, which allows me to see and read their facial expressions. Yours is so bright your whole head seems to be all light. I can't even see your face through it." Rudy said, taking a bite of egg.

"I didn't invent them. Semyon and Valentina Kirlian, a couple of Soviet Scientists invented the camera. I just utilized current miniaturization technology and state of the art optics. I put the electronics into hollow ear pieces made to camouflage a hearing aid, and used the hearing aid control pack as designed adding only the focusing control. Still can't understand why they work for you and not for me." K'narf said, sopping up egg yolk with a piece of toast.

"I think I know why." Rudy said, getting K'Narf's full attention. "You say all you can see is a white haze?"

"Yes, a white haze and what appears to be vague shapes moving around, but that's about all." K'Narf said, scrapping at his plate. "What do you think's wrong?"

"You go put the new batteries in and I'll join you in a minute." Rudy said, standing up and leaving the table.

K'narf, reached over and took an uneaten lamb chop off Rudy's plate; chewing the meat off of it as he watched Rudy walk away. Getting up, he headed for the garage and his improvised laboratory, got out a new set of microdot batteries and started disassembling the power pack for the Kirlian glasses. Just as he finished installing the microdots, Rudy walked in holding two rolls of toilet paper.

"Here, help me unroll one of these." Rudy said, tossing K'Narf one of the rolls.

The two of them stood there, Rudy dead serious and K'Narf feeling foolish, with toilet tissue piling up around their feet. Finally, umpteen hundreds of yards later, they had the cardboard cores Rudy had been after.

"Put on the glasses and turn'em on." Rudy said, taking the cardboard core out of K'Narf's hand.

K'Narf obediently put on the glasses, which acted like ordinary sun glasses until he activated the power switch, then everything went a pale blue white that seemed to pulsate in the lens.

"Now, if I'm right, you're seeing your own aura; so hold these up to your eyes and see what happens." Rudy said, handing K'Narf the cardboard cores.

"Hey! That's it Rudy! I can see you through the tubes." K'Narf said excitedly. "It hurts my eyes though." He added, quickly lowering the tubes and cutting off the power.

"What do you mean, it hurts your eyes?" Rudy asked, not understanding why they would hurt K'Narf and not him.

"The light seeping around the bottom edges of the cores stings and makes my eyes water." K'Narf explained. "I did manage to see your aura though." He added, taking off the glasses and handing them to Rudy.

"Well, at least I was right about why you couldn't see with'em." Rudy said, obviously satisfied that he'd been right.

"You sure were, and you proved your interference hypothesis with a pair of cardboard cores out of a couple of rolls of toilet paper." K'Narf said, smiling as he congratulated Rudy by slapping him on the back.

"Like I said, you were seeing your own aura." Rudy said, happy that K'Narf was happy.

"Well, it's painfully obvious that I can't use them, so consider them yours. I'll order up plenty of spare batteries. Speaking of orders, how about calling Empire and see if they're done with my cores yet?" K'narf asked, turning back to his workbench without waiting for an answer.

Rudy pulled out of the driveway and headed for New River Road. He had said goodbye to K'Narf, but he didn't think it had registered. He had his head buried in some kind of experiment, and had only grunted when he told him he was going into town to do some shopping and pick up the cores from Empire. He also had to check on the people who'd rented his house when he'd moved to New River with K'Narf. He didn't have any family, at least none still living, and up to this point he couldn't say he'd had any regrets about accepting K'Narf's offer. Rather the opposite, he thought, thinking that it had been kind of exciting so far, what with the intrigue and excitement of the casinos and now his new glasses.

Rudy touched his coat pocket, assuring himself that he hadn't forgotten them. Thinking that of the half-a-dozen things K'Narf had created, the glasses were the only invention he had been able to use, much less comprehend, and now they belonged to him.

He remembered how he had almost deserted K'Narf on their way back from Las Vegas when he noticed that the black mark on K'Narf's nose, a birthmark according to K'Narf, was no longer there. He had already figured out that K'Narf wasn't an ordinary person, but the disappearance of the birthmark made him think of an alien camouflaged as a human.

K'Narf had finally convinced him that he was really human; admitting he didn't know what exactly was happening himself, but that he had faith the good Lord would let him know in time. He did believe though, that his desire to get rid of the birthmark and his creating a mental image of what he would look like without it, had combined to eliminate it. He had spent several days at the library when they got back to Phoenix scanning all the medical books he could find; said he was gon'na change his entire face.

Rudy remembered how he had scoffed at him, until he started doing it. That had been over a month ago now, and his face had already started to change. K'Narf said he was holding a very specific image of what he wanted to look like in his mind; but that it took a long time to dissolve and reform calcium and cartilage.

Finally, after fighting through Phoenix's early morning traffic, Rudy pulled into Empire's parking lot. Backing up to their loading dock he got out, opened the van's rear doors and headed for the Supervisor's office.

"Hello, you got them cores ready for Mister Etaguf?" Rudy asked of the large heavyset man sitting behind the desk.

"Yeah, they're ready, but I'll be durned if I know what they're ready for. What kinda nut is this Etaguf anyway?" The supervisor asked, looking at Rudy.

"First thing he ain't no nut, and to you he's Mister Etaguf." Rudy said, backing up as if expecting trouble for defending his friend.

"Okay, don't get all riled up. I was just trying to make conversation. We ain't never seen anything quite like them cores around here before, that's all." The supervisor said, as he got up from behind his desk and headed for the shop.

"What's so special about these cores?" Rudy asked, his own curiosity triggered by the supervisor's comments.

"Take a look for yourself." The supervisor said, stepping up to a wooden crate setting by the loading dock door.

"They look like two halves of a large bagel." Rudy said, looking at the two perfectly round objects in the crate. "A two foot wide bagel." He added, realizing just how big they were.

"Yeah, you might say that. They're both made from ten-point carbon steel. That's the steel that forms these two inches of interior and exterior wall. Our job was to machine the mating surfaces so the two halves would form a perfect union when they're put together; considering that we machined them down to a tolerance of one-thousandth of an inch on both mating surfaces, I'd say we did our job pretty well." The supervisor said, obviously proud of the work they had done as he squatted down and pointed at the outer and inner wall of one of the circular halves.

"The half-inch thick center core you're looking at here." He said, pointing at copper looking troughs in the center of each half. "Is made up of twenty-seven layers of copper interlaced with twenty-six layers of some other kind of metal your Mister Etaguf had electro-plated on over in California. That inside core will create a near perfect three-inch diameter opening in the center of the core when the two halves are put together. I'd sure like to know what he's going to use them for." He said, looking up at Rudy expectantly.

"Yeah, me too." Rudy said, noticing the disgusted look he got from the supervisor as he stood up. He was more concerned by how much these things were going to cost.

"Hey Pete! Nail the lid back on this crate and load it into that blue van." The supervisor yelled out to a man running a lathe. Then he turned and headed back to his office, leaving Rudy to follow.

The sun was less than an hour away from setting when Rudy pulled into the driveway. The van was loaded with groceries, and other sundry items including toilet paper. K'Narf was standing in the door as he pulled up and parked. "Did you get my cores?" He asked, as Rudy opened the door of the van.

"Yep, but you're gon'na have to help me unload the groceries before you can get at'em." Rudy said, walking to the back of the van and opening the doors.

"What's that?" K'Narf asked, looking at the large metal looking table with wheels sitting in the back of the van.

"That's my outdoor barbeque." Rudy said, instant stubbornness showing in his face. "Stopped by the house today and picked it up." He added, stepping back slightly and squaring off with K'Narf.

"What do you need that for?" K'Narf asked, noticing the set expression on Rudy's face.

"Gon'na need it when I barbeque our steaks."

"Steaks! I thought we agreed...."

"No, you agreed. I just went along because you said...."

"But I...."

"No, it's my turn to talk, your turn to listen!" Rudy said, his face set now in a granite-like expression.

K'Narf, again seeing his grandfather in Rudy, could only nod his head in mute acceptance. "I'm listening." He said, backing up slightly and noticing just how serious Rudy was taking whatever this was.

"When you said you wanted me to learn how to cook the vegetarian dishes your grandmother cooked, I agreed. I wrote down and figured out every one of them from your memory of how she cooked them. And I'll be the first to admit that they are excellent and delicious. I also agreed with you about not eating things the Bible called unclean and resting on the Sabbath; but I've been reading the Bible a little myself lately, and it says that an animal that has a split hoof and chews its cud is okay to eat. So if God considers the cow to be a clean animal why can't we eat it?"

"Hormones and antibiotics, that's why. My grandmother wouldn't allow beef in the house cause they pump them full of hormones and antibiotics in those feed lots where they fatten them up for slaughter. Lambs and fish don't get hormone and antibiotic shots." K'Narf said, effectively quoting his grandmother.

"Not if you know where to buy your meat." Rudy countered, fully ready for K'Narf's argument. "I bought our meat from a kosher butcher down in east Mesa. Guaranteed to be hormone and antibiotic free. No different than you're insisting that all our vegetables come from a pesticide free farm."

"Bought?" K'Narf asked, picking up on the past tense of Rudy's statement.

"Yeah, some choice cuts of black angus beef. For starters I got us two nice T-Bone steaks, a rack of beef ribs, some cubed breakfast steaks and about five pounds of hamburger. You've never tasted one of my cheeseburger's, so you've got a real treat in store." Rudy said, watching K'Narf carefully as he finished his argument.

K'Narf, looking at Rudy remembered the roast beef on rye sandwich that hunger had forced him to buy that first night on the road. Mentally reviewing what the Bible said and knowing Rudy to be right, he conceded. "I'll eat whatever you put in front of me as long as it agrees with the Bible except chicken."

"Why not chicken?" Rudy asked, taken back by K'Narf's agreeing to eat beef but not chicken. Chicken was considered clean meat too, he knew.

"When I was growing up, one of my jobs was to take care of my grandfather's laying hens. I had names for each of them written down and for twelve years they were the only friends I had. There is nothing you will ever say or do that will entice me to eat one of them; which is exactly what I would be doing if I ever agreed to eat a chicken." K'Narf said, looking at Rudy with eyes that left no doubt about the seriousness of his decision. "Now, let's get this van unloaded. I want my cores." He added, grinning at Rudy in a way that said everything was all right.

In ten minutes they had unloaded the barbeque, stacked the groceries in the kitchen and Rudy was helping K'narf carry the core halves into his lab.

Rudy watched as K'Narf picked up a sealed metal canister that had arrived by certified mail a week ago. Peeling off the seal he opened it up and started pouring the contents into the copper trough of one of the cores. "What's that stuff?" Rudy asked.

"That's a special metal I had made up. It's highly sensitive to magnetic forces; I had it crystallized and ground into a fine powder. Here, help me put the other half on top." K'Narf said, grabbing the curved edge of the matching half.

After positioning it just right, K'Narf produced three large band clamps from one of his cabinets and clamped the two cores firmly together. "Now I'll have to ask you to leave the lab Rudy. I'm going to be welding and I don't want you to hurt your eyes."

"You ever welded before?" Rudy asked, knowing that K'Narf had bought a brand new Hobart welder but hadn't used it yet.

"No, but I'll learn." K'Narf said uncertainly

"Why don't you tell me what you want welded, and then go in the kitchen and put away the food that needs refrigerated. Don't put anything else away or I'll never find it when I need it." Rudy said, taking the gloves and the fancy new Hobart helmet out of K'Narf's hands.

"I take it you know how to weld?"

"Yep." Rudy answered, putting on the gloves.

"Okay, I know what the book says about welding, but I really don't want to practice on these cores. I need the inner seam and the outer seam welded. You can remove the clamps after you have a good bead started on both seams. Be very careful not to damage these four mini-plugs built into the surface here, here, here and here." K'Narf said, showing Rudy the almost invisible electrical connections built into the cores.

Forty-seven minutes later, an anxious K'Narf came back into his lab to check on Rudy's welds. "They look just like the beads in the welders handbook." K'Narf said, genuinely delighted. "Where did you learn to weld like that?" He asked, blowing softly on the still hot welds.

"Worked at it part time after I retired from the Navy. Got pretty good at it too." Rudy said, obviously proud of his work.

"Well, you sure did a nice job. Now I need you to weld this small control box right here, between the top two mini-plugs. Two one inch welds should hold it solid." K'Narf said, positioning an empty metal box, two by three by one inch deep on top of the core. "I'll just turn my back and close my eyes."

"Perfect, Rudy!" K'Narf exclaimed, squirting water from a squeeze bottle on the still hot welds.

By the time Rudy had the welding equipment stowed and the cables wrapped up and put away, K'Narf had a previously assembled electronic package mounted in the control box, and leads ran to the four mini-plugs. Rudy watched as he wired in what appeared to be a standard light cord and screwed down the cover. "What are you doing now?" He asked, craning his neck to get a better look.

"Wiring in this miniature train transformer you picked up at the hobby shop last week. If Albert Einstein and me are right, then this should be one extremely powerful drive force. The

71

transformer makes it possible for me to control the amount of electrical current I apply. The control box will break down the energy and send it in predetermined pulses to the twenty-six layers of positive-to positive material in the core center. That force will act on the crystallized metal particles, forming them into a perfect circular rod and setting up a gyroscopic spin directly proportional to the energy applied. The bottom of the core will then emit a fan-shaped beam of positively charged electrons, the point of which will react against the negatively charged upper half of the core and its mushroom shaped field; then, as you know, like fields repel." K'Narf said as he finished the wiring.

"Thomas! I can't pet you right now. I'm busy." K'Narf said, ignoring the demands of the grey and white Manx, who had just entered the lab and vaulted onto his workbench. Reaching over Thomas he plugged in the transformer.

"CRUMP!!! ...MEEOOWWWRRR!!!"

"Rudy instinctively threw himself backward; reeling across the garage until he was stopped by the wall. Looking back he saw that K'Narf was sprawled out on the floor. Thomas was nowhere in sight and the core had disappeared. Glancing up he saw the hole in the roof. It was just over two feet in diameter with splinters of wood cascading down through it; mute evidence of where the core had gone.

"Rudy, you all right?" K'Narf asked sitting up.

"Yeah, what happened?" Rudy asked, staggering over to help K'Narf up.

"Not sure, but I think that transformer must have come from the factory wired backwards. It applied full power to the core. I've got to learn to check things like that before I use them." K'Narf scolded himself, as he started pulling Rudy toward the door.

"Where we going?" Rudy asked, grabbing the door jam and stopping K'Narf in mid-stride.

"That core weighs over eighty pounds, and it went *almost* straight up and it's going to come *almost* straight down." K'Narf said, stressing the word almost. "And I intend to be under the van when it arrives!" He added, letting go of Rudy and running for the van.

K'Narf grunted as Rudy slid into him in his haste to join him. "Anyway, the drive core works, which means we'll have to go back to Vegas for more money." K'Narf said, as he scooted over to give Rudy more room.

"Why?" Rudy asked, not really wanting to know.

"Why! So I can build a space vehicle of course!" K'narf exclaimed, as he and Rudy instinctively covered their heads with their arms on hearing the whistling sound of the returning drive core.

Chapter Ten

"K'Narf." Rudy called hesitantly.

"Yes Rudy, what is it?" K'Narf asked, looking up from his drafting board.

"You been sitting there drawing parts and ordering them for the past six days, and I was wondering when we were gon'na go back to Vegas like you said?" Rudy asked, stepping into the garage and looking over K'Narf's shoulder.

"Well, if you'll go to town and order me a new van while I finish up here, we should be able to leave for Vegas this evening." K'Narf answered, stretching his cramped back muscles.

"New van, what's the matter with the one we got?" Rudy asked, surprise registering in his voice.

"Nothing's wrong with the one we've got. I'm going to modify the new one to accept my drive cores. That's why I've been designing and ordering all these parts. I thought I told you what I was doing?" K'Narf asked, looking up at Rudy.

"You probably did, but I don't always understand what you tell me, so do you mind giving it another try?" Rudy asked, still studying the half completed part on K'Narf's drawing board.

"It's simple enough really, I'm going to reinforce the new van so it can take the high energy stresses imparted by the drive cores we're going to install, then modify it so it will be capable of maintaining an internal atmosphere which will support us while we're in space, and by...."

"Space! You mean you were serious about that spaceship stuff!" Rudy exclaimed, as he involuntarily backed away from K'Narf.

"Of course. It's really not that difficult, Rudy. I've worked out most of the details and ordered the parts I'll need already, with the exception of the van itself." K'Narf said, getting up and walking over to the old roll top desk Rudy had bought for him.

74

"You just can't drive a van into space. It just ain't proper. Vans belong on the ground and they ain't gon'na give you no license for no Space-Van!" Rudy sputtered.

"Hey, Space-Van. I like that." K'Narf said, ignoring Rudy's outcry. "That sounds better than space vehicle."

"But you just can't...."

"Don't worry Rudy. When we get through with the modifications, it will be space worthy." K'Narf said reassuringly. Now here's the model list and the option list that goes with it. I've highlighted both the model I want and all the options I need. Don't let them sell you on any changes or substitutions, especially the extended cargo bay or those heavy duty steel belted tires, okay." K'Narf said, handing Rudy the papers he'd plucked from a pigeonhole in the desk.

Rudy, taking the papers, started studying them as K'Narf walked back to his drafting board and sat down. "Ford, I thought you liked Chevies"

"Ford had more of the options I wanted." K'Narf said matter-of-factly.

"Well, I can see one option you can eliminate." Rudy said, looking over at K'Narf belligerently. "You'd be wasting your money on that second heavy duty swivel bucket seat. Ain't nobody I know fool enough to get into that thing with you!"

"Order it anyway, okay." K'Narf said, grinning. "By the time you get back and get us packed for Vegas, I should be through here." K'narf said, turning his attention back to his drawing board.

"Who should I order it from?" Rudy asked, accepting the inevitable.

"I don't care, you know the dealers in the valley better than I do." K'Narf said, ignoring Rudy's parting comments about his smoking something funny again. K'Narf still couldn't understand Rudy's meaning when he referred to his smoking; particularly since he'd never smoked anything in his life, much less in a corn cob pipe.

Late that evening K'Narf locked the front door and headed for the little blue van. Opening the door he climbed wearily into the passenger's seat. "Did you remember to ask Nancy to check on Thomas while we're gone?" He asked.

"Yeah, she said either her or one of her kids' would feed him." Rudy answered, putting the van into gear and heading out the drive.

"Say, I never did ask you how your garden's doing?"

"Two pepper plants and one of the tomato plants died. I managed to save everything else." Rudy stated flatly.

"I'm really sorry Rudy. Of all the places that drive core could have landed; anyway, I'm sorry about your plants. I know how you felt about them." K'Narf said. "By the way, did you have any trouble ordering the new van?"

"No, not really. They couldn't understand why you wanted that small V8 for such a big van, and they tried to talk me out of ordering the midnight black paint job. Said it was too hot in Arizona for that color. I agreed with'em, but ordered it anyway just like you told me too." Rudy said, giving K'Narf one of his *'I did what you told me, but I don't know why I did it'* looks.

"Engine's simple enough." K'Narf explained. "As soon as you drive it home, we're going to yank it out and throw it away. As to the black paint job, I don't want us to light up like a newborn star after we leave the earth's shadow and run into the full power of the sun. Black paint, over-sprayed with a light absorbing finish, should give us a certain amount of anonymity." K'Narf said, finishing his explanation and laughing at the expression on Rudy's face at the same time.

"You might as well get that *us* notion out of your head! This is one trip you're gon'na take solo!" Rudy said grimacing. "How much money you after this time?" He asked, quickly changing the subject as he pulled onto New River Road.

"I figure if we're real careful, and I don't feel sorry for any more old ladies, we should be able to remove three-hundred and fifty thousand from Vegas, and about two hundred thousand each from Reno and Tahoe for a grand total of seven hundred and fifty thousand without arousing any of the local inhabitants. That should take care of expenses for a couple of months anyway." K'Narf said, yawning as he dropped his seat into the sleeping position.

"You sure that's going to be enough. I mean we could go for a million'er two so's we wouldn't have to come back for maybe six months. There's not any reas...." Rudy suddenly realized he was talking to a sleeping K'Narf. All of his sarcasm being wasted on the nighttime breeze coming in the window.

Rudy knew that K'Narf had been pushing himself night and day, ever since that core had blown itself through the roof, and it looked like he had finally reached the limits of his endurance.

Looking at the sleeping form of K'Narf, illuminated by the lights from the dashboard, Rudy noticed that the changes K'Narf had made in his face seemed to stand out in stark relief. His pitch-black hair no longer looked coarse; in fact it looked soft and had a slight waviness to it. The heavy bone of the forehead had finally been dissolved and no longer jutted out over the eye sockets and the eyebrows seemed to have been thinned out and shaped. They even had a respectable open space over the nose where they had almost touched before.

He'd never forget the time he'd sat up with K'Narf when he'd eliminated too much bone morrow, or something like that. K'Narf wouldn't let him call a doctor, so there was nothing he could do but sit with him and watch helplessly as K'Narf held his head and cried when the pains hit. They seemed to come in waves, rivaling a woman's labor pains in their intensity. K'narf finally corrected his mistake, but it cost him a little over three days of excruciating pain. He may be a genius, but some of his knowledge he was paying a high price for, especially this ability to change his facial features Rudy thought.

Looking at K'Narf's face again Rudy realized that the nose and lips seemed to belong now too, they had somehow lost their oversized clownish appearance. The change had been so gradual he'd hardly realized it was happening, but when studied in retrospect the change was quite dramatic. The most striking difference was the chin, where before there had almost been nothing, there was now a very respectable chin showing the beginnings of a cleft. It wasn't a strong jutting macho chin, but it filled out his face and gave him an overall pleasant appearance. K'Narf may not have a movie star face, Rudy thought, but no one would ever call him ugly again. In fact, he may have a surprise waiting for him in Vegas when those showgirls got a good look at him.

Rudy grinned at the mental image he conjured up of K'Narf running from a bevy of half naked showgirls, then settled down to the job of driving as the nighttime highway unreeled steadily in front of him.

"What in the...." K'Narf exclaimed, sitting up and rubbing his eyes as the early morning sun poured through the vans windows. "Why didn't you wake me up, I was supposed to help drive remember!"

"Didn't need you. Besides, you needed your sleep and I enjoy driving at night. I like the peace and quiet." Rudy said, pulling into a motel driveway.

"Where're we at?"

"On a back street of Henderson. Been driving around looking for an out'ta the way motel. Didn't figure you'd want to use the Fox and Hound again. This one's called the George Washington and you can't get anymore inconspicuous." Rudy said, parking the van. "You wait here and I'll go get us a room."

"Where can we catch a taxi?

"Just two blocks over's the main drag. Big taxi stand there." Rudy said, shutting his door and heading for the motel office, leaving K'Narf to his own devices for orienting himself.

Coming back from the motel office, with a key sporting the number twenty-two, Rudy found K'Narf standing on the walkway carrying all four suitcases and both shaving kits. "This way boy." Rudy said, grinning at K'Narf's expression when he motioned him toward the stairway leading to the second level.

"Just put'em down anyplace boy." Rudy said, chuckling quietly at his ethnic humor; humor which K'Narf obviously didn't understand. "I don't know about you, but I aim to sack out for a while."

"Okay, I'm going to take a shower and head for the strip; need to setup a schedule for tonight. I'll call you around six, so don't go wandering off." K'Narf said, heading for the bathroom with his shaving kit.

"Whatever you say." Rudy sighed, as he flopped on one of the beds and kicked off his shoes.

"Hey Rudy!" K'Narf called out, as he stepped from the bathroom wearing only a George Washington towel. "Which suitcase has my light blue denims and turtleneck sweater?" Not getting an answer he looked over at the still fully dressed form of Rudy lying on the bed. He was sound asleep.

Rudy's vitality was such that it was easy to forget his advanced age; however, the dark mahogany face with its sagging facial muscles, wrinkles and grey hair, reminded K'Narf that he would have to take special care not to let Rudy overtire himself again. Tip-toeing softly over to the second bed, he stripped off the covers and gently placed them over Rudy's sleeping form. Finding his blue denims in his smaller suitcase, he quickly got dressed.

Stepping from the room and quietly closing the door K'Narf headed for the taxi stand. He hadn't lied to Rudy, he really did want to check out the Casinos and set-up a schedule for tonight, but his main purpose was to try and find that old oriental woman. Her eyes had haunted him ever since he'd pitched her, head first, over those parked cars. He needed very much to know that she was still alive.

That evening, after a good days sleep, Rudy stepped out of the cab in front of Caesars and looked at his watch. It was five forty-seven, which meant he was thirteen minutes early since K'Narf had said to meet him at six sharp when he'd phoned. He'd never quite understood how K'Narf always knew exactly what time it was since he never wore a watch; said he didn't need one because he'd created one in his head.

Walking into Caesars, Rudy casually put on his Kirlian glasses. He'd been anxiously waiting for his first chance to study the auras of gamblers in their various states of excitement. He was hoping he could tell which gamblers were riding a lucky streak, and which ones weren't. Being early gave him his chance he thought, as he flipped the switch that turned on the glasses.

K'Narf, getting out of the cab at five fifty-eight, paid the driver and headed for the entrance to Caesars, Rudy, looking wild-eyed, almost knocked him down as he came charging out.

"Hey, whoa, slow down!" K'Narf said, as he caught Rudy by the arm. "What's wrong? You look like you've seen a ghost."

"Worsen that." Rudy said, pulling away from K'Narf's grip. "There's more than one of you. I seen'em in there!" He exclaimed, pointing back at Caesars.

"Okay Rudy, calm down and tell me exactly what happened." K'Narf said, leading Rudy off to the side where they'd be less noticeable. "Now what do you mean there's more than one of me?"

"Exactly what I said, there's another Glow-head in there just like you!" Rudy exclaimed again, beginning to calm down a little. "I seen'em with my glasses."

"You mean you saw someone with an aura like mine?" K'Narf asked, a slight tremor of excitement in his voice.

"Yeah, that's what I'm trying to tell you." Rudy said, shuddering as he took a deep breath and relaxed.

"Just one?"

"Ain't that enough!"

"What did she look like?" K'Narf asked, now obviously excited.

"Ain't a she, it's a he." Rudy said, noticing the look of disappointment on K'Narf's face.

"Come on." K'Narf said. "I want you to point him out to me."

Reluctantly, Rudy followed K'Narf back into Caesars and pointed out the young man lounging against one of the mirrored pillars.

Looks Indian, K'Narf thought, remembering the books he'd read on the Indian cultures of America, maybe Nez Perce by the size and look of him. "Okay Rudy, here's what we'll do. I'm going to walk across in front of him and I want you to watch for any kind or form of facial reaction that might show interest on his part. If he doesn't show any, I'll wait a moment or two and come back; only on the trip back I want you to turn on the glasses. It's critical that we know if he can recognize me or not." K'Narf said, leaving Rudy no choice as he walked toward the kid.

Rudy, looking for any sign of recognition, watched as K'Narf casually strolled past the kid. Seeing none, he signaled K'Narf with a 'didn't see anything" shrug and watched as K'Narf started his return trip. Quickly turning on the glasses he watched K'Narf, his head engulfed in a large glowing blue-white ball of light, move through the crowd of normal humans and their slightly shimmering multi-colored auras toward that other glowing blue-white ball of light. Rudy, seeing K'Narf walk within a few feet of the kid with no visible change in either of their auras, gave a sigh of relief. He casually followed K'Narf outside.

"Well?" K'Narf asked.

"If he noticed you, he sure didn't show it." Rudy said, as they stepped out of sight around the corner of the building.

"I couldn't tell anything either. I don't think he knows about the difference in our auras. I wouldn't have known about it if it wasn't for you, so it makes sense that they wouldn't know." K'Narf said, a frown creasing his brow.

"They?" Rudy asked.

"Yeah, they. Don't ask me how I know, but I seem to feel their presence. I don't know who they are, or what they're after, but we'd better be on our guard and extra careful." K'Narf said, a look of intense concentration on his face.

In the next few weeks K'Narf's premonition proved deadly accurate. There were blue-white auras spotted in or around all of the main casinos, but only during the heavy gambling hours; obviously there weren't enough of them to blanket patrol all the gambling establishments. All of them, however, showed a marked interest in any big winner, but only at those games where telekinetic powers could be employed which included the crap tables; so dodging the Glow-heads, as Rudy called them, further complicated the game of outwitting the dealers and cashiers.

The pattern set by the Glow-heads seemed to rule out employment by any particular casino, since they kept up a constant rotation, never being in the same casino twice in succession. They also showed definite signs of telepathic abilities in their method of communicating. A talent K'Narf didn't possess and couldn't figure out, but which made them exceptionally dangerous. They could send out a mental S.O.S. and have help come from every direction. A sight Rudy witnessed one night in Reno.

Two men in a parking lot accosted a very pretty dark complexioned woman with long black hair, who was well stacked, as they would say in the movies. She was a Glow-head so Rudy had been watching her, and before her attackers could get her subdued and in their car there were three other Glow-heads converging on them. One came out of the casino, and the other two roared up in a powerful looking sports car; they made short work of the woman's would be assailants. Rudy's description of her rescue cancelled a plan that K'Narf had been forming in his mind, a plan that would have involved just such a kidnapping.

Twenty-three nerve-wracking days and nights later, they tallied up their take at a little over seven hundred and thirteen thousand dollars. Rudy suggested that they pick up the remainder in Vegas on the way home. K'Narf wearily agreed as they packed their bags and made ready to leave Tahoe.

That evening, setting at a red light in the middle of Vegas, Rudy put on his glasses and turned them on to watch the people in the crosswalk. He gave a start and reached over and shook K'Narf's arm to get his attention. "Two Glow-heads coming across from the left side, big one and a little one." He said.

K'Narf, looking over at where Rudy was pointing, found himself staring at the hobbling form of a little old oriental woman. "It's them!" He cried, excitement showing in his voice.

"Them who?" Rudy asked.

"That's the two who jumped me in the parking lot!" K'Narf said, his eyes glued to the two women as they walked by in front of the van. "Don't you remember? That's the little old lady I felt sorry for at the crap tables. She's the one I tossed over my head in the parking lot fight. Thank God she's all right."

"Hey, you're right. They are the ones." Rudy said, as he got a good look at them. "They're being Glow-heads explains how they caught you." He added matter-of-factly, just as the light changed and he let out the clutch.

"It explains a lot of things." K'Narf said, taking a last glance at the receding form of the brunette. She was just as beautiful as he'd remembered, he thought. "There just might be a way." K'Narf said, his eyes glazing over as his mind concentrated on an elusive idea.

"Way to what?"

"A way to have a *very* private conversation with a *very* beautiful lady!" K'Narf said, emphasizing the word '*very*' as he exploded into sudden laughter. "Let's head for home Rudy. I don't want to take any chances of spoiling things now."

"Sounds good to me." Rudy said, shaking his head and breathing an unconscious sigh of relief.

Chapter Eleven

Pulling off the last of the two-inch wide silver duck tape that he'd used to seal the garage door, K'Narf twisted the handle and lifted it open for the first time since he'd bought the house. The ridge of dried mud and dust, left on the cement where the door had touched, was mute evidence that the tape had indeed protected his improvised lab.

The dealer had called this morning and said that their van had finally come in, and that they could pick it up anytime. Their neighbor Nancy had been nice enough to give Rudy a lift into town; that had been over four hours ago, so K'Narf expected him back at any moment.

Most of the parts for converting it, including the seventeen cores required for its drive system, three hundred linear feet of angle iron needed for thrust reinforcement, and the dual bullet proof replacements for the windows had arrived weeks ago. The special twelve-inch van roof extension designed to house the twenty-four mirror-bowl solar-cells, and the six special order steel encased solar batteries with their silver alloy charging plates for fast recharging, were the only major items yet to be delivered.

Standing there in the open doorway to his garage laboratory with a slight desert breeze stirring the dust at his feet, K'Narf watched as a large black heavy duty Ford van topped the ridge and came barreling down the road, dust boiling out from under her four steel-belted wide track tires.

"Dear Sweet Jesus!" K'Narf said reverently, letting out his breath in a whistle of admiration. Reality is much more impressive than simple visualization, he thought.

As the monstrous black van slowed and turned into the driveway, K'Narf could see Rudy smiling and waving at him through the windshield. Using hand signals he motioned for Rudy to park her in the garage.

"Rudy!" K'Narf said, as he opened the drivers door. "She's beautiful."

"Yeah, I kinda like her myself." Rudy said, climbing down out of the driver's seat with a big smile on his face.

"Let's start by taking off all the chrome parts." K'Narf said, as he walked over and closed the garage door.

"Why?" Rudy asked, the smile fading from his face.

"So you can take them into town, have the chrome stripped and get them painted black." K'Narf said, as he started dismantling a piece of chrome that identified the van as a Ford E350.

"Do we have to?" Rudy asked, reaching for a wrench from his old toolbox K'Narf had hauled in and opened up.

Grunting his answer K'Narf succeeded in getting the identifier off and then meticulously labeled the small nuts so they wouldn't get lost.

Rudy, accepting K'Narf's answer, slid under the rear of the van and started dismantling the bumper. Two hours later he was pulling out of the driveway in the little Chevy van with a full load of chrome parts. K'Narf had given him an address in south Phoenix of a plating shop that he said would strip them while he waited, then on to another shop that in turn would paint them black and bake them dry, also while he waited. Rudy had asked K'Narf how he knew about all them places; K'Narf had given him one of his looks, and said they were listed in the yellow pages. Rudy vowed again, for the umpteenth time, to stop asking fool questions.

It was dark when Rudy finally pulled up in front of the house, and backed the van to within a yard of the garage's side door. Getting out he walked around the van and opened the door. Stepping in he almost tripped over a drive shaft and gearbox. "What in the... K'Narf! Blast you boy! Did you have to put your junk right in front of the door?" he said, yelling at K'Narf's feet sticking out from under the van.

"Did you have any trouble?" K'Narf asked, ignoring Rudy's grumbling at him as he slid out from under the shiny black van.

"Nope, the parts are in the Chevy. They ain't purty no more though." He said petulantly.

"They may not be pretty, but they won't reflect sunlight anymore either. Hey, you look a little bit on the worn out side." K'Narf said, noticing Rudy's drawn face. "Why don't you call it a day and go to bed early tonight?" He asked, putting his arm around Rudy's shoulders and walking him toward the kitchen door.

"Have you had anything to eat?" Rudy asked, ignoring K'Narf's suggestion that he go to bed.

"Not that I can remember." K'Narf said, giving Rudy's shoulders a gentle squeeze before letting him go.

"Well, come on in and set while I fix you something." Rudy grumbled. "You'd starve to death if I didn't make you eat."

"Can I help?"

"You can help by sitting down and staying out of my way." Rudy said, motioning K'Narf toward a kitchen chair.

"Okay, but then you're going to go to bed and get some rest." K'Narf said frowning.

"How about you, when are you going to get some rest?" Rudy asked, as he opened the refrigerator and started removing various bowls, bottles and vegetables.

"As soon as I get the engine out, and why did you fill the gas tank. You knew I had to remove it?"

"Didn't, the dealer did it; said it was their way of apologizing for the van being late." Rudy said, starting to throw stuff into a big sizzling hot skillet.

"Well, I wish he hadn't been so apologetic." K'Narf said yawning. "Took me half an hour with a tin can to drain it."

"You really gon'na try and fly her into space?" Rudy asked, still not quite believing.

"Yep, should be ready for a trial run within the week if the batteries get here." K'Narf said, sniffing at the aroma coming from Rudy's stove. "That sure smells good, what is it?"

"Skillet fried vegetables and beef. Little something I picked up in the orient." Rudy said, stirring it one more time then reaching for a plate.

Early the next morning Rudy awoke to the sound of loud hammering. Getting dressed he headed for the garage. Opening the door he heard K'Narf yell and then let out a pitiful sounding groan, then he started hammering again. Turning around he headed for his kitchen and the coffee pot.

"K'Narf, leave that stuff alone and get in here and eat some breakfast!" Rudy yelled through the open kitchen door.

"What are you doing up this early?" K'Narf asked, coming into the kitchen.

"What do you mean, what am I doing up! How can a man sleep with all that hammering and yelling going on?"

"Sorry about the yelling Rudy, hit my thumb with a hammer."

"Hammer huh, let's see it." Rudy said, walking over to K'Narf. "You're gon'na lose your thumbnail."

"No I won't." K'Narf said, looking at his purple thumb.

"Don't tell me you won't, I've seen to many smashed thumbs and I say you'll lose it." Rudy said, turning back to get the coffee pot. "How you coming on your space van?"

"Real good, I finished stripping out the engine and the radiator last night. Then this morning I positioned and welded in place three of the drive cores to the main I-beam underneath her. I'll need your help setting and welding the rest of them though." K'narf said, gratefully accepting the cup of coffee Rudy handed him.

"Where do they get put?" Rudy asked, as he started cracking eggs into the skillet.

"Two in front behind the grille, a cluster of three on the inside of each side panel. One dead center on top of her, and a five star cluster welded to the inside of her rear doors. The doors will have to be welded shut first though, that's why I didn't want any rear windows." K'Narf said, sipping his coffee.

"Won't they rip themselves loose?" Rudy asked, remembering the patched roof in the garage.

"No, that's why I bought all that angle iron. After we get them all welded in place I'll reinforce each one in its direction of thrust."

"If you say so." Rudy said, shaking his head. "You just tell me what you want me to do and I'll do it."

Two days later, using the van's side cargo door, Rudy helped K'Narf load and weld in place the six large special order solar batteries. K'Narf had welded four steel feet to the axles which were now touching the floor. The batteries' combined weight of eighteen hundred pounds, added to the weight already in her, would have blown her tires if it weren't for those steel landing feet as K'Narf called them. Her insides reminded Rudy of a spider's nesting hole, laced as it was with cross-braced angle iron. This impression was reinforced considerably when K'Narf sprayed the entire inner surface with thick insulating foam that covered everything except the battery terminals, seats, dashboard and the windows.

Then they loaded in and strapped down the four six foot long oxygen cylinders. K'Narf had placed three of the big batteries on each side of the cargo space, creating what looked like two steel segmented boxes, two feet high, twelve inches wide and almost six feet long. Then welded a cradle for two oxygen cylinders horizontally above each one. The cylinders of oxygen, not being covered by white insulation foam broke the spider's nest image in Rudy's mind.

"What's next?" Rudy asked, admiring how the cylinders seemed to balance the entire load.

"I have to wire the window heaters, headlights, tail lights and dashboard for power. Then...."

"Why did you have to put in two pieces of glass in each window?" Rudy asked, interrupting K'Narf's mental list of things yet to do.

"They have a semi-liquid center sandwiched in between them that will darken instantly above a certain amount of light intensity."

"You mean like them sunglasses that darken in the sun and get lighter in the shade."

"Exactly!" K'Narf exclaimed. "Only difference is the time element. My substance will turn totally opaque instantly if exposed to direct sunlight." He added, obviously pleased at Rudy's comprehension of the solar burn protection system he'd built in the van's windows.

"How about calling the rail depot and see if that roof extension has arrived yet. The factory said they shipped it last week, and I'll be ready to mount it by tomorrow if I get the solar-mirrors installed today." K'Narf said, vowing that next time he'd hire a private delivery truck.

"Okay." Rudy said, as he turned and headed for the kitchen, flipping open the new cell phone K'Narf had bought for him as he walked. He could check on the stew he had simmering in the crock-pot while he made the call about the roof extension.

"Thanks Rudy." K'Narf said, turning his attention back to the big, shiny black van.

"It's in." Rudy said, walking back into the garage. "It's too big for me to pick up in the little van, so I called a private delivery outfit. They promised to have it here by five this evening." He added, speaking to what he could see of K'Narf sticking out from under the dashboard.

Early the next morning Rudy helped K'Narf lift the twelve-inch roof extension and carefully place it over the four rows of inverted half-moon mirrors. Two rows of six each on both sides of the drive core welded in the center of the roof. It wasn't too heavy

87

because K'Narf had cut out the center for a window, which he hadn't installed yet.

"Why can't you have just one big mirror instead of all those little ones?" Rudy asked, catching his breath.

"Because each one of those six inch mirror bowls collects direct sunlight, and concentrates it onto the one-inch mirror bowl positioned directly above it; which in turn fires a concentrated beam of compressed sunlight at the high purity silicon solar cell positioned at the center of the six-inch bowl. This solar cell then puts out one-point-five amps of power at point-five volts.

Wired in series they put out twelve volts at thirty-six amps, which will completely recharge all six of those batteries in two-point-three hours. That's why the charging plates in the batteries had to be a highly dense silver alloy; that much concentrated amperage would have melted normal lead plates."

"Yeah, right." Rudy said, again wondering why he insisted on asking fool questions.

"Of course I'll have to hold her steady to the sun while she's charging." K'Narf said as an after-thought.

"Well, unless you need me for something else, I'm gon'na go into town and do some shopping. The cupboards getting a little bare around here." Rudy said, heading for the kitchen.

"Okay, see you later. I have to weld this top on and finish wiring up the solar cells." K'Narf said, stretching. "You'll be back by lunch won't you?"

"Should be, why? Don't tell me you're hungry after eating the breakfast you ate!"

"No, but I'll need you to help me install the glass in the roof section." K'Narf said, heading for his welding equipment.

It was closer to two o'clock when Rudy finally pulled into the driveway and backed up to the front door with a load of groceries. K'Narf hearing him drive in, came out and helped carry in the sacks and then headed back to the garage. Rudy sorted and stowed them and then stepped into the garage himself.

He stopped in the doorway and stared. The big van had taken on an ominous look. K'Narf had reassembled all the parts they'd taken off that first night. He'd sanded and repainted all the scorched spots where the welding had burned through, then sprayed her with a flat dull black finish. She sat there now, big and black, seeming to fill the entire lab with her presence.

"She looks almost ready." Rudy said, speaking more to the van than to K'Narf.

"Yeah, I think we can take her up for a trial run tonight if her pressure system checks out." K'Narf said, stepping out from behind the van. "But right now I need you to help me with her top glass." He added, pulling a five by seven foot sheet of bulletproof glass away from the wall.

Rudy, frowning at K'Narf's free use of the word"we", grabbed the other edge of the glass and helped lift it into place. Then went back to his kitchen. Stew should be just about ready, he thought.

"Rudy!" K'Narf yelled.

"What'cha need?" Rudy yelled back, stepping into the garage with a damp dishtowel in his hand.

"I want you to tell me when her landing feet are exactly three inches above the cement. Here, use this." K'Narf said, tossing Rudy a six-inch scale.

"Okay." Rudy said, catching the scale as K'Narf climbed up into the driver's seat. Sliding under her he yelled, "Ready."

Popping sounds of metal suddenly put under stress, filled Rudy's ears; then miraculously she began to lift. "Two-point-seven inches!" Rudy called out when she stopped. Then watched spellbound as the bottom of the steel landing foot started moving upward again. "Two-point-nine inches!" He called out again. This time, with an almost imperceptible movement, the steel pad stopped exactly three inches off the cement floor of the garage.

"Three inches exactly!" Rudy exclaimed, crawling out from under the van and looking up at K'Narf's beaming face. "How you gon'na get her out of here." He asked, trying to imagine her flying out.

"Oh, she drives just like a ground vehicle when set for surface travel." K'Narf said, opening the door and getting out.

"You mean you can drive her around like a regular van?"

"Yeah, I've got her on a preset power grid and I've hooked up the brake pedal to the front drive cores, and the gas pedal to the rear drive cores. The power setting you just helped me with activates the three bottom cores just enough to keep her weighing about three thousand pounds. She should handle pretty good at that weight." K'Narf said, noticing Rudy's surprised look. "Now what's for lunch?"

"Stew." Rudy said.

That evening, as K'Narf opened the main garage door, he turned and looked at Rudy. "You absolutely sure you won't go with me?" He asked, as he climbed into the van.

"Way I figure it, if God wanted me to fly he'd have given me wings."

"Not really, I spoke with Him for over an hour last night and I didn't get even a hint that he disapproved." K'Narf said, taking Rudy's statement about God at face value.

"You talked to God last night?" Rudy asked, getting nervous all over again. "Did He talk back?" He added, unconsciously stepping back a step.

"No, not in words, he never does, at least not to me. I just know he's there listening when I'm praying. I can feel Him, always could." K'Narf said, matter-of-factly.

"What do you mean, feel Him?" Rudy asked, breathing an unconscious sigh of relief.

"Best way I can describe it is that I feel like I'm wearing a hat, even though I don't have one on." K'Narf said, frowning as he tried to describe the feeling he got when talking to the Lord. "Can't remember a time when I couldn't feel His presence though."

"How old were you when you got saved? That's what you call it isn't it, getting saved." Rudy asked, curiosity getting the best of him.

"Don't know that I ever did exactly. Didn't even know who He was until my grandmother started reading the Bible to me just after I turned six. Just knew He was always there."

"Your grandmother read the Bible to you?"

"Yep, two pages every day." K'Narf said, smiling at the memory. "That way we got through the whole Bible in a year. We were starting on our thirteenth time through when the Lord took her home." He added, his smile fading at the memory.

"That's it then, He's just a feeling that you have?" Rudy asked, feeling relieved but not knowing why.

"Oh no, He's more than a feeling; like there was the time He healed Mattie's broken leg." K'Narf said, remembering what the Lord had done for Mattie.

"Mattie?" Rudy asked.

"Yeah, Mattie, one of my grandfather's laying hens. He had six of them and I had the responsibility of taking care of them. One morning when I went out to feed them I found Mattie on the ground with a broken leg. She had apparently hooked it on the roost and it broke when she tried to get off. I was only nine at the time and felt that it was my fault she got hurt, so I took her in my arms and holding her broken leg asked the Lord to heal her, and He did."

"He healed her leg?" Rudy asked, not wanting to believe, but knowing instinctively that K'Narf was telling the truth.

"Yeah, felt the leg come together while I was holding it." K'Narf said, looking at Rudy with a boyish smile on his face. "You sure you won't come with me?" He asked, this time pleading with his eyes as well as his words.

"Just as sure as I can get, you want company then take Thomas here." Rudy said, bending over and picking up the Manx cat that had been rubbing up against his leg for the last several minutes. Feeling relieved that the conversation about God was over. He'd always had an unreasoning fear of confessing his sins to anyone, much less God.

"Okay, I will." K'Narf said, taking Thomas and putting him in the passenger's seat next to him.

"How long you gon'na be gone?"

"I'll be back before dawn. I'm just going to make a test run around the moon and return." K'Narf said, as he shut the door and backed the big black van out into the night.

Chapter Twelve

Rudy, opening his eyes at the sound of the front door chimes, panicked when he became conscious of the sunlight pouring in his bedroom window. K'Narf should have been home by now. Ripping off his covers he leaped out of bed, grabbing his pants off the bedpost as he charged from the room. Ignoring the front door chimes, which were ringing again, he ran for the garage. Opening the door he stopped cold. The big black van was back, and he could tell by the squashed look of her tires that she was completely shut down and resting on her landing feet.

Just at that second the chimes rang again, activating Rudy's sense of propriety. Seconds later, zipping his pants and buckling his belt, he opened the front door to greet his highly persistent caller.

"Good morning, Rudy."

"Morning Missus Nancy, what can I do for you?" Rudy asked, somewhat confused by the determined look on Nancy's face.

"I would like to see Mister Etaguf, would you please tell him I'm here?" She asked, avoiding Rudy's eyes.

"Uh, he's asleep right now Missus Nancy. He worked all night and I'd be afraid to wake him up. He gets upset and angry if I bother him when he's working or sleeping." Rudy said, thinking fast.

"Well, your Mister Etaguf drove that new black van of his by my place real early this morning, and he was coming from the north. There isn't anything north of my place except mountains. I must admit that I am a wee bit curious as to why he would spend the night in the mountains, and since I've never actually met him, well, I thought it high time I came over and introduced myself. After all, I have been watching your place and feeding that funny cat for your Mister Etaguf each time you two went away." Nancy said, all in one breath, suddenly staring Rudy directly in the eye.

"Well, Missus Nancy, like I told you, Mister Etaguf was up all night and I just wouldn't dare wake him. I know why he spent the night in the mountains though. You see, he writes poetry and he has some silly notion that he can write better when he's communing with nature." Rudy said, trying to avoid direct eye contact with Nancy's piercing stare.

"Oh, well, in that case, uh, please tell your Mister Etaguf that I stopped by and that I would very much like to meet him. If possible I'd even like to read some of his poetry." She said, turning around and walking toward her car. "An you just call on me anytime, you hear."

"Thank you Missus Nancy, I surely will." Rudy said, shutting the door.

"Poetry?"

"What the...!" Rudy cried, giving an involuntary jump. "Blast you boy! Don't sneak up on me like that!"

"But why poetry? I could have been an amateur astronomer couldn't I? And since when do I ever get angry?" K'Narf asked, stepping out of his hiding spot in the hallway.

"Look, you're the one won't meet no one cause of your changing your face around, so don't give me no yap about the excuses I come up with for you!" Rudy half-hollered as he headed for the kitchen and his beloved coffee pot.

"What's the matter with that woman?" K'Narf asked, tagging along after Rudy. "Why's she so interested in me anyway?"

"Nancy? She's just being a woman. All curiosity and she don't need a reason for it, even if you hadn't given her any." Rudy said, turning the fire up under the coffee pot.

"You mean to tell me that...." K'Narf said, stopping in mid-thought.

"Ha!" Rudy chortled, "You're getting the picture."

"But, aw come on, I bought this place so I could have total privacy, and because of that road up into the mountains!" K'Narf cried out, looking thoroughly miserable.

"You still got the road." Rudy said, getting out the coffee cups. "Now tell me about your trip. Did she get off the ground?"

"She sure did, lifted just like a leaf floating on the wind." K'Narf said, forgetting Nancy and getting a faraway look in his eyes. "It was beautiful."

"What do you mean, floated?" Rudy asked, turning from his stove to look at K'Narf. "Didn't you blast off?"

"What for, I wasn't in a hurry. I neutralized her weight and then gave her a thrust of one-tenth of a gravity. That sent her up at about the speed of a rising hot air balloon. Even at that, we were out of the earth's gravitational pull within ten minutes. It was fantastic." K'Narf said, talking with his hands as well as his mouth, excitement sparkling from his eyes. "We'd get caught in the wind and be blown one way, then as we continued to rise we'd run into a stream of air going the other way and would reverse direction. And you should have seen Thomas."

"What about Thomas?" Rudy asked, taking the coffee pot off the burner and turning around.

"He went wild when we became weightless." K'Narf said, still talking with his hands. "He squalled and hollered like nothing I've ever heard before."

"Scared the poor little guy, huh." Rudy said, stepping over and pouring both of them a cup of steaming black coffee. Quickly putting the coffee pot back on the stove and turning down the burner, he turned around and sat down facing K'Narf. Obviously eager to hear what happened.

"No no, he wasn't scared. It was the closest thing I've ever seen to pure ecstasy. His purring, between his squalls of pure delight, was so loud it vibrated the whole van. I can't even begin to describe his fancy acrobatics. He'd launch himself through the air and do two or three somersaults, rolling twists, spread eagle spins and with an uncanny sense of timing land on his feet, only to launch himself again." K'Narf said, trying to roll his hand in an imitation of Thomas' movements in free-fall.

"Well I'll be." Rudy said, obviously surprised. "Kinda figured old Thomas would throw a fit, but not a lik'en one."

"Liking! I almost got loved to death. He kept trying to lick my face each time he flew by my head." K'Narf said, acting out his words. "I did confirm something I've long suspected though. Thomas can read my mind."

"He can what!" Rudy exclaimed, stopping his coffee cup just short of his mouth.

"Read my mind. Oh, not in the sense of what I'm saying, but when I was trying to figure out how to catch him and hold him down while I put the drive cores through an acceleration test. I pictured him in the passengers seat, spread eagled with his claws dug in for support, and he did it."

"You trying to tell me that Thomas saw the picture in your mind and then went back to his seat and copied it?" Rudy asked, incredibility dripping from the tones of his voice.

"That's exactly what he did!" K'Narf said, excitement bubbling in his voice. "And I want you to order me a female Manx. I want to start raising them."

"Where can I get one?" Rudy asked, not quite believing what he was hearing.

"You'll have to order her through a pet shop. And I want a full blooded Manx female from the Isle of Man, not some half-breed look-a-like." K'Narf said, giving Rudy one of his "thou-shalt" looks. "And don't you argue about the price either. Just pay it."

"Why only from the Isle of Man?"

"Because that's the place they originated from. They are the only tame breed that has a semicircular ear canal which gives them a tremendous advantage in falling and turning like Thomas did today in free-fall, and I want another original just like Thomas."

"If they are so rare and expensive, how did you get Thomas?" Rudy asked, sipping at his coffee.

"I have my mother's exuberant desire to spend my father's money, and her guilty conscious to thank for my getting Thomas." K'Narf said, his brow wrinkling at the memory.

"That's the first time I ever heard you mention your folks."

"Yeah." K'Narf grunted, pulling his thoughts out of the past.

"How about her ladyship, how'd she do?" Rudy asked, nodding his head toward the big black van setting in the garage.

"Fantastic! I had calculated her drive cores for one G of thrust per core and she gave one-point-zero-one-five. I had trouble aligning her solar cells to the sun, but with your help I can fix that. I can drill a very small hole in the roof, seal it with glass, and with you shining a light straight down on top of her I'll paint a spot on the floor where the light hits. Then, next time I'm in space and I need to recharge, all I'll have to do is line up the spot of sunlight with the paint spot on the floor. Simple, don't you think?" K'Narf asked beaming.

"Yeah, but what about the moon, did you really fly around her?" Rudy asked, ignoring K'Narf's ingenuity.

"Sure, said I was going to didn't I."

"Then how come it took the astronauts three days just to get there?" Rudy asked belligerently.

"Because they had to coast all the way, I didn't."

"What do you mean?"

"They were under rocket thrust only long enough to break out of the earths gravity, then they had to coast the rest of the way.

Their speed increased only when the moon's gravity started pulling at them. I stayed under a constant one G of thrust three quarters of the way there, then activated the front drive cores to slow me down at one G of counter thrust. I thought the moon's gravity would grab me and slingshot me around her and back toward the earth, but I under estimated the B' Lady's speed and shot on out into space. Had to turn her around and kick her up to three G's thrust just to catch back up."

"B' Lady?" Rudy asked.

"Yeah, she's black, and she's a Lady. Seems to fit, don't you think?"

"B' Lady does have a nice ring to it, but I'd drop the B and just call her Lady if I was you." Rudy said, getting up. "What do you want for breakfast?"

"Oh, half-a-dozen eggs, hash browns and toast, couple of lamb chops if we have any. You know, my usual. You should have seen the earth Rudy, is she ever beautiful." K'Narf said, getting a dreamy look in his eyes.

"That's okay, I'll let you do my seeing for me." Rudy said, not quite as emphatic as at previous times. "What are you going to do now?"

"I need to buy and install some new equipment for the B., uh, Lady." K'Narf stammered, as he consciously heeded Rudy's advice and shortened the big black van's nickname to just Lady. "And I need to get myself a used spacesuit and build in an airtight bubble for Thomas. Then I'm going to load her up and take an extended trip around our solar system."

"Let's back up just a step or two." Rudy said, staring at K'Narf. "Where in blue blazes are you going to get a used spacesuit?"

"From the National Aeronautics and Space Administration. I've been negotiating with them for months on getting a used suit for a mobile space display that I'm putting together." K'Narf said grinning.

"I didn't know you were putting together any...."

"That's right, I'm not, but they don't know that." K'Narf said, laughing at the expression on Rudy's face. "And for a hundred and thirty two thousand dollars they're not asking a lot of questions."

"One hundred and thirty two thousand!" Rudy exclaimed, turning from his stove to look at K'Narf.

"Yeah, I know that's awful cheap for a spacesuit, but it's an old model and they can't use it anymore so they're letting me have it...."

"What do you need it for anyway?" Rudy asked, interrupting K'Narf's explanation of how he got the spacesuit so cheap as he turned back to the business of fixing breakfast.

"Probably don't, but just in case I have to open up the Lady and go outside I want a suit. That's also why I have to build an airtight bubble for Thomas. I'd hate to lose him just because of my lack of foresight."

"What else you gon'na have to get?" Rudy asked, shaking his head at the thought of Thomas being stuffed into a bubble.

"An all channel frequency scanner, CD player and lots of music. I love the old stuff like that one where Snoopy shoots down the Red Barron, and two of the largest retractable antennas *you* can get." K'Narf said, stressing the word "you".

"Why retractable?" Rudy asked, ignoring K'Narf's insinuation that he was going to be doing the buying.

"So I can pull into the garage without getting out and tying them down. I'll also need two of the largest side mirrors you can find, and one of those multi-channel radar detectors with visual and audio warning that gets louder if the radar source gets closer." K'Narf said, looking at Rudy as if everything he wanted was logical, made perfect sense and therefore didn't need any explanation.

"What's all that stuff for, and where do *you* plan to get it?" Rudy asked, putting the buy part back on K'Narf.

"The scanner's so I can pick-up fighter plane chatter if there happens to be any of them in my immediate air space. I got to thinking about how stupid I'd feel getting myself shot down by some jet-jockey."

"You'd feel more than a mite stupid." Rudy said, lifting eggs out of his skillet and laughing.

"As for the CD Player and mirrors." K'Narf said, ignoring Rudy's laughter. "It's way too quiet out there without music, and I can't see behind me worth a hoot in those little mirrors Lady has right now."

"And the radar detector?" Rudy asked, turning off his stove.

"That'll just tell me if anyone has me locked on their radar."

"And where *you* gon'na get all this new stuff?" Rudy asked, stressing the word "you" again as he placed two full platters of food on the table. The one he placed in front of K'Narf being much larger than his own.

"I'm not, *you* are." K'Narf said, looking up at Rudy. "Please Rudy, I have to drive over to Los Angeles to get my spacesuit; the company selling it said I'd have to pick it up in person. Don't worry, everything I need is available right off the shelf down in Phoenix." K'Narf said, giving Rudy a quick grin as he dug into his food.

"You're gon'na drive?" Rudy asked, watching K'Narf clean a lamb chop off with one bite.

"At least in and out of Los Angeles proper." K'Narf said, grinning and speaking with his mouth full.

"How long do you plan to be gone on this space trip of yours?" Rudy asked, changing the subject as he realized K'Narf meant to fly most of the way to and from Los Angeles.

"Oh, at least two weeks, maybe more." K'Narf said, talking around a mouthful of eggs. "Why?"

"Got to pack enough food to last you, don't I?" Rudy said, resigning himself to a trip to town.

"Yeah, and you're going to have to put some of it in vacuum sealed bags in case I have to eat in free-fall. Need to get a portable potty-seat for me and a coverable litter box for Thomas too." K'Narf said, frowning at that last item.

Thirteen days later at three A.M. on a moonless Sunday morning, K'Narf, having rested the whole of the Sabbath, backed the Lady out of the garage. Quietly raising both of the new antennas, and with lights out, drove slowly down the road past Nancy's house. Ten minutes later, to the strains of "Snoopy and the Red Barron" he lifted off.

Immediately upon clearing the mountains, the yellow triangular caution light on the radar detector started flashing, accompanied by the loud synchronized sound of the audible beep-beep warning signal. The all frequency scanner locked on a frequency that sounded like an auctioneer selling used furniture just as Snoopy started rat-a-tat-tatting at the Red Barron.

K'Narf, reacting instead of thinking, started slapping power switches that activated all three of the bottom drive cores at full power. His weight went almost instantly to eight hundred and forty pounds at four gravities. Within seconds his weight dropped to six hundred and thirty pounds as the Lady left behind the singular gravity pull of the earth.

Almost as quickly as it had occurred the bedlam ceased. The yellow caution light stopped blinking and beeping, the auctioneer faded out and Snoopy stopped shooting at the Red Barron. K'Narf, struggling against the three G's of thrust manage to hit the power switches cutting the Lady back to one G, which instantly dropped his own body back to its natural weight of two hundred and ten pounds.

"Perfect lift off Thomas, just like I planned it." K'Narf said, making a mental note that ninety seconds of three G thrust equated to two thousand, two hundred and fifty miles per hour, and that he was now increasing speed at a steady five hundred miles per minute of one G thrust.

"Meowwwrrr!"

"Okay, so it wasn't quite like I planned it. Didn't get hurt did you?"

"Meowrr." Thomas answered, licking his ruffled fur.

"Okay, be a grouch. Let's get lined up and head for Mars, I want to take a look at Phobos and Deimos." K'Narf said, as he steered the van around until he spotted the Red planet. "Then I want to check out the asteroid belt."

"Maybe we'd better top off our batteries first though, the sun gets weaker out there and it'll take longer to charge her." K'Narf said, talking more to himself than Thomas as he cut power and tilted the Lady so her top was facing the sun. Watching the spot of sunlight on the Lady's floor he adjusted her angle to the sun until the sunspot centered on the blue spot of paint on the floor, remembering how Rudy had insisted that the color of the spot match the blue of the seats. Looking at his amperage gauge he let out a whistle. "Would you look at that Thomas, a perfect thirty-six amps. Took us over a half hour of jockeying around last time and the best we could get was thirty-four."

Getting out of his seat K'Narf floated back to the big batteries. Reaching over the packed supplies he lifted the lid to the front battery that had the level of charge gauge built into it. "Ninety-five percent charged Thomas, fifteen minutes and we'll be on our way." Should have built that gauge into the dashboard he thought as he floated back to his seat, dodging one of Thomas' flying attempts to lick his face on the way. "Shouldn't have to recharge until we get back if we're careful."

Fifteen minutes later K'Narf ordered the ecstatic Thomas back to his seat, lined up on Mars, and switched on one tenth of a G thrust; adding another tenth every five seconds. Thomas squalled when he hit one-point-seven G's of thrust. Figuring in the mid-point and switchover he should reach the neighborhood of Mars in less than twenty hours if he didn't reverse thrust and slow down.

Three days later, with Mars only a reddish light behind him, K'narf edged Lady into the area of space known as the asteroid belt. His hand on the power switches as his eyes nervously dissected the space around him. Seeing a glint of something ahead of him he hit the power switches for a short burst of three G thrust, which allowed the Lady to quickly catch up with the errant asteroid. It was about three hundred feet long, shaped kind of like a football with a bite taken out of its side, rotating in a slow lopsided tumbling motion. Then he spotted another glint, and another and another.

Hours later, slowly creeping up on a particularly monstrous asteroid, he was struck by its resemblance to a huge whale. It had a short stubby flat whale looking tail, huge mid-section and head with its mouth gaping open. Circling it he noticed that it even had an eye exactly where a whale's eye should be, at least on the right side of it. K'Narf estimated its length at over a mile with a circumference double that. Moving in close to the mouth he turned on his headlights revealing a one-hundred by four-hundred foot wide gash that angled down to a circular bottom. The whale didn't seem to have any movement at all so K'Narf edged Lady forward until he had been literally swallowed by it. The circular bottom of the mouth turned out to be a fairly flat surface about eighty feet across. Carefully backing out he swung around and headed for the whale's eye.

It was a gaping hole about thirty-five feet in diameter. Moving cautiously, K'Narf edged the Lady's nose into the cave's eye, unknowingly becoming the envy of every spelunker who ever lived.

Moving in about fifty feet, Lady's headlights lit up what appeared to be a huge circular cave, two hundred feet or more across. Edging the Lady on into the center of the cave he started swinging her in a circle lighting up the walls in stark relief. Halfway around he spotted another opening; only this one was just barely fifteen feet across.

Curiosity now in total control, K'Narf nudged Lady toward the new opening. Her headlights revealed an almost perfect tunnel reaching deep into the belly of the whale. Disregarding the warning signals going off in the depths of his mind, he lowered the Lady's antennas and shoved her nose into the shaft. Inching ahead he slowly traversed over a hundred feet of the tunnel. It's size varied slightly, but never enough to stop his progress. Suddenly the walls changed from dark brownish rock to a metallic iron looking mineral with multi-colored highlights. The tunnel's size did not vary, so true to the spelunker's code, he forged ahead. Finally, about one hundred and seventy feet further in, the Lady slid out into an enormous cavern; he was truly in the whale's belly.

Everywhere her headlights hit she exposed beautiful crystal formations. It was like being inside a huge jewel. K'Narf, flying forward with his lights on high beam, spotted the far end of the cavern and estimated its size at a little over ninety yards long and at least fifty yards at its widest point. Lights sparkling and dancing off the crystal formations K'Narf's eyes were suddenly drawn to what appeared to be a waterfall of white crystal at the far end of the cavern, which is exactly what it was. Unbelievably beautiful, everything was beautiful as he swung Lady around. The crystals were formed into large swatches of color ranging from sparkling dark blue with violet highlights, into a white cream blended in and mixed with lavender and dark purple. Going back toward the caverns entrance he spotted a large area of ocher crystals off to it's left, and everywhere he looked in the crystal formations were caves. A myriad of caves and cave entrances both large and small. A man could spend a lifetime just exploring the intricate caves incorporated into the crystal walls.

Reluctantly, he headed for the exit and open space. He couldn't keep wasting energy like this. "Ready to go see Pluto, Thomas?" K'Narf asked, slipping the nose of the Lady into the exit tunnel. "Now why did I say that? I don't want to go to Pluto, I want to go look at the rings of Saturn."

"Thomas, are you putting thoughts into my head?" K'Narf asked, as again he got the feeling he needed to go look at Pluto. Then he got that hatband feeling he knew to be the Lord's presence. "But why Pluto Lord?" K'Narf asked out loud; as usual he got no physical answer, but he knew that he had just been ordered to go look at Pluto. Checking his mental map of the solar system he found Pluto on its way to its outer arc, but still closer in than Neptune.

Outside, headlights turned off, he carefully studied the stars and triangulated the whale's position. He knew he wanted to come back to her and his head was already filling up with ideas about how to do just that.

Maneuvering the Lady out of the asteroid belt, K'Narf lined up on Pluto and set her for a one G thrust. "Let's eat." He said, as he started getting out cold cuts and bread. "Sure do miss Rudy's cooking."

Finishing the meager meal he sat up his portable potty and uncapped Thomas' litter box. Later with everything properly stowed he checked the batteries.

"We've still got eighty-seven percent of our charge, Thomas; ready to check out Pluto?" K'Narf asked, ordering Thomas back to his seat with a picture in his mind of Thomas spread-eagled in his seat with his claws dug in tight. "I'm going to switch to the rear cores and push her up to at least four G's."

"Meowwwrrr!" Thomas complained as he dug in his claws.

"I know, but Pluto's an awfully long ways out there, and we need to build up our speed to at least fifty million per or it'll take forever."

Almost a hundred grueling hours later he was plotting a looping orbit that would take him within a few hundred feet of Pluto's surface. Estimating his speed at that moment he'd be moving at about a thousand miles per hour. Slow enough to give him a good look at her surface and whatever it was that the Lord wanted him to see. He just hoped he wasn't moving to fast to see whatever it was. Then, with the help of Pluto's gravity slingshoting him, he'd be headed back toward Earth and Rudy's cooking, a thought that had been filling his every waking moment of late.

Pluto looked like another version of Earth's moon, cratered as it was. K'Narf nervously fingered the power switches in case a mountain showed up in his flight path, belatedly thinking he'd plotted his orbit a little to close as Pluto's surface filled the van's windshield. Switching on his headlights and putting them on high beam, K'Narf glued his eyes to the fast moving surface as his altitude approached the one hundred foot mark.

Skimming a ridge by what appeared to be less than fifty feet, K'Narf sailed out over what seemed to be a large crater. He wasn't sure because of the sudden bedlam that broke loose, almost worse than when he left earth. The yellow radar detector started flashing and beeping, the scanner lit up and roared with static and the windshield went opaque as a brilliant green laser beam sliced the space in front of him. Hitting half the power switches at once caused the van to leap sideways and up simultaneously. A maneuver that undoubtedly saved his life as another green laser beam sliced the space he'd just vacated.

Turning off the headlights, correcting his orbit to send him earthward and slamming the Lady into her maximum thrust of five G's took place before K'Narf cleared Pluto's gravity. The side windows that had gone opaque at the second laser shot began to clear allowing K'Narf to see the fast receding planet in his rearview mirrors.

Three minutes later the yellow caution signal started flashing and beeping again. The large black cigar shaped ship he'd glimpsed couldn't possible have lifted that fast, but one of those two little ones obviously had. K'Narf listened intently to the spacing between the warning beeps, designed to tell a motorist whether or not a police officer's cruiser was gaining on him.

Several minutes went by before he was sure that the beeps were actually growing farther apart. He was out-running them. Looking in his rearview mirror K'Narf strained his muscles to raise his hand and wave goodbye. It was this act of arrogance that saved his life a second time, because he was looking when the missile was fired. He watched as a red streak of fire pointed itself at him and then winked out. Knowing he had but moments before the missile would hit he flew into action.

Cutting back to one G of thrust he mentally ordered Thomas into his airtight bubble, kicking the little door shut as he grabbed the spacesuit from its Velcro hooks on the ceiling. He had the suit on in thirty seconds flat. In one smooth motion he ripped open the buckles holding two of the oxygen cylinders. Ramming them through his portable potty seat to hold them together, he blew lady's atmosphere, opened her side cargo door and shoved the cylinders outside. Then, slamming the door shut, he leaped into his seat and hit the power switches, throwing the Lady forward at a full five G's thrust again.

Thirty–six seconds later a huge crimson fireball blossomed out behind him. The little yellow caution light winked out and the beeping stopped. He'd guessed right, the missile had been of a metal-seeking type.

"They, they, they tried to kill me!" K'Narf stammered, realizing just how close he had come to death, and for the first time in his life he knew anger, a pure unreasoning anger that seemed to reach in and touch his very soul. With blood vessels bulging on his forehead and neck, he raised his mailed fist and against five gravities of thrust slammed it into the dashboard. He was halfway back to earth before he regained control of his mind, a mind that would never be quite the same again. Anger, controlled anger, an elusive, delicate, balance of emotions, a gift given to the human race when God created Adam and Eve in His own image.

Chapter Thirteen

Rudy, hearing the honking of a horn, stepped over to the front window and looked out. He involuntarily flinched as he watched the big black van attempt a high-speed turn into the driveway, spitting up a wall of gravel, dirt and dust as she slid around the corner. Then, just as she started to tip over, she miraculously lifted about two feet and sailed through the air; simulating the landing of a carrier plane by a rookie pilot. She finally regained both the driveway and control.

"It's a good thing she can fly, because he still can't drive worth a hoot!" Rudy exclaimed, as another urgent sounding blast on the horn galvanized him into action.

Hitting the garage door on the run he opened it, slapped on the lights and literally leaped for the garage door. Whatever had made K'Narf fly the Lady in broad daylight had to be urgent.

"Been getting too peaceful around here anyway." Rudy said, as he heaved up the door and scrambled sideways to avoid the Lady as she came sliding in, sparks flying from her left rear landing foot and a slapping sound as her one antenna hit the roof. Jumping up, he grabbed the door and pulled it down and locked it. Turning at the hissing sound of Lady's pressure being blown.

"Peeuuu! Something stinks!"

"What stinks?" K'Narf asked, opening the van's door.

"The Lady does!" Rudy half-hollered, getting a good whiff of the air pouring out of the Lady as he pulled out a bright yellow handkerchief and held it over his nose. "What in blue blazes happened to the her?"

"What do you mean?" K'Narf asked, stepping out of the van, staggering for a second and then abruptly setting down on the garage floor.

"What do you mean, what am I talking about?" Rudy asked, removing his handkerchief and sniffing at the collapsed K'Narf. "You stink too! And what in blue blazes happened to her?" He asked again, pointing at the Lady.

K'Narf, turning his head and half-twisting his body, looked at the Lady. The long antenna that had been mounted on the driver's side, had been sheared off barely three inches above her roofline, and the left rear tire was almost half gone, rim, brake drum and all. The alien laser had even sheared off a little of the back bumper.

"The bloody Snarks almost got me." K'Narf said, letting out a low whistle.

"Okay, what's a Snark?" Rudy asked, getting frustrated.

"You know what a U.F.O. is?" K'Narf asked, holding out his hand; mutely asking Rudy to help him up.

"Yeah, it's an unidentified flying object, why?" Rudy asked belligerently.

"Well, a Snark is a U.F.O. that's been identified, and believe me, I did a bang-up job of identifying these particular Snarks. Unh!" K'Narf grunted, as he heaved himself up with Rudy's help. "Right about now I'd guess that I'm the one listed as a U.F.O." He said, grinning at the thought that the tables had been turned.

"Meow."

"Rudy, quick," K'Narf said, grabbing at the Lady's open door for support. "Get Thomas out of there and be careful, he's been bruised up pretty badly."

"What happened to him?" Rudy asked, beginning to feel like a broken record.

"My fault mostly. I got excited and threw out two full cylinders of oxygen, so we had to live under five G's of thrust for almost six days getting home; almost didn't make it." K'Narf said, taking a deep breath and exhaling slowly. Need to get Thomas to a vet, have him x-rayed for possible bone damage and pumped full of vitamins."

"I ain't gon'na ask." Rudy sputtered. "I swear I ain't, I ain't gon'na." Rudy mumbled, pulling himself up into the Lady with one hand, while still holding the yellow handkerchief over his nose with the other. "Oh my! Thomas! Oh you poor little thing!" He stammered, backing out butt first holding Thomas in his arms. "I hope you don't think I'm gon'na clean up that mess!" He growled, turning on K'Narf.

"No, I'll clean up the Lady, you just get Thomas to the vet. Tell them he got hit by a car or something." K'Narf said, still hanging onto the Lady's door for support.

"Come on Thomas." Rudy said, cuddling the cat. "Let's go see the doc. He'll fix you up, sure he will." He cooed, opening the side door and heading for the small blue van.

K'Narf stood there listening as the motor caught and Rudy pulled out and left, then turned and half-staggered into the house. Opening the refrigerator he found a plate of cold fried lamb chops. Taking three of them he headed for the bathroom, stopping at the sight of himself in the big hall mirror.

Blood-shot eyes, sunk in pits of tar colored flesh, stared out at him. Six-feet-four inches tall, now a gaunt one hundred and eighty pounds, with two weeks of beard covering his now completed chin with its deep dimple. His open long sleeved white shirt revealing a mass of dark curly chest hair, a dirty, rumpled and stinking long sleeve white shirt if he could believe Rudy since he could no longer smell himself.

He had learned, under the extreme stress of five G's, how to compress the cells of his body to withstand the pressure, but looking closer he noticed changes he hadn't counted on. His skin seemed to have darkened as though he had an exceptional tan. Even his eyes seemed to have a very slight golden glow. Not exactly the self-image he kept in his mind he thought, remembering his grandmother's father. He liked to think that great grandfather Steinbeck, would be proud to claim him as his grandson now that he resembled him closer than a twin would have. At least, that is, if all you had to compare them with was the picture of his grandmother and her parents when she was a young girl as a guide, he thought. Turning from the mirror he headed for the bathroom again, stopping in mid-stride at the sound of the front door bell.

Back tracking, K'Narf walked over to the front window and looked out, instantly recognizing his neighbor Nancy's car parked in the driveway. She'd obviously seen, or heard, him come in and she was also aware that Rudy was gone. "So, she really wants to meet me does she!" K'Narf grunted, ripping a bite out of one of the lamb chops as he walked over to the front door and opened it.

"Good morning, I'm...."

"Ah yes, you must be Nancy. Rudy did mention that you were anxious to meet me." K'Narf said, in a low conspiratorial voice. "Please, do come in." He said, reaching out and taking Nancy's hand, and with a slight tug pulled her into the house, closing the door softly behind her.

107

"I, uh, just thought, uh, maybe we could...." Nancy stammered, backing up against the closed door.

"Exactly, what, did you have in mind?" K'Narf asked, in his lowest softest voice, ripping another bite off one of the lamb chops. Then, placing his left hand flat against the door just above her right shoulder and, according to the 'Theory of Territorial Imperative', deliberately violated her space by leaning in very close to her chubby little green–eyed face, all the time chewing on his mouthful of lamb.

"I, uh, I've got to, I'm afraid I...." Suddenly ducking, Nancy turned and grabbed the doorknob, yanked the door open and bolted for her car, yelling something about seeing Rudy later.

K'Narf, watching her peel out of his driveway, closed the door and roared. He laughed so hard he literally collapsed in the middle of the living room floor, the spasm of laughter leaving him too weak to get up.

Rudy, coming home from the vet's some two hours later, found K'Narf sprawled out on the living room carpet sleeping like a baby. Grumbling about slovenly kids, white ones in particular, he went and got a blanket and taking the half eaten lamb chop from K'Narf's hand covered him up. Then, unable to stand it, he headed for the Lady and the mess he'd sworn he wouldn't clean up.

"How long you gon'na be gone this time?" Rudy asked, holding an agitated Thomas and watching as K'Narf loaded the Lady up with supplies that had him wondering exactly what he was doing up there.

"Oh, using a full five G's of thrust I should be able to get there in just under four hours. Figuring a half hour to unload the welder and I-beams, and a couple more hours to set them in place. Then about the same time to return; I should be back just after sunset tomorrow." K'Narf said, talking more to himself than Rudy.

"You'd think this dumb cat wouldn't want nothing to do with you and your space flying, instead of raising cane about being left behind." Rudy said, tossing Thomas into the kitchen and quickly slamming the door. "That female Manx I ordered is supposed to be here tomorrow. Maybe that'll calm him down."

"Well, take it easy with him. It's only been a little over a week and the vet said he should be kept quiet." K'Narf said, grunting as he tightened one of the straps holding the steel I-beams stowed to the Lady's under-belly. "Go ahead and open the door, we're about as ready as we'll ever be." He added, climbing up into

108

the driver's seat and throwing her power switches, causing a scrapping sound as she lifted her allotted three inches.

Turning out the garage lights, Rudy walked over to the large double garage door, unlocked it and heaved it open. He watched as K'Narf backed out and raised the antennas, new one first and then the old one.

"Would you check on those twenty-four inch solar-mirrors and batteries I ordered, they might come in tomorrow." K'Narf said, as Rudy closed the garage door.

"On one condition." Rudy said, glaring a K'Narf. "You'll tell me what you did to Missus Nancy. Not only will she not talk to me, but she wouldn't even wave at me when I met her on the road today."

"All I did was...."

"Don't give me anymore bull about how you just introduced yourself!" Rudy growled, exasperation showing in his voice. "Oh, go on an git, and watch out for them Snarks, they play kind of rough." He grumbled, slamming K'Narf's door shut and waving him off.

Three hours and forty-seven minutes later K'Narf was very carefully maneuvering toward the eye of the whale. Diving through the eye, he turned on his headlights and slowly circled until he spotted the opening that led to the jeweled cavern. Lowering both antennas and going slightly faster, since he knew where he was going this time, he slid the Lady into the small tunnel.

Still in the tunnel and stopping twenty-five feet short of the cavern, he set the Lady down by applying five hundred pounds of thrust via the single roof mounted drive core. Then, ripping the spacesuit down from its Velcro hooks on the ceiling, he slipped it on and blew the Lady's atmosphere.

Climbing out in the tight confines of the tunnel, K'Narf unstrapped four of the heavy steel I-beams, floating them out from under the van with one finger. Quickly bolting them together with pre-placed bolts, he constructed a steel square equal in size to a standard single car garage door. Hauling out the welder he sealed each seam and bolt head with a smooth bead of welded metal. Then propping it up he started driving steel supports into the iron hard metallic surface and welding them to the steel frame.

Twenty minutes later, with the large steel frame firmly welded and braced in place, he took measurements of the irregular spaces around its edges and backed the Lady up exactly one hundred feet and repeated the entire process.

Leaving the welder, and three full cylinders of oxygen in the tunnel, he backed out and headed for home. Keeping an anxious eye on the small yellow triangle that would warn him if the Snarks had him on their radar screen.

Rudy, standing out at the edge of light spilling from the open garage door, began to get nervous since it would be getting light any minute now and K'Narf wasn't back yet. Suddenly he heard a hissing sound followed by the opening of a door. "Starting to hear things now, must be getting older that I thought." Rudy said, peering out into the gloom of the moonless night.

"Rudy, turn the lights out so I can land!" K'Narf yelled down at the shiny baldhead of Rudy twenty feet below him.

Rudy, whipping his head back and up, found himself looking at the Lady's underbelly and K'Narf, who was half-hanging out her open door. For once in his life he was speechless, but not motionless as he jumped sideways, scrambled to catch his balance and ran for the garage's light switch.

K'Narf, seeing the lights go out, immediately dropped her down and pulled into the garage. Leaping out just in time to help Rudy pull down the heavy garage door and lock it."

"K'Narf." Rudy said quietly.

"Yes." K'Narf said, feeling a bit nervous at the soft sound of Rudy's voice.

"Have I ever told you that the doc said I have a bad heart?" Rudy asked, still in a very soft quiet voice.

"Rudy, I'm sorry, really, I didn't know about your heart." K'Narf said, instantly remembering and regretting all the times Rudy had wore himself out trying to help him.

"Well I don't!" Rudy bellowed, stomping off toward the kitchen door. "But if you ever scare me like that again I will!"

K'Narf, realizing what that strange expression on Rudy's face had been when he looked up at him, and knowing that everything was right with the world, burst into a loud belly-busting laugh. Minutes later, staggering into the kitchen, he found Rudy standing at his stove with a big grin on his face.

"Was kind of funny, wasn't I?" Rudy stated more than asked, as he reached for the coffee pot.

"Yeah, you might say that." K'Narf said, dropping down in a kitchen chair, weak from the sudden release of tension.

110

"Well, did you get built what you wanted?"

"Sure did, everything went together just like we rehearsed it. How about the solar mirrors and batteries, did they come in?"

"Nope, called on them though, said they expected them in this week if they shipped on time."

"That's all right, I have to go buy a half-a-dozen sheets of quarter-inch steel plating and get them cut into a whole bunch of irregular shapes today. Hope to make another run up Saturday evening, right after Sabbath ends." K'Narf said, gratefully accepting the hot cup of coffee Rudy handed him. "Well, who do we have here?" He asked, looking at the newcomer standing primly in the kitchen door.

"That's Judy." Rudy said, seeing the small blue grey cat with the big golden eyes. "She's still not sure she wants anything to do with any of us, especially Thomas." Rudy said grinning.

"She sure is pretty, don't think I've ever seen a color quite like that, have you?"

"Nope, felt the same way myself when I saw her for the first time." Rudy said, lifting a couple of cubed breakfast steaks out of the small skillet."

"Any trouble getting two of those heavy duty spring loaded garage doors?" K'Narf asked, sipping his coffee and carefully reaching down and scratching Judy behind the ear.

"Nope, all we have to do is give them a call and they'll deliver them the same day." Rudy said, turning around and heading for the table with a plate load of food; stopping in mid-stride. "Well I'll be hooted and hollered at! She ain't let me or Thomas even get near her and you walk right in and pet her!"

"I think she likes me." K'Narf said, looking up at Rudy and smiling. "Today's Thursday, so call and tell them you want those doors delivered next Tuesday. I'll be ready to haul them up by then, and how about the oxygen cylinders, did you order that first lot of twenty-five I asked for?"

"Yep, did everything you wanted, even when you didn't tell me what you wanted them for." Rudy said pointedly, as he poured both of them fresh coffee and sat down.

Eleven days later, K'Narf backed the Lady out of the tunnel, and then pulled forward slowly. Coming up on the first garage door he pushed a button newly built into the Lady's dashboard, sending a coded electronic signal to the door. Slowly it opened and he moved forward through it. Pushing a second button caused it to close and seal airtight. Then, moving forward again he reached the second door. Pushing a third button caused a small red light to come on which was mounted just above the door. Five minutes later the red light flickered out and a green light came on telling K'Narf the tunnel pressure matched the pressure in the jeweled cavern. Pushing the fourth button opened the door and K'Narf let out a shout as he shot the Lady forward into his new home and spun her about to look at his handiwork.

The big electric pressure pump hung from the wall where he had mounted it, gleaming like a huge spider with one leg leading into the tunnel and two smaller ones leading into the small ocher cave where he'd stowed six of his special order solar batteries. Which brought him to phase two, rechargeable power.

Moments later, he was back outside with the Lady firmly anchored to the bottom of the fish's mouth by over a thousand pounds of thrust. K'Narf mentally recalculated the angle between the point of entry in the circular flat bottom of the whale's mouth and the ocher power cave where the batteries had recently been placed. Coming up with the same positive answer he closed the contact, which energized the half-inch laser, permanently welded to the Lady's under-belly.

Forty-seven minutes later, a burst of dust from the small hole indicated break-through. Shutting down the laser K'Narf lifted and headed for the eye of the whale and her jeweled cavern. Quickly cycling through his new garage door airlock, he put on his suit, blew Lady's atmosphere and floated down to the power cave. There was his half-inch hole, sucking out the cavern's pressure only seven inches off target.

Unreeling the power cable from the huge roll in the Lady's loading bay, stuck along with the Lady to the wall just above the power cave's mouth, he shoved in two hundred and fifty-seven feet and then sealed the hole with quick setting liquid metal.

Then he attached the new cable to the control box, which had already been wired to battery number one, which in turn had been wired in series to the other five batteries. Going back to the Lady K'Narf tossed out the big wooden reel the cable came on, locked up and headed for home and the solar mirrors.

Eight days, and three trips later he was ready. The twenty-four two-foot wide half-moon solar mirrors were aligned and secured to the flat bottom of the whale's mouth, an exact duplicate of the Lady's power system, only with larger mirrors to account for a much weaker sun.

Maneuvering Lady around to the right side of the whale's head, he carefully moved in until the new reinforced steel extrusion welded to the Lady's under-carriage touched. Then cautiously applied power, watching as the extrusion sunk about three inches into the asteroid's surface before it stopped. Then, slowly building up thrust until at three-point-seven G's the whale began to move.

Six and a half hours and seventeen adjustments later, he had the whale's mouth permanently open to the sun and had managed to put a spin on her amounting to one complete revolution every three-point-nine minutes. Not much, but enough to give the cavern some semblance of artificial gravity. Nothing left but to beef up the oxygen he'd already dumped in her to a breathable mixture and move in, he thought, as he threw the Lady's power switches and lined out for home.

"You're really gon'na take them up there?" Rudy asked, holding Thomas in his arms and scratching him behind the ears.

"Yes Rudy, I really am. I've got power, lights, food, water, heat and most of my lab up there already. I even slept in my new waterbed the last time I was up there and it was fabulous." K'Narf said, his eyes sparkling at the thought of the whale's cavern and the beautiful shimmering purple cave he had found and converted into his bedroom.

"What about those Snarks that shot at you?" Rudy asked, still dubious.

"They're too busy mining to bother with me." K'Narf said, his forehead wrinkling at the thought.

"Mining?"

"Yeah, I finally figured out what they were doing out there. They have an open pit mine bigger than the one over at Ajo. They had to have been working that mine for thousands of years."

"Then you really think it's safe?" Rudy asked, for the umpteenth time.

"Rudy, what more can I tell you. I've been literally living there for the past two months and I'm still alive." K'Narf said, getting exasperated himself.

"Okay."

"Okay what?"

113

"Okay, I'll go up with you and take a look. Been getting awful curious about what you been doing with all that stuff you been hauling up there anyway, specially the kitchen stuff." Rudy said, committing himself as he screwed up his face like he'd swallowed a bitter pill.

"Thank you sweet Jesus!" K'Narf exclaimed, grinning at Rudy.

"Why you thanking Him?" Rudy asked, suddenly getting serious.

"Him?"

"Yeah, Him, Jesus." Rudy explained.

"Rudy, I've been praying for weeks that you'd change your mind and move up with me."

"Well, I ain't said I'd move up there, just that I'd go take a look. You shouldn't be thanking Him for something that ain't happened yet." Rudy said, scolding K'Narf with his eyes as well as his words.

"You're going to love it, I promise." K'Narf said, not fully understanding Rudy's rejection of the Lord, but excited at the thought of showing Rudy the whale's jeweled cavern and the kitchen he'd built for him. "And wait till you see the Waterfall of Tears, you won't believe it even when you're looking at it." He added, and neither will she, he thought.

Chapter Fourteen

The big black van dropped from better than three hundred thousand miles per, to a mere whisper of movement in her final approach. Diving through the whale's eye and into the outer cave she spun around and turned on her headlights. Then, touching down briefly in order to match the whale's rotational spin, she lifted again and moved cautiously forward into the tunnel.

Rudy, hearing the big pressure pump kick-in very carefully stood up, brushed the dirt from his hands and looking at a spot approximately ten feet to the right of where he wanted to land, squatted slightly and leaped; floating across the intervening fifty-plus yards of space with a skill and control indicative of a seasoned space dweller. He noticed that Thomas and Judy had emerged from their ceaseless exploring of the myriad of small interlocking caves and tunnels that constituted the jeweled walls, and were cavorting and cart wheeling through the air with their usual unerring accuracy on a course coincidental with his own. K'Narf's infrequent arrivals were invariably moments of high excitement, since he always had the Lady packed solid with needed supplies.

Doing a mid-air cartwheel split-seconds before impact allowed Rudy to land on his feet, which instantly rebounded him toward the guy-rope he and K'Narf had strung between the landing pad and the pearl colored kitchen cave. The yellow nylon rope spun him around in mid-flight, stretching taut like a bowstring as it absorbed the kinetic energy of his flying body. Then with an over hand crawl he scrambled down the rope toward the landing pad just as the airlock cycled open.

K'Narf, edging the Lady through the second door, fed a pulse of energy to the rear drive core that shot the van into the cavern proper. Then he deftly dropped her to the flat spot they used for a landing pad, noticing immediately that Rudy had strung a new guy-rope that stretched off into the darkness. He must have located a cave he considered suitable for a guest bedroom, K'Narf thought, remembering how picky Rudy had become when he'd told him why he was going to need such a room.

"Did you get my onion sets?" Rudy called out as the hissing stopped and the Lady's door opened.

"Yes, I got everything you asked for except the soil, only had room for a couple hundred pounds." K'Narf said, dodging the flying tongues of both Thomas and Judy as he floated out and started a hand over hand crawl toward the cargo bay door.

"How about those new grow lamps you promised for my garden?" Rudy asked, not quite trusting K'Narf's all-inclusive statement.

"Got you six of them, big ones too, including spare lamp bulbs." K'Narf said grinning. "You'll have to find something else to holler about now."

"Humph!" Rudy grunted, as he shoved off and floated over to the van.

"Did you get a power line strung to the new bedroom?"

"Yes, floors laid and she's wired for lights and power. Just wait till you see what I found. You think that purple cave you moved into is pretty, ain't nothing compared to this new one."

"This I've got to see!" K'Narf exclaimed, as he jumped up and grabbed the new guy-rope.

Rudy, wanting to see the surprise on K'Narf's face when he turned on the lights in the new cave, took mental aim at the rotating darkness and leaped, passing the slower K'Narf as he pulled himself along. At first the distance grew between him and the yellow rope, then he passed the axis point and as the light from the landing pad faded out behind him, his line of flight started converging on the dimly glowing yellow rope. Grabbing it at the last second, he started a one-handed pull and float operation that moved him rapidly forward.

"Rudy! Turn on the lights so I can see where I'm going!" K'Narf cried out, knowing Rudy was somewhere out in the darkness ahead of him.

"Just keep coming, your almost here."

"Must be some cave you've found." K'Narf grumbled, as he pulled himself cautiously forward.

Rudy, watching the outline of K'Narf's form against the now distant lights of the landing pad, reached out and grabbed his hand. "Careful now, you're in a tunnel about seven feet in diameter."

"Tunnel?"

"Yeah, about fifty feet of it. Leads to the cave I found."

"Well, turn on the lights so I can see it!" K'Narf said, getting frustrated.

"Just hold on to your britches. We'll be there in just a second." Rudy said, pulling them both forward with the assurance of a man who knows where he's going.

"What the..."

"Just plant you feet and don't move."

"It's flat!"

"Yeah, you're standing in the middle of the new floor." Rudy said, as he let go of K'Narf's hand and floated over to where he knew the light switch was and switched it on.

"Oh Lord!" K'Narf exclaimed, slowly sinking to his knees. "It's the tears!"

"That's right!" Rudy chortled triumphantly. "There's a big bubble right in the base of the waterfall. Notice how I hid the lights in amongst the walls. Indirect lighting it's called." He added proudly, looking around at the iridescent colors flickering in the layers of what looked like diamond bright tears.

"How?"

"Accident mostly. I was taking a look at the waterfall up close when I noticed a tunnel off to the side of it and this is where it led. What kind of furniture did you get for her?"

"Pale blue rug, white French provincial dresser and mirror, matching chest of drawers and a king size water bed." K'Narf said, still staring in fascination at the glowing walls and ceiling."

"How about night stands?"

"Yeah, I got them too. Bought the whole set right out of the showroom window just like they had it."

"You got all that in the Lady?"

"I had a cabinet maker take them apart, then wrapped each piece in the sheets, blankets and the rug. You'll have to screw and glue them back together again. Got you some touch-up paint too."

"When are we gon'na go get her?"

"Soon as I put together a new pair of Kirlian glasses."

"New pair?"

"Yeah, one I can use."

"What's the matter, you don't trust me to be your lookout anymore?"

"You know better than that! I need a pair I can wear because you won't be there."

"What do you mean, I won't be there?" Rudy asked angrily.

"Just what I said, when I get the passenger seat bolted back in I'll have room for exactly one additional person and it ain't going to be you." K'Narf said, trying to ignore the expression on Rudy's face.

"Why can't I set in the back?" Rudy exploded.

"Because there's always the chance that a Snark might show up, and if I had to make a run for it you'd wind up looking like a piece of hamburger." K'Narf said, turning and looking at Rudy; knowing he was right. "Besides, I need you here to fix up this bedroom for our expected guest." He added, trying to sooth the agitated Rudy.

"Humph!" Rudy grunted, shoving himself toward the tunnel.

Hours later, emerging from his lab wearing a pair of ultra modern bubble lens sunglasses, he flicked on the power switch. He could still see a slight haze of white light around the edges, but it was not enough to prevent his seeing Rudy's aura. Rudy was still acting upset at being left behind, but his aura indicated the exact opposite. He was busy ferrying the bags of soil down to the trench where he had established his garden, obviously excited about his new growing lights and onion sets.

Putting the glasses in their case and clipping it to his belt, he mentally calculated the distance and speed of rotation, then half-squatted and leaped for the dark hole he knew to be his bedroom. Hitting the string switch he'd strung across the top of the cave mouth turned on the bedroom lights, illuminating the beautiful royal purple crystals that formed its walls. Cart wheeling at the last possible second, he expertly absorbed his kinetic energy with his legs and stood up; held to the floor by the slight centrifugal force imparted by the spinning asteroid. Getting out his suitcase he started packing his fancy go to Vegas clothes; turning out the light and leaping toward the landing pad some twenty minutes later.

"You'd better eat something before you go." Rudy said, as they finished reinstalling the passenger seat.

"I am starved now that you mention it."

"Never knew you when you weren't." Rudy said, grinning as he squatted and launched himself toward the kitchen cave.

"Still can't figure out how you make that look so simple." K'Narf said, sitting at the heavy wooden picnic table with its built in benches they had bolted to the floor.

"What's simple?"

"The way you can cook without any real gravity. Every time I tried to turn anything it took off on its own. Never felt so silly in my life as I did that time I turned my half cooked hamburger to quick." K'Narf said, looking up at the cave's opening almost directly overhead. "That louse Thomas nailed it in mid-flight." K'Narf said, grinning at the memory.

"Ain't hard, all you have to do is keep a lid on everything and always move with rhythm, none of your jerky movements or you'll have everything bouncing off the walls."

"I know, I've been watching you. You'd think you'd been born in space instead of on Earth."

"That's funny, sometimes I feel that way myself." Rudy said, moving rhythmically across the kitchen and deftly setting three main course dishes down on the table without so much as losing a single lid. "Two of your grandmother's favorites and one of my own." He added, taking off the lids and letting K'Narf see the steaming veggie specials he had prepared for him.

"You've been practicing!" K'Narf exclaimed, taking a spoon and very carefully and slowly began loading his plate with healthy portions of each.

"Yeah, getting pretty good at it too." Rudy said, pride showing in his voice as he did a quick two-step back to his stove for the coffee pot.

Later, with a full belly and the Lady driving steadily toward the Earth, K'Narf settled back and went to sleep; setting his mental alarm for three hours and twenty-three minutes later when he'd have to reverse his direction of thrust. Having decided that three G's of thrust was more than sufficient to get him back and forth from Earth, even if it did take a little longer.

That night, ten o'clock Vegas time, he dropped rapidly into the desert outside the glowing city, his radar detector blinking and beeping angrily all the way down. Some military scope-jockey should be having fits about now he thought, as he spotted a dirt road and set the Lady gently down. Switching her over to ground power he turned on her headlights and drove toward the main highway.

Thirteen nights later he had accumulated over thirty thousand dollars gambling, most of it legitimately, and knew every Glow-head working the Vegas area. She definitely wasn't among them.

Back at Caesars, sitting quietly in an obscure lounge close to where he had first seen her, he had just made the decision to try Reno or Tahoe when he caught a glimpse of a small dark crippled form. Putting on his glasses and applying power he recognized the blue-white glow instantly. It was the little old oriental woman. "If she's here, I'll bet the brunette is nearby." He said, verbalizing his thought softly under his breath.

Five hours later, watching as the old woman stepped in front of her hundredth slot machine and started pulling its arm, he was about ready to admit defeat when the brunette showed up. Excited at the sight of his prey at last, he retreated to the far side of the casino, keeping track of them by the glow from their auras. By dawn he knew where she liked to gamble, eat, drink and most importantly where she was staying.

The next night he was sitting in the Lady, waiting in an out of the way corner of the M.G.M. parking lot. Her cargo door was unlocked and pulled slightly ajar ready to be opened quickly. He'd checked out of his room early that morning and had spent the day buying supplies, including more garden soil and Rudy's very extensive grocery list. There was no way he'd go back and face Rudy with an empty cargo hold, excluding the brunette of course, he thought.

He'd watched her and the old woman park their car and go in over an hour and half ago. Then, just as he was thinking they should be coming out, she emerged with her hair piled high and glowing from the bright lights of the casino. Her long peach colored chiffon evening gown giving the impression that she was floating across the parking lot instead of walking. He was in luck he thought, as he noticed the old woman stopping to talk with another Glow-head male at the entrance.

Pulling the Lady forward, he eased her between a row of cars that would bring him abreast of the brunette just before she would get to her own car. Shaking off a twinge of guilt, he reminded himself that she had started it when she had had those two goons of hers grab him.

Leaping out of the van he gave her a healthy spray of chem-numb, cutting off her scream with a choking gurgle. Catching her as she started to collapse, he stepped over to the van and opened the cargo door with his foot, gently placing her inside on the layered bags of garden soil. Slamming the door and hearing it lock; he quickly stepped over to the driver's door, pulled it open and leaped for the seat. The clawing hands of the old woman, and her screaming, hit him simultaneously. Reacting to the attack he sprayed the chem-numb, which he was still clutching in his right hand, full into her anger contorted face. Her hands tightened on his arm in a deathlike grip as she fought the paralyzing force of the chemical spray.

Looking up he realized that the other Glow-head, the one the old woman had been talking to, was only yards away and closing fast. Giving a heave he pitched the feather light form of the old woman head first into the passenger's seat, slammed the door and slapped power switches lifting the Lady straight up. The shocked look on the face of the charging Glow-head, as he literally leaped for the van's door, was the last thing K'Narf saw before he was slammed deep into the cushions of his seat.

Minutes later, well out in space he shut her down. Taking the floating body of the old woman by the leg, noticing as he did so the fancy embroidering on the black silk pajamas she always seemed to wear, he shoved her body to the back of the van. Frowning at the problem her unscheduled presence represented. Then, catching the hand of the moaning brunette, he pulled her into the passenger's seat and strapped her down. Turning his attention back to the old woman he suddenly smiled. Ripping the spacesuit down from its Velcro hooks on the ceiling he opened it up and stuffed the little body inside, then closed it back up and stuck it back to the ceiling. She would be protected from the rigors of excessive acceleration, and more important, she couldn't get loose and attack him again.

Orienting the Lady to a course that would intercept the whale he threw the power switches, keeping her down to just a little over one G of thrust because of the twenty four cartons of eggs in the cargo bay; hoping that he hadn't broken too many of them when he'd lifted off.

"What, where am I, please?" The brunette stammered, rolling her head from side to side. "Where am I? Who are you? Please, unstrap my arms." She begged, looking over at K'Narf with watery eyes, her make-up having ran in little rivulets down her face.

"Where you are should be obvious, just look out the window." K'Narf said, the sound of his voice hard and unmoving.

"Oh my God! She wailed. We're in space!"

"That's right! There's no way your telepathic friends can help you way out here." K'Narf said, the tone of his voice tinged with anger.

"How did you... Who are you?" She asked, turning the full power of her dark brown eyes on him.

"I'm the one asking questions, not you!" K'Narf stated flatly, glaring at her tear stained face. "Who are *you*?" He asked, stressing the word *you*. "And why did you assault me last winter?"

"I'm Irena Caves, and I never assaulted you or anyone like you!" She yelled back, countering K'Narf's angry accusation.

"Yeah, think back to last December; the fifth to be exact. You had those two goons of yours grab a big ugly lout of a kid in Caesar's parking lot. Well, I was that kid!"

"It can't be, you're good, uh, good looking. That kid was the ugliest thing T.J. or I'd ever seen. You can't...."

"I not only can, I am!" K'Narf exclaimed, enjoying his moment of triumph. "Now who are you people?"

"T.J. said you were one of us, so we were trying to find out before you got yourself killed."

"What do you mean one of us? And who's T.J.?"

"We're a group of believers that the Lord has blessed by removing our filters."

"Filters?"

"It's an analogy, but it's the best way we've found to explain it. Each one us at some point in our lives, were touched by the Lord in a way that removed the barrier between our conscious and subconscious minds. Science has long known that as normal humans we use only a very small percentage of the brains God gave us, and now after our Lord's touch, we seem to be able to use it all."

"You said believers?"

"Yes, up to now we've never found anyone with our abilities that didn't have a strong relationship with Jesus. You do believe in Him don't you?" Irena asked, looking almost fearfully at K'Narf.

"Yes, yes I do." K'Narf said quietly. "Always have now that you mention it. Now, who's T.J.?"

"I am you big lout! Now get me down from here this instant!" Came a raspy voice from behind, startling both of them.

"T.J., he got you too?" Irena exclaimed in dismay.

"Get me out of this thing!" T.J. screamed. "I need a cigarette."

"Not a chance, you've clawed me up for the last time." K'Narf said, turning around and looking up at the small wrinkled oriental face staring out of the open faceplate of the spacesuit. Noticing again that the black eyes still did not seem to go with the obvious age in the face. The verbal eruption caught him by complete surprise.

Turning to Irena, K'Narf shrugged his shoulders. "Is she cursing?" He asked, over the rapid-fire staccato sounds of T.J's voice.

"Technically no, her original tongue was a high level form of Mandarin and there are no curse words in that language. However, she does know how to insult you and your ancestors all the way back to Adam and Eve."

"Mandarin?"

"Yes, she was apparently a princess of some sort, but she won't talk about it much. She only reverts to her native tongue when she's mad, like now!" Irena said, scrunching down in her seat, in a useless effort to escape the verbal abuse being poured out on their heads.

"What did you mean earlier when you said you were trying to keep me from getting killed?" K'Narf asked, over the din of T.J's voice.

"We're always looking for what we call newborns. When a normal's mind opens up, and he or she realizes they have telekinetic power, they almost always head for the gambling centers. Invariably they start making big wins that defy the odds and it's always a race to see who gets to them first. If we win we educate them in ways of generating funds without risking their lives at the gaming tables. If the casino people find them first they wind up in a shallow grave out in the desert." Irena said, lowering her voice as the verbal din T.J. had been making began to subside.

"You mean to tell me you were trying to save my life?"

"I wasn't, T.J. was. I didn't believe you were really one of us, but she insisted you were."

"Then I'm afraid I owe you an apology." K'Narf said, impulsively reaching over and releasing the straps holding her prisoner.

"It's me you owe the apology to you big lunk! Now get me down from here!"

"Is it safe to let her loose?" K'Narf asked Irena, looking more than a little unsure of himself.

"It'd be considerably more dangerous not too."

K'Narf, still not sure, got up and moved toward the angry little face staring out at him from the spacesuit.

"Oh, please hand me my purse, please!" Irena cried, having seen herself in the rearview mirror.

K'Narf, seeing the small white bag lying on the floor next to the cargo door, reached over the stacks of potting soil and picked it up and handed it to her. Then, taking a deep breath he reached up and pulled down the spacesuit and opened it up.

Eleven hours later, carefully maneuvering the Lady toward the moving target that was the whale's eye, K'Narf was happier than he could ever remember being. They had talked ceaselessly the whole trip out, and he'd learned all about the loose-knit organization T.J. had put together.

They had taught him the complicated process involved in their ability to communicate telepathically. Each person had a mental frequency different than every other person, sort of like fingerprints, and his had been a very high one taking several hours to find; even with him sending out a mental beeper.

Then they showed him how to visualize a huge tuner in his mind and actually dial the person he wanted to communicate with. They each gave him their personal frequency, which was an honor it itself, since there were certain common frequencies everyone used.

T.J. was especially excited about his Kirlian glasses; she asked permission to beam the knowledge immediately back to someone named Toby so he could start making them for their spotters. She said his glasses would save a lot of lives.

Irena fell in love with the Lady and was already planning her own version, but T.J. was mostly interested in his ability to change himself physically. She wouldn't let him have a decent conversation with Irena what with her constant badgering. He'd be able to dump her off on Rudy in just a few more minutes, he thought, as he dove the Lady into the whale's eye and turned on her headlights. Both girls squealed in delight.

Chapter Fifteen

"Are you trying to tell me that he's never known a woman?"

"That would be my guess. He's never actually told me so, but I've been with him since before he learned to change his face, and before that he couldn't of if he'd tried." Rudy said, squirming under the steady gaze of T.J.'s black eyes.

"Well, I can't argue with you there." T.J. said, remembering the monstrous looking lout she'd seen at the crap table that first night. "That'd explain why he's making such a fool of himself. I love that girl like my own daughter, but she shouldn't use her body to tease one man when she has a covenant relationship with another." She added, scowling at the floating flashlight that marked K'Narf and Irena's location and progress.

"Didn't realize that she was taken, leastwise by the ring she wasn't wearing." Rudy said, his sarcastic comment getting an instant, almost violent response.

"A union accepted and blessed by God is a covenant relationship; it's for life *and it don't need a ring to prove it exist*! T.J. Exploded. "She has a good man, that should be enough." She added in a much softer voice.

"What man?"

"Young boy named Toby Zebulon; lost his foot in Israel's six-day war." T.J. almost whispered, her mind drifting back to another more distant war and her own damaged leg.

"Is he a Glow-head?" Rudy asked, breaking T.J.'s reverie.

"What? Oh, yes, he is. The Lord removed his filter about five years ago. Found him at a roulette wheel in Monte Carlo trying to break the bank. Messed him up good when I started deflecting his control." T.J. said, her face crinkling up with laughter at the memory.

"If he's a Glow-head, why don't he just grow himself a new foot?" Rudy asked, watching T.J.'s eyes for his answer.

"Well, I...."

"Humph! Just as I thought, you didn't know you could change yourself." Rudy stated flatly. "That's why you're still in an old lady's body!"

"Which I intend to remedy, if I can just get that big lout away from Irena long enough to find out how he did it!" T.J. growled, leaping for the mouth of the kitchen cave. "Where'd that flashlight go?" She asked, squalling for Rudy as she missed her handhold on the caves edge and floated out into the darkness.

Rudy easily leaped to the edge of the cave, spotted the squirming T.J., mentally plotted his flight path and leaped to intercept her. "Quit wiggling and grab my hand!" He ordered, counting on his momentum to carry both of them to the far side.

"Where'd they go?" T.J. asked, anger tingeing her voice as she grabbed Rudy's hand.

"He's probably showing her the bedroom he built for her."

"The what!" T.J. screamed, as Rudy cradled her in his arms like a baby, tuck-and-rolled into the wall, squatted and leaped; putting them on a return course for the brightly lit kitchen cave.

"What bedroom?" T.J. screamed again, squirming out of Rudy's arms.

"The one he built for her." Rudy said nonchalantly.

"Why that, he's not naïve, he's just plain stupid! Where's it at? Take me there!" T.J. exclaimed, asked and ordered all in one breath.

"Got a better idea." Rudy said, as he took T.J. in his arms then tuck-and-rolled again so as to land feet first, using his legs to absorb their combined kinetic energy; expertly stopping at the edge of the kitchen's entrance. "You stay right here and don't move, I'll be right back." He said, as he squatted and leaped for the power cave. Moments later he threw the main power switch that turned on the lights in the crystal tear bedroom betting that K'Narf wouldn't be able to find where he'd hidden the opposing master switch.

Floating back to the kitchen he found that T.J. was laughing so hard, she'd bounced off the wall and was slowly drifting away as the mouth of the kitchen cave rotated out from under her. "Got your tickle box turned over, did you?" Rudy asked, grabbing her and pulling her back.

"Let's just say that you can see through those crystal walls down there." T.J. giggled, pointing at the brightly lit bedroom at the far end of the cavern. "Moving shadows anyway." She chortled, breaking out in another fit of giggles.

"Come on, you can help me fix supper. I think we're gon'na have a couple of hungry young'uns on our hands in a couple of minutes." Rudy said, as he took T.J.'s hand and jumped for the kitchen floor.

"What kind of meal can you fix way out here?" T.J. asked, as Rudy sat her down at the dining table.

"Tonight, T-Bone steaks, Idaho baked potatoes, sour cream and chives, tossed, or I should say shook salad and a fine dark red California wine."

"This I got to see!"

"Your gon'na do more than see it, your gon'na help me fix it, here." Rudy said, setting a large covered plastic bowl down in front of her. Then, doing his own version of the soft shoe two-step, he moved over to the refrigerator, gathered up tomatoes, lettuce, a cucumber and the little covered jar chopper and two-stepped back to T.J.; his feet never losing contact with the floor.

"Oh, I see." T.J. said, as she took a tomato and put it in the jar, screwed on the lid with its knife and plunger assembly and very neatly chopped the tomato. "You wouldn't happen to have something to smoke would you?" She asked, as she lifted the lid on the large bowl and dumped in the chopped tomato.

"Nope, K'Narf don't allow it up here." Rudy said, resigned to this fact by many long dead arguments.

"I do know of what you speak, Rudy." T.J. said vehemently. "That miserable misbegotten son of a Neanderthal gave me a ten minute lecture on the damage smoking causes to the entire, how did he put it, oh yes, the entire biological system. Just because I asked for one lousy cigarette."

"Yeah, he's talked like that ever since he figured out how to change his face." Rudy said, taking the marinated steaks out of the refrigerator.

"Just how did he do that?" T.J. asked softly, her eyes boring through the back of Rudy's head.

"He just hated that birthmark on his nose so bad he made it go away. Then, when he figured out what he'd done, he went back to the library and memorized all the books they had on the human body."

"That's all there is to it?"

127

"Well not quite, he goofed once. Said something about the DNA chain and an imbalance in his bone marrow. Held his head and cried for better than three days before he corrected his mistake."

"What library did he go to?" T.J. asked, lowering her eyes and concentrating on chopping lettuce.

"The one in Phoenix, the big one down on Central Avenue." Rudy said, doing a fancy half step over to the potato bin. "Why?"

"Oh, no reason, just curious." T.J. said, grinning to herself.

"T.J.!" Irena exclaimed, scolding T.J. with her eyes as she floated into the kitchen holding K'Narf's hand. "You should see the bedroom K'Narf built for me."

"Don't flash me! I'll see it myself when *we* sleep in it tonight!" T.J. said, glaring at K'Narf who was studiously trying to catch Rudy's eye. "We'll need our sleep so we'll be fresh for our trip back home tomorrow morning. Won't we Mister Etaguf?"

"Yeah, uh, do you have to leave so soon?" K'Narf asked, forgetting his desire to nail Rudy.

"Yes, and so do you. They're getting up a party in your honor and I especially want you to meet Toby."

"T.J.!" Irena cried out. "Don't!"

"Don't tell him about you and Toby, that you're a bonded couple. Well, I think he ought to know." T.J. growled, looking straight at K'Narf.

"Toby? Party? What are you two talking about?" K'Narf asked, looking first at T.J. and then at Irena.

"Oh, you'll love it!" Irena bubbled at K'Narf, while slipping T.J. a classic dirty look. "I'll teach you to flash on the way back tomorrow." She said, smiling at him as she took his arm and smoothly turned him away from T.J.

"Flash?" K'Narf asked, getting more confused.

"Flashing is simply using mental pictures and cartoons, along with the spoken word when you talk. Say for example, if I wanted to tell someone to go jump in a swimming pool full of whip cream. I could create a mental picture of that person doing just that and flash it into *her* mind. It's simple really." Irena said, laughing as she walked K'Narf over to look at Rudy's fancy smokeless grill and the steaks that were sizzling on it.

"Ooh!" T.J. shuddered, shaking herself like a wet cat.

"I'm getting confused." Rudy whispered at T.J. "Who you trying to protect, her or him?"

128

"Him of course, any girl who spent three years as an active member of an Israeli Special Forces Commando team doesn't need protecting!" T.J. growled softly.

"Well, don't worry so about the boy, he's just in love."

"In love!" T.J. squalled in a half-whisper. "That overgrown lout doesn't even know the meaning of the word. He's just been smitten with his first rash of puppy lust!" She said, glaring at the backside of the voluptuous brunette.

Thirty-six hours later she was glaring at it again, and for the same reason, she thought. Only difference was now it was covered with white silk, and she had the dark handsome Toby, who was almost as tall as K'Narf, hanging off her other arm.

K'Narf of course, had proven himself to be an extremely popular guest. Each and every one of the other twenty-eight available guests wanted an invite up to his asteroid. Protocol required that they first give him a tour of their private lab sanctuaries which each of them had secreted away. A common facet in their natures, T.J. had secretly developed three of them over the last fifty years herself.

Then, taking a last look at K'Narf, who was glorying in his newfound friends and his ability to flash his thoughts as well as speak them, T.J. turned around and quietly slipped out the door.

"Irena!" Exclaimed a slender, delicate featured black woman with just a touch of grey at her temples. "You've had him long enough. Now it's our turn." She said, taking K'Narf's other arm.

"Oh, okay Wanda." Irena said, reluctantly releasing her grip on K'Narf's arm.

"Toby showed us the Kirlian glasses you invented, and we can't tell you how much we appreciate your sharing the secret of them with us." Wanda bubbled, as she gently pulled him over to a group of women.

"It was my pleasure I assure you." K'Narf said, beaming at the unexpected praise.

"Then tell us how we can build a space-car too!" Piped up a beautiful little blond imp of a child-woman.

"Wonder!" Wanda scolded. "You can't ask Mister Etaguf something like that. It's just not done. How'd you like it if we asked you to share all your secrets?"

"I'm sorry." Wonder said, reaching out and taking K'Narf's hand. "I was just wondering what it would be like to fly in space.

I'm always wondering, mostly about what it'll be like to finally be grown up." She said, looking up at K'Narf with her big blue-eyed doll's face. "That's why they call me wonder."

"Well Wonder, if you'd do me the honor. I'd love to take you up to the whale on my next supply run, that is if you'd like to go?" K'Narf asked, seeing his answer in shining eyes seconds before she leaped up and hugged his neck. "And as for my so called secret of space travel. I'll be happy to teach it to anyone who'd like to know." He added, instantly feeling the hush that fell over the room.

"You'd be willing to share your knowledge of space travel with all of us?" Asked a young Native American who'd been standing quietly beside the fireplace. He was the same young man Rudy had spotted that first night in Las Vegas.

"Sure, way I got it figured, if I ever get into any serious trouble, it'd be nice to have a neighbor to call on for help." K'Narf said, flashing all of them a cartoon caricature of himself standing on the whale yelling "help" at a similar caricature of the young man who he had standing on another asteroid.

"Mister Etaguf, you just got yourself a neighbor." He said, walking over and offering K'Narf his hand. "Name's Brent Conrad." He added, giving K'Narf a firm handshake and a timid smile. "Now about that drive of yours."

K'Narf, smiling at his very attentive audience, grabbed an unoccupied bar stool from Toby's small private bar and drug it over by the fireplace. Then, after waiting until Wonder found another stool and drug it over next to his, he started telling and flashing the Lady's story from conception to her maiden lift-off.

"Well, what do you think of him?" Irena asked, speaking to Toby in a soft but serious voice.

"Well, he's young and naïve."

"You can say that again. I did everything up there but kiss him." Irena giggled. "And the best I could get out of him was a very timid hug."

"Yes, I noticed that he seemed to be unusually intelligent." Toby said, grunting as Iren's elbow caught him in the ribs.

"Rat!" Irena said, flashing Toby a picture of a big fat rat sporting his face with its tail caught in a trap.

"No, I mean it." Toby said, trying not to disturb the attentive silence in the room by laughing. "He's one of us, but he's different at the same time. Most of us are like people with a computer for a brain; we can answer any question you care to ask. He seems to be more like a computer that's learned to reason and he's coming up with his own answers. There's something else about him though, something I can't quite put my finger on. I think it has to do with his level of self-confidence, or maybe I should say his total lack of any self-doubt. Do you know where he went to school?"

"He didn't."

"Why not?"

"Seems he had some sort of mental thing that kept him out of school and when the Lord pulled his filters he ended up going to a library and memorized a bunch of books, at least that's what he told me."

"Sounds like a mirror image of what God did to Moses."

"What do you mean?"

"Well, God made Moses a Prince and put him through the best schools available at the time, and he led his people out of Egypt and into the Promised Land. Now we have him, " Toby said, nodding at K'Narf. " and you're telling me God kept him out of school so he couldn't be contaminated or fettered by any negative modern day ideas, thoughts or philosophies, and from what we've just heard he's going to lead all of us off this planet and into space. Sounds a little like a modern day Moses to me."

"I don't know about that, but he's definitely different."

"Yeah, I can certainly agree with that."

T.J. said she felt it too." Irena said, remembering what T.J. had told her.

"Just look at him." Toby said, staring at the face of K'Narf as he sat there by the fireplace talking. "He's totally guileless."

"Oh, then how come he wouldn't tell T.J. how he changed his face?"

"What do you mean he changed his face?"

"You heard me." Irena said, flashing Toby a private picture of what K'Narf used to look like.

"You're not serious?"

"Yes, and all he'd tell T.J. is that it was too dangerous, and that there were problems he hadn't worked out yet. Speaking of T.J., I don't see those black pajamas of hers." Irena said, looking around her and Toby's large spacious living room.

"That's like T.J." Toby said, as if that simple statement explained her absence.

"You know...." Irena said, pausing thoughtfully. "T.J. has been rounding us up for the past thirty some odd years, but we've always remained a loose knit group, each of us going our own way, meeting only to socialize or pull a duty stint for her at some casino. Looking at him, I get the feeling we're all in for a drastic change in life styles." She mused, tightening her grip on Toby's hand.

"Yes, but it'll be an exciting change." Toby said, feeling a sudden itch on his missing foot.

Late that night, after bidding goodnight to the last of his guests, Toby got his first taste of that excitement when sitting in the passenger's seat of the Lady, as he lifted off for the first time. "K'Narf, it's, ...it's almost like being in church. No, it's more like trespassing where God lives." He whispered softly.

"Well." K'Narf said, as he allowed Lady to drift in a high orbit above earth. "Trespassing is what I wanted to talk to you about."

"If you're referring to Irena...."

"No, T.J. told me in no uncertain terms that you and Irena were a couple or something like that." K'Narf said, looking askance at Toby.

"Yes, you might say we're a couple, but a more proper way to put it would be that we have a covenant relationship approved and blessed by the Lord."

"Covenant Relationship, you mean you're married?" K'Narf asked, slightly puzzled by the new terminology.

"Married is a term normals use, what Irena and I have is similar, but stronger and much more binding."

"Stronger?"

"Yes, uh...." Toby stammered, thinking fast. "Have you ever known or been around a normal couple who've been married a long time?" He asked, struggling to come up with a way to explain a covenant relationship.

"Yes, my grandparents. They were married for a little over sixty-three years when my grandmother passed away. They raised me." K'Narf said, remembering the agony of his grandfather's loss.

"Then you remember the bond they had. How they could almost read each others minds." Toby said, automatically assuming the relationship had been a loving one.

"Yes." K'Narf said, wondering what Toby was driving at.

"Well, when Irena and I went before the Lord and He accepted our petition for a covenant relationship, we were instantly bonded just like your grandparents, only we didn't have to wait sixty-three years for it to happen."

132

"You can read each other's minds?" K'Narf asked, surprised.

"No, no, I can't read Irena's mind." Toby laughed. "Wouldn't want to if I could, but I *can* feel her emotions and she mine. It's the most awesome feeling in the world to be able to share emotions with someone you truly love and who, because you can physically feel her emotions, you know truly loves you in return." He added, looking at K'Narf to see if he was understanding him.

"So you can feel what she's feeling?" K'Narf asked, trying to make sure he was understanding correctly.

"Yes, you might say a covenant couple never have any serious secrets, and believe me, the positives far outweigh any negatives."

"Negatives?"

"Sorry, bad choice of words." Toby said, thinking fast again. "Okay, as my father used to say, listen up. This is covenant wisdom straight from the horses mouth." He added grinning.

"I'm all ears." K'Narf said, not knowing whether to take Toby serious or not.

"There are three things every covenant male needs to know. I'll start with number three, anger. It's real simple, when she's angry and you feel it, run."

"Run?"

"Yes, don't try to figure out why or try to talk her out of it, it'll only make it worse. Most of the time you wouldn't understand the reason anyway. Just get out of the house, take a walk, escape to your lab if possible, but run." Toby said, still grinning.

"And number two?" K'Narf asked, thinking that Toby was trying to pull his leg.

"House cleaning! When she gets in the mood to clean the house, and you're lucky enough to pick-up on it before she actually starts, run. Only this time you need to go a little farther and be gone a little longer."

K'Narf laughed because Toby was laughing, but he did remember how his grandfather would head for the barn when his grandmother got into a cleaning mood. "And number one?" He asked, beginning to wonder if Toby might actually be serious.

"Shopping!" Toby said, a big grin on his face.

Shopping?" K'Narf repeated, wondering why this should be a problem.

"Yes, if she gets into a shopping mood, and gets you to go with her you will wind up, with her hanging onto your arm so you can't get away, checking out every nook and cranny of every store on both sides of the street or mall or both; this can go on for days! "

"You're not serious?"

"Dead serious, women don't shop like we do. We want something, we go into a store and buy it, or better yet order it over the Internet from the comfort of our office. Not a woman, when she *doesn't know* what she wants she goes shopping! If you even think she might be in a shopping mood, head for the other side of the planet, or in your case get off the planet. That's the best advice I can give you."

Toby, seeing the skepticism in K'Narf's eyes, knew that regardless of his warning K'Narf was going to learn this lesson the hard way. "You said something about trespassing?" He asked, changing the subject.

"Yes." K'Narf said, relieved to get back to a subject he understood. "That's actually why I brought you up here tonight."

"Trespassing?" Toby repeated.

"Yeah, by Snarks." K'Narf said, in a soft controlled tone of voice that brought Toby to full attention.

"Sir?" Toby blurted out, not questioning his automatic assignation of rank.

K'Narf gave Toby a long hard look and then started flashing him pictures of his initial meeting with the Snarks. He flashed him a picture of the large open pit mine over at Ajo Arizona, and overlaid it on the even larger pit the Snarks were working. Then a close-up shot of the long black cigar shaped ship and its two inner-system scouts. Ending with picture sequences that detailed the chase, the missile firing, the oxygen cylinder drop and an expanding crimson fireball.

"Those miserable.... They tried to kill you! But it's our, it's our solar system!" Toby erupted, anger growing with each word he spoke.

"That's putting it mildly." K'Narf said, pleased by Toby's outburst.

"You haven't told anyone else, have you?" Toby stated as much as asked, quickly regaining his composure.

"No, I wanted to talk to you first. T.J. told me about your work with the Israeli Military Intelligence and I wanted your opinion. The Snarks have obviously been mining Pluto on and off for thousands of years. However, they've apparently never used force before and I did catch them off guard."

134

"Yeah, I see what you mean, but it's still our solar system, not theirs!"

"Yes, but we're not exactly in a position to go out there and throw them off." K'Narf said, flashing Toby a cartoon of the two of them trying to pick up the enormous black cigar shaped ship and throw it off Pluto.

"What do you suggest?" Toby asked, shaking his head to get K'Narf's flash out of his mind.

"I'm not quite sure. We need to develop a warning system and eventually a self-defense capability. Being forced to run is not exactly palatable to me." K'Narf said, in a soft controlled tone of voice that sent chills up and down Toby's spine.

"Yes sir." Toby said, again assigning K'Narf the superior rank, even though he was his senior in years. "Besides, your running trick will get you killed sooner or later."

"Would you care to elaborate? And quit calling me sir, name's K'Narf."

"Yes, uh, K'Narf, if your radar detector lit up right now, which way would you run?"

"Why I'd, oh," K'Narf said, giving a long slow whistle. "Since I wouldn't know where they are, it'd be a toss of the dice whether I'd run away from or straight at them."

"Yes sir."

"That settles it, would you help me? I can't let our people start settling the asteroid belt without the ability to protect them."

"Yes sir!" Toby answered, the words 'our people' sending a surge of pride through him he'd never felt before.

"Good!" K'Narf said, pleased that Toby was willing to share the burden of responsibility. "We'll be needing a place to work. That's a huge garage you have, maybe we could convert it into a workable laboratory?"

"Possible." Toby said, the hint of a smile on his face. "But if we're going to check it out, we'd better beat the sun back." He added, flashing K'Narf a cartoon of the Lady racing the Sun across the Nevada desert.

"Hang on!" K'Narf said, as he started slapping power switches.

Toby, who had been lifted gently from the earth by the Lady, was suddenly thrown violently back into his seat and pinned there as his body weight doubled and then tripled as she kicked in three of her five rear drive cores. Then, just as suddenly as the crushing force hit him it ceased, but only for the split second it took K'Narf to flip the Lady around and hit the power switches again as the Lady braked for a landing. "Never again, will I ever, suggest you get a move on!" Toby said, gasping as he realized that they were powered down and sitting quietly in his driveway.

"I wanted you to realize how powerful the Lady's drive cores are, keeping in mind that I only used sixty percent of her main drive capability." K'Narf said, blowing the Lady's cabin pressure.

"I, I didn't realize. It's different than what I'd imagined." Toby said, as K'Narf got out and walked around to unlock his door.

"Now, let's take a look at that garage of yours." K'Narf said, as he opened the door and helped the weak kneed Toby out.

"Maybe my basement would make a better place to work." Toby said, trying to hide a smile.

"Basement? Didn't know you even had one." K'Narf said, stopping to look at Toby, quickly seeing through his attempt to hide something. "Okay, what gives?"

"Come on, I'll show you." Toby said, motioning for K'Narf to follow. Opening the front door he quietly led the way through the house to his small private bar. Moving around behind the bar, he touched a hidden switch and stepped back as the entire section of glass shelving, lined with bottles of liqueur, opened out to reveal a brightly lit stairwell. Standing back he allowed K'Narf to enter first.

Stepping past the grinning Toby, K'Narf walked down into what had to be one of the most modern laboratories in the western world. It was as big underground as the house was above ground. "Well I'll, you've got everything here that...." It was K'Narf's turn to stammer with surprise.

"That freight elevator over there's big enough to bring the Lady down here if you wanted." Toby said, still beaming as he watched K'Narf walk from his chemistry section over to his small machine shop.

"Well, you're right about one thing. Your basement will make a better place to work than the garage." K'Narf said, as he stepped into the large freight elevator Toby had pointed out and pushed the button marked up, forcing Toby to jump in or be left behind.

Three months, nineteen days and many sleepless nights later he punched the same button, only this time the elevator groaned under the strain of lifting what looked almost like a twin sister of the Lady's. Actually she was the fourth van that had been converted. She, like Lady-One, was equipped with the new sealed batteries that effectively doubled their cruising range between charges. She had a built-in sensing system that could pinpoint the originating point of any radar beam thrown at her. She could, in an emergency, release a cloud of metallic particles guaranteed to confuse a simple-minded missile, and if cornered she had a few laser-edged teeth of her own.

"Irena, do you know where Toby went?" K'Narf asked, stepping out of the freight elevator and into the garage where Irena was tinkering with Lady-Two, or with Irena-One as Toby called her.

"Said something about meeting T.J. and split. Didn't even ask if I wanted to go along." Irena pouted.

"T.J.! Where's she been anyway? Every time I've asked about her Toby would just shrug and say 'That's T.J. for you.'"

"Hang on a second and I'll see if I can contact them." Irena said, shutting her eyes and relaxing. "Oh yes!" She suddenly exclaimed, opening her eyes and smiling at K'Narf. "T.J.'s back and Toby wants to have a welcome home party for her."

"Great! Ask them if it would be okay to have it in the whale. That way Rudy and Wanda won't be left out." K'Narf said, remembering how Wanda, like Rudy, had had a panic attack when it became time for her to return to earth. She, again like Rudy, couldn't seem to bear the thought of the gravity well that the earth represented. Rudy, looking at K'Narf and getting his agreement, asked her if she'd like to stay up there with him. She'd quickly agreed, but made it plain to Rudy that she'd have to have her own bedroom and a lockable door. K'Narf nodded at Rudy and they both offered her the bedroom set he'd hauled up for Irena.

It only took them a couple of days to laser cut her out a bedroom next to Rudy's in the kitchen cave, but her lockable door had to wait until the next supply run. She'd been there ever since helping Rudy play host. K'Narf was happy for Rudy and, he had to admit, very pleased by the woman's touch Wanda brought to the whale.

"She says yes, how about twenty-two hundred hours Zulu time. She'll ride up with Toby and meet us there."

"Tell her she's got a date, and tell her I've missed her." K'Narf said, really meaning it as he remembered the sparkle in her black almond shaped eyes.

137

"I want to go too." Piped up Wonder, who'd been standing quietly in the corner listening.

"Not this time Wonder, there won't be enough room." Irena said, dismissing the look on Wonder's face as simple disappointment; mentally selecting a few close friends for the party's guest list.

Seventeen hours later, K'Narf and Irena drove through the second airlock door and drifted out into the whale's jeweled cavern. Dropping the Lady down toward the expanded landing pad area, he noticed that all three of the other copies of Lady were already there plus the dark candy-apple red GMC van that Brent Conrad had built. The crystal tear room was brightly lit, so the party must already be in full swing, he thought. Remembering how Rudy and Wanda had converted it into a socializing room, complete with a small bar and an antique jukebox Brent had found for them.

Taking Irena's hand they made a joint leap for the tunnel entrance, hitting it with perfect precision. Floating the short distance down the tunnel to the crystal tear room they emerged into a room packed with twice as many people as he had expected, and standing in the middle of them was the most beautiful creature he'd ever seen. Everybody seemed to sense that this was a special occasion for K'Narf and T.J. as they floated or walked out of their way.

It was T.J. that much he knew, but his mind couldn't connect his memory of a little old wrinkled up woman with this beautiful, voluptuous, long legged oriental girl. She had a full head of luxurious black hair that cascaded down on her bare shoulders and was wearing a long flowing pink silk evening gown; low cut, backless and slit up one leg clear to her hip fully revealing a leg, no longer twisted and marred by a horrendous scar, but now beautiful with flawless skin and muscle tone.

She looked at him and he realized how perfectly those piercing black eyes of hers now went with the stunningly beautiful face he was staring at. They stood and looked at each other for a long stretched out moment when the hatband effect of the Lord's presence descended. He literally felt his heart take a beat.

Suddenly he was seeing T.J. as a young girl badly wounded and being smuggled out of her home on a cart loaded with dead bodies. Then he saw her as a young woman with her terrible scars and her crippled leg; shunned and avoided by all that saw her. He felt her agony as she grew older and no man would even consider her because of her injuries. He felt his heart take another beat.

Then he saw her meeting an evangelist and accepting the Lord as her savior. He felt both her joys and her sorrows after the Lord removed her filter and she started saving lives, creating the loose knit organization he was now part of and he felt her joy now as she looked at him. Then he felt the Lord open up his own memories and the pain they held as his heartbeat again.

He knew that T.J. was now seeing and feeling his own shame as she looked at his memory lists that he had had to review daily so he wouldn't forget how to use a knife and fork, and the family pictures so if one of them came to visit he would know who they were. The hypnotizing stunt of his brother's and the scene of his coming awake in the hospital after the Lord had removed his filter, and the horrifying realization when he first looked in the mirror and truly saw himself. She felt with him the mortifying shame when he found out that his father had spelled his name in reverse so as not to accidentally insult someone with the name of Frank. He felt her heart take a beat with his own.

Looking at T.J. he mentally reached out his hand, feeling her joy as she accepted it, then turning to the Lord they jointly asked permission to be bonded in a life covenant. It was instantly granted and their hearts beat once more in unison and the Lord was gone and like Toby had said, in an instant, in the space of a single heartbeat they had become one in a covenant that could be broken only by death. Knowing each other now in greater detail and depth than a lifetime of living could accomplish. K'Narf could feel her joy, as he knew she could feel his as he looked across the room and into her eyes.

Everyone in the room knew that an offer had been made and accepted and that they had a new bonded couple on their hands. Then suddenly they all started yelling and grabbing their heads.

"It's K'Narf. He's flashing a fireworks display!"

"It's a fourth of July Grand Finally!" Irena yelled, thinking to stop it by covering her ears.

"T.J. tell him to stop!" They all started yelling at once.

"Emergency!" Toby bellowed, effectively stopping K'Narf's celebration and freezing every other thought in the room. "It's Wonder, she's in trouble!"

139

All of them instantly locked onto the emergency frequency and watched through the eyes of Wonder as a large powerful looking alien spaceship converged on her. She had secretly jury-rigged her little Volkswagen with a drive core and oxygen and was heading for the party.

Before anyone could even gasp a pale green beam snaked out from the alien ship and Wonder and her little car ceased to exist.

Brent Conrad started singing a slow rhythmical Native American death chant. T.J. ran to K'Narf's side as he and Toby locked eyes, and K'Narf sealed his second non-verbal pledge in as many minutes, one a promise of life and one a promise of death.

Chapter Sixteen

"Brent!" K'Narf roared, the unyielding authoritative blast of his voice cutting through the sound of the juke box and the Brent's death chant turned war-cry.

"Sir!" Brent answered, flailing with his arms and legs in an attempt to slow his headlong leap at the exit tunnel.

"Where do you think you're going?" K'Narf asked, in a strong tightly controlled voice.

"They just murdered Wonder! I was taught to... I was... I'm going to do to them what they just did to Wonder!" Brent finally screamed out, catching the edge of the exit tunnel and spinning around to face K'Narf.

"How?" K'Narf asked, holding Brent's reason on the end of a tenuous verbal leash.

"I can take that bloody ship! My lasers burned through over a hundred feet of iron and rock when they cut my airlock tunnel, and they'll punch holes through that monstrosity out there like a piece of cheese!" Brent exploded, ending the longest speech of his life.

"And if she destroys you with her long range weaponry first?"

"Then I'll die a warrior's death!"

"No, only a stupid one." K'Narf said mercilessly, locking eyes briefly with every person in the room.

"You got three seconds!" Brent said, glaring at K'Narf.

K'Narf flashed a picture of Brent's red van attacking the alien ship, visualized the green laser vaporizing it long before Brent got close enough for effective return fire, then showed the aliens backtracking to the whale and methodically cutting her up. "You would sacrifice us all to die like a warrior?"

Seeing the uselessness of his death, and the destruction of his friends cooled the blood in Brent's veins. "No sir, but we just can't let them get away with murdering Wonder." Brent pleaded softly, putting into words what was in everyone's mind.

"The problem is not our ability, or inability, to mount an attack!" K'Narf said, his voice strong and resolute. "But rather the absolute necessity for us to destroy their mother ship with our first retaliatory action, before they can load her up and leave *our* solar system!"

"What mother ship?" T.J. asked, confused. Her question echoed by everyone in the room except Toby.

"Oh." K'Narf said, realizing that only he and Toby were actually aware of the true tactical situation. So, for the second time, he played the mental scenario detailing his initial meeting with the Snarks; filling their minds with the crimson fireball as a climax.

"Aiee!" T.J. cried, hanging onto K'Narf's arm.

K'Narf, taking T.J.'s hands off his arm, walked over to the juke box and pulled it's plug. Plunging the room into an eerie silence, and turned around to face his first real command.

"We have to beat that inner-system ship back to the mine on Pluto, and destroy its mother ship while she's setting on the ground. If we don't and she spaces, she'll vaporize us before we even know we're close to her."

"But how?" Toby asked, thinking K'Narf had just outlined the impossible.

K'Narf's face clouded up for less than a heartbeat, then he smiled and flashed them a picture of possibly the strangest ship ever conceived by an intelligent race, civilized or otherwise. "They like to shoot at little Volkswagens, well let them shoot at that one." K'Narf said, flashing them an action scenario showing two of the strange looking fighters, floating nose down out over the mine on Pluto and slicing the huge mother ship up like a warm loaf of bread with their concentrated golden-hued laser beams.

"Sweet Lord Jesus!" Toby said, giving a long slow whistle of admiration.

"Brent, can you borrow two of those seventy foot long steel power poles and get them up here without being tagged? You know the kind that are tapered."

"Yes sir!" Brent answered, nodding at K'Narf in a manner that said he was accepting his authority and command.

"Oh, before you leave. Rudy, help Brent load up twenty four of those old furniture pads down by the landing pad. We have enough battery capability to last well over a week, and the glow from those mirrors could easily give away our location if spotted. We'll need to cover them until this is over. Could you do that before you leave?" K'Narf asked, looking again at Brent.

Brent simply nodded again, as he and Rudy dove for the exit.

"Irena, can you and Debbie procure two late model Volkswagens like the one Wonder had, modify them for space and get them up here within thirty six hours?" K'Narf asked, flashing them a picture detailing two of the small cars outfitted with batteries, oxygen, four drive cores apiece and a seat modified to accept a fully functional and occupied spacesuit.

"Yes sir!" Irena answered, pointing at the mousy little Debbie and pointing toward the exit tunnel that Brent and Rudy had just dove into.

"Minh Le, we'll need seventy-six of the new modified forklift batteries fully charged." K'narf said, watching as Minh Le dove silently for the exit tunnel, knowing that the batteries would arrive on time.

"Toby."

"Yes sir?"

"We need to keep that inner-system Snark ship hanging around for awhile, think you can play fox?"

"You bet your, uh, yes sir." Toby answered, almost coming to attention.

"I don't want even a close contact, I just want you to tickle their radar scopes enough to get them interested, then lead them around to the far side of the system and as far away from Pluto as you can get them. We need all the time you can give us."

"Yes sir!" Toby said, leaping for the exit tunnel.

"Toby!" K'Narf called out. Stop by your lab on the way back, there'll be a load of equipment ready to pick up."

Toby, grabbing at the edge of the exit tunnel spun around and this time came to full attention, saluted K'Narf and ducked into the tunnel leaving K'Narf feeling lonelier than he'd ever felt in his life.

"Got Brent loaded up and he's gone." Rudy said, poking his head back into the room. "Thanks Rudy, now how about getting Wanda to fix T.J. and I something to eat. Tell her it should be about eighty percent protein, ten percent roughage and plenty of calcium for a chaser."

"What ever you say." Rudy answered, having long ago accepted K'Narf's strange requests as normal.

"Oh, and Rudy. When it's ready, have Wanda bring it over to my bedroom. T.J. and I'll be taking up residence there for the next couple of days."

"Yes sir!" Rudy chortled, winking at T.J. on his way out. At least that request he could understand, he thought, grinning to himself.

"Premo, how about taking Sylvia and start rigging up for those power poles Brent'll be hauling in here tomorrow?" K'Narf asked, flashing them a picture of how he wanted each of the power poles suspended in the middle of the cavern using the yellow nylon rope to hold them in place.

"Sure thing K'Narf, T.J." Sylvia said, answering for Premo as she nodded her head at T.J. with that age old understanding one woman has for another. Then, winking at K'Narf she dove for the exit tunnel, quickly trailed by Premo, leaving K'Narf and T.J. alone.

"K'Narf, I, there's something you, I don't think you...." T.J. stuttered, as she turned her back on K'Narf, unable to look at him.

"What's wrong? Are you all right?" K'Narf asked, turning T.J. around and taking her chin in his hand, trying to make her look up at him.

"No!" T.J. exclaimed, twisting away from his hand and grabbing him around the waist; pressing her face against his chest. "You don't understand!"

"Understand what?"

"I can't just, I've never...." T.J. mumbled into his chest, tears starting to form in her eyes.

"Now take it easy T.J." K'Narf said, putting his arms hesitatingly around her shoulders. "Whatever it is we'll work it out." He added, feeling her panic in his mind.

"You still don't understand!" T.J. cried, squirming under the pressure of K'Narf's arms. "I was only thirteen when a shell exploded in my bedroom and destroyed my leg and ripped apart my body. A servant, faithful to my father, smuggled me out of the palace in a cartload of dead bodies and by His divine grace I survived. The damage to my body healed of its own accord, without the ministrations of a court physician."

"That's been so long ago, I...." K'Narf said, trying to sooth the panic he was feeling in T.J.'s mind.

"I can't just go up to your bedroom with you like this, I just can't, I, I've never known a man before!" T.J. cried, interrupting K'Narf as she pressed herself tighter into his chest, tears dribbling down the velvet smooth skin of her face.

"Up to my bedroom, but I didn't mean, you didn't think I meant for us to, so that's why Rudy and Sylvia were acting funny." K'Narf half-laughed, then blushed as T.J. leaned back in his arms and looked at him with her tear stained face.

"Then exactly why did you want me up in your bedroom?" T.J. asked, somewhat icily.

"We've got to change our bodies so they can withstand a minimum of nine G's of drive and braking thrust for a long continuous period of time. You and I are the only ones that have developed the ability to alter our cellular structure, you obviously being much better at it than I, so I'll be needing your help." K'Narf explained, flashing T.J. a mental picture of what had to be done to their bodies. "And since we'll both require absolute quiet for the meditation period, along with a high protein and calcium intake, I just figured my bedroom would...." He stammered, his nice, neat, logical, explanation stopped by the look on T.J.'s face.

"Are you trying to tell me that I'm going to have to shrivel myself up like an old prune? Do you have any idea what you're asking me to do! I've lived well over a half a century dreaming of having a body like this. Why I, why I spent over three weeks in agony just figuring out how to develop my mammaries." T.J. moaned, cupping her hands protectively over her newly developed breasts. "And you want me to shrivel them up!" She screamed, backing away from K'Narf.

"Now T.J." K'Narf said, holding his hands up in front of him and backing up as T.J.'s eyes began to flash fire.

"You miserable, sub-human, castoff, son of a Neanderthal, get out of here!" T.J. squalled, grabbing a small glass stuffed with red and green straws off the bar and throwing it at him.

K'Narf, ducking the glass, dove for the exit tunnel as the air around him filled with colorful straws. Emerging from the tunnel, his ears thrumming to the angry sounds of an alien tongue and not knowing what else to do, he made a fast mental trajectory calculation and leaped for the kitchen cave and Rudy.

"What the...." Rudy said, as K'Narf came flying into the kitchen opening.

"What have you done to T.J. you brute?" Wanda yelled at K'Narf, not waiting for an answer as she leaped for the kitchen's exit.

"Good question, what did you do to T.J.?" Rudy asked, trying to figure out what the funny look on K'Narf's face meant.

"Nothing! That's the problem, I think."

"Ha! If you're not sure, that means you're a learning!" Rudy chortled. "Sit down; I'll get you some coffee. You look like you need it." He said, chuckling to himself.

Half an hour and two cups of coffee later, Wanda came drifting through the cave's opening in the roof of the kitchen. Doing a neat tuck and roll she landed lightly on her feet. K'Narf stood up, not real sure from the look she gave him that the kitchen was a safe place to be any longer.

"T.J.'s in your bedroom waiting for you. I'll bring the food you ordered over in a few minutes." Wanda said bluntly. "Well don't just stand there, git!" She bellowed, her voice echoing throughout the cavernous whale.

K'Narf, jumping to the lip of the cave's mouth, made a fast mental calculation and leaped for the softly glowing purplish-red orb that marked his bedroom's entrance. Instantly regretting his choice, but totally committed by the force and trajectory of his leap.

Forty hours later, as the inner-airlock opened and allowed Toby to enter the central cavern, a strange sight greeted him. The two seventy foot long steel power poles were trussed up like worms caught in a spider web made of yellow nylon rope and illuminated by six jury-rigged spotlights.

Fourteen feet back from the tip of each pole was mounted what used to be a small Volkswagen, one dark blue, one dark green. Protecting each car was a huge funnel shaped nose cowling made of bulletproof two-way mirror, fanning out from a point on the power poles five feet in front of where the cars were bolted on with explosive charges; an escape clause he hoped they wouldn't have to use.

Toby could see Irena and Sylvia, maneuvering one of the big modified batteries into position on the power pole directly behind the dark green Volkswagen.

"Hey, don't just stand there gawking, we've got seventy-one more of these things to weld in place!" Irena yelled at Toby.

"Good, it'll keep you out of trouble!" Toby yelled back, as he leaped for the kitchen. Almost, but not quite panicking as Irena

146

flashed him a picture of a rearranged kitchen. Even so, he was visibly relieved as he sailed through the entrance and found that the stove had not been moved into his line of flight, and that here wasn't a big pot of boiling water on it.

"Toby!" Wanda said. "Am I glad to see you. Are you all right? You look kinda puny."

"I'm okay, just thought for a second there that I was about to be boiled alive." Toby said, staggering as he caught his balance.

"Boiled what? You're not making sense young'un. Come on over here and sit down, I'll get ya some coffee and something ta eat. Bless that Rudy, he's got me talking just like him." Wanda said, chuckling to herself as she did a fancy half step over to the coffee pot.

"You're going to have to teach me how you do that someday." Toby said, admiring the way Wanda moved around the kitchen, her feet never losing contact with the floor in the light gravity of the whale.

"Do what?" Wanda asked, doing a fancy double two step back to the kitchen table without having a single drop of coffee float out of the cup.

"Move like you do. I've been up here just as long as you have, and I still move around like a klutz in this half-baked gravity."

"Watch your tongue young'un. You're talking about my home!"

"Okay, don't get feisty about it. I'm just a little jealous over the way you and Rudy adapted so easily."

"Yeah, know what you mean. Rudy and I have talked about it some. It's like we were born with a kind of natural rhythm for living up here. Don't rightly understand it ourselves, just know we'd rather die than live back down in that gravity well you call Earth."

"Speaking of Rudy, where is he anyway?"

"He took another round of food over to K'Narf and T.J."

"What do you mean, over to them. Where are they at?"

"Up in K'Narf's bedroom."

"Uh, yeah. Up in his bedroom no less. That's, uh...." Toby stuttered, then started grinning.

"It's not what you're thinking." Wanda said, giving Toby one of her infamous eyeball rolling glares. "They're laying up there like two corpses getting ready for a funeral, eating every six hours and then going back to meditating."

147

"They're what?"

"They are over there transforming their bodies into a form that will be able to withstand the extreme acceleration inherent in the design of those two fighters being built out there." Wanda said, dropping her acquired accent totally and revealing the hardcore intelligence burning underneath.

"I thought I'd be the one to...." Toby said, looking confused.

"So did we all Toby, so did we all." Wanda sighed. "But them two over there done figured out something we ain't yet, and if we're going to catch that murderous space traveling Snark ship on the ground we got'ta move fast."

"Why, why such a hurry? How does K'Narf know when they'll lift anyway?" Toby asked, disappointment at not being chosen to pilot one of the fighters showing in his voice.

"He don't, none of us do. You willing to take the gamble on a slow fighter to Pluto?" Wanda asked, smiling at her play on words.

"No, guess not." Toby said softly.

"Here, eat this and then git out there and help git those things built. We're running out'ta time. I can feel it in my bones." Wanda said, putting a huge bowl of stew down in front of Toby. "I can feel it in my bones." She said, repeating herself in a soft whisper.

Twenty-nine sleepless hours later, Toby was holding onto a yellow guy-rope with one hand and Irena's waist with the other. Both of them were looking at the completed fighters hanging suspended in the floodlights.

They had removed the eight new lasers from the Lady and her three sister vans and welded four of them directly in front of each of the sports cars, thus protecting them with the mirror cowling. Then Brent had attached a nine foot piece of neodymium glass rod to the muzzle of each laser, adjusted the rods so that the beams they transmitted, when fired simultaneously, merged into one extremely potent laser beam exactly two-hundred and ten feet in front of the pointed tip of the fighters. Two hundred and ten feet, the distance K'Narf had specified as the optimum height for the one shot firing pass over the Snarks mother ship, if they could catch her still on the ground.

"Do you know where Brent went?" Irena asked wearily.

"No, he jumped in that red van of his and left right after he tested the firepower and accuracy of the lasers. That was over twenty hours ago!" Toby grumbled, fatigue showing in his voice. "I

148

don't know what he's up to, but he sure ain't sharing his plans with us." He added, too tired to care much one way or the other.

"It's not like Brent to desert us."

"I don't know, he got pretty upset when he found out we couldn't use the lasers he'd built for that van of his."

"Yes he did, didn't he? Do you think he had special feelings for Wonder?"

"Definitely, he was just waiting for her to grow up a little more. I thought everyone knew that." Toby said, his voice registering mild surprise that Irena didn't know what had been driving Brent so hard.

Irena, giving a weary shake of her head and shrugging her shoulders accepted Toby's assessment of the situation. "Ready for some coffee?" She asked.

"Might as well, we can't do any more here." Toby said, pulling them both along the guy-rope toward the cavern wall. "Where are Premo and Sylvia?"

"They collapsed after they installed that last drive core on the blue machine. I think they're in the crystal room."

"Do you know Sylvia's private frequency?"

"Yes, why?"

"Flash her and invite her and Premo to meet us in the kitchen. Minh Le and Debbie are already there." Toby said, as they reached the wall where the yellow rope was anchored with a piton.

"She's awake and they'll be there in a few minutes." Irena said, as she mentally calculated a trajectory for the glowing bright yellow orb that marked the kitchen, planted her feet firmly against the wall and leaped, followed by Toby seconds later.

"K'Narf said seventy-two hours, it's been sixty-nine and the fighters are ready, untested but ready." Toby said to the tired and motley group gathered in the kitchen.

"The lasers have been tested!" Debbie blurted out, then blushed when everyone turned to look at her.

"Yes Debbie, but taking a six by six foot by one-inch sheet of steel and welding nine of those drive cores to it, then bolting it to the base of a seventy foot long tapered steel pole could prove fatal when power is applied."

"But we welded seven sets of braces from that drive plate to the power pole using a fifteen inch spread." Debbie said, glaring at Toby. "And Brent said it would hold" She added stubbornly.

149

Toby, seeing that Debbie's faith was in Brent, and not in the shaky engineering of the drive system, conceded defeat with a nod of his head. "All we need now is K'Narf and T.J., guess I'll go over there and wake them up." He said, flashing Irena a picture of a soon to be empty bed.

"Not if you know what's good for you." Rudy said, pouring fresh coffee.

"You know something we don't?" Toby asked, sipping at the hot coffee.

"Yeah, Thomas and Judy are standing guard over there and anybody fool enough to go in while K'Narf and T.J. are sleeping will wish they hadn't."

"So that's where those cats have been. I was wondering about them. Not that I missed them you understand." Toby said, remembering how many times Thomas or Judy had bounced off of him in mid-flight, changing his trajectory just enough to make him miss his target.

"I know what you mean." Rudy said chuckling. "That's why K'Narf ordered them to stand guard. Made'em feel useful and kept them out of everyone's hair."

"Well, someone's going to have to wake'em up." Toby said, fatigue making him slur his words.

"No need to." Wanda said. "They're awake and on their way over."

Involuntarily they all looked toward the entrance landing area, each of them feeling in their own private thoughts, that K'narf and T.J. had spent three days in bed enjoying themselves while they had collectively done all the work. This very normal and human emotion left them totally unprepared for what dropped into the kitchen.

"Oh my God!" Irena exclaimed, looking at the small bikini clad golden black body that came flying in feet first, landing like one of the cats; followed split seconds later by a bathing suit clad male version showing the same agility in landing. Then, turning as one they faced their small audience, the pupils in their eyes enlarged and glowing a soft golden hue.

"Toby, Wanda tells me that the fighters are ready. Do you agree?" K'Narf asked, turning his large golden eyes full on Toby.

"Uh, yes sir. They're as ready as we can make them without additional time sir." Toby stuttered, involuntarily coming to his feet. "Your, your color, how?"

150

"The golden-black skin color seems to go along with the cellular reconstruction, same with the eyes. Our best estimate at this moment is that we can withstand in excess of ten G's with little or no ill effects."

"But you're so thin!" Irena cried.

"I weigh exactly two-hundred and ten pounds, and T.J. weighs one-hundred and thirty-three."

"But you look so...." Irena stammered. "I mean, what happened to your, you're so...!" She almost cried, half pointing at T.J.'s hard flat chest.

"Skinny?" K'Narf interjected, mentally grunting as T.J. flashed him a private message.

Rudy, being the only normal human in the room, and therefore the only one who still depended heavily on facial expressions and eye contact instead of flashing, correctly read the look T.J. gave K'Narf and knew, by dent of many years of experience, that his adopted son was by no means out of trouble with the fiery tongued T.J.

"That's because we have compressed the cells of our flesh. We weigh roughly twice what we appear to weigh." K'Narf said, looking hard at Irena trying to make her shut up or change the subject. "Premo, would you and Debbie please go get our spacesuits and who has a hairnet or something for T.J.'s hair? It could be fatal if it came loose in her helmet at a critical moment."

"I've got one." Sylvia said, breaking the sense of tension and incredibility that had permeated the room and spurring Premo and Debbie into action.

"She wouldn't need one if she had my hairstyle." Wanda said flashing everyone a picture showing what T.J. would look like with an Afro. A picture that caused everyone in the room, including K'Narf, to do a double take as they realized that with the Afro, T.J. and Wanda looked like sisters.

"She wouldn't need one if she had my hair style either." Rudy chortled, polishing his baldpate. Noticing that T.J. started to laugh, then gave K'narf another icy glance, as the comparative mood was broken.

Thirty minutes later Toby watched, too tired now to be envious as the airlock tunnel slowly swallowed K'Narf's fighter. First the nine foot long pointed snout with its four equally spaced neodymium glass rods disappeared, followed by the eight foot wide mirrored funnel. The dark green Volkswagen with K'Narf's

151

spacesuit barely visible through the darkened windows, two rows of eighteen batteries each covering thirty-eight feet of the fighter's main trunk, and finally the last nine feet of heavy steel struts supporting the six foot square drive plate with its nine exposed drive cores.

The airlock door cycled shut and the little red light winked out. The only evidence of their having been there were the two dozen strands of yellow nylon rope, which disappeared from sight as Rudy turned out the jury-rigged spotlights.

It was up to K'Narf and T.J. now, Toby thought as he flashed Irena a message to meet him in K'Narf's empty bedroom.

Chapter Seventeen

Pluto grew from a faint point of light to a huge pockmarked planet. Only three-fifths of Earth's diameter and one-tenth of her mass; she made a stately revolution every six-point-three-nine days. A fact that stretched K'Narf's considerable mental capabilities; forcing him to calculate her advanced orbit and exact position relative to the Snarks mine since his last visit. It was imperative that they keep the bulk of the planet between them and the mother ship during their approach, doing deliberately what he'd done accidentally the first time.

"T.J., see that large crater off to the right of those three small mountain peaks?" K'Narf asked, vocalizing his mental message as he flashed it and a picture of the crater.

"Yes." Came T.J.'s ethereal reply from the vast seemingly empty space that surrounded him.

"Good, I'll go in first. I'll flash you when I'm down." K'Narf said, diving his fighter at the specified crater. Having separated at the beginning of their flight, due to the very real danger of collision at the sub-light speeds they had attained, he was taking no chances in their final rendezvous.

"Have you in my sights." T.J. said, as she flashed K'Narf a picture of his fighter in the cross hairs of her targeting sight. Then dove her fighter for the crater and K'Narf.

"Just don't *accidentally* push that little purple button." K'Narf flashed back at T.J., thinking of the potent weapon under her control.

"You have nothing to fear from my lasers." T.J. replied, braking her fighter and dropping to the floor of the crater; hovering twenty-five feet off to the left of K'Narf's ship. "What I plan for you will be accomplished with nothing less than my own hands, fingernails and teeth." She added, her voice soft and ominous.

153

"Uh, yeah." K'Narf grunted, remembering only to well T.J.'s ability to claw and scratch. "Isn't there something in the Bible against spousal abuse?"

"Don't worry so!" T.J. said, her voice now light and cheerful. "Maybe the Snarks will get you first. Speaking of Snarks, where exactly are they?" She asked, her tone of her voice changing dramatically again.

"Their mine is on the other side of the Planet, almost directly opposite this crater."

"Do you have a plan of attack?"

"Yes, when I surprised them last time they opened fire from a bubble turret in her forward nose section." K'Narf said, flashing T.J. a picture of the turret and the blunt barrel-like protrusion of the laser cannon. "The mental photograph I took shows a second turret at her other end. It apparently had not been activated last time, however...." He added, not having to verbally state the obvious.

"Okay, I presume you want to take out the turrets first."

"Yes, the split second you clear the ridge start firing at the turret. The second you've neutralized it, flip your ship nose down and start a laser cut about one hundred feet back from the turret itself. I'll be doing the same at my end. If we're successful, she'll be sliced into three sections within three minutes or less. Without major repair facilities that should end her career as a deep space ship."

"How do you know one of sections won't be able to fly?"

"I don't, but if I was going to design a ship like that, I'd build a duplicate control bridge at either end and have my power core buried deep in her belly. What we're doing is effectively cutting off both of her heads." K'Narf said, silently praying that the alien ship had only the two control bridges.

"What about that second inner-system ship you just showed me?"

"If it stays put long enough we'll destroy it. If not, I personally intend to find out just how fast this fighter can go with a full nine G's of thrust." K'Narf said nonchalantly, since he had no sound logical plan to deal with the alien's second inner system fighter, especially if it managed to lift off and join the fight.

"That's what I've always dreamed of." T.J. said sarcastically. "Being at the side of the bravest warrior in all the land as he stands

154

firm against hopeless odds." She added, flashing K'Narf a mental image that impugned his chauvinistic male ego.

"Oww!"

"Cut the clowning." T.J. said, getting serious. "Time to get this show on the road."

"Okay my fair lady, follow me." K'Narf said, as he lifted his fighter up over the edge of the crater.

Moments later, all sounds of joviality and false bravado were gone as he flashed T.J. the information that the ridge on the fast approaching horizon was in fact the rim of the Snark's mine. "Keep it low and move over to your left about fifty feet." He ordered, then, just before they cleared the ridge he flashed her the picture of a small red candy heart that said '*I Love You*' on it. He never received her reply, as they were both suddenly involved in a very deadly game called war.

The alien gunner fired a split-second before K'Narf got within range, but his beam glanced harmlessly off of the heavy mirrored nose cone of K'Narf's ship. He never had a chance to correct his aim to the exact center of the mirrored shield, the only vulnerable spot in the fighter's armor, because K'Narf pressed his little purple button that energized the four lasers simultaneously. The alien gun turret glowed for a hundredth of a second then silently erupted into the soundless vacuum of space.

Seeing a similar glow at the other end of the vast ship out of the corner of his eye, he knew that T.J. had successfully completed the initial step at her end of the monster below them as well.

Swinging his fighter so she was hanging nose down, he quickly adjusted her position to an exact two hundred and ten feet. Then, swinging her sideways, he hit the purple button again, the entire maneuver taking less than five seconds.

The beam ate into the black ship like a huge buzz saw cutting a gigantic tree. K'Narf could see the reddish glow from silent explosions taking place within her, and the foggy mist of escaping atmosphere reminded him of an ancient train blowing steam at the end of its run. Only the mist collecting below him as he reached the halfway mark in his cut wasn't steam, it was life-supporting atmosphere.

He really hadn't expected to catch her with all of her internal bulkheads wide open, but as he neared the three-quarter mark in his cut and she continued to boil out her life giving air, he realized that he was watching the death throes of a mighty ship.

Then her entire forward section slewed sideways and broke away from the main body, rolling about thirty yards before coming to rest. He had successfully cut her head off, the still spewing atmosphere mute evidence of the totalness of his surprise attack. It had taken exactly two minutes and seventeen seconds.

K'Narf did not feel the human emotions of guilt or regret; instead he felt a deep satisfaction at having avenged their killing of Wonder. In an odd way the destruction of the alien ship also exorcised his memory of the time they'd tried to kill him, and the anger that had all but consumed him at the time.

His triumph was short lived, for at that exact instant in time the alien scout lifted and shot his tail off, literally. Their beam cut his fighter in half, slicing through the batteries and power pole just five feet behind his little green Volkswagen.

"Help!" K'Narf screamed, flashing an image of his predicament and firing the explosive bolts that released the Volkswagen simultaneously. Knowing instinctively that it would be suicide to give the alien gunner a steady target by running for it, he started hitting the power switches of the Volkswagen's four separate drive cores in a rapid fire random sequence. The result was a bone jarring zigzagging course that quite resembled a drop of water plunged into a skillet of hot grease.

The alien gunner went quietly insane as his beams chased the bouncing Volkswagen all over the crater's floor. It was this single-minded concentration that cost him his ship and his life.

T.J., at the far end of the huge starship was just finishing her cut, with the same grisly results K'Narf had seen when she heard his cry for help. Stopping her cut just short of total decapitation, she lifted and headed for the one-sided fight going on at the other end of the crater. The sight that greeted her was almost beyond her already distorted sense of reality, for hanging just fifteen feet above the alien scout was a dark red van pouring the full force of its twin laser beams into the center of the alien ship. Below, at almost ground level was the ridiculous sight of a very little green Volkswagen playing hopscotch with a deadly pale green beam of cold fire.

Then, seemingly in slow motion, the alien laser flickered and went out and the alien fighter erupted, blowing her guts upward forcing the red van to shoot sideways, barely avoiding certain death. Then, like the baby behemoth that she was, the alien ship plunged to the floor of the crater below.

156

"K'Narf, are you all right?" T.J. asked, flashing the question on the emergency frequency so the stranger in the red van could hear them. Stranger, she thought, it had to be Brent Conrad, who else could it be.

"Yes, I think so."

"Thank God!" T.J. exclaimed, sending him a private picture of a little red candy heart with '*I love You Too*' written on it.

"Brent!" K'Narf suddenly roared, seeing the red van hanging over the wrecked ship.

"Yes sir."

"What in the.... How'd you get here?"

"I uh, I left a little while before you did and I...."

"How long have you been here?"

"I arrived just as you began your cut on that black monster. Then when that inner system fighter lifted I saw my chance to help. Why?" Brent asked, effectively ending the inquisition into his unexpected presence.

"You could have got us all killed! That's why! I ought to...."

"You might try thanking him for saving your worthless hide!" T.J. said, interrupting K'Narf's tirade with a picture of exactly what Brent had done.

"Oh... I didn't realize...." K'Narf stammered, the anger in his voice instantly dissipating. "I guess I owe you...."

"Hey! I just saw something climb into the middle section of that monster." Brent yelled, as he dove his van toward a landing spot right where the severed head section had been. Then, blowing his atmosphere he leaped out of the van and ran for the exposed passageway the alien had disappeared into.

"K'Narf!" T.J. screamed. "Help Brent, he went in after that alien."

"Which passage?" K'Narf asked, jumping his little green Volkswagen over next to where Brent had set his van down.

"The second one up from the bottom on the left side." T.J. answered, flashing K'Narf a picture of the exact opening that Brent had climbed into.

"You get out of here in case that second fighter comes back!" K'Narf ordered, jumping out of his car and climbing up to the indicated opening and charging in. "Brent, where are you?"

"Ssshhh!" Brent replied. "Put your helmet against the bulkhead. Can you hear anything?"

"Yes, just then. There it goes again. He's smashing something." K'Narf flashed back.

"Yeah, that's how I got it figured too." Brent mentally whispered. "I think he's in this...."

"What's happening?" K'Narf asked, moving carefully down the dark corridor.

"I caught him!" Brent yelled. "I'm shining his light out the door, can you see it?"

"Yes, I'm on my way!" K'Narf yelled, running toward the beam of light coming from a room about fifty feet ahead on the right side.

"He stopped struggling after he got a good look at me." Brent said, as K'Narf entered the room, and spotted Brent's large familiar spacesuit holding a creature that appeared considerably smaller than him, mainly due to its skintight blue-green spacesuit and small fishbowl glass helmet.

Stepping over to them K'Narf's boots crunched what appeared to be shattered glass, then their small captive startled them both. Taking one look at K'Narf he started screaming silently into his helmet, his face contorted into a mask of pure terror. Surprising Brent with a violent twist of his body he threw his head at a steel column. The powerful blow cracked his helmet and they both watched helplessly as the little man's life giving air hissed out, his face holding the image of terror even in death.

"What...?" K'Narf asked, looking at Brent.

"I don't know. He took one look at you and committed hari-kari."

"But why?"

"Your guess is as good as mine, unless it had something to do with your eyes."

"What about my eyes?"

"They're glowing, kinda like a cat's eyes at night." Brent said, looking down at the fear-contorted face of the dead alien. Noticing too the fancy gold markings on his shoulders and the emblem on his chest.

"Well, we'll never know now. What was he so interested in smashing?" K'Narf asked, looking around the room.

"Looks like a storage room of some kind." Brent said. "Look at these cylinders, they all have markings etched on the ends kind of like a library book." Brent said, pointing at the round end of one of the cylinders.

"The ships library!" K'Narf exclaimed, looking around the room at what looked like thousands of etched ends sticking out of their cubbyholes. "Do you see a machine that these cylinders fit on?"

"Yeah, over here, but we don't have time to...."

"Can you disconnect it?"

"Think so." Brent said, taking a quick look at the machine. "I'd have to go get my tool kit though, why?"

"Go! No wait, take some of these with you first." K'Narf said excitedly, as he started snapping cylinders out of their cubbyholes and stacking them in Brent's arms, each one close to two inches in diameter and about ten inches long.

Brent, realizing what K'Narf had in mind, picked up his air of excitement and ran for the exit being very careful, as he leaped for the ground and ran to his van, not to break any of the cylinders. Placing them carefully on the van's carpeted floorboard he unhooked his toolbox and ran back toward the severed passageway and the galactic library, almost colliding with K'Narf on his way out with an armload of the glass cylinders.

Twenty minutes later he had the viewing device disconnected and loaded in the van. K'Narf had just headed back to get another armload of the cylinders, so he quickly removed a large round metal object he had strapped into the passenger's seat, grabbed what looked like a piece of a tree and started running diagonally away from the alien ship.

K'Narf coming out of the alien ship moments later, laden down with a full armload of cylinders, spotted Brent about a hundred yards away on his knees digging in the dirt. At least that's what it looked like with all the dust flying from his hands. "Brent! What are you doing? This is no time to play in the dirt! Get back over here!"

"Okay, I'm coming." Brent said, standing up and then strangely, to K'Narf's eyes anyway, he started walking backward swinging his arms and stirring up a small cloud of dust as he moved.

"What were you doing, and what's that?" K'Narf asked, pointing at the thing in Brent's hand as Brent finally turned around and ran the last few yards back to the van.

"Piece of sagebrush." Brent said, tossing it into the back of the van. "Needed it to brush out my footprints." He added, as he turned and started running for the alien ship.

"I don't know how to tell you this, but I think they're going to know we were here!" K'Narf yelled, as he ran to catch up with Brent. Thirty-seven minutes later they loaded the last of the cylinders into the back of the van. "Let's get out of here!" K'Narf said, excitement still marking his voice as he climbed into the red van's passenger seat.

"What about your ship?"

"T.J.!" K'Narf called out. "Where are you?"

"Right over here, darling." Came T.J's voice, flashing K'Narf her location in the shadow of the dead ship.

"I thought I.... Oh, never mind! Do you have enough power left to melt all three pieces of my ship and still get home?" K'Narf asked, referring to the little green Volkswagen as the third piece.

"Yes dear." T.J. said sweetly.

"Then do it, we'll meet you at the crater by the three mountain peaks!" K'Narf said, flashing Brent a mental map of directions to the crater. "Look around for a natural cave or something." He said moments later, as he opened the van's door and hung his head out in order to better scan the area as they dropped into the three peaks crater.

"What for?"

"We can't haul all of these cylinders back in one trip, we'd break too many of them. I want to hide most of them until we can safely transport them."

"How about over there?" Brent asked, pointing at what appeared to be a cave at the crater's edge.

"Perfect." K'Narf said, stepping into the small cave moments later. "Let's get them in here." He added, stepping out just as T.J. arrived in her fighter.

"Stay up there and stand guard." K'Narf ordered, as T.J. started to land.

"Yes dearest!" T.J. replied sweetly on the common frequency so Brent could hear.

"Hey K'Narf!" Brent called excitedly. "Look at this one." He added waving frantically for K'Narf to come over as he was carefully arranging the ones they had decided to take with them on the van's floorboard.

"What is it?"

"Look at the inscription on this one."

"Why, I can't read it." K'Narf said, looking askance at Brent as he took the cylinder from him.

160

"This one you can." Brent said, grinning through his faceplate.

"You got to be kidding!" K'Narf said, staring in unbelief at the etched end of the cylinder. "Check the others and see if they're anymore marked like this."

"Will someone please tell me what's going on?" T.J. pleaded. "What did you find Brent?"

"One of the cylinders has our solar system etched on it."

"Are you sure it's ours?" T.J. asked.

"Unless there are two systems around with our exact number of planets and orbits, especially Pluto's." Brent said, referring to Pluto's odd elliptical orbit as he flashed T.J. a picture of the etching on the end of the cylinder.

"Okay." K'Narf said, climbing into the van and closing his door. "We can strap the rest down with our suits after you get the van's atmosphere recharged." He added, holding the solar system cylinder in his lap.

"Yes sir." Brent said, locking the van's doors electrically, opening the air valves and lifting off at the same time.

"Let's go!" K'Narf said, wondering why Brent was barely moving at less than a G of thrust.

"Just a second, I need to check a few signals."

"Signals. What signals?" K'Narf asked, as he watched Brent doing something with a hand held computer device.

"Good." Brent said, hitting switches and taking off at a three G thrust.

"Yes, let's go home." K'Narf sighed, deciding to ignore Brent's odd behavior as he settled back and started taking off his suit. "T.J., you take the lead, say about three hundred miles or so." He ordered.

"Whatever you say, darling." T.J. half-whispered over the common frequency. The sweet tone of T.J.'s voice made Brent, who had been raised with three sisters and therefore considerably versed in the ways of women, shudder, as he glanced over at the seemingly unsuspecting K'Narf. Then orienting himself, he pointed his van towards the whale and home.

Chapter Eighteen

"Toby, where are you?" K'Narf flashed, the second Brent's van cleared the whale's airlock.

"In the kitchen." Toby flashed back.

"We need to talk. Stay there we'll be right over." K'Narf flashed, as Brent very gently set his van down on the landing pad, extremely conscious of the fragile glass cylinders in the van's cargo bay.

"We?" Toby asked.

"Yes, I'm with Brent. I'll explain when we get there." He flashed. "You need to come with me." He said, turning to Brent. "Toby's waiting for us in the kitchen."

Brent nodded his head in agreement and then, in what seemed to K'Narf to be a single motion, exited the van, squatted and leaped at the kitchen's opening. Leaving K'Narf scrambling to catch up.

"Where's T.J.?" Was Toby's first question as K'Narf sailed into the kitchen.

"She should be moving into the airlock right about now. Don't worry, she's just fine." K'Narf said, dropping toward the floor.

"If you call being mad as a wet hen just fine." Brent said, landing and quickly stepping aside so K'Narf could land.

"Mad. Why's T.J. mad?" Toby asked, looking at Brent and then at K'Narf as they left the kitchen's landing zone and moved very carefully toward him; trying not to bounce off the floor in the whale's light gravity. "You look a lot better." He added, getting a good look at K'Narf.

"Yes, my eyes stopped glowing yesterday and my face is starting to fill out a little." K'Narf said, talking about the changes his body was going through as it began to return to normal.

"What's wrong with T.J.?" Toby asked again, still worried about her.

"Don't worry about T.J., she'll be okay." K'Narf said, noticing that the kitchen had been changed around to accommodate a newly cut doorway. "What's that?" He asked, pointing at the doorway.

"It's a conference room. Gave us something to do while we were waiting." Toby said, accepting K'Narf's explanation about T.J. as he headed for the new doorway followed closely by K'narf and Brent.

"But how?" K'Narf asked, stepping into a large carpeted room with a long highly polished mahogany table, surrounded by no less than fifteen extremely comfortable looking chairs.

"We cut the room out with hand lasers. Minh Le did the carpet work and Premo and Sylvia provided the table and chairs. We thought you might need something like this when you got back."

"Assuming we'd come back."

"To many people praying for you not to come back." Toby said seriously. "Now, what happened?"

"We'll get to that in a moment. Right now I need to know how much power's left in the batteries?" K'Narf said, changing the subject.

"Not much, Rudy's been feeding us cold cuts. Only thing he'll use the stove for is making coffee. Even turned off the grow-lights on his garden." Toby said, knowing what K'Narf was driving at.

"That's what I thought. I'm afraid we're going to have to abandon the whale until we've taken out that second fighter. We need energy and there's no way we can uncover those solar mirrors with that thing running around loose." K'Narf said, thinking about what this would do to Rudy and Wanda.

"That shouldn't be necessary." Brent said, instantly getting K'Narf and Toby's full attention.

"You know something we don't?" K'Narf asked, glancing quickly at Toby who gave him an *"I don't know anything"* look.

"Well, I know that fighter landed next to it's mother ship about an hour ago, and considering the mess you left there she probably won't be lifting off for several days at the very least." Brent said.

"Out with it! Talk!" K'Narf and Toby said in unison.

"Okay, okay, I placed a motion sensor pointed at their landing spot when I was out there and I received a signal from it

163

just a little over an hour ago." Brent said, a grin tugging at the corners of his mouth. "As soon as we unload my van I can skip outside and take the covers off the mirrors and get the batteries charging again." He added, trying very hard not to laugh at the expression on their faces.

"A motion sensor." K'Narf said, repeating what Brent had said. "Will you be able to tell when it lifts off too?"

"Yes." Brent said, giving a direct answer to K'Narf's question. "I'll also be able to tell you exactly where it's at once it does take off." He added, taking a slight step away from the two of them as he spoke.

"How?" Toby asked, beating K'Narf to the question.

"I planted a highly magnetized tracking device in the ground where they land that thing. When they take off it will be firmly attached to the fighter's underbelly and will send out a tracking signal every hour on the hour."

"How did you know where they would land it?"

"Read the ground. They've been landing that thing in the same exact place for thousands of years. Even wore a trail between it and the mother ship where they walked back and forth." Brent said, flashing them a picture of what the ground looked like.

"What if they spot it, your tracking device that is?" Toby asked, again beating K'Narf to the question.

"It can only be spotted by someone looking at it when they lift off, and K'Narf and T.J. made sure that there's no one left alive to do that."

"That's why you were brushing the ground." K'Narf exclaimed, flashing Toby a picture of Brent doing just that. "You couldn't risk them following your footprints and finding it. Wait a minute; you said you could tell us exactly where it was in space. A tracking signal can't do that in dimensional space." He added, thinking he'd found a flaw in Brent's thinking.

"It can if you have at least six directional sightings on the tracking signal. I seeded all of the space around the whale and our approach to earth last week before I headed for Pluto. There are currently two hundred active solar-powered directional tracking relays protecting us and I have five hundred more on order. If that thing comes anywhere near us we'll know it in plenty of time to cover up the mirrors and disappear, at least until we're ready to fight." Brent said soberly, answering K'Narf's concern as fully as he thought necessary.

164

"Let me get this straight, you are going to be able to tell us exactly where that fighter is, whether it's in space or parked on Pluto." K'Narf said, glancing at Toby to see if he agreed.

"You guys are kinda slow, but as they say you're worth waiting on." Brent said, taking another slight step away from the two of them, turning and diving across the long conference table as they made a grab for him. Scrambling to the other end of the room he seated himself in a chair and scooted up to the table, grinning from ear to ear.

"There's only one way out of this room and we're blocking it." K'Narf said, getting a positive nod from Toby, then turning so Brent couldn't see his lips move he added in a whisper. "Question is, should we promote him to head of security, hurt him, or both?"

"Both!" Toby said, looking over at Brent with his little *'got'cha smile'*.

"Here's the deal!" K'Narf said, turning his face back toward the still smiling Brent. "You can try to exit this room without getting seriously hurt, or you can accept our offer of a staff position as Head of Security. Staff protocol does not allow us to hurt you if you're one of us!" He added, making up the rules as he talked.

Brent, looking at K'Narf and Toby realized they were serious, hopefully only about promoting him. "On one condition." He said, getting serious himself. "I want to lead the attack on that fighter when the time comes."

"Staff officers plan fights, they don't do the fighting." K'Narf said, thinking fast again. The last thing he needed was to lose his new security chief in a high-risk attack.

"You did!"

"I had no choice!" K'narf said angrily.

"Neither do I!" Brent said forcefully, knocking his chair over as he stood up.

"On one condition." K'Narf said, quickly calming down as he remembered the feelings Brent had had for Wonder.

"What condition?" Brent asked, calming down as well.

"That you will give me your word of honor that in the future, no matter how badly you may want to get into the action, you will not do so unless you have my explicit permission." K'Narf said, sounding every inch a Commander in charge. "Do I have your word?"

"You miserable piece of space trash!" T.J. squalled, spotting K'Narf as she entered the new conference room. "What's going on

165

in here?" She asked, lowering her voice upon seeing Brent at the far end of the room glaring at K'Narf and Toby. "Are you two bullying Brent? Brent, are they picking on you?"

"Do I?" K'Narf asked again, ignoring T.J.'s angry entrance as he maintained eye contact with Brent.

"Yes sir." Brent said, answering K'Narf. Then turning to look at T.J. he acted like he was going to cry and said. "They're going to hurt me if I try to leave and, and I need to go to the bathroom."

"You big bullies!" T.J. said, hitting Toby because he was the closest. K'Narf immediately dove across the table and made a grab for Brent, who was instantly well out of reach and heading for the now unguarded door. "What happened to that protocol stuff?" He yelled, as K'Narf slid off the end of the table knocking chairs over as he fell.

"Protocol, what's he talking about?" T.J. asked, watching as Brent disappeared into the exit tunnel; realizing that Toby was just standing there grinning as she hit him again.

"Brent just agreed to oversee security." Toby said, looking down at the diminutive T.J. with her dark ebony skin and still glowing eyes, then flashed her a speeded up synopsis of what had just happened.

"Protocol huh, he's the one that needs the protection of protocol!" T.J. said, glowering at K'Narf who was struggling to get up off the floor. "Where is everybody anyway?"

"It's the Sabbath. You caught everyone sleeping I think." Toby said, closing his eyes for a second. "They're all awake, dressed and heading this way." He added, having flashed everyone.

"Sabbath?" T.J. asked, not understanding how it could be the Sabbath.

"Considering all the time zones involved, we decided to use Zulu time here in the whale." Toby explained, flashing T.J. a current image of the international clock called Zulu by the military.

"Good, less than ten minutes left. We need to have a *real* meeting!" T.J. said, stressing her words as Premo and Sylvia came into the room. "Take a seat if you can find one that hasn't been knocked over." She added, her voice and words letting everyone know that the battle was still on between her and K'Narf.

Minutes later, with everyone seated including Brent who had just returned, T.J. checked the Zulu clock in her mind. "Good, the Sabbath is over." She said, and then added. "K'Narf, since this is your meeting, would you like to bring it to order." The sweetness in her voice sending chills down the spines of everyone in the room except K'Narf.

"Uh, yes, uh, let's see." K'Narf mumbled. "We need to let everyone know what happened and what we need to do immediately." He added, noticing that everyone in the room was staring at him.

"Okay, tell us what happened." Sylvia said, trying to give K'Narf a little help. "Did you get their mother ship?"

"Yes, I'll go first, then T.J." K'Narf said, his voice getting stronger as he pointed at T.J. "Then Brent can finish up with his version." He added, getting a surprised look from almost everyone when he mentioned Brent.

"Brent?" Sylvia asked, looking down the table at Brent.

"Yes, I'll let him tell you why. You might also be interested to know that Brent just accepted the newly created position of *Head of Security*." K'Narf said, stressing the title as he started flashing everyone on the common frequency exactly what had transpired from his personal point of view of the fight and the finding of the alien library. Followed immediately by T.J., and then by Brent.

"Oh my God!" Irena cried, those poor people. "They didn't have a chance."

"Neither did Wonder, remember!" Premo said angrily, his baldhead shining with sweat. "Now, tell me more about that viewer and those scrolls." He added, looking down the table at Brent.

"We can bring them in here right now, if it's all right with K'Narf and Toby." Brent said, still not too sure of his new position.

"Good, I've got a pretty good background in electronics. Maybe I can help you get it working." Premo said, getting up from the table even though K'Narf had not dismissed the meeting.

"Are we done K'Narf?" T.J. asked, briefly putting the meeting back into K'Narf's control.

"Yes, let's get that viewer and those cylinders in here, and remember they're glass so don't break any of them!" K'Narf ordered, as everyone started standing up and heading for the exit tunnel. "Toby let's go take the covers off of those mirrors before we find ourselves sitting in the dark." He added, moving toward the exit himself.

Chapter Nineteen

"Well?" K'Narf asked, looking over Brent and Premo's collective shoulders.

"Give us another couple of hours and we'll be ready to plug it in." Premo said, shushing Brent with his eyes before he could protest. "Why don't you go back to the kitchen and have another helping of Wanda's apple pie. You still look like an undernourished teenager."

"What do you mean? I'm almost back to normal." K'Narf said. "I've been eating ever since...."

"Yeah, I know." Brent said, cutting K'Narf off in mid-sentence. "I brought enough food to last me over three weeks, and you ate every crumb of it in the first three days out from Pluto."

"Sylvia told me that you described each and every bite to T.J. before you ate it. Is that true?" Premo asked, chuckling.

"Boy is it!" Brent said. "I've never heard a woman that mad before. She kept flashing Mandarin at us. It was the weirdest thing, kind of like being in the middle of a firefight without a foxhole." He added.

"She's just a little upset because I'm almost back to normal and she's still, uh, underdeveloped."

"That would be one way of putting it." Brent said, grinning at K'Narf. "But you're wrong about her being just a little upset. She's out there in the kitchen with Sylvia and Wanda describing exactly what she's going to do to you."

"Yeah, in color and with sound effects." Premo added.

"She does like to carry on, doesn't she." K'Narf said, an odd smile on his face. "You say it'll take you several more hours?"

"Yeah." Premo said, giving Brent another shushing look.

"Okay, just be sure and yell the second you get that viewer working." K'Narf said, as he turned and headed for the kitchen.

"Yes sir." Premo said, turning his concentration back to the delicate alien circuitry.

"Why did you tell him it'd take us hours; we're almost ready to give it a try."

"Because with him breathing down our necks, it would take us hours." Premo said, sweat making his baldhead shine.

"Ladies." K'Narf said cheerfully, as he carefully walked into the kitchen, trying very hard not to float off the floor and make a fool of himself. "Any of that delicious apple pie left?"

"No, it's all gone!"

"T.J.!" Wanda scolded. "There's plenty left K'Narf. You just set yourself down and I'll get you a nice big double helping."

"The air in here seems to have turned foul, Rudy. Are you sure you put all the garbage on your compost heap?" T.J. asked, standing up and leaping at the kitchen's exit.

"Lord have mercy!" Rudy said, looking at K'Narf and chuckling.

"K'Narf, why don't you two kiss and make up?" Sylvia asked. "Then maybe the rest of us could relax and go back to enjoying ourselves."

"Yeah!" Rudy and Wanda chimed in.

"Kiss! Make up! You've got to be kidding. Me, with a skinny little kid like that!" K'Narf cried around a mouthful of apple pie, flashing them a picture on the common frequency of him as a big handsome muscular individual, standing next to a caricature of T.J. as an extremely skinny, obviously underdeveloped little girl with bow legs.

"Aiiee!" Came a loud mental scream of rage across everyone's mind.

"Rudy, mind if I use your bedroom. I'd like to grab a few winks while they're working on that viewer." K'Narf asked, standing up as he shoved the last bite of apple pie into his mouth.

"What's wrong with your bedroom.... Oh, never mind. I get it. Go ahead, and I'd lock the door if I was you, too." Rudy said, pointing at the bedroom door he had put in to protect himself from Thomas and Judy. They had quickly learned that Rudy couldn't flash a picture of the two of them being doused with a bucket of water if they jumped on him while he was sleeping.

"Thanks Rudy." K'Narf said, heading for Rudy's bedroom and shutting it's door behind him.

"Can I ask a question?" Rudy asked, looking at Wanda and Sylvia.

"Sure."

"Isn't T.J. a little old for K'Narf?" Rudy asked, looking directly at both ladies. "I mean she had to be in her eighties before she changed herself, and I doubt if K'Narf's even turned nineteen yet." He added, noticing that both Wanda and Sylvia seemed to be uncomfortable with his question.

"Sylvia and I've talked quite a bit about this, actually" Wanda said, nodding at Sylvia in a way that said the problem of answering Rudy's question was hers. "I haven't told you about it because, well, the time never seemed just right and I didn't want to embarrass you." She added, looking at Rudy in a way that made him uncomfortable.

"Embarrass me?" Rudy asked, not liking the way the conversation had turned, nor in the way they were both looking at him now.

"Rudy, the Bible and most insurance statistics say that the average lifespan for the human race is about seventy years. Do you agree?" Wanda asked, her voice very soft and gentle.

"Yeah, I remember reading that somewhere." Rudy said, not sure what Wanda was driving at.

"How long in years do you think we can live, and by we I mean all of us, K'Narf, T.J., Sylvia, me, all of us now that we know we can repair our bodies?" Wanda asked, quickly getting to the crux of the situation.

"I don't know, I haven't thought about it?" Rudy said, being honest.

"We have, and we don't know either but we think we can live at least thirty thousand years, maybe much more." Wanda said, watching Rudy very closely as what she had said sank home.

"You're immortal!" Rudy exclaimed.

"No, definitely not immortal. We're just going to live an awful lot longer than you and the other normals down on earth." Wanda said, her eyes beginning to get wet as she looked at Rudy. It was obvious to Sylvia, and everyone else, that Wanda was in love with Rudy.

"Then T.J. and K'Narf are...."

"Yes!" Sylvia said, taking over for Wanda. "On the scale of years we're looking at, they are nothing but very young teenagers. In fact we're all nothing but teenagers and we're growing up without any adult supervision or adult wisdom." She added, putting into words what Rudy was just beginning to realize.

170

"That explains an awful lot." Rudy said, understanding now why Wanda's eyes were watering. He'd known how she'd felt about him for quite a while now, and he also knew in his heart that the feeling was mutual. Now there was this humongous age difference between them. The problem, he suddenly realized, wasn't the age difference between T.J. and K'Narf; it was the one between him and Wanda.

"Hey!" Premo yelled, sticking his head out of the conference room's tunnel. "We've got the viewer working if anyone's interested. Flash everyone will you?" He asked, looking at Sylvia as he ducked back into the tunnel.

"When's Toby and Irena due back?" K'Narf asked moments later, as he entered the conference room. "They should be here for this."

"They just turned back for something T.J. needs." Sylvia said, her face relaxed and her eyes closed, indicating that she was in communication with them at that exact moment.

"They what?" K'Narf asked, turning sharply to look at Sylvia.

"Don't get excited K'narf. They had just barely lifted and it won't take Irena long to go back and pick up a little something for T.J." Sylvia said, grinning over at Premo with a look that said "ask me later".

"What's so important that they had to go back for it?" K'Narf insisted.

"I don't know, T.J. didn't tell me and I didn't ask." Sylvia lied, leaning over Premo's shoulder, trying to get a better look at the flickering screen he was working on.

"T.J.!" K'Narf scolded. "What was so important that Toby and Irena had to turn back to get it?"

"Wouldn't you like to know!" T.J. said, glaring at him.

"Would you two please knock it off!" Premo said, emphasizing the word *please*. "We're trying to get this blinking thing to focus, and your fussing ain't making it any easier."

"Only thing worse than two love birds cooing is two love birds squabbling." Brent said, looking up from the flickering colors of the small screen.

"Hey, what's that?" K'Narf asked, instantly forgetting T.J. and her secret as the small screen cleared and flashed a picture of an alien scout ship like the one Brent had shot down and like the one still running loose.

171

"I think this is the technical manual for that scout ship." Premo answered. "And if we can't figure it out with spoken, written and pictorial examples in front of us, well...."

"I don't hear anything." T.J. said, remarking on Premo's statement about spoken examples.

"That's because Brent's got the only earplug stuck in his ear."

"Oh Brent!" T.J. cried. "Let me listen."

"Uh, okay." Brent said, as he reluctantly pulled the earplug from his ear, wiped it off and handed it over to T.J. and then leaped for the conference room's exit.

"Brent, I didn't mean to...." T.J. yelled at Brent's retreating back, feeling hurt by his abrupt departure after handing her the earplug. Then, following her own natural curiosity she plugged in the earplug. "He sounds like an excited Chinese farmer chasing a chicken thief." She said, referring to the speaker in the earphone.

"He?" Premo asked. "How do you know it's a he?"

"I'm more interested in how she knows what a mad Chinese chicken farmer sounds like." Wanda said grinning.

"I don't know." T.J. said, ignoring Wanda. "It just sounds like a he."

"Here, let me listen to it." K'Narf said, holding out his hand, his face registering mild surprise when T.J. smiled and handed the earplug to him, squeezing his hand slightly in the process.

"Sounds more like a gaggle of geese fighting over a field mouse. I, uh...." K'Narf grunted, as Thomas landed on his right shoulder, followed a split-second later by Judy on his left shoulder.

"If you're going to play with your cats, let me have the earplug." Premo said, reaching over and taking the small instrument out of K'Narf's hand.

"Hey, I wasn't...."

"Well, you weren't listening to it."

"Yeah, but I...."

"Let me have it." Brent said, charging back into the room. "I've got the speaker out of my van." He added, as he took the earplug from Premo's hand and proceeded with rapid movements to cut, strip and wire in the small speaker.

The chittering sound of the alien instructor's voice issuing from the small speaker had the instant, almost chilling effect, of silencing all of the various conversations that had been taking place in the room.

172

"Sounds like a...."

"Shussh!" Three male voices said in unison, as Brent, Premo and K'Narf crowded around the small viewing screen with T.J. and Sylvia leaning over their shoulders.

"That's more than an inner system scout; that's a highly sophisticated fighting ship."

"How in the world did you knock one of those out of action?" Premo asked, looking questioningly at Brent.

"They were so busy trying to nail K'Narf that they didn't see me, why?"

"Impossible!" Premo exclaimed, looking intently at the small screen. "Look at the way she's manned. There is no way that you could have done what you...."

"Unless it wasn't manned by a full five man crew." K'Narf said, pointing at the screen and crossing out two of the positions with his forefinger.

Wanda, who had been so rudely shushed a few minutes earlier, motioned to Rudy that she was going back to the kitchen. Rudy, taking a look at the group of Glow-heads clustered in front of the alien-viewing machine, shook his head and followed her.

"Let's fix some sandwiches." Wanda said, as they entered the kitchen.

"Sandwiches?"

"You don't think your gon'na get any of that crew to leave their new toy long enough to eat a proper meal do you?" Wanda asked, laughing at the look on Rudy's face.

Rudy, putting the lid on a big bowl of sandwiches, picked it up and headed for the conference room. He'd lost track of how many bowls of both hot and cold food, plus the unending stream of coffee he'd hauled into that room in the last five days. Not to mention the dirty dishes he'd had to haul out.

Toby and Irena had become part of the study group immediately upon their arrival; joined off and on by Wanda who, Rudy knew, stayed away from that elite core of Glow-heads only out of loyalty to him. Especially since her ability with the alien language was surpassed only by Brent, who seemed to grasp its strange nuances and meanings like a second tongue.

They were all excited by the massive amount of information on the glass scrolls, and particularly by the fact that K'Narf's drive cores were based on the same scientific principle and natural laws that the alien drive was, except that K'Narf's cores were more efficient on an energy-to-power conversion ratio. At least that was the case if he could believe all the hoo-rawing he received when they figured it out.

"Hey Rudy!" K'Narf called out, when Rudy stepped into the total disaster area that had once been his clean and very dignified conference room. "We're about to decipher the solar system scroll. Would you like to join us?"

"Why? I can't understand any of that foreign talk." Rudy said gruffly. "Besides, I thought you'd already done that."

"Not yet!" Irena said petulantly. "K'Narf wouldn't let us work on it until we'd deciphered all thirty of those stupid technical manuals!" She added vehemently, glaring at K'Narf.

"You can't blame K'Narf for that." Toby said. "We all agreed to save that scroll for last."

"I didn't!" Irena fired back, turning on Toby. "And it was his idea so I'll blame him if I want to." She added, her face puckering up in a pout as everyone started laughing at her.

"It's ready to roll, K'Narf." Premo said, indicating that the solar system scroll was locked into the viewing device.

"Okay, turn it on." K'Narf said, as a hush fell over the small room.

"That's the earth all right." Premo said, stating the obvious. "But the continents don't look right." He added as the alien cameraman focused in on a beautiful blue planet with some slightly scattered cloud cover.

"Yes, I see what you mean. If that's Europe and that's Africa, then that's got to be the Mediterranean Sea." Toby said, pointing at the screen. "But it's dead center on the equator." He added, pointing at the two opposing polar caps.

"Yeah, and look how green it is." T.J. said, pointing out the fact that the entire area they knew as the Middle East was covered with the deep lush green growth of rain forest.

"What's he saying?"

"This is the planet where they found the talking animals."

"Talking animals?" Irena asked, throwing a questioning look at Brent.

"Yes, he said it again; talking animals he calls them. He's noting how they look just like them; but that they have very short lives and their brains don't retain information without considerable effort on their part, if they can do it at all. The, uh, something or somebody, I missed what he called them, started

174

working with them about fifty cycles ago. I think he means years."
Brent said, pausing in his interpretation as the camera moved to
show the most beautiful sight he'd ever seen. It was floating in
space far above the planet's surface.

"It's beautiful!" Sylvia exclaimed, putting into words what
Brent and everyone else was thinking. It was made up of hundreds
of globes of varying sizes, shapes and colors, all interconnected by
crystal clear tubes. The material had a high polish and looked like
glass, especially the connecting tubes because you could see
through them, but it obviously wasn't. The whole structure glowed
with an inner light that seemed to come from the walls themselves.

"That's a city!" K'Narf said. "That thing could hold tens of
thousands easy." He added, getting nods of agreement from
everyone in the room.

The alien voice started talking again and everyone
immediately looked at Brent. "Got it that time, he's saying this is
the city of the helpers."

"Helpers?"

"Yes, helpers, the ones that are working with the animals
that talk. Helpers, he said it again. Think Mother Theresa, Doctor's
Without Borders, The Salvation Army, that kind of thing." Brent
said, holding his finger to his mouth to shush everyone as the
narrator started speaking again. Then the camera panned back
from the city showing how twelve huge black warships had it
surrounded.

"He's saying that the helpers have steadfastly refused to
obey the leader's demands for the personal worship required of all
angels, nor will they tell him the whereabouts of the space people.
They continue to insist that they are the *Sons of God* and will not
deny their *Father* even if it means their death. They also swear that
they don't know where the space people went after they built the
city for them. They have also been ordered to evacuate the planet
and have refused." Brent said, looking uneasy.

"Angels, refusing to worship, the Sons of God, death?
Sounds like something out of the dark ages." Premo said,
remembering how during the dark ages the church had literally
burned parents at the stake for disobeying it and teaching their
children the Lord's Prayer.

"Look!" K'Narf said, pointing as hundreds of small silver
ships suddenly started pouring out of the city and heading for the
planet. Followed immediately by hundreds of small black fighters,

obviously waiting for just such an act of desperation as they boiled out of the warships and took off after the fleeing helpers. Everyone in the room watched in anguish as ship after silver ship was caught and destroyed, some by flashing green lasers and some by missiles like the one they'd fired at K'Narf. Not one of the silver ships tried to fight back.

"Did any of them make it?" K'Narf asked, not having seen any that did.

"No, I don't think any of them did." Toby said, letting out a long held in breath.

"Now what are they doing?" K'Narf asked, speaking for all of them as one of the large warships converged on the city and the narrator started talking again.

"He's saying that now they will be given to the Sun as an offering, and a lesson to anyone denying their leader and following Him; Him being God." Brent said, as they all watched the warship butt up against the beautiful city and begin to push it out of orbit. They could see hundreds of people diving through the connecting tubes as they moved toward the center of the city.

"It's still full of people!" Irena cried, as they all watched in time lapsed photography, about one frame every ten minutes, as the city was slowly pushed into a trajectory that took it into the Sun. It flared briefly just before it vanished. Everyone in the room seemed to be transfixed by the screen as the picture slowly faded out. The spell was broken by the sound of the narrator's voice as the speaker came back to life.

"What's he saying now?" Irena asked, again looking at Brent.

"The fighters are being ordered to root out any survivors that may have been on the planet." Brent said, as the camera suddenly panned on the hundreds of small black fighters descending on a huge white marble city down on the planet and then did another fadeout.

"Now what?" K'Narf asked, trying to figure out where the camera had taken them.

"He's saying he's in a hanger waiting for the return of the fighters. They've been down on the planet for over thirty rotations. He means days." Brent explained, watching as the first of the small black fighters came through a black shimmering force field and into the huge empty hanger. They all watched as two men got out of the fighter and took off their helmets. They smiled for the camera as they saw the narrator coming toward them. One of the

176

men had a seriously scratched up face. The narrator started talking again.

"He's asking them how it went, and if they found any more of the helpers down there. They're saying yes, they think they got them all, but because they were wearing the talking animal's clothes it was hard to tell. Now he's asking the one with the scratched up face what happened. He's saying the talking animal women are very beautiful, but that they put up an awful fight. The other one's saying that they bite, too. See, he's showing him a bite mark on his arm. He's laughing and saying that over half the legion is coming back in worse shape than them. They're all laughing now." Brent said, stating what they all could see.

The camera suddenly took them out into space again, and they found themselves looking at the fleet with hundreds of the small black fighters waiting for their turn to enter their assigned warship. Then the camera zoomed out into space for a close-up of a monstrous asteroid over six miles in diameter and at least nine miles in length. It was being controlled by four of the large black warships, which were pushing it toward the earth. "He's saying no one defies the leader or his angels."

"Angels! You've got to be kidding! He's calling those beasts angels?" Sylvia asked, not believing her ears.

"Yes, he said it more than once and he was referring to them, the fighter pilots I mean." Brent said, watching in silent awe as the alien cameraman, using time-lapse photography again, recorded how the warships released the asteroid on a collision course for the earth. Then he took close-up shots of the asteroid as it began to emit a red glow, quickly turning into a streaming twenty-seven mile long tail of burning gases. Within minutes it entered the densest part of the atmosphere and blew up. Two enormous sections, each weighing billions of tons each plunged into the earth. One of them creating an enormous trench in the floor of the ocean as smaller fragments tore into the ground of what looked like North America.

The earth actually wobbled under their combined impact, permanently changing the tilt of the planet and the positions of both the North and South Poles. Then the earth's crust seemed to crack in a hundred places at once all along the Atlantic ridge, and started spewing out great gushes of black smoke and fire. The beautiful white marble city was devastated by an earthquake, lava and then a tidal wave until the continent itself began to break up and sink beneath the sea, taking the white marble city with it.

"That explains a lot of historical mysteries." Premo said, talking to no one in particular.

"What do you mean?" Wanda asked, giving the pale-faced Irena a pat on the shoulder.

"Well, now I know how that Siberian Mammoth was frozen in his tracks with poppy flowers in his mouth, and the crater like valleys that pepper the landscape around Charleston South Carolina were made, not to mention how the Puerto Rico Trench was gouged into the floor of the ocean." Premo answered, his brow wrinkled in thought.

"Do you think that could have been Plato's Atlantis?" Toby asked, interrupting Premo's deepening insight.

"Well, Plato said it was off the strait of Hercules, or the strait of Gibraltar as we call it today and that matches up. Yes, I'd have to say that what we just saw was the destruction of Plato's mysterious Atlantis."

Suddenly the speaker came to life again. "He's talking about some rare crystal or gem like mineral deposits they found on an outlying planet, and that they plan to mine it for the glory of the empire or something like that." Brent said, everyone automatically thinking of the alien's open pit mine out on Pluto. The one K'Narf and T.J. had attacked.

"Now he's telling everyone that these are space people and they are to be killed on sight." Brent said, repeating what the narrator had just said as a new picture appeared on the screen that made them all gasp. They were looking at a picture of the elusive space people. "He's warning everyone not to be taken alive by these beings. It's better to die as an angel, than be captured and have your brain altered, converted or brainwashed. I'm not quite sure which." He added, frowning as he struggled with his interpretation.

"She's beautiful." Rudy said, speaking for the first time.

"He ain't so bad either!" Wanda said, looking around at Rudy.

"Oh look, she's holding Judy." Sylvia said, causing all of them to look at the beautiful Manx cat the woman was holding.

"They look just like what you and T.J. looked like, except for their hair." Brent said, looking hard at the two figures on the screen. "Their skin is a dark brownish black and their eyes are glowing just like yours did. Other than those Afro hairdos you two looked just like them. This explains why that alien committed hari-kari when he saw you; your eyes were glowing just like them." Brent added, glancing over at K'Narf and T.J. as the figures on the screen faded out and the screen went black. The scroll had come to an end, plunging the conference room into semi-darkness and an eerie silence that stretched from seconds into minutes.

"I need a hot shower, one with real gravity and plenty of water." Toby said, finally breaking the mesmerizing silence. "So if you don't mind I think Irena and I'll head for home before we both collapse with exhaustion." He added, as he looked over at K'Narf and T.J. for agreement.

"Yeah, us too." Premo said, indicating him and Sylvia. "It's been a long five days." He added, having kept track of the time.

"I'm sorry, I'm afraid I can't let you leave just yet." Brent said, causing all eyes to turn to look at him.

"*You,* can't let us leave, why?" Sylvia asked, too exhausted to care if she was being rude or not.

"First, because based on Zulu time the Sabbath starts in less than an hour and your traveling would violate it, and second because that alien fighter lifted yesterday and I don't want anyone to leave the whale until I've had a chance to verify exactly where it's headed." Brent said, asserting his new authority for the first time.

"Then, you're getting a tracking signal?" K'Narf asked, realizing what a functioning tracking signal would mean to the safety of all of them.

"Yes, but I don't have any of my relays that far out. Right now I can only tell you that they are on the move and heading this way, and that they will be seriously hunting us." Brent said, looking at K'Narf and Toby for support.

"One night in sleeping bags won't kill us." Toby said, taking Irena by the arm. "But that van floor is not the softest thing I've ever slept on." He added, nodding at Brent as they headed for the exit.

"We have an air mattress and if you need us we'll be in the crystal room. Van's a little to cramped for the two of us." Premo said, as he and Sylvia followed after Toby and Irena. "You know, the hospitality of this place is outstanding, but the accommodations are deplorable. What do you think Toby, should we write a letter to the management?" He asked, his voice fading as they all disappeared into the exit.

"Speaking of exhaustion, you look terrible Rudy." K'Narf said, noticing just how haggard and tired Rudy appeared to be.

"He is!" Wanda said, glaring at Rudy. "I managed to get him to lie down a couple of times, but he'd only sleep for a few hours and then he'd get right back up!" She added, angrily. "Had it in his head that as long as the bunch of you were in here working, he needed to be up taking care of you."

"That's been over five days." K'Narf said, knowing just how tired he was as he looked at Rudy. "Go to bed Rudy, I don't want to see you up and about for at least twenty-four hours." He added, seriously worried by the utterly exhausted look on Rudy's face.

"What about you?" Rudy asked. "You a pot calling the kettle black?"

"Don't worry about K'Narf." T.J. spoke up, understanding what Rudy was trying to say as she took K'Narf by the arm. "He's going to be in bed within the next ten minutes. I'll see to that." She added, looking seductively up at K'Narf and pulling him toward the exit.

"Now that's a happy man." Rudy said, watching as T.J. pulled the smiling K'Narf out of the conference room."

"Won't be for long." Wanda said, as she and Rudy entered the kitchen. "Sit down, I'll get us some cold soymilk and some of those peanut butter cookies you made yesterday."

"What do you mean by that?" Rudy asked, not liking the way Wanda was smiling.

"Well, you know those well developed mountains of trembling flesh under T.J.'s sweater that K'Narf couldn't keep his eyes off of."

"Now that you mention it, I do recall something like that." Rudy said, grinning in spite of himself.

"Well, Irena bought T.J.'s in a department store in Vegas." Wanda said, setting two glasses of cold soymilk down on the table.

"You trying to tell me them was phony, rubber phony?" Rudy asked unbelievingly.

"That's what I'm telling you. T.J. had Irena get her three sets of them so it would look like they were getting bigger as they grew back. K'Narf shouldn't have made fun of her flat chest, cause that's what he's gon'na find when he gets her sweater off; which should be any minute now."

180

"Oh that poor little white boy! He...." Rudy said, stopping when he heard K'Narf's frustrated bellow echo across the vast chamber from his bedroom, followed immediately by T.J.'s pealing laughter; laughter which quickly turned into a scream.

"You don't think he's actually hurting her do you?" Rudy asked, starting to get up from the table.

"Not a chance." Wanda said smiling. "Just you sit yourself back down. He's only doing what she's wanted him to do right from the first." She added, laughing as T.J. squalled again.

"If 'en you're sure." Rudy said, slowly dropping back into his seat, giving the impression that he wasn't fully convinced by Wanda's assurances.

"To the newly weds!" Wanda said, raising her glass of soymilk.

"I don't recall any preaching ceremony between those two." Rudy said gruffly.

"Weren't none." Wanda said, smiling patiently at Rudy. "But the vows they flashed to each other that first night in the crystal room were more binding than any piece of paper ever thought of by your bureaucracy."

"Oh, uh, then to the newly weds." Rudy said softly, returning Wanda's toast with his own glass of soymilk; his mind quickly turning to thoughts of an uninterrupted twenty-four hours of much needed sleep.

181

Chapter Twenty

"Toby!" K'Narf flashed. "Are you up yet?"

"No, what do you want?"

"We need to have a meeting before everyone leaves." K'Narf flashed back, realizing he was waking Toby up.

"K'Narf, we've been in a conference room with you for a little over five straight days, and *now* you want to have a meeting, why?"

"Minh Le and Debbie are on their way. They'll be here by the time Sabbath is over and I want to talk to everyone before they leave." K'Narf repeated.

"You're changing the subject, and why are they traveling during the Sabbath. It won't be over for another five hours, and where have they been?" Toby flashed, getting frustrated.

"Minh Le has been gathering up his family and moving them from Vietnam to the States and Debbie has been acting as his pick-up pilot. He's got them all out now. They're staying at a farm he bought for them in California, and his great grandfather is one of us. He has respectfully requested that we teach his venerable ancestor how to reverse the aging process before the old one dies." K'Narf flashed back.

"And traveling on the Sabbath?" Toby flashed, pushing his first question.

"They aren't on Zulu time. Their Sabbath ended a little over three hours ago, and like I told you, they'll be here by the time our Sabbath ends and I want to have a meeting before everyone leaves." K'Narf answered. "Look, go back to sleep. I'll see you in the kitchen as soon as the Sabbath ends and we'll talk. Just don't let anyone jump the gun and leave before I have a chance to talk to them, okay?"

"You're still in bed aren't you?" Toby asked, flashing his question as he received a mental picture of K'Narf snoring.

"Coffee?" Wanda asked, as Toby and Irena dropped into the kitchen just minutes after the Sabbath ended, holding hands as they landed.

"Where is he?" Toby asked.

"He's already in the conference room." Wanda said, knowing he meant K'Narf. "T.J. and Brent are in there with him talking to Minh Le and Debbie." She added, watching as Premo and Sylvia came flying in a little to fast, bouncing off the floor instead of landing on it. Stepping over she grabbed Sylvia's foot and pulled her down to the floor as Sylvia grabbed Premo and pulled him down with her.

"I still want my hot shower, so let's get this over with." Toby said, taking a cup of the coffee Wanda had poured out for them and heading for the conference room, followed by Irena, Premo, Sylvia and finally Wanda. K'Narf had insisted everyone be there, including Wanda. Rudy was still in bed recovering.

"Well?" Toby asked, looking at K'Narf as he took a sip of his coffee.

"Good, everyone's here." K'Narf said, seeing Wanda come in behind Sylvia. "Please, everyone take a seat." He added, pointing at the empty seats around the conference table.

Toby looked at T.J. as he pulled out a chair for Irena, getting an *"I don't know"* look back as he pulled out the chair next to Irena and sat down.

"There's a lot of things we need to do, and we need to do them as fast as possible, but before I talk about them there is another problem we need to address." K'Narf said, standing up and making eye contact with everyone around the table. "It's something I hesitate to bring up, but I don't see a way around it." He added, making it obvious to everyone in the room that he was embarrassed about what ever it was he wanted to talk about and also that he felt he had no choice.

"What problem?" Toby asked, voicing the question for everyone in the room.

"Money!" K'Narf said, speaking the word like it had a disease. "We are going to need quite a bit of it. I currently have a little over seventy thousand, and I know I can raise another two to three hundred thousand at the gaming tables given a little time, but that's not going to be near enough. I need your help." He added, relief showing in both his voice and his face now that he had the problem out on the table.

183

"K'Narf." T.J. said, standing up. "Do you mind if I take over for a few minutes, I think I can help?" She added, looking at K'Narf and seeing the relief in his face as he nodded his head and sat down.

"Okay, everyone, let's take it by the numbers just like I taught you." T.J. said, looking and sounding exactly like a college professor with a room full of students. "Let's tally everything up in U.S. Currency. You do want everything in U.S dollars don't you?" T.J. asked, getting a timid nod from K'Narf as she looked at him. "And don't count any of your stock holdings, the market is too volatile right now and we don't' want to add to the problem."

"Should we look at any of our operating capital accounts?" Toby asked, frowning a little as he concentrated on the problem of adding up his various accounts.

"No, just your reserve cash accounts. Again, convert everything into U.S. currency rounded up to a thousand. We want everything in apples, so don't mix in any oranges."

"What about the 'if sold' value of my paintings?" Debbie asked, referring to the paintings she had hanging in galleries all over Europe.

"No, just cash that can be liquidated without causing alarm, preferably without being noticed by the financial community." T.J. said, answering Debbie's question so it included all of them.

"Ready, then you go first Toby." T.J. said, pointing at Toby.

"Okay, Irena and I pooled everything and we can put three million, seven hundred and thirteen thousand on the table. About two million of that will have to be converted, so it might take about a week to get it into U.S. banks."

"Good, Premo?" T.J. said, pointing at Premo and Sylvia.

"Well, most of our holdings are right here in North America, so getting at our available cash is relatively easy and not counting anything but reserve cash, we can put on the table right now one million four hundred and forty three thousand."

"Brent?"

"Most of my holding are in Asia and Europe, so it will take a while to get it converted and transferred to the U.S., but if you'll give me a little time I can throw an easy seventeen million into the pot." Brent said, the amount surprising everyone but T.J.

"Debbie?"

"Well, most of my money is in Europe, but I can put nine hundred and seventy-seven thousand into the pot as Brent says, within a week or two."

"And Minh Le?" T.J. asked, indicating that he was the last one.

"Please forgive me." Minh Le said. "But I spent most of my ready cash buying my family a vineyard in Napa Valley, so I can only offer to help with six hundred and nine thousand." He added, obviously bothered that the amount was so low.

"Oh, I'm sorry. Wanda?" T.J. asked, turning to look at Wanda who had been sitting slightly behind her.

"Yeah, me too. Sorry that is, I put everything into stock right after I moved up here, so until you let us sell some of it, I can't be of any help I'm afraid.

"That's okay, before this is over you'll have more than your share of ways to help." T.J. said, smiling at Wanda.

"And you?" Toby asked, taking everyone's attention off of Wanda by directly addressing T.J. "How much can you throw into the pot?" He added, getting everyone's attention. They all knew how tightly T.J. kept her affairs to herself, especially when it concerned money.

"Well, I've been trying to add it up. It's not that easy as some of my accounts go back well over a hundred years."

"A hundred years!" Irena repeated, surprised by T.J.'s comment.

"My family had holdings in many parts of the world." T.J. said, looking at Irena. "After their deaths it all fell to me. Much of it was in the form of very old land grants as well as business interests and gold; I have added considerably to what they left me. K'Narf," She said, turning to look at him. "We all know that our fortunes and very lives will mean nothing if those creatures come back and start throwing asteroids at us again, so I pledge to you not only my fortune, but the combined fortune of my family of whom I am the only surviving member. I can as of right now, put in the pot as Brent puts it, one billion dollars as available cash for whatever purposes you may deem necessary in your fight against those beasts. Lack of funding, as far as you are concerned, should not be an option." She said, as she sat down to a stunned and silent room.

"You're a billionaire?" K'Narf asked, looking almost fearfully at his wife.

"Yes, actually about thirty times over if you count both holdings and stock." T.J. said, stunning her small audience a little more, especially K'Narf who was just sitting there staring at her.

"Well, at least we know she didn't marry you for your money." Toby said, breaking the silence as they all looked at the speechless K'Narf. "Uh, if you ask T.J. real nice, she'll probably let you keep your seventy thousand for pocket change." He added, getting even with K'Narf for waking him up.

"You said there were other things that needed to be done." T.J. said, ignoring Toby as she looked at K'Narf; urging him to stand up and continue what he had started.

"Uh, yes." K'Narf said, standing up. "We need to start a couple of schools."

"Schools?" Toby asked, beating everyone to the question by a few nanoseconds.

"Yes." K'Narf said, his voice growing stronger. "And I'd like you two to set up and run one of them." He added, pointing at Premo and Sylvia.

"Could you elaborate a little bit?" Premo asked, not sure what K'Narf was driving at; taking a quick glance at T.J. and Toby to see if they knew.

"Yes, yes I can. We are going to be deluged by new Glow-heads, as Rudy calls us, many of them coming in like Minh Le's grandfather, barely alive and needing immediate instruction in how to repair their failing bodies. They will be coming in from all areas of the planet, speaking hundreds of dialects and reflecting just as many cultures."

"But how can we, I mean...." Premo stuttered.

"Here's what I have in mind. We don't have time for everyone to go to the library like I did, so you know those hand held readers that can be electronically programmed with thousands of books?" K'Narf asked, getting yes nods from everyone. "We can program those as teaching aides, and since we don't have time to translate into all the languages we'll be dealing with, I want you to program the first one as an English primer capable of taking someone from their beginning ABC's to a doctorial level vocabulary as quickly as possible. Speed and time will be vital in many of the critical cases that will be brought to you. A medical primer will follow this reader immediately on all the vital organs and the nervous system just in case they've had a stroke. They'll need to know how they function down to the lowest cellular and hormonal level so they will be able to repair the particular organ or nerve damage that is threatening their lives."

"Yes!" Premo said, beginning to get a glimpse of what K'Narf wanted. "I think, no, I know we could do that." He added, excitement showing in his eyes as he turned and looked at Sylvia to make sure she agreed.

"Good, your next readers would continue educating them until they had all the medical and physiological knowledge needed to alter and repair their bodies and reverse the aging process." K'Narf said, seeing the excitement taking hold in Sylvia's eyes as well as Premo's. "Some of them might even want to grow their hair back if they've gone bald." He added, getting a chuckle from everyone as Premo immediately polished the top of his head.

"Is that all? What about the sciences and the arts, wouldn't they need to be taught those subjects as well?" Sylvia asked, looking at K'Narf and then at T.J.

"Yes, that will be the next stage of their education. They will need to be brought up to speed on everything from Algebra to Zoology. Nothing should be left out; we don't know what skill set may trigger an observation or idea at a critical moment and we are going to need all the help we can get. Again, can you do this, and if so how soon can you be ready with the first two readers?" K'Narf asked, driving for a commitment.

"Two weeks." Premo said, getting an agreeing nod from Sylvia. "Do you have any thoughts on just how many students we might be expecting?"

"I have no biblical proof for this, but if I were you I would plan on at least one hundred and forty four thousand coming through in the next couple of years." K'Narf said, knowing everyone would recognize that particular number.

"Those numbers refer to the Jewish tribes, and other than Toby and Irena none of us that I know of are Jewish." Wanda said, looking around the table for agreement.

"*That you know of!*" K'Narf repeated, pausing to make sure he had everyone's attention as he too looked around the table. "The Bible tells us that the Jewish tribes were scattered to all corners of the world, and the fact that they now ethnically resemble the various races they live among tells us that down through the last two millennia they took wives and sometimes husbands from the indigenous people they were living among."

"Yes, but how does that..."

"It only stands to reason that there were just as many marriages where a Jewish person was taken in by a gentile family and the connection to a particular Jewish tribe was lost as there were of a gentile being taken in by a Jewish family." K'Narf said, answering Wanda's question before she could finish asking it.

"Yes, but if the connection was lost, how can we..."

"Lost only to us, not to God." K'Narf said, again answering Wanda's question before she finished asking it. "If there is so much as a drop of Jewish blood in us, God knows about it." He added, as heads began nodding around the room.

"Then you believe that God is choosing us based on our blood connection to a particular Jewish tribe?" Brent asked, being sensitive to a tribal culture.

"Yes, God said he would choose twelve thousand from each tribe, that's why I believe we'll be finding Glow-heads, in every corner of the world, not just here in America." K'Narf said, again seeing heads nodding as he looked around the table.

"Okay, we'll plan for those kind of numbers." Premo said, getting another nod of agreement from Sylvia.

"Good. Minh Le's grandfather will be your first student, so let him know when you're ready. "Now as for you." K'Narf added, looking at Brent. "I'd like you to set up a training school for agents."

"What kind of agents?" Brent asked, his facial features frozen in place as he looked in a totally uncommitted manner back at K'Narf.

"We're going to need to infiltrate every country in the world looking for new born Glow-heads, and I would like you to set up a school to train agents to do this; paying particular attention to caretaking centers for the aged. Your agents will need to know how to change their appearance to match the ethnic background they are working in, and you might consider some training in self defense just in case. Pick up can be arranged whenever you can get one of our vans on the ground without it being noticed." K'Narf said, looking for a sign that Brent would be willing to take on this added responsibility.

"I'm not sure I have time to...."

"Delegate!" K'Narf said, stopping Brent before he committed himself to a negative position.

"I know you can't do everything yourself, but you can oversee everything if you learn to delegate responsibilities. Minh

Le, would you be willing to act as Brent's assistant and head up the actual school for him?" K'narf asked, carefully putting into action his plan to recruit Minh Le as Brent's second in command as both he and Brent looked at Minh Le. Brent's responsibilities were growing and he was not going to be able to do everything himself.

"Yes, I am very honored to be considered." Minh Le said, giving a slight bow to Brent.

"Good, then it's settled." K'narf said, pushing Brent for an agreement as everyone looked at him.

"You'll have your school." Brent said, the look in his eyes said he was already working on how to do it.

"As for you two." K'Narf said, turning his attention to T.J. and Wanda. "I need, and I do mean need, for the two of you to take a reader and program it with our history. I...."

"History?" Wanda asked, not letting K'narf finish his thought.

"Yes, our history. I want to treat the information about who we are and where we came from like classified graduate school information. Premo, don't put anything into your training about us. I want a single reader developed with that information and I would like it presented to your graduates here in the whale."

"Why here in the whale?"

"What was your impression the first time you were lifted into space and brought to the whale? Any of you." K'Narf asked, looking around the room.

"Awe struck!" Irena said, speaking for all of them.

"That's what I want them to feel. If they are loaded into one of those long stretch limos and lifted into space and brought here, then handed a reader programmed with all the history about us, how T.J. originally started rounding everyone up, what we've learned about our origins and what lies ahead of us. Well it should be both impressive and the quickest way I can think of to get them on board and ready and willing to join us as we prepare for an invasion that we all know is coming." K'Narf said, finishing on a serious note.

"What do you mean, who we are and where we came from?" Wanda asked, looking perplexed.

"That last scroll didn't conflict with what we know about ourselves, it actually confirmed what we know based on the Bible." K'Narf said, causing everyone to start reviewing the Bible in their minds.

189

"You mean about our origins." T.J. said, beginning to understand what K'Narf was driving at.

"Yes, the first thing we know is that there were survivors to that asteroid attack on our planet; we're living proof of that. The scroll also said those helpers, do gooders as my grandmother used to call them, considered themselves to be *sons of God*, and the Bible tells us in Geneses '*That the sons of God saw the daughters of men and that they were fair; and they took them wives of all which they chose*'. Modern DNA tests can trace every woman on the planet back to one woman, but the same DNA tests tell us that men *do not* go back to a single ancestral source, so the scrolls are backed up by both the Bible and modern science." K'Narf said, quoting the Bible as well as current data.

"And those beasts that attacked them?" Irena asked, remembering how the two fighter pilots had bragged about what they had done.

"Again, the Bible tells us that, '*God saw that the wickedness of man was great in the earth... and it repented the Lord that he had made man... and the Lord said, I will destroy man whom I have created from the face of the earth.*' The seed of your beasts injected so much wickedness into our blood that God had to purge us with a flood, a flood that is so well documented even the most diehard atheist admits that it happened." K'Narf said, again quoting the Bible to back up what they had seen on the scroll.

"But what about Noah, didn't he..."

"*But Noah found grace in the eyes of the Lord.*" K'Narf said, quoting the Bible again, as he cut Irena off in mid question. "We obviously go back to Noah's sons and their three wives and yes, I believe Noah had to be a direct descendent of one of those *sons of God* or we wouldn't be standing here talking about him. Unfortunately one, if not all three of his son's wives carried the blood of those beasts as you call them, judging by what God did to Sodom and Gomorra after the flood." K'Narf added, seeing sudden understanding shining in Irena's eyes.

"And the stretch limo, when did you come up with that idea?" T.J. asked, understanding what K'Narf wanted her and Wanda to do as she changed the subject back to the problem at hand.

"A few minutes ago when I found out that money was '*not*' an object of concern." K'Narf said, grinning at the look on T.J.'s face as he stressed the word "*not*". "No, seriously, bringing them up here a few at a time wouldn't be practical. We have enough chairs in this room to bring up thirteen at a time and a stretch limo would be the most practical way to do it. It won't be hard to convert one of them for space and it would be an extremely impressive way to bring them into the fold. We'd need thirteen copies so each person could have their own reader, and you two are in the best position to program them and set everything up."

"Thirteen copies." Premo repeated, thinking of how many readers he was going to need.

"Yes, they shouldn't have to share and even though we know that they wouldn't be here if they hadn't repented and accepted our Lord as their savior, their knowledge of the actual Bible may be scant. You might want to consider adding it and maybe some secular history like what Josephus wrote." K'Narf said, spelling out what he wanted a little clearer.

"Who's Josephus?"

"Thank you Irena, you just made my point." K'Narf said grinning.

"But not until that thing out there has been destroyed." Brent said, bringing everyone back to reality and the situation at hand. "And I don't want anyone leaving until I've verified that fighters location." He added, looking at K'Narf and Toby for support before Irena could think of a comeback for K'Narf's nailing her because she hadn't read Flavius Josephus.

"Brent's right." Toby said, making eye contact with everyone in the room. "And not only do you need his permission to leave, but each and every time you make a trip up here in the future. No one comes or goes without Mister Conrad's permission until that fighter out there has been dealt with. Is that understood?" He asked, as he made direct eye contact with everyone a second time. "This goes for K'Narf and me as well." He added, making sure everyone knew just how serious he was.

"Okay, we've all got our assignments, but I haven't heard a word about what you two are going to be doing." Premo said, causing everyone in the room to look at Toby and K'Narf.

"We're going to go buy a factory." K'narf said, taking over for Toby. "I'd originally thought of trying to build a squadron of fighters in Toby's basement, but it wouldn't be easy or practical and I know a man whose business specializes in buying and selling defunct factories." K'narf added, creating more questions than he answered.

191

"I know money's not an object." T.J. said, saying it before K'Narf could. "But why do you need a defunct factory?"

"Okay, what I mean to say is that we need to find a small town with an abandoned factory, a town where most of the people have left and where we can buy it up piecemeal. That way we can control it in a way that will keep out the curious and suspicious. This is going to be a very long term project involving a lot of our people and they'll need a place to live so why not buy a whole town along with the factory we need?" K'Narf asked, letting everyone know that he had thought the project through and what he was proposing was actually logical.

"And exactly who is this man you know who sells defunct factories?" T.J. asked, curious about K'Narf's strange friend; especially since he was a friend she knew nothing about.

"My father." K'narf said, surprising all of them.

Chapter Twenty-One

"Are you sure I look all right?"

"K'Narf, for the hundredth time, you look just fine. That's an Armani suit T.J. bought you, the Rolex is serious bling, your shoes are shined and your socks match, so relax." Toby said, as the taxi pulled up to the curb.

"My grandfather always wore a stickpin." K'Narf said, opening the door and stepping out.

"You don't stick holes in an Italian patterned silk tie. If you don't trust me, trust T.J. She wouldn't present you to your father in anything less than the best, and if you try to take that tie off again she will do serious damage to your body. Here, help me with these blinking crutches." Toby grunted, handing K'Narf his crutches as he struggled out of the taxi.

"How's the new foot?" K'Narf asked, as he helped Toby get his crutches under his arms and steady himself.

"Started imaging it last week, but it didn't really start growing until night before last. It's starting to form the ankle now. It hurt when I tried to put my prosthesis on this morning so Irena ran out and got me this pressure boot. Makes it look like I just have a sprained ankle." Toby said, as they started toward the buildings entrance. "What floor is your father on?"

"According to the register his company occupies the thirty second floor." K'Narf said, leaning back and looking up at the building towering over them. "Why do they have to use glass for outside walls, it doesn't look safe." He added, as he stepped forward and opened the door for Toby.

"His company occupies the whole floor?" Toby asked, ignoring K'Narf's worries about the building being safe.

"Yes, I gather they're pretty well known." K'Narf said, remembering the phone calls he had made.

"And very successful if they take up a whole floor, especially in this kind of a building." Toby said, as they reached the elevator and stepped in. "The thirty second floor it is." He added, as he pushed the button.

"Thank you for coming with me." K'Narf said, pulling at his tie.

"Just leave the tie alone, now, do you still have the business cards we made for you?" Toby asked, ignoring K'Narf's "thank you" since it wasn't the first time he had said it that morning.

"Yes, and the picture." K'Narf said, pulling out his picture for Toby to see.

"So that's your great grandfather." Toby said, looking at the picture of K'Narf's great grandparents posing with his grandmother when she was a young girl. "You really did a good job morphing yourself. Looking at you is like looking at him, it's almost as if your great grandfather just stepped out of the picture." He added, handing back the picture as the elevator door opened on a large marble rotunda with at least a dozen exit doors built into its sides.

"That's Miss Willetta." K'Narf said, surprise showing in his voice as he looked at the woman setting behind a formidable mahogany receptionist station.

"You know her?" Toby asked, looking at the heavyset woman who was now carefully appraising them from across the room.

"Yes, she came to our house once when I was five. I heard my mother greet her as Miss Willetta and came out of my room to look at her. She was wearing the same style of gray suit she has on now. The only difference I can see is that braided bun on top of her head is also gray now." K'Narf said, trying to keep his voice down as they walked toward her. "She gave me a look that could frost the tail off of a polar bear." He added, flashing Toby instead of talking.

"What happened?"

"Nothing really, I ran back into my room and hid in the closet until she left." K'Narf flashed, just as they reached her desk.

"Good morning, may I help you?" Willetta asked, in a tone of voice that backed up what K'Narf had said about her ability to "frost the tail off of a polar bear", giving Toby and his crutches a look of distain that matched her voice.

"Yes, I would like to speak with Mister Joseph Fugate." K'Narf said, handing Willetta his card.

"K'Narf Etaguf, that's all, no company affiliation?" Willetta asked, looking at K'Narf's card. "Do you have an appointment?" She asked, staring up at him.

"No, but I...."

"No appointment." Willetta said curtly, glaring up at him as she offered his card back. "I'm afraid it would be impossible to...."

"Just give him my card, Willetta!" K'Narf said just as curtly, cutting her off in mid sentence as he glared right back at her.

"How did you, uh, yes." Willetta said, obviously flustered by K'Narf's use of her first name as she reached over and pushed a button. Seconds later a young woman walked into the receiving area and Willetta handed her K'Narf's card. "See if Joseph has a minute or two he can spare for these gentlemen." She said, then turned back to her computer as though K'Narf and Toby no longer existed. Less than a minute later the young woman returned.

"Right this way please." She said, holding the door open for them.

"Do me a favor." K'Narf said, flashing Toby a picture of his father. "Tell me if you see any kind of reaction when he realizes who I am."

"Why?"

"I've never seen him show any emotion, and I'm curious if my new face will crack his facade in any way." K'Narf said, as they followed the young woman into a large spacious office resplendent in polished wood with carefully placed art pieces and there, sitting behind a large carved and very impressive desk, was Joe Fugate, his father.

"Do you mind telling me how you came upon this name?" K'Narf's father asked, motioning to the chairs in front of his desk. Chairs designed to put the person, or persons setting in them just slightly lower than K'Narf's father thus giving him the advantage of looking down on them. A fact instantly recognized by Toby as he dropped into one of the chairs and took the load off of his one leg. K'Narf remained standing.

"Not at all. You gave me the first name, and I chose the second, father." K'Narf said, as both he and Toby watched his father's face for any sign of a reaction. "Here, this may help in identifying me." K'Narf added, exposing his Rolex as he took his picture out of an inside pocket and handed it to his father.

"I see." K'Narf's father said, looking at the picture and then back at K'Narf. "I presume you had yourself made over to look like your great grandfather. Surgeons are really quite good today, aren't they." He added, making a statement rather than asking a question as he handed the picture back.

"Yes, I didn't think grandmother would mind." K'Narf said, deliberately allowing his father's assumption that the skills of a plastic surgeon were responsible for his new face as he put the picture back into his pocket.

"Your mother will be pleased, I'm sure. Now what can I do for the two of you?" Joe Senior asked, dismissing the changes in K'Narf as he looked over at Toby. "And do please, sit down." He added, pointing at a chair for K'Narf.

"This is my associate Toby Zebulon, and we're looking for a factory." K'Narf said, forcing his father to look back at him as he sat down. "You told me that one of the aspects of your corporation was to audit businesses for sale and verify assets prior to a purchase. Is that still one of the services you offer?"

"A factory you say?"

"Actually we're looking for more of a town with a factory." Toby said, pitching in as K'Narf settled himself. "An abandoned factory along with a town that was shut down and deserted when the factory closed may be a better way of putting it."

"And the amount of capital you're willing to invest?" Joe senior asked, leaning back into his chair.

"Funding is not an object of concern." K'Narf said, trying very hard to keep a straight face as he looked over at Toby for agreement.

"No, as K'Narf said, funding is not a concern." Toby agreed, flashing K'Narf a picture of T.J. strangling him with his tie. You never tell someone that funding is no object when discussing a business deal, he scolded.

"In that case I may have just such a property. It's a solid redbrick building built back in the early fifties, about one hundred thousand square feet of assembly space and a very nice office complex sitting on about twenty-five acres. It even has a railroad spur and three recessed loading bays for the trucking trade."

"Where?" K'Narf asked, getting excited. "I mean is it here in the U.S.?" He added, having just received a nasty flash from Toby about looking eager.

"Yes, it's located on the outskirts of a small town in Iowa called Sutton Wells." Joe senior said, looking curiously at K'Narf.

"Do we have anyone in Iowa? K'Narf flashed at Toby.

196

"I'm checking." Toby flashed back. "Keep him talking."

"Go on." K'Narf said, looking at his father and not knowing what else to say.

"Well, like I was saying, based on your criteria. There are twelve very nice executive level houses in the town that come with the factory, and as you put it, most of the town was shut down and deserted after the factory closed." Joe senior said, as he put the tips of his fingers together. Carefully scrutinizing K'Narf and Toby.

"One of our people, a friend of Irena's, is visiting her sister in West Des Moines. Her name's Joy and she has a motorcycle." Toby flashed, showing K'Narf a picture of a very pretty girl getting on a rather large bike and burning rubber as she took off with her front wheel a good foot off the ground. She knows the town and says it's less than twenty miles away by the freeway. Keep him talking." Toby said, trying to listen to K'Narf's father and flash Joy at the same time.

"How's grandfather?" K'Narf asked, not knowing what else to talk about.

"Your grandfather." Joe senior repeated, unprepared for the question. "Is doing just fine. Joe Junior is living with him now and running the farm for him." He added, his voice registering annoyance at the change of subject.

"Junior is living with Gramps!" K'Narf said, grinning at the thought. "What happened to his going to college?"

"He's now taking correspondence courses to become a master gardener instead of an engineer." Joe senior said, noticing that Toby seemed to be only half listening to them. "Your grandfather said he would deed the place over to him if he could prove that he could run it properly." He added, the tone of his voice now saying that he was not particularly happy with Junior's decision, though his face continued to show no discernable emotion at all.

"And mom went along with all this?" K'Narf asked, wondering how Junior had convinced his mother to let him drop out of college.

"Yes, after your grandfather showed them his books and they both realized that a fully functional organic farm in today's market was a highly profitable enterprise. As a matter of fact there was a gentleman who came by just last week and contracted for everything they can grow at full market value."

197

"At full market value, all of it?" K'Narf asked, surprised because he knew that marketing their crops was what used to take up most of his grandfather's time.

"Yes, all of it, as long as they continue to rest one of the greenhouses and three of the fields each year like your grandmother used to do. The man's company is going to send a truck three times a week for everything they can grow."

"Three times a week?" K'Narf asked, getting a flash from Toby that Joy was entering the town right now and flashing him pictures.

"Yes, your grandfather and Junior seem to be quite happy with the arrangement."

"What about mother, does she approve?" K'Narf asked, realizing as he asked the question that his father had already said that she did. "I guess she does since she let him do it, how is she, I mean how is mother anyway?" He added, trying to recover his fumble.

"Your mother is doing just fine. Now, back to this factory we were talking about. Would you like me to arrange for you to take a tour of the site?" Joe senior asked, putting all things personal aside and getting back to the business at hand.

"You shaved your Van Dyke. Did mom make you do that?" K'Narf asked, getting desperate.

"Here's what we've got." Toby flashed, showing K'Narf flashes of a small main street town with boarded up houses and businesses. One working gas station, a small grocery store and what appeared to be a functioning white steepled church, followed quickly by flashes of the factory taken by Joy as she flew around the property and drove through an open bay and into the building itself. Some of the windows were broken and there were a lot of bolts sticking up out of the concrete floor where heavy machinery had been mounted. "It's everything we were looking for." Toby flashed.

"No, your mother does not dictate my personal appearance, now do you want me to arrange a site tour or not?" Joe senior asked, coming very close to a display of emotion as he forced the conversation back to the business at hand.

"No, I think we'll just buy it." K'Narf said, getting looks from both his father and Toby. "Well, if I can't trust the word of my own father, who can I trust? Now how much do they want for it?" He asked, flashing Toby a "Why not, we want it don't we?" in flashing neon.

"They're asking one hundred and fifteen million." Joe senior said, seemingly unfazed by K'Narf's response. "That includes the twelve executive houses of course."

"How much do you want down to start the process?" K'Narf asked, pushing forward with the purchase.

"Twenty percent is customary with the balance at closing." Joe senior said, again leaning back and putting his fingers together as he studied K'Narf and Toby's reactions.

"That's an even twenty-three million. How soon do you need it and in what method do you prefer to be paid?" K'Narf asked, flashing Toby at the same time with a how soon can we get it question.

"A cashier's check made out to my company would be sufficient to get the process started." Joe senior said, beginning to realize that K'Narf and Toby were actually serious.

"We can have it on his desk before five o'clock today." Toby flashed, struggling to get up. Knowing that this meeting was over and thinking he would strangle K'Narf when they got outside, if he could beat T.J. to it. Nobody spent that kind of money without bargaining a little first, and they hadn't even created a company name for themselves yet.

"The check will be on your desk before the close of the day." K'Narf said, standing up and giving Toby a hand with his crutches.

"Is there a way to get in touch with you?" Joe senior asked, looking at K'Narf's card, a card that had only his name on it.

"Here." Toby said, taking the card and scribbling a cell number on it. "Call that number and someone from our organization will call you back within the hour. We'll both be notified immediately of course."

"Give my best to mother and tell Gramps and Junior I'll be dropping in to see them sometime." K'Narf said, holding out his hand to his father, followed by Toby as they all shook hands and turned to leave with K'Narf holding the door for Toby.

"Did he react at all?" K'Narf asked, the minute the door shut behind them.

"Your father, not that I could tell. I'd say that he's the coolest customer I've ever met." Toby said, glancing at K'Narf. "I'd sure hate to play poker with him." He added.

"I didn't see any reaction either, except in the tone of his voice, anyway we've got our factory!" K'Narf flashed, nodding at Willetta as they passed her desk, then trying to imitate exploding fireworks again as he flashed T.J. the news.

"Tell her we need to send people in to start buying up the town, businesses and all, before they find out the factory has been sold." Toby said, realizing that K'Narf was flashing T.J. with the news. "Tell her the prices will go through the roof as soon as the word gets out." He added, as they stepped out onto the sidewalk.

Chapter Twenty-Two

"T.J. said I'd find you two goofing off in here." Brent said, instantly getting a violent response from K'Narf and Toby as he stepped into what had been a fairly decent personnel lounge in the old factory. It was now a disaster area; drawings and sketches were taped all over the walls and scattered helter-skelter over an improvised worktable, along with discarded paper wadded up and thrown everywhere.

"Goofing off!" Toby yelled, looking around for something more substantial than paper to throw at Brent.

"It's been almost two weeks, where have you been?" K'Narf asked, his voice almost as gruff as Toby's. "Minh Le didn't even know where you were."

"I had things that needed doing." Brent answered, stepping a little further into the room.

"Where, on the other side of the planet?" Toby asked, giving up on finding something to throw as he sat back down on his drawing stool, obviously tired and more than a little stressed out. "We've been trying to flash you for over a week. You and your pilots are going to get killed if we don't come up with an effective fighter design!" He added, waving his arm at the drawing table and at the obviously failed attempts wadded up and scattered about the room.

"I thought that might be a problem, so I brought you this." Brent said, holding out a small flash card.

"And what's that?" K'Narf asked, his curiosity overriding his irritation at Brent's not staying in touch.

"It's a complete readout on that small two man fighter we saw on the solar scroll." Brent said, calmly watching their reactions. "You remember, the black ones that shot down all those silver ones." He added, flashing them a picture of the deadly black fighters.

"You've been to Pluto." Toby stated rather than asked.

"Yes, I found a picture of that black fighter etched on the end of one of the scrolls we left in that cave. I ran it through the viewer in the whale on my way back and copied it onto this flashcard." Brent said, seeing Toby straighten up as he looked at the small device in Brent's hand. "I also took six of the largest spacesuits I could find from their mother ship, enough for three two man fighters. Our spacesuits are far too bulky and clumsy for the type of fighter we're going to need." He added, enjoying the dumbfounded looks on both Toby and K'Narf's face.

"So that's what you've been up to." K'Narf said, as he reached out his hand for the flashcard.

"Among other things." Brent said, a bare touch of a grin on his face as he stepped forward and handed the flashcard to K'Narf.

"What other things?" Toby asked, catching the *"other things"* comment as he stood up and walked around the table so he could get a closer look at the flashcard in K'Narf's hand.

"I had some of my guys working on the *'getting one of our vans on the ground without being noticed'* comment K'Narf made at our last meeting." Brent said, walking over to a window that looked down on the factory floor where he had parked his van. "Good, you can see it from here."

"See what?" K'Narf asked, moving toward the window where Brent was standing.

"That." Brent said, pointing at a beat-up looking dirty white van with "Conrad's Electric Service" written across it in faded red lettering.

"Where'd you get that thing?" Toby asked, as he came up beside K'Narf and looked out the window.

"Watch." Brent said, as he took a small hand held computer from his shirt pocket and started pushing buttons. The van started changing colors and quickly turned into the dark apple red space van that everyone knew belonged to him.

"How?" K'Narf and Toby said in unison.

"There's a new technology on the market that allows a decorator to change the color of individual walls by using computer induced current to the individual paint pixels instead of repainting. I had my guys use the same technology on my van. I can make it look like a trade or delivery van in almost any culture on the planet." Brent said, as he changed his van back into a beat up looking electrician's van and turned to face K'Narf and Brent. "Problems with our being noticed when we pick up newbie's from

202

various parts of the world should be minimal now if my guys are careful, including coming and going from this factory." He added, looking at K'Narf since it had been his comment that had been addressed.

"When can we get the rest of the vans converted?" K'Narf said, asking the obvious question.

"I'll need to take them to my shop in Korea where it'll take approximately twenty-four hour's to paint and bake them dry. I'll show you how to program the new paint when I bring the first one back." Brent said, stepping away from the window and walking back into the center of the room. "You also need to drop by the school and see Minh Le. Tell him I said to update the two of you on self defense." He added, turning to face his superiors.

"Why?" K'Narf asked, noticing the hard way Brent was staring at him and Toby.

"The two of you have been holed up in this room so long you've allowed yourselves to become antiquated." Brent said, fully expecting the reaction his words would cause.

"Antiquated! Why you little...." Toby said as he bent over and grabbed a wadded up piece of paper to throw at Brent. "My legs, I can't...." He stammered, as he slowly collapsed to the floor, followed seconds later by K'Narf as he tried to take a step and collapsed next to Toby.

"How?" K'Narf asked, looking up at Brent.

"You told me to develop some self defense techniques for my agents. Minh Le and I have done that, and the two of you need to get over to the school as quickly as possible and learn how to defend yourselves." Brent said, a slight grin tugging at the corners of his mouth.

"Why, what's the urgency?" Toby asked, struggling to sit up as he realized he was numb from the waist down.

"Because T.J. and Irena should be at the school right about now reviewing the reader on both self defense and *offense* that Minh Le and I put together." Brent said, openly grinning now as he stressed the word "*offense*".

"Couldn't you have just told us?" K'Narf asked, physically pulling his legs around in front of him so he could raise up into a sitting position like Toby had done.

"Minh Le and I have found that a physical demonstration is much more effective in getting a students full attention." Brent said, still grinning.

"And after the student recovers?" Toby asked, his meaning clear as he glared at Brent.

"You will recover the use of your legs in about five minutes, by that time I will be long gone, and again, I strongly urge you to go see Minh Le, and Premo while your at it; you really do need to update your knowledge. I wasn't kidding when I said that you have allowed yourselves to become antiquated." Brent said, given them a slight bow and as he headed for the door. "Oh, and T.J. said to tell you that your father called and wants you to call him." Brent added, as he disappeared through the door.

"That is one dangerous man." Toby said, rubbing at his legs.

"Yes, and I'm sure glad he's on our side." K'Narf said, as he tried to wiggle his toes. "And in the future, if I was you, I'd think twice before threatening him with anything, even a piece of wadded up paper." He added, as his toes began to tingle.

"I'll agree with you on that." Toby said, wiggling his toes. "I wonder what your father wants, we finished all the paperwork on this place over a week ago." Toby said, massaging his legs as they started to tingle.

"Don't know, but I might as well find out. Can't do anything else at the moment." K'Narf said, as he pulled his new cell phone out of his shirt pocket and punched up his father's personal phone number. "Father, What can I do for you?" He asked, as his father answered the phone.

"Your mother would like you to come over for Sunday dinner." Joe senior said, getting right to the point.

"This Sunday?"

"Yes, I do believe that was her intention."

"Uh, okay, but tell her to set an extra plate, I'll be bringing my wife with me." K'Narf said, listening to the dead silence on the other end of the line; thinking for a moment that his father had hung up.

"I will let her know." Joe senior said finally, after a full moments silence. "Eight o'clock it is then." He added, seconds before the phone went dead as he really did end the connection.

"Well, that was short and sweet." Toby said, moving his right leg a little.

"My mother wants me to come by for Sunday dinner. I told him to tell her that I'd be bringing T.J." K'Narf said, realizing he could feel both of his legs now.

"Then we need to get over to Brent's school and see Minh Le as fast as we can." Toby said, as he got his knees under him and started crawling toward his drafting stool.

"Why?" K'Narf asked, turning around so he could get his knees under him.

"Irena is over there right now with T.J. learning to do what Brent just did to us and more." Toby said, using his arms to get up on his stool. "I'm telling you, we'd better know how to defend ourselves before we run into either of them." He added, as he watched K'Narf slowly crawl toward his stool.

"Toby was quite right you know." T.J. said, checking herself one more time in the rearview mirror. "What Irena had planned for the two of you would have been unpleasant to say the very least."

"Why, what exactly was she going to do?" K'Narf asked, getting out of the van and walking around to open T.J.'s door.

"She was going to paralyze you and make you go shopping with us. She had two attendants standing by with wheelchairs and an itinerary that covered half of New York." T.J. said, taking K'Narf's hand as she got out of the van. "It would have taken days, so it's just as well you didn't fall into her trap."

"You were going to let her do that?" K'Narf asked, looking down at his unbelievably gorgeous wife as she smiled up at him.

"Of course, she's my sister, besides she thinks she still owes you one for that stunt you pulled on her in Vegas." T.J. said, taking K'Narf by the arm and heading for the parking garage's down elevator.

"She's still upset about that?" K'Narf asked, surprise showing in his voice.

"Sweetheart, you really need to understand this, Irena spent three years in an elite Israeli commando unit and you took her out like she was a newbie on her first mission. She'll never forget it, or totally forgive you until she evens the score. Toby was being targeted simply because she knows how much he hates to go shopping, but you were her main target." T.J. said, smiling sweetly up at K'Narf as they stepped into the elevator and K'Narf punched a button for the third floor and his parent's suite. "How did you manage to get your hands on that defense reader before she spotted you anyway?" She asked, holding onto K'Narf's arm as the elevator started dropping.

"That was Toby's doing, he scouted that school like it was an enemy held position. We finally approached it on the north side where all the deep shrubbery is. He made me crawl through the brush behind him until we were directly under a second story window, then he flashed Minh Le to drop a reader out the window to us. It didn't take ten minutes to figure out what they had discovered about the nervous system and how to stick mental pins into it, or how to protect oneself." K'Narf said, answering T.J.'s question. "That bit about cutting off the blood supply to the brain and cold-cocking someone was a little bit spooky, but I can see where it would come in handy it you were under attack." He added, as the elevator stopped.

"Yes, I don't think we have to worry about his agents anymore. Brent does know how to take care of his own." T.J. said, stepping out of the elevator and looking around. "So this is where your parents live, but why the third floor. I'd think they'd want to live higher up with a nicer view?"

"My father would love to, but mother wants to be within reach of a fireman's ladder." K'Narf said, walking over to the door he knew belonged to his parents; a door he hadn't been through for thirteen years and knocked. "Hello mother." He added, as his mother opened the door.

"Oh my!" Robbie said, throwing her hand up to her mouth. "Joe said you looked like my grandfather, but I didn't think...." She stammered, standing in the doorway staring at K'Narf.

"Mother, I'd like you to meet my wife." K'Narf said, stepping slightly to the right so his mother could see her. "This is T.J., may we come in?" He added, asking the question as his mother stepped aside and let them in, closing the door behind them without saying a word.

"I'm very pleased to meet you." T.J. said, turning and holding out her hand to her obviously stunned mother-in-law. "I hope we're not too early." She added, leaving her hand extended.

"No, no." Robbie said, coming alive as she took T.J.'s hand and shook it. "I'm just a little surprised by my son's appearance, that's all. May I take your wrap?" She asked, quickly getting her composure back.

"Yes please." T.J. said, slipping off a beautiful silver mink stole and exposing both her shoulders and a beautiful and fragile looking jade and emerald studded necklace.

"So you're my son's wife." Robbie said, taking the mink stole and giving T.J. a long measured look. "I don't see any rings?"

"We believe rings to be a bit pretentious." T.J. said, glancing at the eye-catching diamonds sparkling on Robbie's hand.

"And that's not?" Robbie asked, rudely nodding at T.J.'s necklace.

"Oh this." T.J. said, fondling the necklace. "I inherited it from my great grandmother. I thought the green of the stones and the gold filigree would go nice with the green of my gown. Don't you agree? I so wanted to make a good first impression."

"Father." K'Narf said, breaking the pregnancy of the moment as his father entered the room. "How are you?" He asked, as his father walked over and shook his hand.

"Fine, and you?" Joe senior asked, as he got a good look at T.J. and K'Narf ceased to exist.

"I'm T.J." T.J. said, holding out her hand. "I'm K'Narf's wife." She added, allowing her new father-in-law to take her hand and touch it lightly to his lips as he bowed slightly to her.

"Please, call me Joe." Joe senior said, slowly releasing her hand.

"Ada Louise should have dinner ready to serve by now." Robbie said, as she took her husband by the arm. "We shouldn't keep her waiting should we?" She asked, as she turned and moved toward the dining room, taking her husband with her.

"Well, your father liked me." T.J. flashed, taking K'Narf by the arm as they followed his parents.

"So we both noticed." K'Narf flashed back, smiling down at T.J. "But he still didn't lose it."

"Lose it?"

"Yes, I've never seen my father lose his cool. Toby said he has the best poker face he's ever seen." K'narf flashed, trying to explain his father's extreme level of self-control.

"So, where did you two meet?" Robbie asked, after they were all comfortably seated.

"We sort of ran into each other in Las Vegas." K'Narf said, trying to imitate his father by not showing any emotion. "T.J. and a friend of hers went on an excursion with me." He added, trying not to lie, but not wanting to tell the absolute truth either.

"I see, and where did you get your surgery done?" Robbie asked, looking sharply at K'Narf. "I know something of cosmetic surgery and I know of no one capable of doing what's been done to you." She added, looking pointedly at K'Narf and then at T.J.

"She won't believe anything you say, so let me handle this." T.J. flashed, squeezing K'Narf's hand under the table.

"She's all yours." K'Narf flashed back.

"You are quite right." T.J. said, instantly getting Robbie and Joe's full attention. "The changes you see in your son were not done by a surgeon, they were done by K'Narf himself. We have the ability, through a very slow and sometimes painful process, to change the cellular structure of our bodies." She added, having decided to tell the absolute truth rather than try and concoct some farfetched story.

"We?" Robbie asked, picking up on the pronoun that included T.J.

"Yes, K'Narf and I both have this ability."

"Then you've changed yourself too." Robbie said, quickly putting two and two together.

"Yes, I...." T.J. said, stopping when Ada Louise entered the room and proceeded quietly to serve each of them from off a highly polished stainless steel serving cart.

"I'm sorry, Ada Louise is it?" K'Narf asked, as she put a beautifully broiled bacon wrapped filet mignon steak on his plate. "Is that bacon?" He added, asking the question as he pointed at the steak.

"Yes sir, is there something wrong?"

"Just have her take it back and trim off the outer edge where the bacon touched." T.J. flashed, again squeezing K'Narf's hand.

"Yes, my wife and I don't eat pork in any of its forms. Could you please take our steaks back and remove the bacon and trim off the outer edge of the steak where it was touched by the bacon?" K'Narf asked, giving Ada Louise a smile that said everything was okay and not to worry.

"Yes sir, if you'll give me just a moment. I'll be right back." Ada Louise said, taking both plates and heading for the kitchen.

"That's just the way they come when you buy them." Robbie said, trying to justify the use of the bacon as soon as Ada Louise was out of earshot.

"Grandmother would turn over in her grave." K'Narf said, looking at his mother; knowing he was right.

"Be nice!" T.J. flashed, she's your mother.

"Yes, she probably would." Robbie said, remembering her mother. "I just didn't think it would matter if you didn't actually eat the bacon." She added, as Ada Louise came back with the trimmed steaks for T.J. and K'Narf. Saying nothing more as Ada Louise finished serving each of them and quietly left the room.

"You just had a birthday, didn't you?" Joe senior asked, looking at his plate as he started cutting up his steak into bite size pieces.

"Yes, two weeks ago as a matter of fact." K'Narf said, attacking his own steak with a very fancy bone handled steak knife. "Turned nineteen on October the eleventh." He added, looking up at his father.

"And you my dear." Robbie said, not about to miss a chance to find out her new daughter-in-law's age. "Have you had a birthday recently?"

"Not recently, no. I did turn eighty-seven on August sixteenth last, though." T.J. answered, looking up at Robbie as she flashed K'Narf to look at his father. "I think he just lost that cool you were talking about."

"Father, are you all right?" K'Narf asked, looking at his father with his jaw hanging open showing a mouthful of half masticated steak.

"Joe!" Robbie said, getting up and slapping her husband on the back. "I think he's chocking on something." She added, slapping him again.

"I'm, I'm all right!" Joe said, coughing as he closed his mouth. "Did you say eighty-seven?" He asked, looking at T.J.

"Now you've done it." K'Narf flashed, looking at the stunned look on his father's face.

"You said you wanted to see him lose his cool." T.J. flashed, smiling as she looked back at Robbie before she answered. "Yes, I was born exactly eighty-seven years ago in the year of the Monkey." She added, calmly taking a bite of salad.

"Yes, but I didn't think he'd have to have a heart attack before he'd lose it." K'Narf flashed, wondering if his father really was having one.

"Then you must have changed yourself as much as he has." Robbie said, ignoring her husband as she pointed at K'Narf.

"Yes, the changes were rather dramatic." T.J. said, noticing that K'Narf's father was beginning to regain his composure.

"How is Junior doing?" K'Narf asked, trying to change the subject.

"I'm getting a flash from Wanda, Rudy's had a stroke." T.J. flashed. "Wanda wants us to get there as quickly as possible. Do you have your phone on you?"

"Yes."

"Pretend you're getting a call, I'll flash and you talk." T.J. flashed, trying not to show any emotion to the closely watching Robbie as she took a sip of water.

"Junior is...."

"Excuse me, mother." K'Narf said, cutting her off as he pulled his cell phone out of his pocket and pretended to answer it. "What's wrong?" He asked, for the benefit of his parents.

"Wanda says he is all right, but he can't move his right side. She wants us to hurry. Say 'I see, we'll get there as soon as we can'." T.J. flashed, looking at K'Narf like she was concerned about his phone call.

"I see, okay we'll get there as soon as we can." K'Narf said, turning off the phone and putting it back into his suit pocket.

"I'm terribly sorry mother, but a very close and dear friend of ours has just had a stroke and we're going to have to leave." K'Narf said, pushing his chair back and standing up.

"But you just got here!" Robbie cried, visibly upset that her dinner party was being spoiled.

"I know mother, but Wanda said Rudy is asking for me, and we need to leave *now*." K'Narf said, stressing the word *now*, as he pulled out T.J.'s chair and helped her up; watching as his father stood up at the same time. "We'll get together another time. Maybe Junior and Gramps will be able to join us." He added, thinking there'd be more witnesses and fewer questions next time.

"Very well, let me get your wrap dear." Robbie said, accepting defeat as she stood and followed them toward the door.

"Where did you park?" Joe senior asked, as they reached the door.

"On the top level of your parking garage." K'Narf said, watching as his mother returned with T.J.'s stole and handed it to his father, who in turn helped T.J. adjust the silver mink about her shoulders.

"Why in the world did you park on the top level?" Robbie asked, picking up on the conversation.

"We didn't exactly park." T.J. said, as they stepped over to the door. "We more like landed." She added, taking K'Narf's arm.

"You flew here!" Joe senior stated, rather than asked.

"Yes, and we have a long trip ahead of us so we're going to have to rush off I'm afraid." K'Narf said, offering his hand to his father and then giving his mother a quick hug.

"It was nice meeting you dear." Robbie said, giving T.J. a quick cursory hug.

"Yes, it was." Joe senior said, giving T.J. a very slight bow just as they turned and opened the door and headed for the elevator. Pushing the button for the top level and waving goodbye as the elevator doors closed.

Chapter Twenty-Three

"Do we need to stop off and get you a change of clothes?" K'Narf asked, as the van quickly lifted through the glowing New York sky and into the blackness of space.

"No, I can get a change of clothes from Wanda, we're not that much different in size." T.J. said, settling back into her seat.

"No, I guess you're not now that I think about it." K'Narf said, remembering his first impression of Wanda as being dainty; an impression quickly driven out of his mind by the strength of her character. "I'd better try and contact Brent and see if it's safe." He added, getting quiet as he started flashing Brent on his private frequency.

"You got through?" T.J. asked, seeing K'Narf's face relax.

"Yes, he's already heard about Rudy and had just finished checking on our friendly aliens. They're back on Pluto at the moment so there shouldn't be any problems." K'Narf said, as he slowly added power to the van's drive cores.

"Good, we have enough problems of our own right now." T.J. said, feeling herself being pushed deeper into the cushions of the seat. "Your Mister Conrad is really something, isn't he?" She added, asking the question as K'Narf energized core number four.

"Brent, what about him?" K'Narf asked, deciding four G's of constant thrust was more than enough to get them there in a hurry.

"Well, we haven't figured out how to measure intellect like the normals do, but when we do I think we'll find your Mister Conrad standing head and shoulders above the rest of us." T.J. said, turning a little as she tried to get comfortable. "You know he redesigned your Kirlian glasses don't you?"

"No, what did he do to them?" K'Narf asked, trying to get comfortable himself, knowing it was going to be a long grueling trip.

"He designed a contact lens so you could view the Kirlian effect through it, then attached a small light absorbing core to the inside of a regular pair of glasses to block out the wearers personal glow. Mister Conrad said your bubble lens sunglasses attracted too much attention, something his agents didn't need." T.J. said, relaxing as much as possible under the four G's of pressure and closing her eyes.

"Did he do it, or did his guys as he calls them do it, and who are they anyway?" K'Narf asked.

"Mister Conrad's guys are a group of young geniuses he has rounded up over in Korea. He has a rather extensive lab set up over there with a fair amount of manufacturing capacity. He pays them extremely well, and I mean extremely well, including full medical benefits so they won't even think of leaving him and going to work for someone else." T.J. said, turning her head so she could look at K'Narf as she talked.

"So that's why he keeps calling them his guys." K'Narf said, as he calculated how long it would be before he would have to reverse thrust. "And why do you keep calling him Mister Conrad, why not just Brent?" K'Narf asked, having noticed the formal way T.J. always referred to Brent.

"He may look small and somewhat insignificant, but he's a direct descendent of Chief Joseph of the Nez Perce and deserves all the respect that fact alone demands. Adding in his own personal skills and accomplishments, of which you and Toby are just becoming aware, makes his deserving of the personal respect and title that I extend him." T.J said, falling back on her own background and culture to determine status and class of an individual. "You were truly blessed when he accepted your 'Head of Security' position, and you couldn't have chosen a more qualified man if you'd had thousands to choose from." She added, rolling her head back into its forward position and closing her eyes.

"I'll agree with you on that, but if he calls Toby and me antiquated again I'm not going to be held accountable for what we do to him." K'Narf said, feeling he owed Brent one for both the insult and the paralyzing lesson.

"That was a good call on your part to have him look for Glow-heads in retirement and rest homes." T.J. said, allowing K'Narf to think she was changing the subject, even though she wasn't.

"Really, what has he found?"

"Well, I spent over thirty years checking out casino's looking for what I thought were geniuses with telekinetic abilities. During that whole time I found and trained exactly fifty-three of them, and that doesn't count you. Now you, your Mister Conrad and that new core of agents he and Minh Le have put together, have discovered better than fifty during the last week alone, most of them in the retirement and rest homes where you suggested they look." T.J. said, squirming under the gruesome pressure of a constant four G's of drive force. "Some of them were even under Hospice care when they found them." She added, finally getting around to the subject she wanted to discuss.

"Hospice care?" K'Narf asked, searching his mind for a definition.

"Means they're closer to death than life, and are being allowed to die a natural death with the help of drugs like morphine to keep them pain free in the process."

"They keep them drugged?"

"Yes, but only if they're in pain. Mister Conrad's agents now take a special reader in the field with them just in case."

"In case of what?"

"In case they find a Glow-head too close to death to risk transport." T.J. said, opening one eye and looking at K'Narf.

"What's in the reader?"

"That's where you and I have a problem." T.J. said, closing her eye and frowning.

"How come *we* suddenly have a problem?" K'Narf asked, stressing the word "*we*" as he looked over at T.J.

"Your Mister Conrad has his agents teach them English, then the workings of all the vital organs; the nervous system and the circulatory system just like you suggested." T.J. said, making sure K'Narf was getting a clear picture of the situation.

"What's wrong with that?"

"Nothing, until they show them *two* before and after examples to prove that they have the ability to fix the immediate damage to their bodies." T.J. said, taking a moment to let her words register in K'Narf's mind. "I understand their presentation is quite effective, especially the '*two*' before and after examples they use." She added, stressing the word "*two*" both times she used it.

"He didn't, he wouldn't dare...." K'Narf stammered, unable to finish his thought as he caught onto what T.J. was saying.

"Not only would he, he did! His agents are not only showing them pictures of how seriously I had aged before I reversed the process, they show them a picture of my damaged leg! Then they show them a picture of me in that dress I wore to the party with a

214

slit all the way up the side so I could show my leg off after I had regenerated it! All he did to you was show a picture of what you used to look like and what you look like now!" T.J. said, red spikes of anger coloring her unseen aura.

"How could he do that, I don't even have a picture of what I used to look like myself!" K'Narf said, wondering how Brent had acquired such a thing.

"That may be our fault." T.J. said. "I mean Wanda and I. We needed material on you for the history reader we were working on, and Wanda asked Brent to see if he could find out where you grew up and went to school."

"But I never went to school, so I don't have any records to look up!"

"You have a driver's license don't you?" T.J. asked, knowing how easy it was to trace.

"Oh no, Sheriff Anderson!" K'Narf said, understanding what T.J. was driving at. "That would lead him straight to the farm and Gramps."

"That would explain the picture he has of you." T.J. said, knowing how K'Narf felt about the way he used to look.

"And this is the man you want me to call Mister!" K'Narf said, gritting his teeth at the thought. "I'm going to...."

"First, he still deserves our respect, especially yours, and you're going to do nothing at the moment." T.J. said, cutting K'Narf off before he committed himself as she opened both eyes and turned and looked at him. "Second, we are going to wait and see if he survives the attack on that alien fighter."

"And if he does?"

"Then we are going to be very patient and bide our time. Right now he has his guard up and it would be extremely difficult to surprise him." T.J. said, looking at K'Narf in a way that made him suddenly feel sorry for Brent. "But when the time is right we will, as you say in your western slang, *'skin him alive and tack his hide up on the barn wall to dry.'*" She added, stressing each and every word and syllable.

"Ouch!" K'Narf said, knowing why he suddenly felt sorry for Brent.

"Now, try and get some rest; sleep if you can." T.J. said. "Just wake me up before you flip us around and reverse thrust. I don't want to be jerked around like that while I'm asleep." T.J. said, closing her eyes and leaving K'Narf to thank the Lord a little more

215

earnestly than he had, about giving him Mister Brent Conrad as both a friend and colleague, especially considering the challenges that still lay ahead of them. Then spent more than an hour praying earnestly that neither Brent, nor any of his team, would die in the battle to come.

He also pointed out to the Lord that Brent needed to learn that it was not nice to make examples out of people without their permission, especially if one of them was his wife, T.J.

"I thought you were going to wake me up when we hit mid-point." T.J. said, waking up and realizing they were already in the asteroid belt.

"You were sleeping so soundly that I decided to ease off and turn us around at one G, then very slowly increased us back to four. You never noticed the change so I let you sleep. You seemed to need it." K'Narf said, as he spotted the whale.

"I must have because I never felt a thing." T.J. said, stretching now that they were in freefall; watching as K'Narf approached the eye of the whale and started matching her spin.

"Why don't you flash Wanda and let her know we're coming in." K'Narf asked, as he dove the lady into the whale's eye.

"That was an awful fast trip." Wanda said, as T.J. and then K'Narf dropped into her kitchen. "You were in New York when I flashed you, weren't you?"

"Yes, we pushed four G's all the way." K'Narf said, helping T.J. set down at the familiar picnic table with its built in bench seats he and Rudy had bolted down so long ago.

"Let me get you some coffee first." Wanda said, as K'Narf joined T.J. at the table. "I'll fix you something to eat after we talk." She added, reaching for the ever-present coffee pot.

"Where did those come from?" K'Narf asked, suddenly pointing at some familiar looking cardboard boxes stacked in the corner.

"Those." Wanda said, looking at what K'Narf was pointing at. "Brent brought us some of the best veggies we've ever gotten in those. He said they came from your grandfather's farm in upstate New York." Wanda said, looking at the logo on the end of one of the boxes that read "Stienbeck's Best" in big bold red letters and "Organic Produce, Est. October, 29th, 1916" in smaller black lettering on the next two lines. "Is that true?"

"Well, we were right about how he got your picture." T.J. said, as she read the label on the box and recognized the name.

216

"Yes." K'Narf said, answering Wanda first. "It also explains who it was that contracted to buy all Gramps and Junior's produce." He added, remembering his father's comment as he answered T.J.

"Here." Wanda said, as she set three steaming cups of black coffee down on the table and sat down opposite K'Narf and T.J. "Now, about Rudy. The numbness in his right side has worn off and he seems to be okay at the moment, but it sure gave me a start when he couldn't move, talk or feel anything on the whole right side of his body." Wanda said, the fear of that moment showing in her face.

"Where is he now?" K'Narf asked, glancing at the closed door of Rudy's bedroom.

"I told him to go lie down and take a nap when T.J. flashed me that you were coming in. He ought to be asleep by now." Wanda said, as she took a sip of her coffee. "He naps a lot lately, so he didn't argue with me." She added, looking at K'Narf.

"Has he accepted the Lord yet?" T.J. asked, blowing on her coffee. Trying to cool it off enough to take a sip.

"No, I think he wants to, but something in his past is, in his mind, unforgivable." Wanda said, her eyes getting moist.

"I think I know what it might be." K'Narf said, getting both Wanda and T.J.'s full attention. "Rudy told me once that he had spent thirty years in the Navy as a cook, all of them at sea. He said that's why he never married. I think our Rudy might have had a girl in every port, so to speak." K'Narf said, remembering the porch conversations he'd had with Rudy.

"Is that all!" Wanda said, looking relieved. Having thought of much worse things. "If I know my Rudy, he had more than one girl in every port, and have you ever noticed the scars on his knuckles?" She asked, looking at K'Narf.

"Yes, I have. Being black at that time, I'm sure he had his share of fights." K'Narf said, remembering the fight he'd had with Herman's gang. "But have you noticed that there are no scars on his face, that they're all on his knuckles. I think our Rudy was a pretty good fighter." He added, thinking again of Herman.

"I'll bet he was. Now if I can just convince him that he hasn't committed an unforgivable sin, or sins, and that our Lord Jesus is more than willing to forgive him if he'll just forgive himself and repent." Wanda said, smiling with relief.

217

"I can help you with that. I've counseled and led more than a few to the Lord during my years." T.J. said, reaching over and touching Wanda's hand. "By the way, do you have some clothes I can borrow? I really need to get out of this." She added, opening her mink stole so Wanda could see her dress.

"I thought you looked somewhat over dressed for my little kitchen. You really do look nice though, and that necklace is a stunner." Wanda said, looking at T.J.'s antique necklace. "K'Narf, why don't you go look at what Brent and Debbie did to the crystal room while I get T.J. something more comfortable to wear."

"What did he do now?" K'Narf asked, getting tired of being surprised by something Brent had done.

"They turned it into a memorial chapel. Rudy and I didn't think you'd mind." Wanda said, standing up. "It's actually very beautiful, especially the picture Debbie painted of Wonder and the cross she created."

"Cross?"

"Yes, she went up to the top of the waterfall of tears and cut out a Cross, then fused the tears with her laser so you can't even see where she got it from. All the wood stuff Brent got from an old church in England, I think. Anyway, you go take a look at it while I'm getting T.J. some clothes." Wanda said, taking T.J. by the hand and heading for her bedroom door; a door that was adjacent to Rudy's but not connected. "Take your time, we'll be a few minutes trying on different outfits." She added, as she shut the door behind them leaving K'Narf no choice but to go look at the new chapel.

"Oh sweet Lord Jesus!" K'Narf said, as he turned on the lights in what had been the crystal room. Instantly feeling the presence of the Lord.

Brent and Debbie had placed an eight-foot Cross, the one Wanda said Debbie had cut out of the crystal waterfall, into the far wall wiring it in a way that made the entire Cross glow when you turned on the lights.

They had also covered the floor with a dark purple carpet, and placed twelve beautifully carved antique pews, six on each side of the room, creating an aisle that led directly to the Cross. Up front and slightly off to the left, they'd placed the most beautiful wood podium, worn and polished with age, he had ever seen. What made it even more beautiful was that all ten of God's commandments, the original ones, were deeply carved into it's front.

Taking a few steps further into the room he could see the memorial portrait Debbie had painted of Wonder hanging on the wall just to the right of the Cross. He knew Debbie was an artist, but until now he had not realized the extent of her talents. The picture of Wonder looked like it could come alive and speak. It could hang in any museum in the world with pride.

K'Narf, feeling the strong presence of the Lord, dropped to his knees in front of the Cross and began quietly and simply to talk to the Lord; praying about something that had been on his heart for months now.

"Dear Sweet Lord Jesus." He said softly. "When I was a small child, I sat crying in my grandfather's hen house holding a hen named Mattie who had broken her leg. I asked you to please heal her, as I was the one responsible for her and that she was my friend.

You took pity on me that day, and healed her. I felt the bones come together as I held her leg in my hand. I come to you today asking again for a friend; a friend I desperately don't want to lose. He is the first person who ever took a real interest in me, and I would not be here now if it were not for him. Lord, I don't want to lose Rudy to age, illness or anything else. I know you can't pull his filters unless he repents and accepts you as his Lord and Savior, but in my heart I know he will.

We're all praying for him, and T.J. is going to be helping Wanda convince him that You can and will forgive him. What I'm asking is that the minute he asks for forgiveness and accepts You as his Lord and Savior, You will heal his mind just like you did Mattie's leg, putting it back together like it was when You created Adam in the Garden of Eden. No left, no right, no conscious and no unconscious; just a single unified brain functioning like you originally designed it. Please Lord Jesus, pull the filters in Rudy's mind the second he accepts You. We can show him how to heal his heart, or his nervous system if that's the problem, but only if You heal him first.

That's what I'm asking for, that's my prayer. I'm beginning to see the path you've placed before me, and I'm asking that Rudy be allowed to travel it with me. He's my friend Lord Jesus, he's my friend." K'Narf said, tears welling up in his eyes.

"K'Narf, are you there?" T.J. flashed. "Rudy's awake and wants to see you." She added, knowing K'Narf was hearing her.

"Amen." K'Narf said, as he wiped at his eyes and got to his feet. "I'll be right there." He flashed, as he headed for the chapel's exit tunnel.

Dropping into the kitchen, K'Narf saw Rudy's face split in an ear-to-ear grin when he saw him. If there was anything wrong with him he sure didn't show it. "I thought you were sick!" K'Narf said, landing too hard and bouncing off the floor.

"I may be sick, but at least I know how to keep my feet on the floor." Rudy said, laughing as K'Narf floated two feet off the floor, his arms flailing at the air like windmills until Wanda reached up and pulled him down.

"You just wanted some attention, didn't you?" K'Narf asked, making light of Rudy's condition as he grabbed the table and sat down before he floated off the floor again.

"Got it, didn't I." Rudy said, winking at T.J. who was now dressed in what appeared to be a form fitting white sweat suit.

"Toby's been trying to get through to you, said you weren't responding. Is something wrong?" T.J. flashed on the common frequency, so Wanda would know what was being said.

"No, nothing. I was talking with the Lord and didn't want to be interrupted, that's all." K'Narf flashed back. "Wanda, that chapel is unbelievable." He added, speaking so Rudy could hear.

"Yes, it is." Wanda said, smiling at Rudy. "I've been there quite a few times lately praying for this big lug here." She added, hitting Rudy with a love tap on the shoulder.

"No need to be wasting God's time on me, I'm going to be just fine." Rudy said, suddenly embarrassed at being the center of attention.

"K'Narf, it's Toby again." T.J. flashed.

"Yes, I have him. What is it Toby?" K'Narf flashed back, again using the general frequency so Wanda could hear them. Noticing, by the look on Rudy's face, that he knew they were flashing.

"You need to get back here before I lose control or lose my mind, whichever comes first." Toby flashed.

"Why, what's going on?" K'Narf flashed back.

"What isn't?" Toby flashed. "Premo and Sylvia moved into the old High School and Brent and Minh Le took over what used to be the grade school and they brought all their newbie's with them!"

"What's wrong with that?" K'Narf flashed, still wondering what had Toby so upset. "That's why we bought up the whole town, isn't it?"

"What's wrong is now they're all out here wanting to help. They've fixed all the broken windows, cleaned or painted everything in the place. Some of them are outside landscaping and starting what they're calling a factory garden!" Toby flashed, sending pictures of the outside of the factory being overrun by dozens of newbie's of every size, shape and sex.

"I'm still not sure why that's a problem?" K'Narf flashed, looking over at T.J. and Wanda.

"K'Narf, they know about that alien fighter, they know about you and the whale, they know about the history reader they will get to see when it's their turn to go to the whale, and they all want to help! If I hiccup, one of them will be standing there with a glass of water!" Toby flashed, visibly upset and obviously overwhelmed.

"What about the design for the fighter, how are you coming on that?" K'Narf asked, changing the subject.

"It's done, parts are already starting to arrive. They'll probably have all three fighters ready to go by the end of the week!"

"By the end of the week, how?" K'Narf flashed, starting to get as excited as Toby.

"Four of the newbie's used to be top aeronautic engineers, they looked at the readout Brent brought us on those black fighters, and said they could design a fighter that could outmaneuver and outfight one of those things any day of the week. Brent told them what he wanted yesterday morning and they had a full set of specifications ready by nightfall. K'Narf, these guys don't sleep, they were ordering parts before you and T.J. landed in New York to shop for that new dress T.J. wanted." Toby flashed, excitement showing in his flashes.

"Buying parts?" K'Narf asked, thinking that was to be his job.

"K'Narf, they know every manufacturer on the planet, and they're pulling strings all over the place, it's awesome!"

"What about the battery problem?" K'Narf asked, knowing the oversized forklift batteries and charging them with solar mirrors had been their biggest design problem.

"Brent took care of that."

"How?"

"He sent one of his agent teams out to Pluto and had them remove three of their atomic batteries from that mother ship."

"Go on." K'Narf flashed, sensing there was something Toby didn't want to tell him.

"Brent said that your battery system was nice, but it was too Rube Goldberg for use in a fighter." Toby flashed, pausing for a second before he continued. "The new batteries are smaller, about the size of a water heater, and have a radioactive core. Brent said we developed a similar version here, but the large power companies had them shut down as being too dangerous."

"Are they dangerous?"

"Not according to Brent, he said the core is wrapped in two inches of hardened steel, six inches of lead then another two inches of hardened steel. He says getting contaminated by the core is next to impossible, and that they will produce electric current for a hundred years or more before they burn out." Toby flashed, obviously proud of Brent's ingenuity.

"And he sent one of his teams to the mother ship to get them?"

"Yes, he said to tell you that he's learning to delegate just like you taught him."

"I taught him?" K'Narf flashed, questioning Toby's allegation that he had taught Brent anything.

"Yes, I don't know what to tell you, but Brent listens and reacts to everything you say, I think he really looks up to you." Toby flashed.

"Anything else?" K'Narf flashed, passing on Toby's assessment of Brent, and thinking there had to be more than this to rattle Toby.

"If by else, you mean the six new vans they hauled in and are disassembling all over the factory floor, or their new paint booth they're setting up so they can paint them with Brent's new color changing paint, or do you mean the stretch limousine they brought in this morning?" Toby asked, flashing them a picture of the pandemonium on the factory floor.

"Stretch limousine?" T.J. asked, jumping into the conversation, remembering when K'Narf had suggested it to needle her, at least that's what she thought at the time.

"They know about K'Narf's wanting to bring them up, thirteen at a time, to the whale in a limousine so they went out and got one. They're down there now happily tearing it apart and converting it for space." Toby flashed. "And tell Wanda and Rudy to get ready for visitors, they're going to have a lot of them and how soon can you get back here?" He added, sounding better having vented some of his frustrations on K'Narf.

"Hang on a second." K'Narf flashed, looking at T.J. "Are you going to stay here?" He asked, knowing the answer before he asked the question.

"Yes, Wanda and I are going to gang up on Rudy." T.J. said, smiling at the expression on Rudy's face and flashing K'Narf an "*I Love You*" on their private frequency.

"Give me about five hours." K'Narf flashed, letting Toby know that he'd push all five drive core's and get there as fast as possible. "Rudy, I'm leaving you in good hands, but what's happened to Thomas and Judy. I haven't seen hide or hair of them since we got here. Don't they like people anymore?"

"They're over in your bedroom with the kittens." Rudy said, answering K'Narf now that the conversation had moved back into the audible realm. "They're almost a week old now, and Thomas and Judy are having trouble controlling them." He added grinning.

"How many?" T.J. asked. "Can I go see them?" She asked, before getting an answer to her first question.

"Six of them, and yes, anytime you want. Thomas and Judy don't mind." Wanda said, getting up from the table at the same time K'Narf did.

"Flash me a picture, but not for the next few hours, I didn't get any sleep on the way out here, and I'm wiped out. I should be able to get a good four hours on the way back." K'Narf said, leaning down and kissing T.J. goodbye. "Take good care of him." He added, nodding at Rudy as he leaped up at the kitchens exit, feeling a sudden urgency to get back to the factory and Toby.

Chapter Twenty-Four

"Toby, are you awake?" K'Narf flashed, as he approached the factory in the early morning light.

"Yes, where are you?"

"Coming up on the factory right now, and since when do we have gate guards?" K'Narf asked, as two men stepped out of a refurbished and newly painted guard shack and motioned for him to stop. One of them was wearing a pair of the bubble lens sunglasses he had designed.

"Yes sir, can I help you?" The first one asked.

"He's one of us." The second one said, removing the sunglasses. "Ask him for the password."

"Toby, they want a password!" K'Narf flashed.

"Etaguf." Toby flashed back. "The password is Etaguf."

"But that's my name! Brent did this didn't he?" K'Narf flashed, not knowing whether to be flattered or angry.

"Sir?" One of the guards said, making a question out of the word as he stepped closer.

"Etaguf, the password is Etaguf." K'Narf said quickly.

"And your name sir?" The other guard asked, trying to get a peek into the Lady's cargo bay.

"K'Narf, K'Narf Etaguf." K'Narf said, noticing that his name seemed to shock both of them.

"You're him!" They both said in unison, snapping to attention like a pair of Marines just out of boot camp.

"Toby, they're standing at attention, what should I do?" K'Narf flashed, getting worried.

"Say 'as you were gentlemen' and then ask permission to enter."

"As you were gentlemen, may I proceed now?" K'Narf asked, quickly following Toby's directions.

"Yes sir!" They both said, as they stepped aside and smartly waved him through the gate.

"Toby, I'm in, but where should I park? The parking lot's full of all kinds of cars and trucks."

"Pull around front. You'll see my van. It's still black like yours and I reserved you a spot next to it. I'm on my way out and I'll meet you there." Toby flashed.

"You said it was a mad house, but I didn't expect it to be this bad." K'Narf said, opening the Lady's door as Toby came running up. "And is that a train?" He asked, looking at the nose of what appeared to be a locomotive poking out from behind the factory.

"Yeah, they just unloaded three fuselages. Had to bring them in on flatcars." Toby said, like it was the most normal thing in the world to be doing.

"Fuselages?" K'Narf asked, hurrying to keep up with Toby as they headed back into the factory.

"Yeah, Karl said that starting with something that had two tandem seats and was already designed to fly would cut assembly time in half. Uh, better watch out, I think they know you're here." Toby warned, noticing all the people rushing into the lobby area from every direction.

In moments no less than fifty people, all clapping their hands, surrounded K'Narf and Toby. Every one of them looking and smiling directly at K'Narf. "All right, you've all seen him, now shoo!" Toby said, waving his hands and shooing everyone back to wherever they came from. "You're lucky we don't have a band, he would have had them playing 'Hail to the Chief'." He added, grinning at K'Narf.

"By 'he', you mean our young Mister Conrad." K'Narf said, as everyone smiled and nodded at him as they turned and headed back to whatever it was they were doing.

"Let's just say that Mister Conrad and his agents make sure that you and T.J. get full credit for their being found and rescued." Toby said, grinning. "He's made both of you rather famous, at least with our people."

"T.J.'s going to kill him." K'Narf said, stating it as a fact, not a possibility.

"I figured as much when I saw the pictures he was using of her. I asked him why, and he said he needed something dramatic and you two were the best he had at the moment." Toby said, leaving the lobby and leading K'Narf down a long narrow hall. "And from what I understand, the shock value of those pictures have been instrumental in bringing several of them out of their death spiral." He added, as they stepped out onto a platform that allowed them to look down on the factory floor.

"I don't think that's going to be enough to save him." K'Narf said, remembering the look in T.J.'s eyes when she said she was going to skin Brent alive. "Where is he anyway?" He asked, quickly forgetting his question as he stepped up to the rail and got a good look at the factory floor. It had been one hundred thousand square feet of empty, lightless and dirty floor space the last time he had seen it. Now it was sparkling clean and lit up like Times Square on New Year's Eve.

In the far right corner was the stretch limousine with its guts spread all over the floor. Next to it and all down the whole right side of the assembly floor were all six of the new vans Toby had spoken of, all in the process of being converted seemingly at the same time. Unneeded engines and transmissions were neatly stacked against the wall, and the flickering of welding torches lighting up each one in turn like the on and off blinking of Christmas lights. On the left side, divided into three equal areas, were sitting what looked like three world war two fighters without wings; which is exactly what they were. Everything on the floor was lit up by overhead and improvised floodlights.

"What are they unloading?" K'Narf asked, pointing at over a dozen men carrying boxes and stuff out of a semi trailer that had been backed up to one of the docks at the back of the building.

"I have no idea, all I know is that Brent makes the drivers wait in town while our people drive their trucks over here and unload them." Toby said, quickly scanning all the different activities going on. "There's Karl waving at us." He added, pointing at a man in white coveralls who was waving at them to come down.

"Who's Karl?" K'Narf asked, turning away from the rail and following Toby back into the narrow hallway.

"He's in charge of the design team. I think he was part of the team that designed the German Messerschmitt." Toby said, opening the door to a stairwell and motioning K'Narf to go in ahead of him. "I know he came over from Germany after the war, and that he was one of those who were very near death when one of Brent's teams found him." He added, following K'Narf down the stairs.

"You never answered me about Brent, you do know where he's at, don't you?" K'Narf asked, opening the door and stepping out into the assembly floor proper.

"Oh yes, he and his five carefully chosen fellow pilots, are lying down, meditating and stuffing their faces over in one of those company owned executive houses of ours." Toby said, baiting K'Narf as they headed for the now smiling Karl.

"Meditating! You mean goofing off!"

"Yes, just like you and T.J. did when we built those first two fighters for you, remember!" Toby said, not being able to resist pointing out how they'd felt when it had been K'Narf and T.J. lying down. "At least we know what they're doing this time!" He added, making his point as they joined up with Karl.

"I am so glad to finally be able to meet you!" Karl said, holding out his hand to K'Narf.

Twenty-two exhausting days later, he was standing in the exact same spot with his arm draped over Karl's shoulder looking at the most beautiful flying machines he had ever seen. Working continuously around the clock, resting only on the Sabbath and napping in between when the opportunity presented itself, they had managed to strip down, redesign and build back up the three original fuselages into three gleaming silver, teardrop shaped fighting machines.

They looked almost identical to the small silver ships that they had watched being destroyed on that solar scroll. The major difference was where those pilots had given up their lives without a fight, these ships were heavily armed with lasers, rocket launchers and a lethal looking cannon that made the black enemy fighters look like starter toys. A team of pilots flying one of these machines would not give up their lives so easily.

Brent had showed up right after last Sabbath with his team mates and had been training on the new machines seemingly around the clock ever since; spooking everyone out with the darkness of their skin and their golden glowing eyes.

"K'Narf!" T.J. flashed, calling him on their private frequency. "Something's wrong with Rudy!"

"What's wrong?"

"We don't know. Wanda finally got him to understand that he hadn't done anything so terrible that our Lord Jesus wouldn't forgive him. Then we talked him through repentance and he accepted the Lord as his savior." T.J. said, flashing K'Narf a picture of Rudy huddled in a corner with his knees drawn up against his chest.

"I don't understand, I thought that's what we wanted him to do?" K'Narf asked, trying to make sense out of the picture T.J. was sending him.

"Yes, it was, but I think it may have caused him to have another stroke." T.J. said, sending K'Narf a second picture of Rudy huddled in the corner of the kitchen, only this time with Wanda squatted down beside him.

"T.J., go into Rudy's bedroom and find those Kirlian glasses I made for him." K'Narf flashed, sending her a picture of what the original glasses looked like. "Hurry!" He added, signaling Toby to come over.

"Found them." T.J. flashed, sending a picture of the glasses in her hand.

"Good, put them on and see if they're working." K'Narf said, sending her a picture of the battery control and pointing out the 'on' switch.

"Oww! I can't see anything." T.J. flashed, turning the glasses off. "That hurt." She added, taking them off.

"Okay, quick, go in the bathroom and get a roll of toilet paper then go back in kitchen." K'Narf flashed, not taking time to explain.

"Okay, now what?"

"Put on the glasses, close both eyes and turn them on, then hold up and look through the toilet paper core with your left eye only, keep the right one closed." K'Narf flashed, giving T.J. specific directions. "Is Rudy's head glowing?" He asked, holding his breath as he asked the question.

"Yes! Yes it is! It's so bright I can't even make out his face!" T.J. flashed, taking off the glasses and yelling at Wanda to come take a look.

"I'll flash you right back!" K'Narf flashed, terminating the connection with T.J. as Toby came running up.

"What wrong?" Toby asked, knowing by the look on K'Narf's face that something serious had happened.

"Where's Brent?" K'Narf asked, looking around. "Get him over here, we need to talk."

"What's up?" Brent asked, not real happy that a training session had been interrupted as he joined Toby and K'Narf.

"Is it safe for me to take one of your vans and go to the whale?" K'Narf asked, knowing he had ignored Toby's question.

"Yes, our friends apparently found out that we've been visiting their mother ship and are hanging around Pluto guarding it, why?"

"Rudy's had his filters pulled by the Lord, and Wanda and T.J. think he might have had another stroke. Your vans have three seats and I need to get up there as fast as possible, and I want to take Premo, Sylvia and a copy of all their readers with me." K'Narf said, finally answering Toby's question.

"Yes, of course. Here, take mine." Brent said, pulling out a hand held computer and punching buttons. "There, it's dark red again and it's parked out front by yours." He added, handing K'Narf a set of keys.

"Thank you Mister Conrad." K'Narf said, formally addressing Brent as he took the keys. "Sabbath starts in a few hours. Will you and your pilots be ready to take off as soon as it over?"

"That's what we've been planning on." Brent said, duly noting the respectful manner in which K'Narf had addressed him.

"May the blessings of our Lord Jesus go with you." K'Narf said, holding out his hand. "And Brent, when this is over, could you and your pilots come to the whale. We're going to have another meeting and I'd like you and your team to be there." He added, shaking Brent's hand and making the request personal by using Brent's first name as he nodded at Toby in order to include him in the decision and the invitation.

"Will our ships fit through your airlock?" Brent asked, using the question as a way of saying yes.

"You have exactly one point seven inches of clearance, Karl and I made sure of that."

"You know Karl was one of those on whom yours and T.J.'s pictures had a profound effect." Brent said, nodding toward Karl who was over polishing a spot on fighter number three.

"How so?" K'Narf asked, not sure he liked talking about what Brent had done with his and T.J.'s pictures. It was still a sore subject as far as he was concerned.

"We found him in a full service home under hospice care out in California. He was just shy of one hundred years old and drugged up with morphine because his heart was failing. We transferred him to the van's bed and took him out into space where there was no gravity to pull on his heart, let the morphine wear off and started showing him the readers. He resisted us until I showed him your pictures. It was those pictures that gave him hope. You might say he's here now because of them." Brent said, knowing that K'Narf and T.J. had been upset with him and thought to use this chance to explain. "For whatever it's worth." He added, nodding at Toby as he turned and walked away.

"Told you." Toby said, grinning at K'Narf.

"I still don't think that's going to be enough to save him." K'Narf said, remembering again the look in T.J.'s eyes when she said she was going to skin him alive.

"I need to get over and pick up Premo and Sylvia, could you flash them and tell them what's happening and that we need to be in space within the hour?" K'Narf asked, turning and heading for the front office area. "Tell them to bring a full set of their readers."

"What about the Sabbath, it starts in an hour?" Toby asked, hurrying to catch up.

"Once we're in space we'll be on Zulu time, and we'll have just enough time to get to the whale before the Sabbath starts there." K'Narf said, grabbing his briefcase and a coat from the office and heading out the door. "As soon as the Sabbath is over gather up Minh Le, Debbie and Irena and bring them up. We have a lot to talk about."

"Like what?" Toby asked, trying to get a handle on what K'Narf was driving at.

"This battle isn't the end, it's just the beginning." K'Narf said, turning and looking at Toby like he should have known better than to ask such a question. "Tell Minh Le we'll expect a full report on his recovery operations and agent training, current and projected." He added, as he turned and broke into a run for Brent's dark red van with its extra seat for Sylvia."

Five hours and seventeen minutes later he was in the asteroid belt approaching the whale. Premo and Sylvia were still having a contest to see who could snore the loudest, making him wonder how could they teach everyone else to repair their bodies and not be able to fix their own adenoids. Reaching over he shook Premo by the shoulder and woke him up.

"What, are we here already?" Premo asked, rubbing at his eyes as he automatically reached back and shook Sylvia.

"Yes, we're almost there and you'll want to be ready when we land." K'Narf said, diving at the whale's eye. "Rudy may not be in any danger, but I don't want to take any chances." He added, as Sylvia started coughing and clearing her throat.

"My God, what happened to you?" T.J. asked, as K'Narf landed in the kitchen and she got a good look at him, jumping up from the table and grabbing him as he staggered trying to regain his balance.

"Nothing, why?" K'Narf asked, getting out of the way so Premo and Sylvia could land.

"Because you look like death warmed over." A familiar voice said. "Ya never did know when to pull the plug." Rudy added, grinning at K'Narf from across the room.

"Rudy!" K'Narf said, leaving T.J. standing in the middle of the floor as he made a beeline for Rudy. "You're all right!" He added, as he grabbed him and gave him a full double arm wrap bear hug.

"Was, until you decided to squeeze the life out of me." Rudy said, trying to get K'Narf off of him as he looked over at Wanda. "Sabbath started yet?"

"Yes, just minutes ago, why?" Wanda asked, knowing the question had been directed at her.

"Lord said to rest on the Sabbath, so this boy is going to bed!" Rudy said, taking K'Narf by the arm and pulling him toward his bedroom. "Your bedroom ain't fit, so you're going to have to use mine." He added, opening his bedroom door and shoving the unresisting K'Narf toward his big king size bed.

"What's wrong with my bedroom?" K'narf asked, not really caring as he flopped down on the bed and let Rudy pull off his shoes and cover him up, clothes and all.

"It's infested by a bunch of kittens that'll attack you the second you go in there." Rudy said, looking down on the exhausted face of his best friend. "And they scratch." He added quietly, as he slipped out of the bedroom and closed the door on an already sleeping K'Narf.

Twenty-three hours later, K'Narf opened his eyes to a darkened bedroom and the sound of loud voices and laughter. Getting up he staggered over and opened the door on a wild scene of celebration. Minh Le, Debbie, Primo, Sylvia, Wanda, Rudy, Toby, Irena and T.J. were all jumping up and down, hugging each other and praising the Lord at the top of their lungs. "What's going on?" He asked, standing in the doorway, his hair and clothes looking as rumpled and befuddled by sleep as he was.

"They did it!" Toby yelled, being closest to the door when K'Narf stepped out. "They got those miserable misbegotten murdering scum!" He added, the anger and vehemence in his voice dampening the laughter in the room.

"But how, they couldn't have got to Pluto that fast. They haven't had time to...." K'Narf stammered, beginning to understand what had happened.

"They didn't have to, they came to them." Toby said, calming down a little. "They left Pluto and headed for earth, Brent and his fighters intercepted them coming in just this side of Mars and took them out in less than ten minutes."

"Did any of our guys get hurt?" K'Narf asked, seeing the answer in everyone's face before he heard it from Toby.

"No! Not even a near miss if I understood Brent right! I don't know what he did, but none of his ships were hit and they're on their way here for that meeting you wanted." Toby said, as T.J. got to him and gave him a big hug. "I guess we're all here for that meeting you wanted." He added, looking around the room at everyone crowded into the kitchen.

"How much time have I got?" K'Narf asked, trying to stop T.J. from brushing at his hair with her hands.

"Brent and his ships should be getting here in about two hours." Toby said, seeing the surprise in K'Narf's eyes. "Those ships of his are faster than anything we ever thought of designing." He added, reminding K'narf of the pitiful designs they had started out with before Karl and Brent had gotten involved.

"Good, I have time to clean up, get something to eat and have a little prayer time before they get here." K'Narf said, as he gave T.J. a quick hug, turned and headed for the bathroom in Rudy's room.

"Please!" Debbie said, getting up and offering K'Narf her seat at the table when he returned. "I'll go see about the kittens." She added, leaping for the exit.

"Here you go." Wanda said, as she set a big bowl of lamb stew down on the table in front of K'Narf. "Saved you a piece of apple pie too, but you better eat it quick with this bunch hanging around." She added, stopping as K'Narf bowed his head and asked for the Lord's blessing before putting the pie on the table.

"I must say you do look a lot better." T.J. said, getting a nod of agreement from Wanda. "You had me worried yesterday, and I agree with Rudy. You really don't 'know when to pull the plug.'" She added, quoting Rudy as she snuggled up against K'Narf's side and wrapped herself around his left arm; forcing him to eat with his right.

"Where's Rudy?" K'Narf asked, speaking with his mouth full.

"He's in the conference room with Premo and Sylvia. They've taught him to flash using the common frequency, but they haven't found his private frequency yet. I think it's like yours, a very high one." Wanda said, turning and heading for the refrigerator.

"Where's everyone else?" K'Narf asked, trying to swallow at the same time.

"All over the place." Wanda said, coming back from the refrigerator with a large glass of cold soymilk. "Minh Le's in the conference room too. He has flip charts for his report and recording devices all set up for the meeting. I think Toby and Irena are in the Chapel, and Debbie just told us she was going over to your place to play with the kittens." She added, setting down opposite K'Narf and T.J.; watching quietly as K'Narf devoured everything in front of him.

"Well, if you ladies don't mind, I'm going to head for the chapel and get in a little time with the Lord before this meeting starts." K'Narf said, draining the last drop of milk from his glass and standing up.

"Do you want me to go with you?" T.J. asked, knowing he didn't, but bound by politeness to ask.

"No, you and Wanda just try and get everyone into the conference room when Brent gets here." K'Narf said, leaning over and kissing T.J. on the top of her head. "And save me a seat!" He added, leaping at the kitchen's exit.

"Lord, this place is beautiful." K'Narf said, feeling the Lords presence as he stepped into the dimly lit chapel a few minutes later.

"K'narf, we were just leaving." Toby said softly, greeting K'Narf as he and Irena got up from the second pew on the right side and quietly headed for the exit.

Feeling the presence of the Lord getting stronger, K'Narf walked forward to the same spot where he had prayed for Rudy and dropped to his knees; light from the crystal Cross shined on his face as he again began to quietly and simply talk to the Lord; and as before he started praying about something that was heavy on his heart.

"Dear Sweet Lord Jesus." He said softly. "These people You are sending me are all, each and every one of them, brilliant, talented, innovative and extremely independent. If I don't use and say the right words in this meeting they will start abandoning me and go their own way out into the world or into the safety of space.

I am asking You, imploring You, to please help me when I stand before them. You told Moses '*I will be with thy mouth*' when he had to speak before Pharaoh. I am asking for that same blessing.

They must understand that not only will the evil we have discovered out on Pluto return in force, but that our world is getting ready to live through the horrible prophecies of Daniel eleven and twelve. That as soon as those seven years Daniel describes are finished, You will be returning to build your Holy City and live amongst us. They need to know and understand in their hearts that we must stand and fight, that running away into space as the space people did, would be to abandon not only our planet and the souls living on it, but You and Your Holy City as well.

That's what I'm asking for, that's my prayer. I see the path You've placed before us, and I'm asking that You give me words that will reach down into the very soul of each and every new unveiled believer You send us, and by the words You give me that they will take up Your banner and be loyal to Your cause. We're going to need them all, and I don't know where to begin or even how to thank You for what you did for Rudy." K'Narf said, tears welling up in his eyes.

"K'Narf, are you there?" T.J. flashed. "Brent just arrived." She added, knowing K'Narf was hearing her.

"Amen." K'Narf said, as he wiped at his eyes and got to his feet. "I'll be right there." He flashed, as he headed for the chapel's exit tunnel.

234

Chapter Twenty-Five

"What's this?" K'Narf asked, stepping into the conference room and looking around. Brent and his five pilots were seated around the back of the table, still in their blue and green spacesuits, but without their fishbowl helmets. Giving a surreal atmosphere to the room with their dark skins and golden glowing eyes. Two of them, he noticed were women, something he hadn't realized at the factory because of the skullcaps they had been wearing during training.

Everyone else was seated on either side of the big oblong conference table, the front of it being left open for him; each of them setting back in one of the deep cushioned conference room chairs leaving only a small straight backed chair unoccupied at the head of the table.

"Sixteen people, fifteen chairs, last person in gets what's left." Toby said, grinning at K'Narf who was frowning at the small bedside chair he knew had come from Rudy's bedroom. "You'll be standing most of the time anyway." He added, noticing that everyone seemed to agree with him except T.J.

"Sorry sweetheart, I tried, but they outnumbered me." T.J. said, frowning at Toby who had taken the last of the good chairs.

"It's okay." K'Narf said, taking the small chair and setting it off to the side. "And what's that?" He asked, as he stepped up to the front of the table and pointed at a six-inch silver globe setting on a small pedestal in the center of the table.

"That's a digital recording device. Every expression and word spoken in this room will be recorded." Minh Le said, leaning forward in his chair. "I will do the editing later." He added, nodding politely to everyone in the room as he leaned back into his chair again.

"Thank you Minh Le." K'Narf said, knowing it was necessary, but feeling like the globe was suddenly looking at him personally; a feeling shared by everyone in the room. "First I'd like to welcome our five pilots to this, our second meeting in the whale." K'Narf said, giving a bow of recognition to Brent's pilots.

"Have them introduce themselves." T.J. flashed, not wanting to coach K'Narf openly.

"Mister Conrad, would you like to introduce your team?" K'Narf asked, stepping back and leaning against the wall behind him, effectively giving the floor to Brent.

"It would be my pleasure." Brent said, standing up. "Sitting next to me is my co-pilot Hacker, who also happens to be Minh Le's grandfather. Our Marines gave him the name of Hacker during the Vietnam War because he always carried a big machete around with him.

Next to him is my second Pilot Dan Ripplinger and his bond mate and co-pilot Susan Ripplinger. My third pilot is Peter Vanlieu and his bond mate and co-pilot Antoinette Vanlieu." He added, pointing at them in turn as he sat back down.

"Thank you Mister Conrad. We're very proud to have all of you here and we'll be hearing about your recent exploit in a few minutes." K'Narf said, forewarning Brent that he would be the first speaker as he stepped away from the wall and back up to the head of the table.

"Next, it is my great privilege to welcome, with the Lord's recent blessing, another *full fledged* member to our little council, Mister Rudy Marcus." K'Narf said, stressing the words *'full fledged'* as he joined everyone in giving Rudy a round of applause.

"And his bond mate Wanda Marcus!" T.J. flashed, giving K'Narf a verbal dig in the ribs for not mentioning Wanda.

"Wanda!" K'Narf blurted out loud. "When did this happen?" He asked, still talking out loud.

"That's the other reason we were celebrating when you woke up!" Toby said, picking up on what was going on and realizing that K'Narf didn't know that Rudy and Wanda had been presented and accepted by the Lord as a bonded couple. "If you didn't spend all your time sleeping you'd know about these things!" He added, grinning from ear to ear as he looked at K'Narf's confusion.

"Now don't you go picking on K'Narf for getting a little sleep!" Rudy said, quickly speaking up in defense of K'Narf, remembering how he had driven himself to exhaustion getting Premo and Sylvia up to the whale just for him.

"I'll second that!" T.J. said, twisting around and hitting Toby on the shoulder.

"Okay, okay! I give up!" Toby said, laughing as he leaned away from T.J.'s blows.

"Wanda, you have my utmost apology and congratulations. You couldn't have found a better man!" K'Narf said, as he gathered his wits and bowed at the smiling Wanda. "Now, let's get a little dignity back into this meeting." He added, raising his hand to silence the tittering going on around the room.

"Oww!" K'Narf wailed as a kitten sailed into the room and latched onto his shoulder, digging in it's claws so it wouldn't bounce off. Turning as he grabbed for the kitten allowed the second incoming kitten to hit him square in the chest; again claws digging in for support. Looking up and seeing two more coming straight at him he managed to duck just in time to avoid being hit again.

T.J. seeing what was happening, and being the closest, jumped up and caught the next one that came sailing in just inches away from K'Narf's face, only to have the last of the six kittens hit her directly in the back. Writhing in pain she tried to twist her arm up behind her just as Toby reached her and carefully removed it, trying not to snag her jumper in the process.

The two kittens that K'Narf had dodged, had by this time hit the wall and rebounded at the unsuspecting K'Narf who, because he was standing and therefore the tallest person in the room, was their obvious target as one of them hit him directly in the back and the last one landed on his head and dug in; it had taken the high ground which was the top of K'Narf's head.

K'Narf, tossing the kitten he had taken from his shoulder at Sylvia, quickly grabbed at the one on his head, trying not to draw more blood than had already been drawn as he pulled it off the top of his head. T.J. quickly tossed her kitten to Debbie then grabbed at the one on K'Narf's chest. Minh Le, having been in the first seat on the other side of the table, had jumped up and was industriously trying to get the last kitten off of K'Narf's back without tearing his shirt.

Just as quickly as the attack had happened it was over, with six kittens safely captured and secured as K'Narf tossed his last kitten to Wanda. "Now, where was I?" K'Narf asked, brushing his hands through his rumpled hair and again raising his hand for

237

silence; allowing everyone time to get control of themselves. Even Brent's pilots had been unable to keep themselves from laughing.

"Saying something about dignity." Brent said, starting the tittering all over again.

"That, I'm going to delegate to you. Are you ready to tell us what happened out there?" K'Narf asked, reaching over and getting his chair and setting it down next to T.J., who immediately started brushing at his hair with her fingers as Thomas and Judy calmly walked into the room and looked around for their errant kittens.

"When our instruments told us that the alien fighter had left Pluto and was heading in the direction of earth, the timing could not have been better." Brent said, as he walked up and took his place at the head of the table. "The Sabbath was over and we had just finished attaching our four paintball missiles to Dan and Pete's fighters."

"Paintball?" Toby asked, not having heard anything about paintball missiles when they were building the fighters.

"Yes, paintball. I knew that ordinary explosives would do very little damage to our heavily armored friends out there, so I had my guys make me up four missiles filled with paint and very small particles of highly magnetized iron." Brent said, turning the full attention of his golden glowing eyes on Toby. Letting everyone in the room know that he did not like interruptions as he turned and looked at K'Narf as well.

"We were in space within minutes and had applied all eleven G's of thrust, setting us on a course that would intercept them just this side of Mars. We calculated a trajectory that would allow us to swing around behind them and match their speed before they were aware of us.

Everything went as planned and the first they knew of us was when Dan and Pete fired their missiles at them. The missiles were designed to corkscrew going in, making it almost impossible to hit them, but those gunners were good. Only two of our missiles got through, but two of them were enough. The paint instantly coated and blinded all of their optics and the magnetized particles created havoc with their inside tracking instruments at the same time.

While they were busy firing at the incoming missiles, Hacker had moved in and positioned us directly under their belly and I had opened fire with a highly concentrated quarter inch laser.

Having scouted their downed fighter out on Pluto, I knew exactly where their power controls were located. It took exactly eighteen seconds to cut through the four inches of hardened steel armor and hit their power panel.

As soon as we had them shut down, we slapped a super sensitive listening device to their hull and proceeded to drill holes into their ship with our laser at everything that moved or made a noise. We could hear them breathing, so none of them survived." Brent said, ending the saga of their fight with his chilling words of death. "We're going to haul their ship back to Pluto and salvage it next week. We can repair the damaged control panel and our laser holes will be easy to plug." He added, as he calmly walked back to his seat and sat down, having put a chill on the room with his report.

"The Lord's will be done." K'Narf said, motioning at Minh Le to make his presentation, knowing that killing evil people who were trying to kill you did not violate God's commandment against murder.

"I have nothing quite so dramatic to report." Minh Le said, stepping up to the front of the table and setting up a standard off the shelf flipchart. "I apologize for the quality of my charts, I could have made a very nice computerized presentation had I time to properly prepare." He added, looking directly at K'Narf so everyone would know who was to blame.

"As you know, Brent and I have designed our search teams around three people, all of them trained in each others specialty; interchangeable if you would prefer to think of them that way. There is the pick-up person who is responsible to bring the van down when the ground team is ready to be taken out. The ground team always consists of two people so they can carry a person who may be incapacitated and also to be able to protect themselves. The van is equipped with three acceleration chairs and one adjustable bed that can be tilted for acceleration also, but not recommended unless the patient is extremely stable.

As of right now we have nine teams in the field with six more van's being prepared for fieldwork at the factory. Volunteers for fieldwork are not a problem as almost everyone wants to be on a team. We have so far found one hundred and ninety seven newly unveiled believers, newbies or Glow-heads if you prefer those terms. All but thirty-two of them were spotted in retirement or nursing homes, and we have barely scratched the surface so to speak.

As you can see by this chart, the number of identified homes for the aged in California alone number more that seventy thousand, and that's just the larger ones we've managed to identify. Having a team visit each one of them will take more time and resources than we have at the moment, and I am still talking only California. As a result I am projecting, as you can see by this next chart, an immediate need for six hundred teams and, as he flipped the chart again, with three times that number as we branch out into Europe and other parts of the world.

We are of course working closely with Premo and Sylvia as to numbers of students, both current and projected, and again I apologize for the quality of my little presentation." Minh Le said, looking at K'Narf as he moved his flip chart out of the way and sat down.

"Premo, do you and Sylvia have anything you want to add?" K'Narf asked, leaning forward and looking down the table at Premo and Sylvia. "If nothing else, you might tell us where all that new hair came from." He added, causing everyone to grin as they looked at the full head of hair Premo now sported.

"Don't go talking about my hair, Brent might decide to use me for show and tell." Premo shot back, turning the tables on K'Narf by reminding everyone of his and T.J.'s before and after shots. "But I do have sort of a warning for Rudy and Wanda." He added, drawing everyone's attention to Rudy and Wanda as he looked across the table at them.

"My students have completed that stretch limousine of theirs and have been drawing straws to see who gets to come up here first. They've already identified the first five groups and are drawing straws for the sixth." Premo said, noticing the puzzled look on Rudy's face, not having been aware of what K'Narf had put into motion at their last meeting. "They've turned that limousine into a real luxury transport. It seats fourteen, counting the driver who they assume will be one of us, and they've put in a small restroom and refrigerator so they can have snacks on the way up and back. They even set it up with small tables so they can play that 'Four Kings' card game they're all hooked on right now. Like I said, just a little heads up for Wanda and Rudy." He added, looking back at K'Narf as if to say that's all I've got.

240

"Tell them they better bring more than snacks if they want us to cook a meal for them while they're up here!" Wanda said, speaking for Rudy as well as herself. "And I want to know ahead of time that they're coming, no midnight surprises. In fact, tell them they have to schedule all trips up through us!" She added, pointing at Rudy and then at herself.

"Okay, I'll tell them, what frequency should they contact you on?" Premo asked. "Or do you want them to go through me?"

"Through you, it will get too confusing otherwise, and we'll need an edited copy of this meeting to add to our history reader before any of them can come up here." Wanda said, glancing over at Minh Le and then down the table at K'Narf to let him know that she was through and the meeting was his again.

"Well, I guess it's my turn." K'Narf said, standing up and moving to the head of the table. *"There are things we need to talk about."* He added, bringing to Toby's mind all the things that had transpired since the last time K'Narf had called them all together because he had *'things he wanted to talk about'*.

Chapter Twenty-Six

"Our Lord has presented us with an opportunity to serve Him." K'Narf said, looking solemnly at everyone around the table. "However, as always when He presents us with a task He would like us to do, He also presents us with choices, at least two paths we can take. Not necessarily a choice between good and evil, but simply a free will choice.

And, as you know, the world, for both us and the normals, is currently standing on the brink of the prophecies in Daniel's eleventh and twelfth chapter. In those chapters he talks of three men, three contemporaries living in the same century; men according to Daniel that are all alive at the same time and place in history. These are the three men the Bible refers to as the three sixes, six being the number of a man according to John in his book of Revelations. These are the men that will usher in the final seven years, as prophesied by Daniel, prior to our Lords return." K'Narf said, pausing to take a breath as he looked around the table. Noticing that he had everyone's full attention.

"The first man is obviously the leader of a nation," K'Narf said, continuing. "Because Daniel says his predecessor will '*Set his face to enter with the strength of his whole kingdom, and upright ones with him*' which means he goes out and starts a war. The '*and upright ones with him*' indicates he will have a coalition of other countries going to war with him which is exactly what President Bush did, which positively identifies the country Daniel is talking about as the United States. Then Daniel says the first of his three contemporaries, his three sixes, '*shall stumble and fall, and not be found*'. This tells us that the first man dies in some manner that is not natural such as his plane being lost at sea. This first man has to also be a setting President of the United States." K'Narf said, seeing the shock of his statement travel around the table.

"How do you figure that?" Premo asked, echoing the question that was instantly in everyone's mind.

"Because his predecessor was, and Daniel said the third man, the man of evil, would do '...*that which his fathers have not done, nor his fathers' fathers; he shall scatter among them the prey, and spoil, and riches.*' This, if you know your world history, is something all of the old world nations have done down through the centuries, with many of their officers and enlisted men becoming quite wealthy as a result of the wars they fought.

"You mean spoils of war?" T.J. stated as well as asked, remembering how her family's estate had been gutted by an invading army.

"Yes, exactly, how many here have read Jane Austen's *'Persuasion'*?" K'Narf asked, seeing every hand in the room go up except Rudy's and Premo's. "The story was set in eighteen-fourteen England, and involves a penniless Navy Captain named Wentworth who goes to sea in the year six of eighteen hundred as Jane Austen writes it, and returns eight years later a very wealthy man due to the spoils of war." K'Narf added, looking around the table. "Rudy, in all your years of service in the United States Navy have you ever known of any officer or enlisted man getting rich on the spoils of war?"

"Not if they wanted to stay out of the brig." Rudy said, beginning to understand what K'Narf was driving at.

"*Not if they wanted to stay out of the brig!*" K'Narf repeated, then added. "The glaring exception is the United States, which has never allowed anyone in the military to take even the smallest spoil during any of its wars. Daniel's verse refers to, *and can only mean*, the United States of America which concurs with their predecessor being a United States President too." K'Narf said, challenging anyone to contradict him.

"You said the third man." Toby said, changing the subject back to the three men.

"Yes, but first Daniel says a second man stands up in this first man's estate, that's how we know they were contemporaries, otherwise he couldn't take the first man's place. Then Daniel says this second man doesn't live but a couple of days because as Daniel tells us '*Then shall stand up in his estate a raiser of taxes in the glory of the kingdom; but within few days he shall be destroyed, neither in anger, nor in battle*'.

I believe what Daniel is telling us is that a natural disaster, such as the great earthquake described in the sixth seal, takes out this second man because the final and third man, a vile and evil man according to Daniel, then stands up in this second man's estate."

"You're saying the second man is a Judas goat." Toby said, realizing what K'Narf had just described.

"Exactly! His purpose would be to get the entire functioning government of the United States assembled in one place so it can be destroyed along with him. A *'Judas goat'* as you put it. Getting everyone to attend his inauguration as the new President would easily fulfill that prophecy." K'Narf said, looking at Toby.

"Having everyone attend the funeral for the first man would do it too." Premo said, realizing that a state funeral would have the same effect.

"Yes, that would do it too." Toby said, agreeing with Premo as he nodded at K'Narf.

"Anyway, it's this third man Daniel speaks of that we will be forced to acknowledge." K'Narf continued. "He will not be elected by the people, but rather a man who *'shall come in peaceably, and obtain the kingdom by flatteries,'* according to Daniel, something he could only do if the United States government had been severely crippled by the same natural disaster that took out the second man, the *'raiser of taxes'* as Daniel calls him."

"So what you're saying is that the first two men both have to be duly elected Presidents of the United States, if the third man ends up as the un-elected leader of the nation?" Premo asked.

"Yes, that's exactly the way Daniel spells it out, and it's this third man who we will have to contend with if we decide to stay and serve the Lord." K'Narf said, pausing to see if there were any more questions at this point.

"What kind of trouble will we have with him, I mean will he be able to cause us any real trouble?" Dan Ripplinger asked, joining in for the second time.

"Yes and no. Yes we will have problems when he comes into power, including what can and cannot be bought in areas under his control; and no, we can always move facilities into space and arrange to buy necessary products from countries not under his control. It's the normals living under his rule that won't have any choice.

Understand that this third man, according to Daniel, is a nasty piece of work that will rule most of the western world for a little over seven years; in essence he'll be a dictator with little or no control on his power. During this time he will be responsible for causing severe religious persecution and at least two major wars; however, the world will also have to contend with rampant diseases, mass starvation, droughts, floods, fires, storms and earthquakes during this same seven years.

You must also understand that even if we manage to find and recruit all of our one hundred and forty four thousand unveiled believers, there would still be little or nothing we could do to help. When you compare us to almost eight billion people in distress, we wouldn't even be a drop in the bucket as they say." K'Narf said, looking around as each person in the room realized the enormity of what he was talking about.

"I'm not saying we won't try to help, but you must realize that what I am talking about has been prophesied in God's word, and it will happen as God said it would. This is something we will have to deal with if, and I say if, we decide as a group to stay and serve the Lord, because what needs to be done will take all of us working together."

"What exactly needs to be done?" Brent asked, speaking for all of them.

"We're to protect this planet throughout the one thousand years that our Lord will be living with, and reigning over this world's inhabitants." K'Narf said simply. "He is going to return to this world at the end of our third man's reign of terror, destroy him and all those who support him, then build an earthly city and set up an earthly government. As John said in Revelation, those *'which had not worshipped the beast, neither his image, neither had received his mark upon their foreheads, or in their hands shall live and reign with Christ a thousand years'*.

Our Lord will be walking among them looking as though He was one of them, but it will only look that way. He will be God in man's flesh just like He was the first time He walked among them; only this time He will be walking among them in power and glory with His angels at His side. Understand, *He does not need our protection*, the planet and His sheep as He calls them do, and remember, we are His sheep too."

"You said *'if we decide to stay'*, exactly what did you mean by that?" Brent asked, pushing his chair back and standing up.

"That's our other choice. There is an interstellar ship lying out there on Pluto that can be repaired. We could build enough of your fighters to protect us and head for deep space like the space people mentioned in the solar scroll did. Deep space would be the '*unknown risk and possible danger*' I mentioned earlier as one of our choices." K'Narf said, seeing traces of anger as he looked around the room.

"If you know the Bible as well as you say you do, then you know that when God made Adam and Eve He created them in His image!" Brent said, raising his voice as his temper flared. "You also pointed out once that our very existence proved that there had been survivors, and that we had descended from them through the blood of Eve! Is that correct?" He asked, sounding more and more like a man getting ready to lose his temper.

"Yes." K'Narf said, silently praising the Lord for Brent's anger.

"Then you ought to know that one of the gifts God gave us through Eve's blood is anger; anger if someone wrongs you, tries to kill you, or in any other way violates you! Those people who fled into the safety of space and who died without putting up a fight did not have that gift! And if you are going to stand there and tell me that it's our option to let them come back and throw another asteroid at our home planet because we chickened and ran, you're going to find out just how angry I can get!" Brent said, his voice and manner saying he was ready for a fight right now as all of his pilots agreed and stood up with him.

"Does everyone in this room agree with Brent?" K'Narf asked, slowly looking around the room as each person in turn stood in solidarity with Brent and his pilots, including T.J. "Then it's settled, the option of absconding is off the table." He added, as one by one they slowly sat back down.

"Good! This is exactly what I prayed for, now does everyone understand that God gave us all a free will, and it was a very real physical choice we all had to make. I could not make it for you, and every new unveiled believer that sees the minutes of this meeting will have to make it too." K'Narf said, watching as Brent, the last one standing, slowly sat back down.

"Now, lets talk about what needs to be done!" K'Narf said, now that the touchy business of choosing to do, or not to do, the Lord's bidding was out of the way. "Toby, what do you see as our most pressing problem?" He added, finally getting the meeting around to the subject he really wanted to talk about.

"The fact that we're going to be attacked in force when they find out what we did to their little mining operation." Toby said, thinking he had expressed their most pressing problem.

246

"That's our most immediate pressing problem for sure, so lets take it first." K'Narf said, his mind going a mile-a-minute. "Brent, when this meeting breaks up, would you send one of your teams back to Pluto and have them ransack that mother ship until they find the captain's log. It should tell us where they came from and how long it took them to get here. It might even tell us when they were supposed to depart." K'Narf said, seeing Brent's eyes light up.

"If that information's there we'll find it, sir." Brent said, again assigning leadership to K'Narf.

"See if your team can find out what they were mining too. What is it that is so valuable or rare that they were willing to come all the way out here to our little solar system in order to get it?" K'Narf asked, scratching an itch that had been bothering him since he'd first realized that the base on Pluto was an open pit mine.

"Yes sir." Brent said, thinking he was going to do that anyway.

"Toby, with the information in the Captain's log, will you be able to calculate how long it will be before they come looking for their missing people?" K'Narf asked, making Toby the new center of attention.

"Giving them just enough time to put an expeditionary force together and launch it, we should be able to pinpoint their arrival to within a few months." Toby said, realizing what K'Narf was asking of him.

"Brent, on that solar scroll there was a fleet of twelve large warships. Did all of those warships launch fighters and if so, how many fighter's were launched?" K'Narf asked, turning everyone's attention back to Brent who was quickly reviewing the solar scroll in his mind.

"All of them launched fighters, and if I counted right they launched eighty fighters from each warship for a total count of nine hundred and sixty fighters." Brent said, looking slightly strained.

"Then, considering that fleet to be the least amount of warships they will initially send against us, how many fighters are you going to need to throw against them?" K'Narf asked, keeping the pressure on Brent.

"At least a two thousand, we always fight in teams of two, they don't." Brent said, envisioning the fleet of fighters he was going to need.

"And the warships? What about massive multi-warhead launchers for your paint ball missiles, and robots that can attaché themselves to their hulls and fire and drill small laser beams at every power source or person they sense moving inside?" K'Narf asked, throwing ideas at Brent that would keep his "guys" busy for years.

"I'll have my guys start working on robotic prototypes immediately!" Brent said, excitement showing in his voice.

"Toby, how long will it take to gear up the factory to produce two thousand fighters?"

"We'll have them done in plenty of time to meet that incoming fleet!" Toby said, committing himself as he added. "I guarantee it!"

"What if a tornado hits our factory, or a flood, fire, or an earthquake destroys the factory of a critical source? Not to mention that third man we just talked about, what then?" K'narf asked, putting pressure on Toby to start thinking of multiple factories and multiple sources for everything.

"I see what you mean." Toby said, frowning as the magnitude of both the manufacturing and supply side hit him.

"Minh Le, we are going to need thousands of newbies. Do you believe you can meet everyone's needs including your own?"

"As I showed you in my presentation, with the resources I have asked for, and the Lord's blessings of a steady supply of new unveiled believers, it should not be a problem." Minh Le said, having been the only one who had already projected his future needs.

"Premo, can you and Sylvia process and train the numbers of new students Minh Le is projecting?" K'Narf asked, turning his attention to Premo and Sylvia's school.

"Not in the building we're in, but based on the need for duplication you have pointed out to Toby, if you and your father can find us another factory town where we can set up a second school I'm sure we could." Premo said, throwing the proverbial hot potato back at K'Narf.

"I will let him know of our need as soon as I get back to Sutton Wells and our factory." K'Narf said, pleased by Premo's response.

"When Toby said this attack was our most pressing need, you said *'That's our most immediate pressing problem for sure.'*

What did you mean by that?" T.J. asked, having carefully followed the conversation.

"Because our *most immediate need* is information on our enemy." K'Narf said, extremely pleased by T.J.'s very astute question.

"Let me explain. Brent, when you defeat this fleet that comes to find out what happened to their ore ship, and we all know you will, how big will the fleet be that comes to investigate the loss of twelve warships and nine hundred and sixty fighters, and what kind of resources will you need to defeat them when they show up on our doorstep?" K'Narf asked, putting Brent on the hot seat again.

"I don't know, I...."

"Exactly! What are the military resources of our enemies? Can they field another twelve warships, or will they send a hundred warships? That's what we desperately need to know, that is our most pressing need!" K'Narf said, nodding at T.J. and then turning his attention to Toby and then back to Brent.

"There is no way my agents can get that kind of information!" Brent said, recognizing the impossibility of sending a team to the enemies system and expecting them to return.

"I believe there is." K'Narf said, getting everyone's immediate attention, especially Brent's.

"Go on." Brent said, listening intently.

"I believe there is a man, possibly more than one, walking this planet that has that information. He, or they, are survivors of that asteroid attack, some of our paternal ancestors if you want to think of them that way."

"How do you see this?" T.J. asked, reverting to speaking English under the influence of her native tongue.

"First let me ask you all a question, how long do you think you can live now that you know how to repair your bodies?"

"Thirty thousand years or more." Wanda said, having spent some time thinking about that very subject.

"Yes, at least that long!" K'Narf said, excitedly agreeing with Wanda. "That asteroid was thrown at our planet much less than thirty thousand years ago according to our own geological records of the flood and the genealogy records our Lord gave us in the Bible! He also left us a clue that at least one of those survivors may still be alive today, and He even told us who to look for!" K'Narf said, seeing surprised looks on most of their faces.

249

"Who?" Half a dozen voices said in unison.

"First let me ask you this, if you had been living in the time of our Lord, and He had told you to lay low, survive if you will until His return. How would you do it, keeping in mind that these bodies of ours can be destroyed, anyone?"

"Stay away from airplanes!"

"And ships, they tend to sink!"

"Cars too, they tend to crash!"

"Okay, okay, you get the point." K'Narf said, holding up his hand to stop the onslaught of ideas. "So, where would you go to avoid situations that could kill you, adding things like hurricanes, tornadoes, earthquakes, droughts, famines and wars to your list, where would you live?"

"A monastery far back in the mountains would be the safest place, that would be my guess." Brent said, deciding to play K'Narf's guessing game.

"That would be my guess too. Now if this person exists, and I believe he does, he will have turned the ability of being inconspicuous into an art form. He would also be able to change himself to look like the local inhabitants, both speaking their language and, if he's not wearing monk's robes, then dressing like them as well. Is there anyway you can think of to positively identify him besides the fact that his head will be glowing when you look at him through your Kirlian glasses?" K'Narf asked, looking at Brent.

"Yes, language. If my agents were trained in ways to trick him into answering in the scroll language, we'd have him!" Brent said, getting a strong nod of agreement from both Toby and K'Narf. "Now who is he, you said you knew who he was?"

"Yes, I believe I do." K'Narf said, pausing to gather his thoughts. "When the Lord was here on earth, He gathered about Him twelve men we know today as the apostles. One day when He was speaking to them He said something that was copied down and recorded as scripture. It has intrigued Bible scholars to this very day." K'Narf said, searching scriptures in his mind so he could quote their words exactly.

"The Lord '...when He had called the people unto Him with His disciples also, He said unto them, ...verily I say unto you, that there be some of them that stand here, which shall not taste of death, till they have seen the kingdom of God come with power.'

'*Not taste of death*'! He had to be talking to survivors of that attack. People like us that have the ability to repair their bodies and live for the thousands of years required. If they were going to be alive when our Lord returned, and the only time He's described as returning in Power and Glory is in the same second coming that we are waiting for, and He said '*some of them*' meaning more than one!" K'Narf said, excitement showing in his voice.

"You said you had a name?" Brent asked, pushing his original question.

"Yes, I do. There was one of the apostles that our Lord favored above all the others; most scholars think it was because he was the youngest. He was the one the Lord turned to when He was hanging on the Cross. The one He asked to take care of His mother. The one that laid on His chest like a child, a lost child, an orphaned child, that apostle's name was John."

"Why do you...?"

"Because all the other apostles were publicly stoned, crucified, or executed except John. In fact secular history says that they tried to boil John in oil and couldn't, so in a panic they imprisoned him on Patmos where he wrote the book of Revelations.

It all makes sense if John was one of the survivors, possibly a child or young man when the attack came. And when our Lord said that '*that there be some of them that stand here*' He was telling '*us*' that more than one survivor existed so that we'd know to go looking for them someday.

I believe, no, I know the apostle John is still alive somewhere on this planet and we need to find him. He and his friends, if they have survived with him, have the information we desperately need. In fact, if we don't find John, or one of his friends who are like him, we may not survive that second attack because we won't be prepared for what they send against us, it's that simple." K'Narf said, looking at each person setting around the table before turning his attention back to Brent. "Brent, I am charging you with this one and only task until it's done, put together as many special teams as you possibly can and find the Apostle John. All of our combined resources are at your disposal. Now I would like to have a closing prayer." He added, watching each person around the table as they closed their eyes and bowed their heads.

"Dear sweet Lord Jesus, we humbly ask that You allow us to find Your servant John and his friends, so that we can know and understand the true nature of the evil we are facing. We desperately need this knowledge as we prepare to defend both the solar system and this planet we call home. We ask this blessing in Your name Lord Jesus, because this need to defend will also include Your earthly city when You come to live amongst us as You promised in Your word.

I also want to thank You for the words spoken here today. Words that confirm and strengthen our commitment to You and the task You have laid out before us. Words that will also confirm and strengthen the commitment of each and every new unveiled believer who sees and hears the minutes of this meeting in the months and years to come. In the name of the Father, Son and Holy Spirit, Amen."

Finishing his prayer, K'Narf watched as heads were raised and all eyes turned to him. "This council is adjourned." He added, as he stepped over and took T.J's hand, helping her as she stood up.

###

Other works by
Steven A. Vaughn
@
godsrockingchair.com

Non-Fiction
Coming Prophecies!!!
My Mother's Prayers
Spiritual Pathways

Short Fiction
God's Gift Giving Day

Novellas
The Missing Link Church
We Cannot Afford

Full Length Novels
Series Reading Order

Book 1 - **Temani: Odd Angel Out**
Book 2 - **Temani: Odd Angel Out II**
Book 3 - **K'Narf Etaguf**
Book 4 - **K'Narf Etaguf II**
Book 5 - **Holpen**
Book 6 - **Holpen II**
Book 7 - **Holpen III**

Written for Christians by a Christian, please tell a friend!

Made in the USA
Monee, IL
18 September 2020

42907310R00140